Wind Up Dead

About the author

Sam Tobin was born in Recife, Brazil and ended up in Manchester, England. He's been a BAFTA-nominated producer, worked in kebab shops and studied law. He's lived in Moss Side, Brixton and Hollywood.

WIND
UP
DEAD

SAM TOBIN

HODDER

First published in Great Britain in 2023 by Hodder & Stoughton
An Hachette UK company

This paperback edition published in 2023

1

A CIP catalogue record for this title is available from the British Library

Paperback ISBN 978 1 399 71384 9
eBook ISBN 978 1 399 71385 6

Typeset in Monotype Plantin Light by Manipal Technologies Limited

Printed and bound in Great Britain by Clays Ltd, Elcograf S.p.A.

Hodder & Stoughton policy is to use papers that are natural, renewable
and recyclable products and made from wood grown in sustainable forests.
The logging and manufacturing processes are expected to conform to the
environmental regulations of the country of origin.

Hodder & Stoughton Ltd
Carmelite House
50 Victoria Embankment
London EC4Y 0DZ

www.hodder.co.uk

To Ann and Dave

Prologue

The lights were on in the small, ground-floor flat on the edge of Moss Side. Standing outside in the darkness, the man looking in through the window was as good as invisible. He was free to take in the scene. Bide his time. Wait for just the right moment to make his move.

What he saw disgusted him.

The sofa was missing all the cushions. A filthy duvet had been thrown over the bare base to try to give some impression of domesticity. All it achieved was to make the room look even more squalid.

The floor was covered in burn marks and debris. Takeaway wrappers, cigarette butts and drugs paraphernalia.

People had defaced the magnolia walls with marker pens, blood and what looked like faeces.

In the quiet outside the window the man turned and silently spat on the ground. He hated junkies.

When he looked back up, for just a moment before his eyes adjusted to the light levels, he caught a glimpse of his own reflection in the glass. A broad, white face, hair shaved to reveal the ridges of his skull at the sides and swept back on top. There was an unrelenting motion to his eyes, never at rest, always alert. His nostrils wide and flared, sucking in the night air.

As his eyes refocused, in one corner of the room he saw a mattress that looked recently slept on. The door to the living room hung open. Through the crack in the open window he could hear movement. The person he was waiting for.

A young, black teenager walked into the living room, his face glued to his phone. He had the height of an older man but his soft features betrayed every one of his sixteen years. Even if he had looked up he wouldn't have seen the man outside standing in the dark. But the man saw him and smiled. It was nearly time.

He felt his heart begin to race. Not with fear but with excitement. This is what he lived for. Savouring the moments of quiet before the storm. His dry mouth tasted metallic with the anticipation of what he was about to do. His heavy fists clenched and unclenched; he jogged from foot to foot as the adrenaline built up inside him. He looked like a professional athlete gearing up to play.

In a way he was. He'd made his living turning his innate love of extreme violence into a profitable career.

In the flat the oblivious teenager turned and walked back out of the room.

The man outside ran his tongue around his lips, licking the empty gap in his gums where his front teeth once were. Then he slowly pushed open the ground-floor window and hauled his short, squat body into the flat.

It smelt worse than it looked. Stale body odour and smoke. The marks on the wall definitely were shit. Human shit by the looks of it. The man felt not a glimmer of doubt about what he was about to do as he walked through the living room and into the hallway where the teenager was still on his phone.

The man was breathing heavily now, ready for action. The sound of his breath whistled through the gap in his teeth. It was the first indication the teenager had that he was not alone in the hallway.

The boy turned and had just enough time to register the appropriate reaction of fear before the man was on him.

The first blow knocked the teenager clean out, his body falling awkwardly against the wall and down to the floor.

But one punch wouldn't be enough. Not by a long shot.

It was only a matter of seconds but what followed was a blur of fists and feet. Blows struck without any regard for their target.

All the while the man hissed softly to himself, 'Fuckin' . . . fuckin' . . . fuckin' . . .' His own private hymn to his frenzied brutality.

Then as soon as it had started it was over. The man stood upright, sucking in a lungful of air. He felt his head clear and the painfully tight knot in his guts eased just a little.

On the floor the teenager was making wet groaning sounds.

The man was about to pick up the body when the door to the bathroom opened and he found himself face to face with a wretched-looking man in his thirties: lank hair, blotchy, ulcerated skin and the rheumy red eyes of a junkie.

Once more the knot in the man's guts pulled itself tight and he pounced.

1

Malton was late for a murder. It was a warm Saturday night in early August and thousands of bodies filled Manchester city centre, blocking his way as Mancunians and visitors alike spilled out of bars, restaurants and clubs over the pavement and into the road.

Sat behind the wheel of his vintage, green Volvo estate, Malton watched packs of middle-aged men from out of town, their bellies hanging over skinny jeans, their sunburned arms dangling from shirtsleeves as they shouted and swaggered their way across the city centre. He saw endless groups of hens; from the women all dressed as superheroes to the party wearing T-shirts with the mortified hen's face printed on them. They all moved with purpose. Determined to squeeze as much fun as possible out of their big night out in Manchester.

He had got the call ten minutes ago. A boy called Zak Alquist had turned up dead. Slaughtered in his own home. Because of who his father was, soon enough the whole of the Greater Manchester Police would be mobilised to find the killer.

Malton's job was to beat them to it.

A drunk banged his hands on the roof of Malton's car. A red-faced man, his shirt untucked, sweat pouring off him. As he came level with Malton's side window the smile left his face. Looking back at him from inside the car was an eighteen-stone, shaven-headed, mixed-race man with a deep scar running down one side of his face. His expression was unmistakably hostile.

The drunk held his hands up in surrender and stammered something that Malton didn't have time to hear. He was already in motion. He needed to get to Zak's apartment.

Malton wasn't police. Not even close. He owned Malton Security, a firm that ran doors, protected property and provided security to high-net-worth individuals. But that was just the tip of the iceberg.

Craig Malton was the man who Manchester's criminal fraternity turned to when they needed to get to the bottom of something and would rather not get the law involved. He solved crimes for criminals.

After finally managing to weave his car through the crowd of bodies, he turned off the inner ring road into the newly minted neighbourhood of Ancoats. Towering mills had been filled with apartments, their ground floors a carefully curated selection of international cuisine, themed bars and artisanal eateries. What had been a neglected backwater just a decade ago, was now teeming with life.

One of the men responsible for this miraculous change was Nate Alquist. Nate was as close as it came to Mancunian royalty. A property developer with the council's ear. Through his company, Upland Living, Nate owned half of Moss Side as well as several tower blocks in the city centre. He had spent the last decade remaking Manchester in his image, cheered on all the way with generous government grants and glowing press coverage.

But now his son was lying dead in one of the apartments he himself had built. And it wasn't the police who Nate turned to. It was Malton.

Manchester had long since shed its image of post-industrial deprivation. But just under the surface, the grime and filth were still there. Nate Alquist knew that as well as anyone. You didn't get to be as rich as Nate without brushing up against the dark underbelly of the city. Greater Manchester Police would get their turn but Nate had the money and connections to reach out to someone like Malton. Someone who saw how Manchester really worked.

Malton knew every criminal in the city. The families out east involved in the wholesale importation of drugs. The gangs that clustered around the deprived northern edge of the city centre selling those drugs. The various criminal firms around Salford and Chorlton whose exploits ebbed and flowed across multiple generations. Malton could talk to people who would never speak to the police on pain of death. He could go places the police would be scared to even think about treading. And he could do things the police would never dream of doing. Whatever it took to get answers.

Malton parked his car down a cobbled backstreet and walked through the shadows cast by the towering Ancoats mills. His footsteps echoed on the same streets that hundreds of years ago workers trod as they poured out of their slums ready to break their bodies on the wheels of industry. Manchester used to sell cotton. Now it sold apartment living and men like Nate Alquist had made their fortune doing it.

It had been twenty minutes since Nate made the frantic phone call to his lawyer Bea Wallace begging for help. Malton was that help.

He emerged from the canyons of converted mills and out into what was left of the evening sun. Ahead of him lay the last remaining patch of green space in Ancoats. An empty field threatened on all sides by development. The tramline ran across the far end of the field and beyond the tram stop loomed dozens of newly constructed apartment complexes. Nate Alquist had told Bea that in one of those flats Malton would find the body of his son Zak Alquist.

Malton picked his way between the groups of people sat on the grass, drinking in the evening light. A tram pulled in from East Manchester disgorging dozens of clubbers all too excited by the night ahead to pay much attention to him as he stalked towards Zak Alquist's canal-side apartment block.

Malton noted with satisfaction an absence of police. He could hear only the distant, ambient sirens of a Saturday night in Manchester. He had made it clear that if Nate wanted his services he needed to be the first one to see Zak's body. The crime scene would be his and his alone.

He didn't have to wait long before someone emerged from the front entrance and he slipped past them before they even had a chance to decide whether or not they wanted to challenge the grimly determined man striding away through the lobby and slipping into the stairwell. By the time Malton reached Zak's floor he was jogging. He didn't want to spend any longer than he had to in the building. Bea had instructed Nate to wait half an hour and then call the police. With Malton on the job he would need the plausible deniability of police involvement.

The door to flat 304 was ajar. Malton paused briefly to slip on a pair of blue latex gloves and a facemask. He was walking into a crime scene; he didn't want to leave anything of himself behind. Looking left and right to make sure the coast was clear, he took a breath and stepped into the apartment.

He was greeted by an abattoir.

The lights were off but in the glow thrown from the flats across the canal he saw a body sprawled on the floor of the small, open-plan apartment. But only the body. The neck ended in a ragged gash of flesh. Where the head used to be was little more than nauseating, wet pulp. Meat and jelly and bone. Malton recognised the round indentations of a hammer beaten into the bloody floorboards. Whoever had been wielding the weapon hadn't stopped until there was nothing left. Extreme overkill. Looking up at the ceiling confirmed it – the wild blood splatter of a frenzied attack.

The unmistakable smell of viscera filled the flat. An earthy, salty stench.

A large pool of blood was spreading out from the body, across the wooden flooring and soaking into the nearby rug. Zak Alquist hadn't stood a chance.

Malton took a step back and looked around. Aside from the gore the flat was immaculate. High-end appliances, hardwood floors, elegant Scandinavian furniture and brash modern art hanging on softly pastel walls. A flat like this would easily cost a couple of thousand a month. Not for Zak though – his father owned half the block.

Scattered all around the flat were piles of money. Paper money. Tens of thousands of pounds. Some in bundles, some loose notes. All of it covered in blood.

In the distance Malton heard a single, determined siren. He froze. It was getting closer.

Malton bent down over the human remains. Something caught his eye, the start of a tattoo beneath the scoop neck of Zak's T-shirt. Malton gently lifted the T-shirt. There on the right breast a tattoo that read: CARRIE 4EVA. The stylishly modern font contrasted with the ironically old-school text.

He was getting up when he saw something he'd missed. Leaning in closer, amongst the cash he instantly recognised what he was looking at. Bright and white in the half-glow. A kilo brick of cocaine. A dealer's amount. And something else, a mark on top of the brick.

The siren was definitely getting louder now. Other sirens joined it. A murder would be a top priority. Police all over the city centre racing to get a piece of the action. It was time to get out.

Through the gloom, Malton squinted at the brick of cocaine. There on the top was an imprint. A signature. Whoever had pressed the cocaine into a brick had also branded their logo onto the top of it. In drugs as in most things nowadays, branding was everything.

As his eyes acclimatised further he made out the marking. It was a circle inside of which was the outline of a hand grenade.

By the time the police stormed Zak Alquist's apartment Malton was already walking out the underground car park and taking the long way round to his car.

Whoever had killed Zak Alquist had done so with such a high level of violence that there was only one thing Malton could say for sure. It wasn't the first time they'd killed a man and it wouldn't be the last.

2

The whole of Moss Side rang to the sound of bass. The fat sound ricocheted off the terraces and echoed through the parks. It filled backyards and crept in open windows. The Moss Side Caribbean Carnival after-party had been going for several hours now and was showing no signs of slowing down.

Far from it. Now the parade was done with and the events in Alexandra Park were starting to wind down, the real party was only just beginning. Half a dozen unofficial sound systems were set on street corners, and throughout the narrow streets of Moss Side impromptu barbecue stalls had sprung up, serving jerk chicken and brutally spicy homemade sauce.

Dean was looking forward to the party stretching on into the early hours.

Officially he was here on work. Unofficially this was just the latest encounter in his growing love affair with Moss Side. Next to him, his girlfriend Vikki seemed equally thrilled, their white faces standing out among the crowds of revellers.

Dean was tall and thin. A boyish face made younger still with a look of constant curiosity. Vikki was not quite as tall as Dean but she was far more powerfully built. Solid and athletic she had the natural beauty of someone confident in their own skin. While Dean wore jeans and a T-shirt, Vikki was in baggy combat trousers, platform trainers and a crop top. Dean loved watching Vikki dance; seeing her lost to the dense, throbbing music.

Suddenly a new sound system erupted from further down the road. A cheer went up as competing bass lines smothered each other, flooding the road with joyous noise. Vikki turned to the sound and started swinging her hips appreciatively, her arms in the air, one hand clutching a can of beer.

Dean worked for Malton Security. More accurately he worked with Craig Malton. When an old friend had asked Malton to provide unofficial security for the after-party, Dean had been tasked with organising a crew. Amongst the police and official marshals, Dean had made sure that a dozen of Malton Security's best guys were spread over Moss Side. Watching for known faces. Stopping trouble before it had a chance to get started. Like Malton himself, the men Dean had chosen were all Moss Side, guys who had grown up in the area and knew what made it tick.

Dean was there to make sure everything went smoothly. But that didn't mean he couldn't enjoy himself while he did so. After all he was now a Moss Sider too.

He'd been living with Vikki in her flat in Salford but last month, fearing another Grenfell, the council had stripped the entire block of all its cladding. Without external insulation, every flat in the block was now either unbearably hot or impossibly cold.

It was Craig Malton who had stepped in with a solution in the form of a terraced house he owned in Moss Side.

Dean and Vikki had only been going out for a few months but now they found themselves living together. A few miles from the city centre, Chorlton and Hulme, Moss Side was ideally placed to enjoy the best of Manchester. They had laughed about how they'd suddenly ended up like an old married couple but deep down, the longer it went on, the more Dean found himself enjoying the arrangement. The times when Vikki was late back from the fashion course she was doing at Salford Uni and he got to tie on an apron and bash together their evening meal. Or when he'd come home and she'd surprise him with tickets to a gig or a trip to a brand-new bar.

Domesticity had been sprung on him but now Dean couldn't be happier.

It was very different from his previous living arrangements, back in the flat he had shared with his mum. Dean had dreaded telling his mum that he was moving out. But far from being inconsolable, she had already cleared out his old room and was in the process of turning it into a small yoga studio.

From working with Malton Dean knew all too well about the reputation of Moss Side. The random violence. The gangs and the guns and knives. As if a curse hung over the place, dragging generation after generation through the same point-less suffering.

But living in the area Dean had discovered the real Moss Side. The families. The communal pride. The history that despite being an integral part of Manchester, went largely unknown, with the world preferring to dwell on all the worst aspects of the M14 postcode. Dean already knew half the peo-ple in the street they were living on. He was on first-name terms with the couple who ran the chippy, the family who owned the corner shop and the Halal butcher across the road.

For everything it had endured, Moss Side had never given up.

Looking at the girl he loved, dancing in the street alongside the hundreds of revellers, Dean couldn't think of any better place to be.

It was then he saw the gun. Almost hidden, sticking out the back of the trousers of a young man stood a few feet away from another group of youths. Dean instantly recognised his body language: hopping from foot to foot, walking back and forth. He even seemed to be talking to himself. Psyching himself up.

Vikki was busy dancing with an elderly Rastafarian. Dean looked up the road. He saw one of the Malton Security guys defusing a drunken argument with laughter and good humour. A quick scan of the surroundings told him that no other backup was nearby.

Dean had to act and he had to act now. A gun being pulled wasn't just a lethal threat in that moment. What would follow would be worse: the retaliation in the hours and days that fol-lowed. The spark that could set off a beef that could run for years and ruin countless lives. Dean had only lived there a few months but already Moss Side felt like home. He'd do whatever it took to defend his home.

Thinking quickly, Dean grabbed a box of jerk chicken that was being prepared at a nearby barbecue. Before the waiting customer had a chance to complain Dean handed him two twenty-pound notes, smothered the chicken in hot sauce and was on the move.

As he passed Vikki he whispered in her ear: 'Be careful.' There was no time for anything more.

Dean sped up and crossed the road. Holding his box of chicken out in front of him, he could smell the sweet and spicy sauce. Thick and sticky.

A thick, sticky sauce that went all over the tracksuit top of the boy with the gun as Dean walked right into him, dropping his chicken over the pavement.

The young man spun round. He was about Dean's age with a scruffy moustache and braids. Whatever he had been trying to talk himself into doing was forgotten as he turned all his anger on Dean.

'You fucking div,' he screamed in Dean's face.

Dean noticed both the boy's hands were raised, gesticulating. As long as they were nowhere near the gun everything would be fine.

'Oh, I'm so sorry,' said Dean as loudly and as whitely as he could. A few faces turned to look. He heard a laugh.

'I'll fucking end you, you lanky dickhead,' spat the guy, all his anxiety and indecision suddenly forgotten.

Dean leaned over and made to brush the sticky mess off the tracksuit top.

'Don't fucking touch me, bro,' shouted the young man, springing backwards from Dean's touch, his hands still up. A small crowd was gathering. Voices joining in. Phones coming out.

'I didn't see you,' said Dean apologetically. Over the lad's shoulder he saw that one of the Malton Security guards was already coming over.

13

'Nah, no way you leaving me like this.'

Just as the guy's hands went down and towards his trousers the Malton Security guard was there. He was a large, first-generation Somalian Manc called Djama. He'd joined around the same time as Dean. The two of them sometimes had lunch together when their shifts overlapped, Dean pumping Djama for titbits of information that could prove useful down the line.

'What is this? What is this? What is this?' said Djama, a huge smile on his face.

'I'll pay for the dry cleaning?' offered Dean.

'Fucking dry cleaning?' spat the young man. He took a step towards Dean again but then, taking a look at the six-foot-two Djama, turned and stormed off into the crowd.

'White guy at the Moss Side Carnival,' said Djama loudly, playing to his captive audience. The crowd burst into laughter. Dean mugged for their benefit before finally slipping back to Vikki, the flashpoint defused with humour.

Vikki had been standing watching the exchange. She looked like she'd seen a ghost.

'You OK?' asked Dean.

'That guy, the one you bumped into. He walked past me. He had a gun in his trousers.'

'Did he?' said Dean innocently.

3

DI Benton looked around and tried for a moment to think more like a teenage boy and less like a middle-aged, female detective still furious at being sent out on a random missing persons case despite her recent promotion to the rank of Detective Inspector.

She was stood in the cramped bedroom of a boy who had been missing for the past forty-eight hours. The window had been hauled open a crack but the air was still thick with undertones of sweat, masturbation and top notes of Lynx body spray.

Crammed into the space was a single bed with a plain blue duvet, a wardrobe and small desk. The desk was piled with schoolbooks, and a large TV balanced on a nearby chest of drawers with wires leading out to a PS4. The wardrobe didn't quite fit. It covered half the window making the room feel even more claustrophobic.

Several shoeboxes were stacked on top of the wardrobe and the clothes basket bulged with dirty washing. Benton suspected the mother had cleaned the room before she came over. Something that was both unnecessary and unhelpful for Benton's purposes.

More than anything the room felt small. The kind of place that made a teenage boy restless to find his place in the world.

Benton thought back to her own teenage daughter's room. Even before they'd moved in Jenni had demanded the largest room in the house. And got it. She slept in the master bedroom along with all the best furniture. Benton was home so little it didn't seem worth putting up a fight.

'Can I help you?' came a voice from downstairs. The mother of the boy who had walked out of this very house forty-eight hours ago and had yet to return.

'I'm nearly done,' Benton called back.

Her eyes went around the room. She'd checked under the mattress, gone through the drawers and the wardrobe. She was running out of places to look.

She caught herself in the mirror on the back of the door. She had a police metabolism. Always on the go, always eating, never stopping. It meant that she was solid but she was surprisingly fit. With no time for anything more than moisturiser, her skin had a healthy pink glow. A stern face framed with choppy, brown hair. Benton cut her own hair; it was quicker that way. She had more than enough to do without wasting half a day on a haircut. Years of this habit had given her a very distinctive look. One she confidently owned.

After shutting the bedroom door, Benton climbed onto the bed and took down the first of the shoeboxes. She was dismayed to find some shoes inside.

She replaced the box and tried the next one.

Shoes again.

The next one wasn't shoes. It was filled with old Pokémon cards.

She replaced it and as she took a step back she suddenly lost her balance. Benton grabbed at the top of the wardrobe knocking the shoebox full of Pokémon cards down and scattering them all over the floor.

Her arms shot out and she braced herself against the bedroom walls. Her heart racing, she quickly checked she wasn't in any immediate danger of falling on her arse before turning to see what had happened.

One foot had sunken down into the mattress.

Benton very carefully lifted her foot out of the mattress and made sure it was firmly planted on the floor before she let herself down and knelt in front of the bed. Lifting the mattress, she saw that someone had cut a hole in the top of the divan base. When she'd looked before she'd not seen it but now that her foot had gone through it, it was unmissable.

She leaned forward, holding the mattress up on her shoulder as she stuck a hand into the base and rummaged around. As she fumbled in the divan she suddenly remembered a flash of her police training. A warning about sticking hands in suspicious places. Knives and syringes and worse. It was the sort of advice Benton relished ignoring.

Her fingers came across something hard with a taut elastic band around it.

She pulled out what looked like a stack of bank cards and IDs. The top one was a white man in his thirties who from the look of him Benton would say was more than a little fond of drugs. Definitely not the teenage boy whose room she was currently searching.

Benton pocketed the stack of ID cards and reached back into the hole. Just from the feel of it, she knew exactly what the next thing she found was before she'd even pulled it out.

Her heart sank as she pulled out a quarter kilo brick of cocaine, wrapped in cellophane and tape. It had suddenly become a very different sort of missing persons case.

***

'Did you find anything helpful?' asked Tejumola, the mother of Femi Musa, the boy in whose bedroom Benton had just found enough drugs to send him away for a double-figure stretch.

Benton gazed at all the photographs covering the walls of the front room. Femi with his mum and dad dressed for church. A young boy in a bow tie stood between two beaming, proud parents. Here was Femi getting an award for spelling. Here he was captain of his football team and here on a visit to Westminster as part of a government scheme. Femi had more talents than there was space on the wall.

'Maybe,' said Benton cagily. She didn't know whether or not Tejumola had the first clue what Femi was up to but, from experience, Benton knew just how far mothers would go to protect their sons. For Femi's sake Benton needed nothing but the truth.

Since her divorce Benton was living in a rented house. There was nothing on the walls. The whole place was full of packing boxes from her old home. Both her stuff and her ex-husband Simon's things. Simon's outnumbering Benton's ten to one. She was trapped living in a cardboard labyrinth of her failed marriage.

On top of the rent for her own place she was also paying the rent on the bedsit Simon had moved to. With his refusal to get a job it was the only way to get him out of the house without throwing him onto the streets. Something which, for the sake of their daughter, she wouldn't do. No matter how much it appealed.

Tejumola's house felt like a proper home. You could feel the love. Everything was immaculate. The bright peach wallpaper, the shining, clean laminate. Every picture frame dusted and lined up. It was just like Femi's mother Tejumola herself. She perched on the edge of the white, leather sofa in a knee-length dress and blazer, her short, straight hair glossy and immaculate. Benton had caught her on her way out to church.

Benton felt almost rude being here. She was in her work trousers and a jumper. Her purple anorak lay balled up beside her. Looking down she could see a ketchup stain on her left thigh from two days ago. She smelt of the mint bodywash they put in the showers at the Hulme police station she worked out of.

Benton was finishing her tea when Tejumola spoke. 'I'm not stupid. I know that my son was no angel.'

Benton put her cup down on the doily that Tejumola had provided and wondered just how much Femi's mother knew.

'Oh?' she said, not giving anything away.

'If I could afford to move I would have done. Before Femi went to secondary school. But after my husband died . . .' Her eyes went to the photo of the man on the wall. 'Not everyone here . . .' she looked into the distance, searching for the words '. . . is a good person.'

Benton couldn't argue with that. Femi's house was on the edge of Moss Side. Separated from the terraces by Wilbraham Road, he was within walking distance of a postcode that seemed utterly resilient to the forces of gentrification that were washing over the rest of Manchester.

'This isn't the first time he's gone missing,' said Tejumola. Benton could hear the heartache in her voice.

'What's different now?' asked Benton.

Tejumola took a breath; she was trying not to cry.

'Lately Femi has been acting . . . differently. He hasn't wanted to leave the house. He's been jumpy. Restless. It was like he was scared.'

'What of?'

Tejumola looked pained. 'He is a teenage boy. He doesn't tell me anything.'

'I've got a daughter. Girls are no better.'

For just a moment Tejumola smiled, a shared shred of normality passing between the two mothers. Then the smile went, leaving just a mother's concern for her child.

'Ordinarily I wouldn't have called the police but a few nights ago I found Femi in his room. He was crying.'

Tejumola welled up at the thought of her son's distress. Benton kept quiet.

'Ever since he was a little boy we have taught him about Jesus Christ. But the last few years, he stopped going to church. Stopped talking about Jesus. Shut him out of his life completely. But that night, when I found him, he asked me to pray with him.'

Tejumola sniffed back a tear.

'What did he want to pray for?' asked Benton.

'Forgiveness,' said Tejumola.

4

It was a beautiful cottage. Halfway up the valley from Uppermill out to the east of Manchester. High up enough to command views down across the picturesque town filled with stone terraces and a canal winding through it. On the other side of the valley were dotted similar farms and cottages. Barely an hour's drive from the middle of Manchester it felt like another world.

Malton wondered if that was the point.

He looked down at the cottage from some distance away. With only one road leading to it he couldn't afford to be any nearer. Still, with his binoculars he could see what he wanted to see. The heavily pregnant woman and her father who lived there. Emily. The woman he thought he would be spending the rest of his life with.

Last time he'd seen Mayer Haim he was telling Malton to never again come near his daughter. Last time he'd seen Emily she was telling him she was pregnant with his child and that the best thing he could do was to stay out of their lives.

Growing up in Moss Side Malton never felt he belonged. Mixed-race with a white dad and a dead mother, he spent his teenage years trawling the city looking for meaning, gazing towards the white affluence of Didsbury and beyond. Convinced that if he tried hard enough and grafted long enough he could somehow earn his way into finally feeling like he had a home.

Malton Security had given him more money than he could spend. His work for the Manchester underworld had meant that there was nowhere in the city he couldn't go. No one he couldn't get to. But it had been Emily who'd given him a brief taste of happiness.

True she was a junkie when he met her. And yes he had been hired by her father Mayer to rescue her from her pimp boyfriend. But he and Emily had found something in each other. They'd made a home and for a few years he'd almost known what it meant to belong.

But then she'd had a glimpse of who he really was. What he'd had to do to make himself someone worthy of someone like Emily. She'd seen the real Craig Malton and run.

Down in the valley a steady stream of Sunday visitors was beginning to fill up the car parks. While in the fields farmers were already several hours into their day. Malton sat in the gentle chill of the morning watching.

It wasn't hard to find Emily. To his mind he'd kept his promise. He wasn't in her life. But ever since he'd discovered where she was he'd been coming here a couple of times a week. Sometimes in the morning like today, other times late at night. Always keeping his distance, always just watching. Never making contact.

Malton had always feared having children. Partly it was his own upbringing and a desire to never inflict that on anyone else. But mostly it was his life now. Surrounded by death and violence. Malton had chosen to make Manchester's rotten underbelly his home. He put his mind and body to the test staying alive as he plied his services to some of the most dangerous people you'd never want to meet.

Emily had already paid the price for that. Malton was a one-man army but she was not. So when the past that Malton couldn't leave behind caught up to Emily she was utterly helpless.

The past's name was Keisha Bistacchi. Keisha and Malton had grown up together in Moss Side. They had planned to make a life together. But, racked with self-doubt, Malton had turned his back on her and Keisha had never quite forgiven him. She had very nearly burned the city down seeking her revenge before fleeing Manchester to who knows where. But the damage was done.

Now, despite carrying Malton's baby, Emily had shut him out of her life.

Malton couldn't blame her.

Through his binoculars he saw her standing in the kitchen. She was in a baggy nightshirt, her neat, jet-black bangs grown out. Her stomach bulged fit to burst. Malton moved his gaze to another window where he saw Emily's father Mayer preparing breakfast. Mayer looked great for his age, slim with neat, grey hair, dressed in the casually expensive manner of a man with millions in the bank. Mayer had always been good to Malton. Treating the brutal, mixed-race man from Moss Side who had taken up with his white, Jewish daughter from Cheadle as nothing less than family.

Malton's binoculars moved back and forth between Mayer and Emily. Their mouths were moving. Smiling, laughing. Things that came at a price in Malton's world.

But compared to James, Emily had got off lightly.

Malton had always slept with men and women. At first it had bothered him. It was why he'd left Keisha, rather than have her find out the truth about him. But then he met James and fell in love. James was unlike anyone Malton had ever met. Unafraid, unashamed, irrepressible and for some reason wildly in love with Malton. For the first time in his life Malton felt the heavy fist around his heart unclench just a little.

Then one day someone had snatched James off the street and cut him into tiny pieces.

Malton learned his lesson. He'd let himself love someone. Let himself be weak. Someone exploited that weakness. He wouldn't let it happen again.

However far away Malton went, his child would always be his weakness. And so he came to the cottage and watched. Expressing his love in the only way he knew how. Protection. He earned his place in this distended family by never daring to presume he belonged inside the cottage. Always on the outside. Always watching. Always juggling that nagging fear.

When he'd looked down at Zak Alquist's murdered body, Malton had felt that fear nearly overwhelm him. He knew in that moment that he could never be part of his child's life but he could never, ever stop watching from a distance.

He turned the keys in the ignition and drove up and out of the valley, leaving Emily and Mayer to their breakfast. He only knew one way to drag the dread that threatened to overwhelm him back down into a dark recess of his soul. He had to turn Manchester upside down to find Zak Alquist's killer.

5

The bin liners full of that Sunday's food waste felt like dead weights in Lesha's hands as she backed out of the kitchen door and into the alley behind Kieran's Place, the café she ran with her partner Graham.

Despite cleaning it every day the alley always had the same familiar, sweet tang of rotten food from the communal bins that lined it.

After dumping the bags on the ground, Lesha heaved open the bin's heavy lid. Her arms bulged with the effort, throwing into muscular relief her tattoos. On her left arm was written: IF LOVE COULD HAVE SAVED YOU, THEN YOU WOULD HAVE LIVED FOREVER; while on her right was a portrait of a young man, smiling out at the world. Frozen forever in flesh. Lesha's deep-red hair was tied back in a ponytail and what little make-up she wore couldn't disguise the relentless determination that shone in her face.

One after the other Lesha tossed the bags into the bin before letting the lid slam back down. She paused for a moment and took a breath. It was five years ago today that she lost Kieran. She hated the anniversary. She'd made sure to keep herself busy all day. Never giving herself the chance to stop and let the memories catch up to her.

Kieran's Place didn't give her the time to stop. A year after Kieran's death she'd set it up in his memory. A café in Moss Side run by volunteers and donations where no one would be turned away. She wanted to make sure that when Moss Side thought about Kieran Thompson they thought about good things. About the decency and humanity in Moss Side. Not the other side of the place.

Now every day she served lunch to nearly a hundred different people. What had once been a terraced house off Claremont Road was now a welcoming space where people could sit, eat and talk. She'd built a state-of-the-art kitchen out over the backyard and turned the upstairs into a community meeting space. Moss Side had nearly dragged Lesha under but now she was working every minute of every day to fill it with love.

She let herself back into the café and began stacking away the tables and chairs. Her partner Graham worked as a carpenter. They'd first met when Lesha hired him to do some renovations to the café. That was two years ago. He was still hanging around. When he wasn't on jobs he was at the café, working side by side with Lesha. Right now, he was at the house they shared in Whalley Range cooking tea. Lesha hadn't mentioned the anniversary. Graham had already done more than enough to bring Lesha back from the brink. He didn't deserve the burden of her grief.

Late at night when he'd gone to sleep and she was the only one awake in the house, then and only then she might just let the mask slip and shed a tear. But Lesha still had more to do before she could finally give in to anything as self-indulgent as grief.

She'd loved Kieran but it hadn't been enough. So now she treated every single customer like her own family. She didn't just feed them. She heard their problems, took their side, fought their corner.

Lesha knew pretty much every member of Manchester Council's housing department, dozens of policemen, probation officers and support workers. She'd built a giant network of support, held together by her determination to never let another mother go through what she did.

After she checked the back door and set the alarm, she picked up one final lunch from the counter and locked up.

She still had to check on Tommy.

Tommy had been a regular from the start. He was what social services would describe as a vulnerable adult. Lesha made it her business to make sure that anyone caught taking advantage of that vulnerability knew just who they were dealing with.

Lately she'd been worried about Tommy. He'd been coming in less often. And when he did show up he was quiet. He didn't eat his food or want to talk to Lesha. The other day he'd got into a fight with another customer. Lesha had to drag them apart and lay down the law. Fighting wasn't tolerated in Kieran's Place.

Lesha walked between the terraced streets, parallel to Princess Parkway, the four-lane road that divides Moss Side in two. She passed by the park where a handful of mothers watched as their young children played on the grass. Chasing balls and calling to each other. Their voices bounced off the backs of the terraces facing the park and for a moment Lesha was back there all those years ago with Kieran. Watching a shy little boy delighted to be included in a game of football. Talking to other mums, hoping against hope that they didn't know who Kieran's father was.

Lesha sucked in a gutful of stale, summer air and held back her tears. She wasn't finished yet. There was still Tommy.

Tommy lived across Moss Side towards the brewery in a block of new-build flats managed by a housing association. As a vulnerable adult he was meant to have support workers and constant help. Lesha had seen how council cuts meant that those promises were more like lofty ambitions than reality. As the money had been sucked out of the country by decades of austerity, it was the kind of people who needed Kieran's Place that suffered the most.

Tommy's flats were built in a horseshoe shape, facing onto a scruffy communal garden. The bright red brick clashed with the Victorian terraces. Lesha had heard rumours the flats were to be knocked down. The council had built them in the Nineties when the idea of anyone wanting to live in Moss Side was a joke. But now the city centre was finally expanding out to meet Moss Side. A prime patch of land next to the brewery had been earmarked for a new food hall and Moss Side was going to change. Out with the vulnerable adults, in with boutique living.

The main door to the flats was open. It usually was. Either the mechanism was broken or people living in the flats propped it open. It meant a regular flow of bodies in and out, putting people like Tommy especially at risk.

Lesha walked in, shutting the door behind her. In her hand, she held Tommy's lunch – sausage rolls donated from the local Greggs, a couple of curries handmade by a collective of Muslim women from Chorlton, some bottles of water and pop from a wholesaler who supplied Kieran's Place at below cost and a bag of fresh fruit from a trader in Smithfield Market who was born in Moss Side and was only too glad to be giving something back. The very best of Manchester coming together to help the very neediest.

Lesha made her way down the corridor to Tommy's flat. The lights in the hallway flickered and the sound of several different stereos filled the poorly insulated building. The whole place always smelled heavily of cannabis smoke.

Tommy's door was ajar. Lesha had told him before about keeping it locked to stop people just wandering in.

She knocked before pushing on the open door and was about to launch into yet another lecture about keeping safe when she saw Tommy sat on the sofa facing her.

His flat was destroyed. The walls smeared with human waste, the floor covered in drug paraphernalia. And there in the middle of it all sat Tommy.

Half his head was missing, a bloody claw hammer – its handle wrapped in puckered packing tape – lying on the coffee table in front of him.

6

'You think it's got anything to do with Carrie Lewis?' asked Dean, looking over at his boss from the passenger seat.

That had been Malton's first thought when he got the phone call asking him to go to the scene of Zak Alquist's murder. Having had time to sleep on it Malton wanted to hit the ground running. After leaving Emily's cottage he'd picked Dean up mid-morning and they were heading over to Salford to meet Nate Alquist and, Malton hoped, get a clearer idea of what exactly it was he expected from Malton.

Dean had been working for him for over a year now. Where Malton intimidated, bribed and threatened, Dean relied on charm, curiosity and a natural openness that led to people consistently underestimating him. They made an odd pair. Malton – squat, mixed-race with his heavily worn aura of violence. And Dean – gangly, white and with an almost childlike innocence about him.

But in his time at Malton Security, Dean had been nearly beaten to death by a mass murderer and been shot in the face by Malton's ex. He'd unravelled murders and helped bring killers to heel. Malton didn't have any doubt that he could rely on Dean completely.

On the drive from Moss Side to Salford, Malton brought Dean up to speed and then let him think out loud as he drove.

'Everyone knows Zak Alquist killed that girl a year back. Rich kid at a posh school starts going out with a scholarship girl. Decides he wants to play at being gangsters and bites off way more than he can chew. If it wasn't for his dad's money he'd be doing life right now.'

His dad's money and Bea Wallace, thought Malton to himself.

Carrie Lewis had been found stabbed to death in a drug dealer's squat. She and Zak had met at school and been going out for several months. When the police found Zak, he had all but confessed on the spot. But at trial the jury had found him not guilty. It was a verdict that took everyone by surprise. Not least Zak.

It was all down to one woman. Criminal lawyer Bea Wallace.

She was five foot four of blonde, Geordie legal genius. She had made a name for herself defending gangsters and drug dealers. The worst of the worst. As long as they could afford her, Bea represented them and more often than not she got them off too.

Malton had been sleeping with her for nearly a year now. A fact that he suspected would risk making everything a lot more complicated.

Malton turned off the M602 and headed towards Worsley, the upmarket suburb of Salford, which looked, acted and cost like it was in Cheshire.

'If Zak killed Carrie why would he have her name tattooed on his chest?' asked Malton.

Dean looked out over the parkland that had suddenly sprung up along the edges of the M60 as they approached Worsley.

'Bravado? Overcompensating? Guilt?' said Dean.

'Maybe he got it before he killed her?' said Malton. 'If he really did kill her. Remember he was found not guilty.'

'Only by the court. Carrie's parents were there every day,' said Dean. 'Sat with Bibles and crosses. When Zak Alquist got off the first thing they did was forgive him. If they didn't think he did it then what were they forgiving him for?'

Malton smiled. He liked how Dean thought. Just like him. Questioning everything. Assuming everyone was lying until proven otherwise.

Bea's trick to getting Zak acquitted had been to scour the police evidence and find DNA suggesting a third party had been at the scene of the murder. Despite Zak being found at the scene and his refusal to name anyone else as being involved in his girlfriend's death it was enough reasonable doubt for the jury to not find him guilty.

'Was there anything else in Zak's flat? Apart from the drugs and the money?' asked Dean.

Malton shook his head.

There *was* something else, but for now Malton was keeping it to himself.

The lack of defensive wounds from a front-on attack suggested to Malton that Zak knew his attacker. He wasn't scared. That or the attacker had moved with such speed as to hit Zak before he knew what was coming. Not only that but he hit him so hard that after the first blow it was all over. That meant someone who was used to fighting with weapons and had the kind of damaged mind that wouldn't think twice about crashing a hammer into the face of a teenage boy.

That narrowed it down a little.

They were in Worsley now. Trees lined the roads. A cluster of half-timbered cottages thronged a village green while thatched roofs and the vast, semi-detached homes that once belonged to the Victorian middle classes sprung up all around. Only the constant hum from the nearby motorway broke the illusion of a rural village.

'Either way I think you should check out Carrie Lewis's parents. Cross them off the list,' said Malton.

Dean nodded enthusiastically as they pulled into the driveway of Nate Alquist's home.

It was an enormous, turn-of-the-century mansion house nestled at the edge of woodland. Dozens of windows and sloping roofs. Ornate brickwork, gables and finials. Everything made with impossible complexity, beauty and scale. Giant, fully grown trees towered over the back of the house from the garden behind and beyond that Worsley Park golf course. Standing on the paved driveway looking up at the house it felt like it wasn't in Salford but some remote English shire.

A few little touches gave away that behind the Victorian façade something very different was going on within. The double-glazed uPVC sash windows. The CCTV cameras and the outline of a huge glass and steel extension coming out the back of the house.

Malton was used to seeing the houses of those high up in the criminal underworld. They were invariably garishly modern, flaunting wealth and power at every conceivable opportunity. Nate's house was very different. It didn't need to flaunt anything. It sat as a statement to the timeless nature of true money and power.

Even Malton was impressed.

As he pressed the doorbell and listened to the faint echoes of chimes reverberate throughout the house, for a second or two he almost forgot about Emily and his unborn child.

7

From the looks of the scene in front of her, someone had beaten Benton to the punch.

Having checked the cocaine she'd found in Femi's mattress base into police evidence, she'd taken the top card from the stack of photo IDs she'd found with it and decided to pay a visit to its owner.

That owner's name was Tommy Fenwick and the flats where he lived in Moss Side were already surrounded by police cars when she arrived.

When Benton had been taken off Serious and Organised Crime and put into the general pool she had known better than to make a fuss. Greater Manchester Police were currently in the midst of a large-scale intel-led operation to sweep up all the organised crime in Manchester. An encrypted criminal network known as DLChat had been hacked and now GMP had the chat logs of every major criminal in Greater Manchester. The sheer volume had meant that other departments had emptied out and now ironically experienced detectives like Benton were forced to leave Serious and Organised to fill the gaps.

If Benton had spent more of her career getting drunk with the right people, going on the right training courses and looking the other way then maybe she'd be higher up the chain of command and involved in the DLChat operation. As it was she was an unusually experienced DI and that meant having to cover missing persons cases.

Knowing full well you could never be too successful for GMP not to clip your wings or too mediocre not to end up with a dizzying professional ascent, Benton had made discreet, low-key invisibility the hallmark of her career. The best revenge she had against the powers that be was to simply do her job better than the whole lot of them.

Benton tucked the photo ID in her pocket, it wouldn't hurt to have an ace up her sleeve, and approached the nearest uniformed officer – a young woman in glasses looking a little lost by a police van.

'DI Benton,' said Benton sternly. 'Who's all this for?'

Panic flashed across the young officer's face. But before she could answer a voice came from over Benton's shoulder.

'Are you in charge here?'

Benton recognised a full-throated Moss Side accent when she heard it. Turning round, she saw a flame-haired woman with a photo-realistic tattoo of a handsome young man on her right arm.

'DI Benton,' said Benton, more warmly this time. 'And you are?'

'Lesha. I run Kieran's Place. I found Tommy.'

'Tommy Fenwick?' said Benton, thinking back to the name on the ID card in her pocket.

'Yes, that's Tommy. He was murdered. And I know who did it.'

Benton studied the woman's face. She half recognised her. She ran some kind of café. One of the dozen or so charities that had sprung up in recent years to do what the state seemed incapable of doing – protecting the most vulnerable people in society.

'You saw the killer?' asked Benton, unable to restrain her curiosity.

'No. But I know who did this. Or at least who gave the orders.'

Benton relaxed a little. This wasn't a witness statement; this was a theory.

'If you've got information then you need to speak to an officer.'

'I'm speaking to you.'

Benton smiled awkwardly. 'Yes, but I'm not here for Tommy.'

Lesha frowned.

'Then what the fuck are you here for?'

'I'm investigating the disappearance of Femi Musa.'

The name had an immediate effect.

'Femi? He probably killed Tommy himself,' said Lesha, her voice suddenly raised in anger.

Benton's missing persons case had suddenly become a lot more complicated.

'You're accusing Femi of murder?'

Lesha shook her head and looked frustrated. 'He's one of them, isn't he? A Chopboy.'

The Chopboys.

That was a name that rang out from Benton's time in Serious and Organised. On current police intel there were at least nine different street-level gangs operating in and around Moss Side. Less gangs and more loose affiliations of friendship groups based around streets and schools. None of those gangs let their lack of rigid structure get in the way of drug dealing, violence and the occasional murder.

The Chopboys were easily the longest-running gang. They'd changed their name over the years but were still held together by a couple of older ex-gang members.

Over Lesha's shoulder Benton could see a detective she recognised talking to a crime scene coordinator. DI Boyle was Serious and Organised. She could easily sweep away Benton's investigation into Femi Musa before she got the chance to go anywhere interesting with it.

'What can you tell me about the Chopboys?' asked Benton, turning back to Lesha.

Something changed in the woman's demeanour. Benton wasn't sure if she was about to break down in tears or attack. She did neither. Instead she spat on the pavement and glared at Benton.

'I can tell you they killed my son,' replied Lesha, then she turned and started to walk away.

Finally Benton remembered where she'd first seen the woman before. Where the face tattooed on her arm was from. Kieran Thompson. He was shot dead five years ago. An unsolved case. His grieving mother had set up a café in his memory. Lesha. As in Lesha Thompson.

A queasy churn of guilt sprung up in Benton's gut.

She glanced back to check Boyle hadn't seen her before chasing after Lesha.

'I'm sorry,' said Benton. 'I didn't realise who you were. I thought you had just walked up. We get that at crime scenes. Members of the public who want to help.'

Lesha stopped and looked Benton up and down. Benton couldn't help taking another glance at Lesha's tattoo. There were dates beneath it. A birth and a death. The death was five years ago that day.

'I just need to get home,' said Lesha. 'I'll contact the police tomorrow, tell them what I found.'

Benton had made her peace with being shunted into the general detective pool but if there was a chance of getting back to Serious and Organised Crime through the back door there was no way Benton was letting this one go.

She reached into her anorak pocket, pulled out a card and handed it to the woman in front of her.

'This is my card. If you want to talk, call me. About Tommy, about Femi, about what happened to Kieran. Anything.'

'Why would I talk to you about Kieran?'

'Because he deserved better than what he got.'

Lesha stared hard at Benton, her eyes scraping away any hint of artifice, trying to discern just what she was playing at. Benton didn't flinch until finally Lesha turned and walked away. Benton watched her go. Today wasn't the day to push it. Five years ago today her son was murdered. Not only did they never catch the killer, she also never got to bury a body.

Kieran Thompson was gunned down in the street. Then in an act of deliberate cruelty his body was spirited away.

But Tejumola was a mother just like Lesha, just like Benton. And that meant that whatever Femi Musa did or didn't do, Benton was going to do everything in her power to bring him home.

She just wasn't sure if she would be bringing home a missing boy or Tommy Fenwick's killer.

8

Nate Alquist's office was epic in scale. It occupied the whole of the angular, modern extension at the rear of the house– a two-storey-high, metal cube with a glass ceiling and glass walls that slid aside, opening out into the garden beyond. It was the nerve centre of Upland Living, Nate's company which was currently responsible for billions of pounds' worth of developments across the city.

Malton had grown up blown away by the confidently affluent taste of the homes in Didsbury and Chorlton where he'd found himself taken by posh, white girls after a night out in town. Those houses spoke to him of somewhere beyond his small terrace in Moss Side and his alcoholic father. Somewhere he might like to belong. But this was on a whole new scale.

Nate's desk was the size of a double bed and situated in the centre of the room. It was covered in papers and several laptops.

The brick walls of the original house blended into the steel and glass of the extension and were hung with framed posters from famous Manchester gigs. The Happy Mondays playing the Haçienda. The Smiths playing the Ritz, Oasis at Maine Road.

In the midst of the cavernous space three antique sofas had been arranged around an original fireplace, which stood empty in the late summer heat.

It was on these three sofas that Malton, Dean, Nate and his wife Amelia now sat.

Nate and Amelia looked inconsolable.

Malton recognised Nate Alquist from the myriad of PR pieces, building launches, council events and conferences he attended. He was one of a handful of Mancunian faces who seemed to pop up everywhere and attach themselves to everything. The money behind the machine that was Manchester.

Nate was always there with a sound bite and his signature shaggy long hair, looking more like a rock star than a property developer.

Right now he looked like a father who'd lost a son.

'Did you see him?' asked Nate, his voice faltering.

Malton nodded slightly, thinking back to the scene last night. 'Remember him how he was. What I saw, that wasn't your son. Not anymore.'

Amelia let out a little gasp. Even in grief it was clear to see that she was beautiful. Good genes and Nate's money meant that she would always enjoy an ageless, tasteful grace. But today her strawberry blonde hair hung limp; her eyes were swollen and red with tears.

Nate stiffened his expression and sucked in air through his nostrils. He looked ready to throw up.

'Bea says you do this sort of thing all the time?' he said, looking up hopefully.

Malton already had the job. He didn't need to give his résumé but he knew what they wanted to hear. That somehow despite the terrible, irretrievable loss, their money and connections meant that there was still something to be done, even in death. Like the private hospital or the fee-paying school, just another chance to push to the front of the queue.

'I will find whoever was responsible for what happened to your son,' he said. 'How did you know something had happened to call Bea?'

Nate's eyes darted away for a moment then he asked, 'Are you a parent?'

Malton silently shook his head. Nate leaned forward and fixed Malton in the eye. It was the kind of staged sincerity that made Malton think he was being lied to.

'I'm a dad. And when you're a dad, you just know these things. If your kid's in trouble. Like a sixth sense,' said Nate. Malton was right. He was being lied to.

Amelia shook her head just a touch. Nate didn't seem to notice and continued, 'Obviously the police are involved now,' he said. 'Bea told me to call them half an hour after I'd called her.'

'That's not a problem,' said Malton. 'I don't work with the police. I don't work against the police. I work for you. You don't need to know how. It's better that you don't know how. That's what you pay me to worry about. But I can promise you this: there is nowhere in Manchester I can't go. No one who won't talk to me. Eventually. From what I saw in your son's flat I already have several leads. People who the police don't know about.'

'How could you know more than the police?' burst out Amelia. She looked up from her private grief, staring Malton straight in the eye with an angry disbelief. 'I'm sorry but I don't know why my husband called you. Who even are you?'

'We've talked about this!' Nate snapped at his wife, his frayed nerves at their very limit.

Malton weighed up the situation. Nate Alquist was not his usual client. Usually he worked for people who knew exactly what he'd do. The bones he'd break and the threats he'd make good on to get to the bottom of whatever it was he was looking into. Nate Alquist wasn't anything like them. Through Bea he'd been offered the chance to go off the beaten path and come to Malton. Whether or not he regretted it, it was too late now.

But if Malton was going to do this he needed to make sure the Alquists were on board.

'Remember last year, the man who shot all those people in a casino in town?' said Malton calmly.

Amelia looked suddenly scared. 'You know him?'

'I stopped him. He was planning to do much worse. I got involved and he gave himself up to the police. My colleague here . . .' he nodded to Dean '. . . saved Bea Wallace's life when that same man tried to kill her in a police custody suite.'

'The paper said it was Bea. She told us she stabbed him in the neck with her heel,' Amelia said.

Malton nodded. He'd asked Bea to leave Dean out of her account of what had happened in that room and Bea had been more than happy to take all the glory.

He motioned to Dean to speak.

'Before that happened,' said Dean, 'I fought him off.'

Up until now both Alquists had been focused on Malton. The shaved head, the scar, the enormous bulk. But now they looked at Dean afresh, trying to reconcile the lanky youth who sat in front of them with what they'd just been told.

'That's what you're paying me for,' said Malton. 'To work behind the scenes to make sure everything turns out . . .' He paused, searching for the word. 'As well as it can do.'

Amelia looked at Malton once more and burst into tears.

'What does it matter? He's dead,' she cried through her sobs.

Above the fireplace stood a giant painting in smudgy pastels of Nate, Amelia and Zak. It reminded Malton of the job in hand. He looked to Nate.

'Who do you think did this?' he asked.

Nate looked sad. 'We all know what happened with Zak. The court case. But that was nearly a year ago. Since then he's turned his life around. He packed in all that gangster shit.'

Amelia let out a little snort but with a look from Nate she turned away and wiped her tears rather than elaborate.

'He'd got a new girlfriend, was going to university. He'd turned his life around,' said Nate in a tone that made it clear the matter was no longer up for discussion.

'At Zak's trial Bea said there was a third person there when Carrie was killed, do you know who that was?' asked Dean.

Nate frowned and started to shake his head.

'What's that got to do with anything? That was a legal thing. Bea's department. Reasonable doubt.' Nate's tone was different to how he spoke to Malton. Whatever heroics Dean had or hadn't done he was the junior person in the room and Nate was speaking to him accordingly.

'So there wasn't anyone there?' said Malton, coming to Dean's defence.

'I don't know. It doesn't matter,' said Nate reining in his frustration. 'Zak didn't kill Carrie; that's all that matters. You said you had leads. Follow them.'

'I will,' said Malton. 'I've just got one last question. Why not just let the police handle it?'

Amelia shot Nate a loaded look. Nate hardened.

'I'm worth nearly half a billion pounds. I've single-handedly changed the face of this city. For the better. You don't do that without making enemies. When Zak was on trial it was really me up there on trial. People wanted me to be punished. I'd been too successful. Too outspoken. A working-class lad from Eccles who never knew his place. Bea saved Zak's life and she made the GMP look like the clowns they are. You think I trust them to investigate my son's murder? Whatever you find out, you tell me, not the police. When you find Zak's killer, it's my decision what happens next. Do you understand?'

Malton knew exactly what he meant. He wasn't a killer but that didn't mean he didn't know men who were. For a price. If Nate Alquist was worth half a billion pounds Malton was sure he could afford that price.

Nate was walking them out when he stopped Malton on the doorstep. Dean was already halfway to the car. A look from Malton and he kept going until it was just Malton and Nate.

'Bea couldn't speak more highly of you,' said Nate. 'If she trusts you, I trust you. But what I said back there, about Zak turning his life around. That's not entirely true.' Nate looked pained. 'I want Amelia to remember our lad how he was. Do you understand?'

Malton nodded.

'And I want to help you,' Nate continued. 'That's why I've got you Zak's girlfriend. It was her who found his body and called me.'

'Really?' said Malton, quietly gratified that his read on Nate had been the correct one. 'If you're going to lie to me, that makes things complicated. It stops me doing my job.'

Nate held his hands up in mock surrender. 'I know. My bad. Like I said, I just didn't want my wife thinking the worst about her boy. From here on in, nothing but the truth. The only thing that matters is finding out who did this to Zak.'

'I'd like to speak to the girlfriend,' said Malton.

Nate nodded. 'I thought you would. That's why I'm keeping her in a hotel in town. For her own protection,' he added. 'You get her first. Before the police. Get ahead of the game.'

Malton couldn't tell if Nate Alquist was simply displaying the natural ruthlessness that got him a house like this, a wife like Amelia and half a billion pounds in net worth or if there was something else going on. Something that behind all the money and reputation and grandeur was something he was all too familiar with.

Nate had already lied once. Was he working an angle?

It didn't matter to Malton. Either way he would find out and so he simply nodded and asked Nate to set up a meeting.

9

Graham would be at home wondering where she was but Lesha couldn't go home just yet. Not while she still felt like this.

The horror at finding Tommy and the grief of Kieran's anniversary that she'd been running from all day long had finally started to overwhelm her. She marched the pavements she'd known all her life suddenly feeling lost. The familiar sights of Moss Side felt like an echo of a memory. Someone else's past and not her own.

The death of her son had severed something inside Lesha. The feeling of safety that can only come with belonging. Moss Side was her home and it always would be. But Moss Side had also taken her son.

Or more accurately Ani Delgado had taken her son.

The Chopboys were the latest incarnation of a gang that went back nearly three decades. Survivors of the Nineties Gunchester days. While most of the gang members from back then were dead or in prison, there were the ones who got away. Some grew up and moved on. But some stayed in the life. Rebuilt their power with new, younger recruits. Hiding behind the respectability of middle age they let teenagers and even young kids take the risks and commit the crimes.

Lesha knew for a fact that even after all these years Ani Delgado still had sway with the Chopboys. If he wanted something done then it got done in the worst possible way.

Lesha crossed over Wilbraham Road and headed for the Rathbone Park Estate.

Wilbraham Road marked the edge of Moss Side. A four-lane road that crossed Princess Parkway and carried on down to Chorlton. But before it did that, it spawned the Rathbone Park Estate. A post-war estate of cul-de-sacs and mature trees.

In the early 2000s a huge programme of intensive, community-led policing had effectively ended a major gang war. Freed from the shadow of gang violence the Rathbone Park Estate was now a thriving community of families living their lives.

Ani Delgado had never left the estate. He'd lived in the same house for the past thirty years. Ani and his twin brother Lani. After becoming the prime suspect in a vicious arson that had taken the life of a young mother and her son, Lani had left Moss Side and vanished off the face of the earth.

But Ani was still there in the house he grew up in. Now living with his wife and six kids.

Everyone knew Ani. Some knew him as a community leader. Some knew him as the dad always on the school run. Some knew him from his involvement in a local football club, others as the guy who'd lend you anything you needed from a cup of sugar to a couple of grand.

Lesha knew him as the cold-hearted sociopath who had ordered the murder of her son.

Ani had been in the gang that became the Chopboys right from the start. He quickly moved from street violence to drug dealing and robbery. He saw the writing on the wall and transitioned to respectable adulthood but it was an open secret in Moss Side that he'd never really left his street days behind him.

Lesha knew exactly where he lived. Everyone did. Everyone knew Ani. He hid in plain sight. All these years she'd spent studiously avoiding him. Not today. Five years to the day he'd killed Kieran and now Lesha was finally done running.

Ani's house was no different to any other on his road. A modest, two-storey semi with a small front garden and driveway and a garden round the back that was accessed via a communal alley that ran between the two semis. Loud music could be heard coming from the back garden.

Lesha didn't even bother to knock on the front door. Heading to the back she could feel her heart beating out of her chest. She touched her tattoo of Kieran for courage and then let herself in to Ani Delgado's back garden.

10

'We lost a daughter. Nate Alquist has lost a son. Two young lives extinguished before their time. Reunited now in heaven.'

Dean looked around the church. St John's in Heaton Mersey was a decent-sized building, with high ceilings, heavy brickwork and carved wooden pews. It had the deep, open cold that you only got in old churches. Along with a smell of dust and soap that took Dean straight back to junior school harvest festivals.

Diane Lewis stood at the front of the church reading her words from a piece of paper. She looked just like what you'd want in a mum. Solid but kind with it. Beside her stood her husband David, taller and with a beard and next to him a younger man who Dean guessed must be Ryan Lewis, Carrie's older brother. Back when Carrie's case was all over the papers the family were rarely off the front pages. Especially Ryan.

Ryan was dressed like his parents, in the respectable shirt and chinos casual of a regular churchgoer. His hair cut neatly and his shoes brightly shined. Only the hand-poked tattoos on his face and hands gave away anything of the previous life that had fuelled so much press speculation.

'When Carrie was taken from us we forgave Zak Alquist. I hope that with God's blessing Nate will find it in his heart to forgive those who so cruelly took Zak's life.'

Having left Nate's house just over an hour ago, Dean didn't hold out much hope for that.

The church was half full. Not a bad turnout for a last-minute memorial service for Zak Alquist. At the front were two blown-up photos surrounded by floral tributes. One of Carrie and one of Zak. It had been over a year since Carrie died and only a few months since Zak's trial. In that time Carrie's parents had pushed themselves front and centre. Talking about how their Christian faith had carried them through. How they decided to forgive and the strength that decision gave them.

On the way over Dean had listened to half a podcast where they were interviewed. The interviewer was amazed at how brilliantly brave they were to forgive Carrie's killer.

Every face in the church was locked on Diane as she spoke. Several people were openly weeping. Many others were smiling, drawing strength from Diane's words.

Dean had seen first-hand the flipside of forgiveness. That was the business he and Malton were in. The people who hired Malton, by and large, were looking for someone to take out their abject lack of forgiveness on.

After hymns, prayers, more hymns and a poetry reading by Carrie's father, David, the service broke up and a large crowd formed around the Lewises. Diane and David fielded questions and condolences. There was even a young woman there wearing a BBC News lanyard.

Dean was thinking how he was going to get a moment alone with them when he saw Ryan Lewis stood to one side in the shadows, watching the scrum from a distance.

Dean stopped by the refreshment table, picked up two cups of watery tea, several packets of sugar and headed over.

'That was really powerful back there. What your mum had to say,' Dean said, offering Ryan one of the cups of tea. Ryan took the tea from Dean but simply held it, not making any move to drink.

'I'm sorry about your sister,' said Dean, trying a different tack.

Ryan turned to look at Dean. He was tall, less lanky than Dean but still not carrying a lot of muscle. A teardrop had been tattooed under one eye along with CB on his right cheek and a skull in the middle of his forehead. Ryan's eyes were vacant. Dean wondered if he was on some kind of medication.

The papers had hinted at it but a quick trawl of Facebook comments under articles around the time of Carrie's death quickly gave the full picture of Ryan Lewis. He had been a junkie, living in supported accommodation in Moss Side at the time of Carrie's death.

Several Facebook commenters heavily implied that Carrie's murderer was far closer to home than even Zak Alquist. During Zak's trial those same commenters kept popping up to suggest that everyone *knew* the real identity of the third person at the murder scene.

'You want sugar in your tea?'

Something stirred behind Ryan's eyes and he nodded softly. Dean held out four packets and watched as one by one Ryan tore them open and emptied them into his tea. He then gave the steaming liquid a stir with a tattooed finger before downing it with a grimace.

Revived, he looked across to the photos on the altar.

'It's all bullshit,' he whispered.

Before Dean could ask anything else he saw Diane was coming over, smiling aggressively at them both.

'Hello!' she almost shouted at him. 'Please don't mind Ryan. He's back on his medication. This business with Zak. It's brought it all back.'

'I was really inspired by what you said up there,' said Dean, pivoting to Diane. She beamed enthusiastically.

'It's been so hard. I just want some good to come from it all.'

Diane had a careworn face. The best sort of lines, from smiling and laughing. Dean wondered how much of either she had done this last year.

'Like Ryan here,' she said, rubbing Ryan's arm affectionately. 'When I think what he was like back then. I might have lost a daughter but I got my son back.'

Ryan smiled weakly.

'He's even got a job at the garden centre. I'm so proud of him,' said Diane.

Dean could feel the desperate optimism radiating off her. He understood completely. He couldn't imagine losing a child but he could imagine the urge to simply push on through the pain. To choose love and hope.

Working with Malton he was so used to meeting people who chose quite different things that Diane's outlook made a welcome change. Her defiance in the face of tragedy.

It made him feel very bad about what he said next.

'You talk about forgiving Zak. But the jury found him innocent. So, shouldn't it be about forgiving whoever really did kill Carrie?' said Dean doing his best to sound naively curious and not suspiciously accusatory.

Diane kept smiling but her eyes darkened.

'Thank you for coming,' she said, before grabbing Ryan by the arm and leading him over to a group of people who turned to welcome him and closed back around him.

Already Diane was back to working the crowd. Fighting to stay one step ahead of the still-raw grief of burying a child. For just a moment she turned away and looked straight at Dean.

The smile was gone. In its place a stolen moment of anger so deep and strong that it could split stone.

11

'She's fucking nuts this one,' said Ani Delgado with a smile.

He was sitting on a plastic chair in a back garden that was crammed with both furniture and people. Several kids, half a dozen adults, a barbecue and a table covered in supermarket multi-packs of beer and cider. All torn open and well on the way to depletion.

'Tell you what, have a drink? You want a drink?'

Ani Delgado was around Lesha's age. They'd grown up together. As teenagers they'd even moved in the same circles. Ani was still just as handsome now as he had been back then. These days his afro was a little neater, his goatee a little more grey but he still sported the boyish smile that somehow let him get away with murder.

'Your boys killed Tommy Fenwick,' said Lesha. She was shaking, struggling to keep her voice under control.

'My boys? They're all here,' said Ani, gesturing to the kids running riot in the garden. Something caught his eye and he lifted himself up out of his seat and bellowed, 'Get off the fucking fence, Konnor. How many fucking times?'

A blank-looking little boy hopped off the fence and ran off to find something else to climb. Ani turned back to Lesha.

'He told me what was happening,' she said, taking a step towards him. 'Lads coming round his flat. Stealing from him. Selling drugs. What happened? Did he finally stand up to you?'

Ani laughed and clapped his hands together. A couple of nearby cronies sniggered.

'Go on,' he said, playing to the gallery. 'I'm enjoying this.'

'You think you can just get away with it.'

Ani lowered his gaze and exhaled. He looked like he was trying to appear diplomatic.

'I know what day it is today. It must be hard for you.'

Lesha lost it. 'You had my son killed. And here you are, on his anniversary, drinking and laughing like it was nothing to do with you.'

A darkness came over Ani's face. 'You're upset, so you're saying stuff that you shouldn't. And because it's today, I'm going to let it go. Now get the fuck out of my back garden.'

Ani moved to grab Lesha, but she squirmed and shook him off. Still he advanced on her. She stepped backwards, nearly tripping over a child's bike that had been discarded on the ground.

'Maybe if you'd brought your son up not to grass he'd still be here today,' he said through a condescending grin.

Lesha stumbled back into the garden table covered with drinks. Ani was on her but she stood her ground.

'You never cared about anything except your little fucking gang.'

Ani stopped. 'From what I remember, your son was the one in a fucking gang. And then he was the one who lost his bottle and went to the police.'

Lesha felt her blood turn solid. Her muscles tensed and a dull roar began somewhere at the base of her spine and spread through her brain, drowning out the surrounding world.

All she saw were the faces in that garden. Ani's stooges. The hangers-on who had lived their entire lives fuelling his ego. The people who knew exactly who he was and stuck close to him through awe, or fear, or the hope that some of that Ani Delgado magic might rub off on them.

This was the world he'd created for himself. The Ani Delgado show. Everything Ani needed right there in that back garden. His reputation, his mystique, the legend of Ani Delgado.

There in the middle of them all was Ani, untouched by age or conscience or grief. Smirking down at her.

Before Lesha had time to think her hand was already slapping Ani across the face. The first she realised what she was doing was when she heard the impact of her open palm ring out. Then came the reaction from everyone in the garden. Their fear at knowing just what a line she'd crossed.

But it felt so good that Lesha didn't care. She turned on her heel and walked out of Ani's garden.

She was halfway down the road before her heartbeat slowed to something like normal and it hit her just what she'd done.

12

Anyone can sell drugs on the street. You might get robbed, you might get shot, you'll almost certainly end up arrested but the only entry-level requirements are an indifference to those risks and access to the drugs.

Selling drugs to drug dealers – that's a very different skill set. While there were far too many street dealers for Malton to ever keep track of, the further up the chain you went the fewer players there were to be found. Gangs who'd pooled their resources and bashed down a kilo to get into the whole-sale game. Faceless cannabis farms staffed by smuggled Vietnamese immigrants. Enterprising students on the Dark Web. Moving up from the street there was a wide variety of different parties involved.

That was where Malton could pick up the trail. A businessman who'd diversified out from mobile phone covers to cocaine would have a house and a family and a life. All things he stood to lose unless he could give Malton what he wanted. Raiding a cannabis farm and burning the crop would quickly bring whoever held the controlling interest to Malton's door. Higher up the chain there was not only the threat of the law but of larger gangs deciding to use violence to protect their own share. The difference from the street was vast. Not just in profits but in risk.

At the very top of the pyramid sat the sprawling international networks who brought the drugs into the country in the first place. People far beyond Malton's everyday dealings.

But in the middle, between the narcotic gods and the rabble on the street sat a very specific class of criminals. Like Malton they weren't backed up by muscle but by something much more fearsome – reputation.

The brokers.

Men who helped move huge quantities of freshly smuggled drugs. Protected by the profits they were making for those higher up and trusted by those below due to the fact that they were the earthly representatives of the cartels who produced the drugs in the first place.

The drugs trade is built on the constant application of fear and brutality. But somewhere along the line there needs to be trust. And that was where the brokers came in.

Men like Adam Parley.

Sat in Adam's kitchen in Bramhall, Malton couldn't help notice how the house felt, in its way, like a miniature version of Nate Alquist's. It too was a large, detached Victorian home with a modern rear extension jutting into the garden. But unlike Nate's the scale was merely impressive, not impossible.

Adam's kids were in the garden playing on a large trampoline while his wife sat on tasteful garden furniture beneath a pergola watching them bounce higher and higher.

From the sound of their voices it was clear that the drugs trade had been good to Adam. To hear the round, posh vowels of privilege coming out of the children's mouths you'd never guess Adam got his start in Salford.

'I'm thinking of moving to the States,' said Adam, sucking on a vape pen.

Malton had done several jobs for Adam. Tracking down non-payers, finding stolen shipments. Adam relied on his reputation and that meant ensuring no one ripped off him or his suppliers.

'This country's fucked,' continued Adam.

Malton kept silent. He had no opinion either way. Growing up as he had Malton had never expected anything from Britain.

Adam blew a cloud of strawberry-scented smoke up towards an open skylight and continued. 'If it's not the Albanians wanting to control every step of the chain, it's kids who think if they can turn me over that makes them the new Adam Parley. You hear about Saz?'

Malton had indeed heard about Saz, a retired dealer who made the mistake of not cashing his chips in and leaving Manchester while he still could. The legend of the retired dealer with a couple of million in diamonds held in a safe in his house in Sale proved too tempting for whoever it was who had broken into Saz's house, tortured him and his wife before fleeing empty-handed. Saz died of his wounds. His wife would never walk again. There never were any diamonds.

Malton knew that was the flipside of reputation. It kept you safe until someone got brave or, even worse, someone got foolish.

'Fucked,' repeated Adam. He thought for a second and then a smile broke over his face. 'But you're not here to listen to me bitch and moan. Look at us, right pair of old bastards!'

He laughed and Malton managed a smile. Adam had every reason to be scared. Malton had never had a family, never had children. That way when they came for him they had to come for *him*. Not his dependants. He called the shots and he paid the price.

In a way he was relieved about what happened with Emily. She and the child had got out while they still could. Emily had realised that the best thing she could do for the child was to flee Malton. Malton, for his part, had let her go.

But he wasn't here to reminisce about the good old days. The brick of cocaine in Zak's flat had been imprinted with a grenade. No one knew the ebb and flow of the drug trade like Adam.

'Who prints the grenade logo onto their gear?' asked Malton. He knew if Adam had answers he'd give them. There was no point fucking around.

Adam rolled his eyes. 'The fucking idiot. Yeah, you're after a guy called Jordan Weekes. From what I've seen you better get your skates on. Weekes is a popular lad.'

'Police?' asked Malton.

Adam smiled and blew a small, strawberry smoke ring. 'If he's lucky.'

13

Femi Musa's mum had told Benton he was praying for forgiveness and now Lesha Thompson had as good as accused Femi of being Tommy Fenwick's killer. If Femi had got caught up in something bigger than he could handle then, unless Benton could find him fast, the police could well be the least of his worries.

DI Boyle was already all over Tommy Fenwick and there were still two dozen cards in the stack from under Femi's bed but Benton decided to roll the dice and see if her other piece of evidence could speed things up.

Now, as she checked the cocaine out of evidence she quietly cursed her call to go with the ID cards first and visit Tommy. If she'd just taken a few moments to examine the cocaine before she checked it in there might have been something that could have got her closer to Femi without the risk of getting sucked into Boyle's murder case. But now the cocaine was in a sealed evidence bag awaiting forensic examination. Given that it was a missing persons case that could take months.

Alone in the evidence suite Benton turned the bag over in her hands trying to see if there was anything obvious she could see. It was the size of a large chocolate bar and professionally wrapped in cellophane. Femi hadn't got round to doing whatever it was he was intending to do. Whether that was sell it on, bash it down or even just take it himself.

Benton could feel herself starting to sweat under her purple anorak. The evidence suite was a tiny, windowless meeting room. One chair, one table, nowhere to hide. Cameras inside and out, once something was checked in this was the only place she could see it without contaminating the chain of evidence.

This case felt like something more than a missing person and she sure as shit wasn't going to hand it over if she didn't have to.

Benton took off her anorak and made sure the door was shut before clambering on the chair and then onto the table, clutching the evidence bag of cocaine.

The room was lit by a single, bright LED bulb in the centre of the ceiling. Benton held the bag up to the bulb as close as she could.

Light poured through the small block of pressed drugs, working like a kind of makeshift X-ray. Squinting at the light, Benton peered close. There was something there beneath the wrapping. Some kind of marking.

★★★

Jordan Weekes. A hard-working thief who'd turned his hand to dealing and was rumoured to stamp drugs with a grenade logo.

It had taken Benton little more than a couple of keystrokes to get everything she needed to know about Weekes and his cocaine branded with a hand grenade.

Since DLChat had been compromised, GMP had access to a searchable online database of hundreds of thousands of communications from drug dealers all over the north-west. Not just texts but photos and videos. While some criminals were content to use DLChat to communicate in oblique code with a minimum of information, others had ended up treating it like a group WhatsApp.

There were jokes, memes and even family photos. A treasure trove of identifying details. It was policing on easy mode.

All around her in the office detectives were so absorbed processing this mountain of data that there was no one there to question what Benton was doing in her old stomping grounds of Serious and Organised.

Serious and Organised's office was in an anonymous building just east of the city centre. After checking the cocaine back in at Hulme it had taken Benton half an hour to make her way across the city centre and out towards Clayton.

If it wasn't for its location you'd never notice it. But while all around it had been turned into low-rise estates, this single building had been left to climb a modest few storeys above everything around it. Walking past it along the canal you might wonder why suddenly there were solid, spiked grilles bolted to the nearby bridge to prevent anyone climbing up from the canal. If you took a closer look you might even notice the CCTV cameras and the Union Jack flag flying from the building.

But unless you knew, there was nothing to tell you that this was where GMP were coordinating their strip-mining of the Manchester underworld's phone data.

Benton looked what else Jordan Weekes's name turned up. Clicking the search function, her screen filled with hits. Scrolling down the assorted messages her eyes widened.

IT'S WEEKES. HE'S THE GRASS. HAS TO BE.

I'LL DO IT MYSELF.

WHO ELSE KNEW EXCEPT WEEKES?

TEN GRAND AND I CAN GET THE LITTLE CUNT BLIND AND IN A WHEELCHAIR.

HAS HE GOT A WIFE AND KIDS?

It seemed Jordan Weekes had found himself on the wrong side of the underworld gossip mill. With the DLChat hack GMP were making the sort of arrests that previously only deep intel or an informant could garner. Now the police had the DLChat logs it was clear fingers were getting pointed. You don't deal drugs without developing a healthy sense of paranoia. That paranoia was now off the scale and Jordan Weekes was in the firing line.

Benton knew she wouldn't be the only one looking for Weekes.

She was about to get up when a thought struck her. She cleared the search box and typed in 'Femi Musa'. Nothing. Femi was too far down the food chain for anyone to be bringing up his name on an encrypted phone network that charged criminals tens of thousands of pounds just to get on it. Benton felt a little wave of relief. She couldn't deny that Femi was involved in drugs but she desperately wanted it to be the case that whatever story she would eventually tell his mother, she would at least be left with the memory of that smiling little boy in his suit and tie, on his way to church.

She wondered what it was Femi had wanted forgiveness for? Had he found it or had his sins caught up with him before he could be granted absolution?

'Oi, Benton,' came a Northern Irish voice from across the office.

Benton looked up and saw DI Boyle smiling and walking across the office towards her. Boyle was tiny. Thirty years ago she'd never have got into the police. But thanks to the graduate programme she'd slid right into plain clothes and had been making herself indispensable ever since. She was also loud. As if her voice was making up for her stature.

Benton turned off her screen and spun round in her chair.

'Been busy?' asked Benton innocently.

'The uniform guarding my crime scene said she saw you and some woman arguing. Looks like I saved you the trouble of finding me to tell me what that's all about,' said Boyle in her full-bore Belfast accent.

Benton liked Boyle. She reminded Benton of herself. That didn't mean she was going to tell Boyle any more than she had to. Like for instance Lesha Thompson's theories on who murdered Tommy Fenwick.

'I was telling an interested passer-by what a professional and thorough job would be done now that you were on the case,' said Benton, the very picture of innocence.

Boyle shook her head and despite herself a thin smile broke over her face.

'And you wonder why they keep shitting on you?'

'I thought everyone loved me?' said Benton with a grin.

'Much as I enjoy this mutual exchange of bullshit I've actually got something I need you to do,' said Boyle shaking off the small talk.

Boyle held up an evidence bag with a phone in.

'This was found in Tommy Fenwick's flat. Now if this goes off to evidence that's weeks before I get anything back. But if I can just get the owner to open it for me . . . With consent, obviously,' said Boyle with a grin.

'So where do I come in?' asked Benton.

'I don't want to turn it on. Get pulled up for not having consent or a warrant. But I did check the SIM card, and got a name. Femi Musa.'

Benton's ears pricked up.

'And I understand you're looking for young Femi?' said Boyle hopefully.

Benton kept her excitement close to her chest. Femi's phone at a crime scene would definitely put him on Boyle's radar but if there was something on this phone then maybe she could get to him first.

'Looking is the operative word. Can I see?' asked Benton.

'Keep it in the bag,' said Boyle, handing over the evidence bag containing the phone. 'And obviously, I only do this because I know it'll be helping out on your case.'

Benton nodded in solemn agreement. 'Of course. But if I do find something that helps you, by coincidence.'

'Purely by coincidence,' said Boyle with a straight face.

'Thing is, Femi's a minor,' said Benton taking the bag. 'And I've spoken to his mum. And she wants him found. And if I were to tell her that we have his phone . . .' Benton fumbled with the bag and managed to turn the phone on.

'I think she'd be all for it,' said Boyle.

Benton smiled, they were speaking the same language. Two women who knew that whatever they did between institutional misogyny and the rolled-trouser brigade they were already on the losing team. The least they could do was a little mutual corner cutting.

The phone came on. It was locked. Boyle audibly groaned.

'It was worth a shot,' said Boyle, the disappointment obvious in her voice.

But Benton wasn't listening. There on the lock screen was a photo of two boys. One of them was Femi Musa sat astride a scrambler bike. The other, stood next to him holding a lock knife, was a face she recognised from that day's papers.

Zak Alquist.

14

'But what if he had shot you?'

Dean and Vikki were having their first argument.

'I knew what I was doing,' said Dean from the small kitchen at the back of the terraced house in Moss Side. He was making dinner. The kitchen windows were misted up with steam. The reassuring smell of beans on toast poured out of the kitchen, filling the back room of the terrace.

Vikki was curled up on the sofa, her laptop on her knee, as she scoured through Pinterest, creating a mood board for her fashion course. The back room was organised around a wood-burning stove that sat where the fireplace had once been. Vikki's Staffie Fury was curled up on the carpet in front of the wood burner, dozing.

As well as the sofa there was a small dining table by the back window, looking out on the yard. There was no television but neither Dean nor Vikki had the time or the patience for TV.

'You saw what happened. It was fine. Djama handled it,' Dean called out.

'And what happens when you're walking down the road in a week's time and Djama isn't there?' said Vikki, not looking up from her laptop.

Dean went quiet. He'd been so wrapped up in working out how he could speak to Ryan Lewis without his mother there to protect him, that he hadn't given what happened at the carnival the other night a second thought. From Ryan's tattoos and demeanour it seemed like the Facebook brigade was right: Carrie's brother was far more involved in her death than had ever made it into the papers. If he was the third person at the scene of her murder it would be unlike Bea not to throw Ryan under the bus. But maybe even Bea Wallace had her off days.

'You're not Craig Malton. You're Dean. You get involved in that world, it only ends one way.'

'I'm not involved,' said Dean.

Vikki laughed. 'Why? Cos you don't want to be? Cos it's just a job? You provoke people like that, you're involved. You go places like that? You're involved. You don't get to turn it off. Once you're in you're in. On the streets, at home, wherever.'

Dean felt suddenly sick. He turned the heat down under the beans and stood in the doorway looking into the back room.

But Vikki wasn't finished.

'I remember growing up with my dad. No one got the last word. If you beat him in a fight he'd come back tooled up and put you in the hospital. Men like that can't live with themselves if they think anyone's got one over on them. It eats them up.'

Dean was quiet. He knew all about Vikki's dad. Vikki's dad had tried to kill him.

'It'll be OK,' said Dean with absolutely nothing to back that up. When he'd told Vikki about his ploy, spilling food on the kid back at the carnival, he'd expected her to be impressed with his quick thinking. Instead she was horrified. Trying to change the subject, he sat down on the sofa next to Vikki and looked over at her laptop. 'What you doing?'

For just a moment he saw onscreen a half-completed application form. At the top of the form was the logo for Goldsmiths College London.

Vikki quickly shut her laptop and turned to Dean.

'I'm worried about you. Everyone Malton gets involved with winds up dead or in prison. Which way are you going to go?'

Before Dean had a chance to argue that maybe he was the exception, the doorbell rang.

'That'll be Edith!' he said, glad of the interruption.

As he turned to go Vikki grabbed his arm. 'Just promise, you won't do anything like that again. You don't have to try and save everyone. OK?'

Dean saw the quiet steel in her eyes.

'I promise,' he said.

Vikki looked up at him for as long as it took for her to feel like maybe she could believe him. Then finally a smile came over her face and she let him go.

'Don't want to keep Edith waiting!' she said as the doorbell rang a second time.

Since moving to Moss Side Dean had got to know a good number of their neighbours. The elderly married couple who owned the immaculate vintage Mercedes that when it wasn't parked outside their house was replaced with a pair of traffic cones. The music student who practised her viola in the back-yard when it was sunny. The unmarried son and his mother whose house was falling down but who always seemed well turned out and full of local gossip for Dean.

As he went to open the front door he tried to put Vikki's words out of his mind. He told himself that what happened at the carnival was a one-off. The guy he'd stopped was probably glad Dean saved him from an almost certain bloodbath. Besides, Zak Alquist was a nice safe job. A favour to one of Bea's rich clients. A world away from the monied psychopaths they usually worked for.

He opened the door to see Edith from next door looking excited and clutching her red notebook.

'He's back!' said Edith, her voice lowered.

She threw a glance over her shoulder to a house on the other side of the road a few doors down. Parked outside was a grey people carrier with blacked-out windows.

The street was one of the few in Moss Side where the terraces had their own small front garden, a strip of ground not much wider than a wheelie bin but somewhere to grow a hedge to obscure the view into your front room and a small pathway to your front door so that you weren't coming out of your house directly onto the pavement. They were neat, pretty little houses and in the late evening sun the road looked almost suburban.

No sooner had they moved in than Edith had been knocking on their door, determined to find out if they owned or rented, how long they were staying and where they were from. Having answered all her questions the next thing Edith wanted to know was whether or not they were joining the neighbourhood watch.

The neighbourhood watch was in reality a network of households in the road, all of whom reported to Edith every single detail of anything out of the ordinary. Every house they suspected of being a party let or an illegal HMO or simply abandoned. Their local councillor received near daily updates from multiple residents and the local police received multiple calls every time something happened. All coordinated by Edith.

In her own way Edith reminded Dean of Malton. She refused to accept the world as she saw it and had no sense that there was anything she couldn't achieve with enough ingenuity and daring.

Number Twelve opposite had been on Edith's mind for the past few months. It was a mystery. There was no loud music and no sign of life save for the people carrier, which would arrive a couple of times a day and park directly outside the front door. One time Dean had seen a woman walk into the street to smoke. What struck him was the way she was dressed. Lucite heels and a dress that looked more like lingerie. Midway through her cigarette another woman, similarly dressed, had come out and started an argument before both of them went back inside.

The first time there'd been any real disturbance had been earlier this week when Twelve was having some kind of building work done and Edith had been sure to knock and make certain Dean had heard it too. But now that had seemingly finished Number Twelve was back to its usual routine.

'Those poor girls,' said Edith, marking down the date and time in her red notebook.

They stood together and watched as the front door opened and a couple of women walked to the vehicle. The clicking of their heels echoed off the terraces.

'And on a Sunday too,' said Edith as if that somehow made what they were seeing infinitely worse.

They heard the door to the people carrier slam and it drove off, slowly making its way in the direction of town.

'First Ten and now Twelve,' said Edith sadly. Number Ten adjoined Number Twelve but, rather than being a house of ill repute, Number Ten was barely a house at all. The lower windows and door were covered with steel shutters. A4 notices of possession had long since been torn off them or lost to the elements. Ivy grew up from the front garden and covered most of one side of the house. Higher up at the roofline the guttering was gone and the roof wasn't far behind. When it rained water cascaded down the front of the house feeding the ivy and hurrying the eventual collapse of the whole building.

Dean nodded but he realised he was no longer thinking about people carriers and abandoned houses.

He was more worried about what Vikki was doing applying to Goldsmiths. A university all the way down in London. Hundreds of miles away from Moss Side, guns and Dean.

15

Southern Cemetery was Manchester's very own city of the dead. A vast complex sandwiched between Chorlton and Didsbury, it was home to thousands upon thousands of Mancunians. Its diversity mirrored Manchester's own. Here was the Polish section, looked over by its memorial to the Katyn massacre, there Greeks gathered, while Hindus, Jews and Italians all clung to their own for comfort. In death as in life.

At this time of night, the lamp posts that lined the paths of the cemetery had begun to come on, creating narrow corridors of light between the endless, dark spaces beyond. It was almost serene. But the piles of cellophane-wrapped flowers, water-damaged teddies, rain-worn photographs and long since illegible cards all made sure that it was impossible to forget what it was that lay in those dark spaces beyond the illuminated safety of the path.

Lesha walked among the graves. In the fading light she picked out names and dates and final words that someone's loved ones had chosen to remember them by. She kept a brisk pace, never stopping, never taking time to reflect as she passed the giant tombstones of city elders and the half-finished inscriptions of families separated in death.

Fleeing Ani's house she had walked, almost without thinking, down Princess Parkway to the cemetery. The place she came so often looking for comfort and relief. To be with Kieran's memory. Thousands of graves but not one of them held the body of her son. Kieran was out there somewhere, a lost boy in unknown soil.

As her heart slowed and the sweat from her walk began to dry, salty and rough on her skin, it started to dawn on her exactly what she'd done.

Ani Delgado was an expert in fear. He sat in Moss Side, a king in his own mind. His fiat was terror and with guns and knives the Chopboys enforced his will. Ani didn't have money. He'd never been driven to amass the impossible fortunes that drug trafficking could provide. That wasn't what Ani wanted. He wanted respect. He wanted his name to ring out. He was the last man standing from three decades of strife and he wanted everyone to know it.

So to do what Lesha did, slap him, in his own back garden. In full view of his craven sycophants. That was unforgivable. It was only Ani's shock and Lesha's quick exit that had prevented something far worse from happening. But Lesha knew that Ani would never back down now. To forgive a display of disrespect like that would be to undermine everything he craved.

He'd already ordered the murder of Kieran and almost certainly had a hand in Tommy's death too. Why would he hesitate to kill Lesha?

Names flashed by from stone markers as Lesha marched past, slowly taking in the full horror of what she'd done.

Her mind went to Graham at home. He was a big man who could easily take care of himself but even so she'd have to tell him what had happened with Ani. That thanks to Lesha's actions his relationship with her made him a marked man.

That was how Ani operated, death was only one option. Ani knew he could only kill you once. He preferred you to live in terror. He would go after your family, your home, your business, anyone who you cared about was fair game.

Finally, at the edge of the children's graveyard, Lesha stopped walking. A few seconds later her scrambled thoughts caught up with her and before she knew it she was laughing.

Terror? Ani Delgado had killed her only son. He had brought down a parent's worst nightmare upon Lesha and she was still standing. Ani could kill her but nothing he could do would match the cruelty and sadness of Kieran's death.

She looked out over Southern Cemetery and the moment of triumph quickly passed. She wished more than anything she knew where her son was. Lesha turned to look down at his face, smiling out from her tattoo. Until she laid him to rest properly he would lie with her.

As long as Kieran was with her, Ani Delgado couldn't hurt her.

Lesha felt the chill as evening began to approach. The light was gradually fading as clouds filled up the pale blue sky.

She was about to leave and finally return home to Graham when she saw someone she'd not seen in decades. She recognised him instantly. The thick, squat outline of his powerful body, the shaved head and light brown skin. He was standing in the middle of the children's graveyard, bent down looking at something. A bouquet of flowers in his hand.

16

'If things go well with Nate, I've got other clients I'd like to introduce you to. Big names who could use a man like you.'

After leaving the cemetery Malton had gone to Bea's flat with the intention of asking her more about Nate Alquist. Nate's case was the first time Malton and Bea had mixed work and pleasure and he wanted to make sure he had all the information possible. Instead he'd found himself laid out flat on Bea's giant, Caesar-sized bed while she sat astride him and rode out the day's frustrations on his hard body.

Bea lived at the top of the tallest of three tower blocks that overlooked the Mancunian Way as it merged into Regent Road. To one side all of Manchester's future spread out before you. To the other the Salford suburb of Ordsall with its overlooked estates and industrial units. As dominating as the three skyscrapers were, already yet more tower blocks were being built all around. Soon enough the three towers would no longer stand out on the gateway to Salford but simply be yet another vertical punctuation mark on the Manchester skyline.

Malton and Bea lay side by side on the bed, Bea's post-coital brain now firmly back on work.

Malton had hardly put up any resistance to Bea's seduction. Lying next to her on the bed he began to wonder why that was? For the time that they'd been together Bea had made his life easy. She didn't need him. He didn't have to save her from anyone. When they were together it felt almost like a business relationship. It was Bea who had taken things to the next level and suggested feeding her clients to Malton.

The Nate Alquist job was the first fruits of that arrangement and the way it was going it could well be the last. Having had time to think it over, Malton was now certain that Nate was holding back more than just Zak's new girlfriend. Something was definitely wrong about the whole situation. Nate was a man who'd played the system his whole life. Why would he stop now? Finding out that he had a witness in Zak's girlfriend all pre-packaged and ready to go was just too convenient. Malton knew when he was being fucked with.

The more he thought about Zak's flat the more questions he had. All that money and the drugs. It felt like someone was trying too hard to make Zak's murder look gang-related. Malton didn't know any criminal who'd resort to that level of violence and then leave thousands of pounds of cash and product just lying there.

Whoever killed Zak Alquist wanted him found like that. But why? And what was the real reason behind his death that they were so desperate to cover up?

More than anything he wanted to know whether or not Bea was in on whatever it was that was going on. But until he had a clearer idea of exactly what it was that Nate was up to he decided to keep quiet.

'So, what did Nate say to you?' asked Bea, innocently.

'That he wanted me to find his son's killer,' said Malton blankly.

Bea rolled over onto her front, propped herself up on her elbows for a moment before dropping her head onto Malton's chest. Her blonde hair flowed out over his scarred torso. Compared to Malton she was tiny. A small, soft, white body filled out with full breasts and hips. A tattoo of a worker bee on the base of her spine, which doubled as the logo for her law firm.

'We're a team on this you know? Anything I can do to help you just ask.'

'Did you know Zak's new girlfriend was the one who found his body?'

'Poor girl,' said Bea.

'And that Nate's keeping her hidden in a hotel in town.'

'I'm not surprised,' said Bea, running her fingers around the solid muscle of his chest. Her face felt warm against his skin. 'This is why he wanted you. After what happened with his son's trial he doesn't trust GMP. And why would he?'

Bea's lack of surprise about Nate Alquist hiding a material witness from the police was as much of a red flag as Nate doing it in the first place. Malton was glad they'd already had sex. His head was clear.

'What really happened with his son's trial? Beyond what was in the papers?' asked Malton casually.

Bea broke into a smile, her lipstick-red lips framing her perfect, white teeth.

'I did my job,' she said.

'Who was the third person Zak claimed was there?'

'It doesn't matter. The DNA showed there was someone else there. It's the police's job to find out who. All I needed was the reasonable doubt.'

'And you didn't ask Zak who that was?' said Malton.

'You of all people should know why he wouldn't want to give a name. He didn't offer and I didn't ask,' said Bea, rolling off the bed and heading into the shower.

As the shower started Malton sat alone on the bed and looked around at his opulent surroundings. This was the world he'd beaten and bullied his way into. Thirty years of building from the ground up. From the pavements of Moss Side to the penthouses of the town centre.

Not once had he ever lost the fear that he could end up right back where he began. That was what had kept him on top all this time. Never truly trusting anyone. Never owing anyone a thing. Never letting himself be dragged into someone else's life so completely that he couldn't step away at a moment's notice.

Zak Alquist never had any of that. He was born into money. When he went to Moss Side to live out childish fantasies he knew whatever happened, with one phone call his dad could sweep in and save him with his money and his connections.

That's exactly what Nate had done. Paid Bea Wallace to get his son off a murder charge. If Zak thought he could get away with murder just how far would he push it? Far enough to wind up dead?

The shower stopped and Bea emerged, dripping wet, her skin glowing softly pink. She wrapped her hair into a turban with a towel but left the rest of her naked.

'I almost forgot to tell you,' she said casually. 'I came across something the other day. It might be nothing but if you want I can follow it up.'

Malton sat up in bed. There was something off about Bea's tone. He didn't know why but suddenly he had a sinking feeling in his gut.

'What?' he asked calmly.

'A witness statement, just one line in about sixty pages. Mentioned a murder. Well torture and then murder. Over in Liverpool. Around the same time as what happened to your ex. James.'

17

Sergio and Raheem messily gobbled up their dinner while Lesha knelt between them rubbing their ears and digging her fingers into their soft white fur. She'd bought the two Akitas shortly after Kieran died. The house felt so empty without him and without a body to bury her grief had become an open wound. Desperate for something to hold on to Lesha had found the dogs, but she always felt that really they had found her.

As she fumbled her way into the painful new world of being a bereaved parent, Sergio and Raheem were always by her side. They were powerfully built with giant, muscular heads and thick, staunch bodies. When Lesha watched TV they would jump up beside her, their warm, soft bodies pressing in tight on either side. At night they would sleep at the foot of her bed watching over her. Sergio and Raheem were the first inkling Lesha had that life might still go on.

Now she doted on them. Regular appointments for grooming their fluffy white fur. Only raw dog food, nothing processed for her two boys. She walked them twice a day and couldn't wait to get home to find them excited to see her.

Luckily Graham was a dog person. When they first met he fell for Sergio and Raheem just as much as he fell for Lesha.

Lesha watched as he heated up the dinner that had long gone cold after her walk to and from Southern Cemetery. He didn't mind. Graham never did. He had never married and was in his forties but still running marathons and working full-time as a chippie. He was tall and heavily built with short, salt and pepper hair and a beard to match. A man's man.

He was there when she woke up crying. He knew when to ask and when to be silent. Lesha had no idea what a man like him thought he was doing with someone like her but she was more than glad of him.

Graham set two plates down on the table. Steam rose up from the freshly microwaved food. The kitchen smelled of garlic. Graham had done chicken Kievs, mashed potatoes and peas. Lesha's favourite. Stodgy, reassuring comfort food. Graham was no cook but he could just about manage Kiev and mash.

Lesha rose, leaving Sergio and Raheem noisily demolishing their dinner. Putting off the moment she would have to tell Graham what had happened this evening a little longer, Lesha crossed the kitchen and went to draw the curtains.

The kitchen looked out over a small front garden onto a scruffy, suburban street, just behind Alexandra Park.

As she went to close the curtains she glanced out and froze. Across the road, illuminated under a street light was a teenage boy. He was dressed all in black, his eyes peeking out from between a hoodie and ski mask. He was staring straight at her.

Lesha hauled the curtains shut and turned away. There waiting for her in the warm kitchen light was Graham and the dogs and the meal he'd cooked on the anniversary of her son's murder.

There was nowhere left to go.

'I fucked up today,' said Lesha flatly.

Graham didn't move or stop eating, he just watched her, giving her the time to find the words.

'You know I told you about Kieran? How he was killed?'

Graham swallowed. 'What those bastards did, it's unforgivable,' he said, darkly.

'I think the man who killed Kieran had Tommy killed.'

Graham looked shocked. 'Tommy Fenwick? From the café? He's dead?'

Lesha nodded. Graham couldn't hide his anger.

'We need to tell the police. Maybe this time they'll finally catch him.'

'That's the thing, they won't do anything. The man who had Tommy killed. He didn't do it himself. He'll have got some kid to do it. Just like he did with Kieran.'

Graham digested this information. A troubled look came over his face.

'The way you're talking. You sound like you know who he is.'

Lesha had always known this moment would come. She'd told Graham everything about Kieran. Her precious boy. How he laughed, how he loved playing football. How he was ticklish and would sleep in with her when he got scared in his own room. The only thing she hadn't told him was who had killed him. The name Ani Delgado meant nothing to Graham. She had hoped to keep it that way.

'I do,' said Lesha sadly. 'With the anniversary today, hearing about Tommy. Something snapped. I confronted him.'

'The man who killed Kieran? He's here in Moss Side?'

'He never left. He never will. This is where he feels most at home.'

Graham was on his feet. 'Fuck him. He won't feel at home when I'm done with him.'

'No! You don't get it. I went to confront him and I fucked up. I lost my temper and I slapped him.'

'I'll do more than that.'

'You're not listening!' Lesha realised she was shouting. Graham stopped mid flow, caught out by her tone.

'Sorry,' he said and let out a deep breath. 'So, you slapped him, sounds like he got off lightly.'

Lesha shook her head. 'He won't leave it there. I disrespected him. In his own backyard. For him that's the worst thing anyone can do. He'll not leave it now. He'll be coming for me. For both of us.'

'Let him try,' said Graham.

'Go to the window,' said Lesha flatly.

Graham rose with a quizzical look on his face and crossed the kitchen. He lifted the curtain and looked out.

'You see?'

Graham dropped the curtain and turned back. 'I see. And I'm here for you. You did the right thing. Showed him the respect he deserved. I'm proud of you.'

Lesha felt herself welling up. She had been ready for Graham to turn and run but before she could burst into tears he was across the kitchen and wrapping his strong, solid arms around her. Sergio and Raheem nuzzled at their feet and finally Lesha let it all out. The reservoir of grief that had come to a head on this dreaded anniversary.

She raised an arm to wipe her tears, embarrassed at the display of emotion.

'I love you, you know that right?' said Graham.

'I love you,' said Lesha.

'So who is he? This bastard?'

Lesha knew this was coming.

'His name's Ani Delgado. He's Kieran's father.'

18

Benton hung up the phone and felt guilty. She'd just called home to tell Jenni to have tea without her. That meant yet another ready meal out of the freezer to be eaten alone while her mother was working late again. Even worse, Jenni had been meant to be at her dad's tonight, before he had called Benton to cancel last minute. Now both parents had let her down.

In the space of a day Benton's missing persons case had wandered into Serious and Organised territory before somehow connecting itself to the most high-profile murder investigation in Manchester right now – that of Zak Alquist. Now Benton really would have to be careful if she didn't want to find herself sucked into the orbit of a much bigger operation.

In a perverse way Missing Persons suited Benton. It let her work alone. No one cared so no one was watching. People were simply grateful to even see a police officer, much less expect any actual results. Under the cover of low expectations Benton did her best work.

Armed with what she'd discovered that day Benton bedded down in the office to go through the evidence. Femi was definitely in the flat when Tommy Fenwick was murdered. Or at least his phone was. And thanks to that phone she knew Femi and Zak Alquist were connected. On top of that Femi was somehow involved in the supply chain of a dealer called Jordan Weekes. Despite the rumour mill churning away on DLChat nothing Benton had found suggested Weekes was grassing on anyone. Unfortunately for Weekes the police had yet to make public the DLChat hack and so in the absence of a better explanation for previously untouchable operations getting rolled up Jordan Weekes had found himself the fall guy.

Somewhere in the intersection of all this information was hiding a young boy called Femi Musa.

By the time Benton looked up from her desk it was dark and the office deserted. But before she could go home and grab a few hours' sleep there was one last call to make.

Standing outside the shabby block of flats on the edge of a junction in Levenshulme, she composed herself. The landlord clearly entertained visions of grandeur and had erected a sign across the front of the collection of terraces and shops he'd converted into a clumsy mess of flats. It read 'Hawksmoor Court'.

Benton took a moment. In her line of work you never quite knew what to expect when you knocked on the door. She'd seen bodies, looked down the barrel of a gun and on more than one occasion been knocked off her feet by someone less than keen to speak to her as they made good their escape. She put her game face on and was about to knock when the door opened and she was greeted by the sight of her ex-husband Simon dressed in a Manchester United kit, clearly on his way out.

From the look on his face he knew he'd been caught.

'So this is why you couldn't have Jenni over tonight?' said Benton, looking Simon up and down.

Benton was doing her best to make the divorce easy on her daughter. No mean feat with a sixteen-year-old who shared all of her father's selfishness and all of her mother's belligerence. Part of that meant shuttling Jenni between the rented house she was now staying in and Simon's flat.

Benton waited for Simon's excuse. She'd heard them all.

Why he quit his job. Why he needed to retrain as a massage therapist. Why now wasn't a good time to go into massage therapy and could Benton please pay for him to do a course in landscape gardening?

Benton was a firm believer in lost causes. As a junior detective she'd single-handedly gone door to door on a murder case that had nothing more than a torso in a suitcase to go on. Eventually thanks to her shoe leather a killer had been brought to justice. Benton had once called the mobile phone of the deputy commissioner in the middle of the night and convinced him that a group of heavily armed men were driving to Hale and unless he authorised an immediate firearms response there was going to be a bloodbath. And it was Benton who persuaded her boss to release a teenage tearaway called Craig Malton who'd been arrested for breaking into cars. Benton was born to back the loser.

But in the case of her ex Simon even Benton finally had to admit defeat and cut her losses. As she was the one with the job, he moved out. To the flat in Levenshulme. A flat that she was currently paying for.

'I need some me time,' said Simon.

'You need something,' said Benton and, turning on her heel, left her ex-husband stood on the doorstep looking for all the world like a naughty child.

***

By the time she got back to the house she was sharing with her daughter, Benton was just about ready to crash. Letting herself in she dodged around the stacks of boxes in the hallway. She could hear Jenni's music from upstairs. It was loud. Jenni was angry. Benton couldn't blame her. She was angry too. Unfortunately for Benton the focus of her daughter's anger was her.

Both her parents had blown her off but it was Benton who would get the blame.

Benton spent the next ten minutes opening boxes, looking in vain for the kettle. She found Simon's collection of *PC World* magazines from the Nineties. A box full of his various unfinished language courses (French, Spanish and Russian) and a box full of hardback rule books for Dungeons and Dragons. But no kettle.

Giving up, Benton settled down on the sofa in the front room and closed her eyes. At least she was finally off her feet.

Beside her sat a police radio that she had 'borrowed' long ago. She liked to leave it on and let the sound of Manchester's suffering soothe her to sleep. All the bad things that constantly happened and would be there waiting for her when she awoke.

Benton let the white noise of police calls wash over. Domestics, social media rows, road traffic collisions and the occasional actual crime.

In the dark of the front room she smiled to herself. Everyone was looking at the murder of Zak Alquist. No one was looking at the disappearance of Femi Musa. She might not have the resources or the profile but she had one thing that Zak's case didn't – the cover of low expectations.

19

Nate Alquist wasn't sparing any expense in keeping his son's girlfriend out of the way. Paramore was a striking black cube of a building on the edge of the city centre. Nate had sprung for one of the largest suites. Everything was decorated in tastefully muted tones of black and grey. From the king-sized bed to the sunken jacuzzi.

In any other situation staying here would be the height of indulgence.

The young woman Malton found himself talking to looked anything but indulged. Despite a balcony giving views over the city, the blackout curtains were drawn. It was only midday but inside the suite it may as well have been the dead of night.

Her name was Izzy and as she sat perched on the edge of the sofa answering Malton's questions, she looked terrified. Malton wasn't sure if it was Zak's murder that had her spooked or whatever hold Nate had over her that let him shut her away like this. But he was going to find out.

Malton had already accepted that everything he would be told would be lies. But that was no problem. The more a person lied the more Malton could tell what it was they weren't saying. Lies were the shadow cast by the truth.

Izzy was stunning. Tall, athletic and black, her closely cropped hair drew even more attention to her striking features.

She sat with her hands clasped together in her lap, her knees pressed tight and her head low. She avoided eye contact as she spoke.

She was very still, but when she did move, for just a moment Malton caught sight of what looked like a bruise beneath her vest, around her collarbone. She didn't look the clumsy sort.

'Tell me again how you found Zak?' said Malton.

Izzy grimaced and in a low voice started talking. She had a Moss Side accent. Ever since she started talking Malton had unconsciously been mirroring her. Letting his own Moss Side accent come to the fore. Giving her something familiar to reach out to in this most unfamiliar of situations.

Malton waited until Izzy had recalled the scene much as he remembered it. The money, the drugs and Zak's body. If she wasn't there then she'd been very well briefed.

'The drugs in his flat,' said Malton. 'Whose were they?'

Izzy shook her head sadly. 'Zak's. He got them on credit. He was planning to sell them. I told him a kilo was much too much. Zak wouldn't listen. Then they started calling him. Asking for their money. Dozens of times a day. He was scared,' said Izzy slowly.

'And did he sell them?' asked Malton.

Izzy shook her head. 'Zak was a posh boy. He was . . . it wasn't his thing. I was coming round for eight. We were going out to eat. And I was late. My Uber didn't turn up. And when I got there I was in a hurry. The front door was open. I got in the lift. Alone. And when I got out I went straight to his flat. But the door was open. It was never open like that. He was too paranoid to leave it open. So I went in and . . .'

Izzy started crying.

Malton was unmoved. This was the third time of asking about finding Zak and every time the details had been identical. Nothing added. Nothing altered. Either she had an amazing memory or someone had been making sure she said the right thing.

In Malton's line of work people didn't talk. He dealt with drug dealers and murderers. Everyone from professional hitmen to deranged psychopaths. None of them ever volunteered information. Years of working with the worst the city had to

84

offer meant that Malton had refined his toolbox accordingly. He could cajole and threaten, bribe and blackmail his way to the truth. Only very occasionally would the gloves come off and even then he often found that having taken a reluctant party somewhere no one would ever hear them scream, very often they had a very sudden change of heart and told him everything without him ever having to lay a finger on them.

But to be led to a plush hotel room and presented with a willing witness giving him a blow-by-blow account of every detail? For Malton that was more than a red flag.

'Did Zak ever talk about Carrie?' asked Dean.

'We're not here to talk about Carrie,' chastised Bea from over Malton's shoulder.

When he had arrived at the suite he'd only been half surprised to find Bea there waiting for them. She told him that Nate had requested she be present. Make sure Izzy was taken care of.

Last night Bea had dropped a bombshell. The mention of a scant single line in a much bigger testimony. But in the course of that one line it was as if an earthquake had rocked the fiercely guarded walls within which Malton held inside all the pain and sadness that he'd both suffered and caused.

James's death had left an indelible stain on Malton's soul. In the immediate aftermath he'd torn through Liverpool in a desperate, grief-fuelled hunt for James's killers. He'd found nothing. In all the years that passed James's killers grew more and more distant.

Until last night.

Malton knew Bea had chosen this exact moment to tell him about this lead. She had taken a risk letting a client like Nate hire Malton. She wanted to make sure that Malton played ball.

Malton knew what she was doing but if it meant getting closer to finding James's killers he was happy to be played.

'He never talked about Carrie,' said Izzy.

'We're not here to talk about Carrie,' said Bea more firmly, her cool RP accent slipping just a little into her native Geordie.

Izzy hung her head.

'OK,' said Malton. 'How long were you going out with Zak?'

Izzy thought for a moment. 'Three months?' she said, almost as a question to Malton.

If Nate Alquist was to be believed Zak had turned his life around since his acquittal. Three months put the relationship squarely around the time Zak got off from a murder charge. Something about a schoolboy like Zak from Worsley and a woman like Izzy from Moss Side didn't add up.

'How did you meet?' asked Malton.

Izzy paused. Her eyes roamed the room then she let out a nervous laugh.

'A bar, in town. The Ivy.'

Malton nodded. A girl like Izzy could find someone to pay for her to drink wherever she wanted. Still, the Ivy seemed a strange place for Zak to be hanging out. It was an opulent bar and restaurant housed in the ultra-modern Spinningfields complex. Classy and luxurious but hardly the sort of place a wannabe drug dealer would turn up. But then Zak Alquist had his father's money. Malton had long ago learned that the rich didn't live like everyone else. Could that be what Izzy saw in a teenage Zak Alquist? His father's money?

'When you found Zak, why did you call his father and not the police?'

Izzy screwed her eyes up.

'I was scared. I wasn't thinking. Nate's all right. He's keeping me here,' she said, quickly adding, 'for my own protection. He's paying for all this. I trust him and I wanted to help Zak.'

'But not by calling the police?' said Malton.

Izzy looked at him and for the first time since she started talking, Malton saw something in her eyes. Not just the dull fear but the tiniest flicker of defiance.

'You're from Moss Side,' she said. 'Would you call the police?'

Malton smiled and conceded the point.

'If everyone always called the police, you'd be out of a job,' said Bea breezily.

Malton wasn't sure if Bea thought she was successfully steering him away from what he wanted to know or if she thought that this was all a game that the two of them were playing. Either way it was becoming clear that whatever was happening here, if he was going to get to the bottom of it he'd need to isolate Bea from his hunt for Zak's killer. Let her feel like she was in the driving seat while he got on with discovering the truth.

'I've only got one more question,' said Malton, clasping his huge hands together and leaning in. He'd saved this one until last.

'The people who were selling Zak drugs, the drugs Zak was trying to sell. The ones that were in his flat when he was killed. The people he was scared of. I need a name,' said Malton. Whatever compassion he had in his eyes faded to black and he held Izzy's gaze.

In Malton's line of work things were never this easy. Clues were never handily left next to bodies and there was never a witness waiting for you in a plush hotel suite to put it all together. He'd heard enough to know that everything he'd heard in this room had been theatre. Created by Nate Alquist for his benefit.

Until he could find out why, all he could do was play his part.

Whether what Izzy said next was the truth or a lie, if he had a name it would be one more thread to pull.

Izzy looked Malton in the eye.

'Jordan Weekes.'

20

Normally Lesha enjoyed the walk from Whalley Range into Moss Side to open up Kieran's Place. Not today. Graham had insisted on coming with her and so they walked side by side in silence through scruffy suburbs towards Alexandra Park.

Ordinarily she'd cut down a path to one side of the park but today she made sure she walked straight through the middle. Smiling at every jogger and dog walker she saw. Safety in plain sight.

The fear of the night before had given way to something unexpected. Hope. Graham wasn't part of this world. He'd been brought up in Burnley and moved to Manchester in his late teens. The dense, local mythology of Ani Delgado meant nothing to him. Lesha saw Ani through Graham's eyes and suddenly he didn't seem nearly so frightening.

As long as she had Graham and Kieran with her she could weather any storm.

They crossed Princess Parkway and headed up Claremont Road. There was still a lot of litter left over from the carnival. Bins overflowed with torn bin liners piled up beside them and yet more litter strewn across the pavements and gutters.

This was Moss Side. It wasn't Ani Delgado's personal kingdom. It was her home.

As she turned off onto the road to Kieran's Place all that hope fell away.

The front of the shop was gone. Someone had not just smashed the windows, they'd torn out the frames and half demolished the front wall too. It looked like someone had rammed a car into the café.

Lesha was running now. She needed to see it up close and begin to make her peace with the reality before her imagination could run away with her. Graham kept pace behind her.

She staggered through the shattered frontage and found the inside of the café in pieces. Every bit of furniture had been smashed to splinters. Red paint had been thrown over everything. Like blood.

But the thing that let her know that this was just the beginning was still waiting for her.

There, sat in the middle of the floor amongst the broken furniture and paint was a giant pile of freshly laid human shit.

As the weight of it all threatened to crush her she felt a solid hand on her shoulder. It was Graham. Upright and strong beside her.

'Dirty bastards,' he muttered. 'Fuck 'em. Let me make a few calls, get some of the lads round. We'll have this place back together in no time.'

With Graham's calmness, all at once the spectre of Ani Delgado began to pale in the Moss Side sunshine.

'Who the fuck does this Ani think he is?'

'Are you open, Lesha?' came a voice from outside.

It was Phil, one of the regulars who came early and liked to help Lesha set up for the day. He was a giant, nearly seven foot, completely bald and easily four hundred pounds. But he had the mental age of a child.

Phil stood in the ruins of the shop looking confused.

'What happened?' he asked, an edge of fear to his voice.

Before she could answer Graham smiled and said, 'All right, Phil! We're having a bit of a redesign today. You want to help?'

Phil's face lit up and Lesha knew that with Graham at her side Ani Delgado could never win.

21

It wasn't hard to find the garden centre where Ryan Lewis worked. Centring his search around St John's Church, Dean simply looked for any garden centres within a five-mile radius and started with the nearest.

He got lucky.

Sunshine Plants and Flowers sat between Didsbury and Cheadle within spitting distance of the motorway. The frontage had seen better days but inside it was packed with retirees browsing garden ornaments while outside there was an extensive collection of plants and flowers of every description.

Dean had woken up wanting to talk to Vikki about what he'd seen the night before. The Goldsmiths application. When Vikki had started her fashion course at Salford Uni, Dean couldn't have been more encouraging. When he first met her he'd only just started working for Malton Security. Vikki was sixteen, just a couple of years younger than Dean, and living alone in Salford having been abandoned by her drug addict father. He'd immediately felt the need to do everything he could to help her.

What he hadn't expected was the transformation that took place. In a few short months Vikki had gone from a broken scared girl to a vibrant young woman who knew exactly what she wanted to do with her life. What's more she was good at it. Throwing herself into every project. Volunteering to work for free doing costume for film and music students. Making friends and making connections. Vikki seized every opportunity.

By the time he realised he'd fallen for her the feeling was mutual.

As happy as he was for Vikki, Dean realised he'd started to wonder where he fitted in to. it all. Why on earth would this confident, ambitious new Vikki need someone like him? Dean hadn't gone to university. He'd barely scraped his GCSEs. Working for Malton was his life.

Every time Vikki took him to a new club or introduced him to a new group of friends he found it harder and harder to see just what it was she still saw in him.

But when he'd woken up this morning Vikki had already gone. To rub salt into the wound she'd made him a stack of pancakes and left it with a note – LOVE YOU! V XXX

Dean ate his pancakes in silence. Delicious ashes in his mouth.

But finding Ryan Lewis so quickly gave Dean something else to focus on. He wanted to know what Ryan had to say about Zak and the trial. Was Ryan quite as forgiving as his parents? More importantly, was he the third person at the scene of his sister's murder?

Ryan was working in the far corner of the outdoor area at Sunshine Plants and Flowers. Past the fruit trees towards the back he was loading a trolley with bags of compost, struggling to wrangle the huge, wet sacks.

Just as it looked like Ryan was about to drop the bag he was in the process of loading Dean rushed in and took one end, helping him place it on the trolley.

'Can you take a break?' asked Dean wiping compost off his hands. Ryan looked Dean up and down, trying to work out exactly who had just come to his aid. Whatever suspicions he had quickly vanished when Dean added, 'Do you smoke?'

They sat shielded from view of the shoppers and staff, hidden in a small, plastic smoking shelter tucked away behind some trees. It was perfect.

Ryan had already smoked down his first cigarette before Dean even got a chance to speak.

Dean watched him suck the hot smoke into his lungs with the professional hunger of an ex-addict.

Today Ryan was in the black trousers and polo shirt uniform of Sunshine Plants and Flowers but his tattoos were clearly visible. His hands and face were covered in them. More like scribbles than anything.

Dean wondered about the CB on Ryan's cheek. If the C stood for Carrie, what did the B stand for?

'What are you on?' asked Dean as Ryan lit his second cigarette.

Ryan turned and looked at Dean through foggy eyes, as if trying to will his thoughts into focus.

'Methadone,' he said slowly as he lit the cigarette and inhaled.

'I'm sorry about your sister,' said Dean. 'And Zak.'

Ryan snorted. It sounded smothered, as if coming from somewhere lost deep inside him.

'It's great what your parents do. Forgiveness.'

Ryan's jaw clenched, he pulled the cigarette out of his mouth and turned to Dean. 'When do I get forgiven?'

His head turned away and he looked up at the trees sheltering them.

'It wasn't your fault your sister died,' said Dean, delivering his line not quite as a question but not quite as a statement either.

'I was ill,' said Ryan to himself. 'It's an illness.'

'You can't help being ill,' said Dean.

'And they know that. They use you.' Ryan's voice finally sounded awake. Something was stirring.

'Who are they?' asked Dean.

Ryan ignored him. 'They make out like they're your friends. Come over. Give you gear. Next thing you know they're beating the shit out of you. Locking you in your own flat. Fucking everything up.'

The cigarette he was holding burned down to his finger. He looked down curiously as the hot ash met his flesh. He didn't seem to feel it.

'Let me get you a new one,' said Dean offering another cigarette.

Ryan didn't take it. He stubbed his old cigarette out between his fingers and continued. 'So when they find out Carrie was going out with a rich kid they tell me, *Do this one thing and we go.* One thing. And it'd all be over.'

Dean put the cigarette back in the packet and said, 'What thing?'

Ryan closed his eyes and began to rock. 'Idiot. Idiot. IDIOT!' His hand swung up and he punched himself in the side of the head. Again and again.

Dean dived on him, holding his arm back. As he got wrapped up with Ryan he found himself looking into his face. He could smell the fresh tobacco on his breath. See his ruined yellow teeth up close.

'It wasn't your fault,' said Dean.

'They said they were only going to rob him,' said Ryan pitifully. He gave a loud sniff and pulled himself together. Holding up his arms in surrender to indicate to Dean that whatever had gripped him had passed.

He wiped his nose with the back of his hand and shook his head.

'Fucking Femi,' he muttered to himself. 'Set the whole thing up.'

22

Benton opened her second can of Diet Coke and peered closer at the TV screen. The TV was ancient. A portable combi television and DVD player. Benton was old enough to remember when GMP still used the VHS combis.

An image of Zak Alquist's flat filled the screen.

Benton didn't watch much television but when she found herself watching a crime drama, of all the many inaccuracies that infuriated her, the sight of dozens of suited-up crime scene investigators and a couple of detectives traipsing through a crime scene was right up there.

In reality a single investigator films the scene from every angle. Recording everything just as they found it. Then and only then do the crime scene investigators begin the painstaking process of gathering evidence.

Meanwhile detectives must make do with watching the tapes in the back of a police van. A van just like the one in which Benton was now sitting. Turning up outside Zak Alquist's Ancoats flat with a badge, a box of Krispy Kreme doughnuts and a smile, she had managed to find her way into the back of the CSI van with the television and for the past half hour had been taking in what she saw.

Zak Alquist had been beaten to death with a hammer. His flat was littered with money and drugs. Everything about this said gangland feud. Benton thought back to her last gang case. She'd been handed intelligence that had led to the winding up of a major organised crime gang. Almost single-handedly she was responsible for nearly wiping out the drugs trade in Bolton. For at least the couple of weeks it took for someone else to step in and fill the vacuum.

That was what Benton loved. Putting the pieces together. Wading in where most people would be terrified to show their face. Benton knew gangsters intimately. The ones who came from violent homes and knew no better. The nasty ones who got off on knowing people feared them. The greedy ones who thought they were smart enough to get away with it. A whole ecosystem of human weakness. Benton was in her element.

The cocaine from Femi Musa's bedroom was back in evidence but it had given her a name – Jordan Weekes. The man who branded his drugs with a grenade logo. As much as she wanted to talk to Weekes she decided first to head over to the Alquist murder scene to try and learn as much as she could while everyone involved was still running around chasing those early leads. Once the investigation cooled down she would have a lot more explaining to do as to why her missing teenager case had anything to do with Zak Alquist.

Right now all she had to connect Femi to Zak was a photo from a phone. Femi's phone, which had been found at the scene of Tommy Fenwick's murder. Two hammer attacks leading to two bodies. And one boy missing. For all Boyle knew the hammer recovered from Tommy's flat was the one that had killed Zak Alquist.

The video came to an end. Benton took out the DVD and put in the next one in sequence. Now the CSIs were in shot, slowly and systematically removing the evidence.

Benton hit fast forward. She knew exactly which piece of evidence she was looking for. After a little back and forth she found her place.

A CSI was kneeling over what Benton recognised from the earlier tapes as a brick of cocaine. But more than that. She paused the DVD.

Printed into the cocaine was a circle enclosing a hand grenade. Jordan Weekes's brand.

Benton took a photo of the screen with her phone and started the DVD playing again. The CSI on screen was picking up the brick of cocaine when the doors to the van flew open.

'Benton! What are you doing in my van?'

Benton closed her anorak and turned round with a smile to meet a voice she recognised. DCI Steven Priestly.

Priestly was younger than her. He was a graduate detective. One of the new breed who had leapfrogged years in uniform mopping up human misery and gone straight into plain clothes.

He was from Liverpool but posh enough to have just a very slight lilt to his voice.

'I was just passing and wondered if you needed a hand?'

'We're doing just fine,' said Priestly assuming the demeanour of his senior rank.

Priestly was a typical graduate copper. In his mind the pinnacle of policing was to get to a rank where your main duties involved mismanaging resources, doing press conferences in your dress uniform and waving a flag on the police float at Pride.

Benton had found her rut and she was quite happy in it. Or at least she had been before the DLChat goldrush gave the higher-ups the excuse they were looking for to put the boot in.

'You were there at the DLChat briefing; I saw you. You were eating a sausage roll,' said Priestly peevishly. 'You heard the plan. We need veterans like you to hold the fort while the DLChat operation soaks up manpower. The most important thing you could be doing is keeping the wheels turning.'

He'd got over his initial annoyance at finding Benton in the van and now it sounded like he was winding up to giving a pep talk. If it was a toss-up between a bollocking and a motivational chat from Priestly, Benton would take the bollocking every day of the week.

'Sorry to tread on your toes, sir,' said Benton with a deferential nod.

'Bit of professionalism next time,' said Priestly, already growing bored of her.

'Sir,' muttered Benton as sincerely as she could stomach.

She watched as he strode back towards the crime scene.

But Benton didn't mind. She'd not just seen the matching grenade logo. She'd seen something else on that tape. Something that she was betting Priestly wouldn't spot for at least another couple of days.

A couple of days would be all she needed.

23

A low, canine growling was coming from behind the six-foot electric gates that barred the way to Jordan Weekes's Heaton Moor home.

Across the front of the solid wooden gates, in bright red letters, someone had spray-painted:

JORDAN WEEKES = GRASS = DEAD.

Malton pressed the intercom once more and then he and Dean stood waiting for an answer.

Malton knew what would have to come next. He couldn't leave without knowing for himself whether or not Jordan Weekes was inside. Both the broker Adam Parley and Zak's girlfriend Izzy, in her heavily scripted account of Zak's murder, had named Weekes. And from the graffiti it was clear Malton wasn't the only one after him. That meant it was even more vital to lay hands on him.

Dean had filled him in on his meeting with Ryan Lewis. Ryan had been cuckooed. A drugs gang had taken over his flat and tormented him until he agreed to set up his sister's boyfriend Zak Alquist to be robbed. Whatever happened with that robbery ended up with Carrie Lewis getting stabbed. Who by, Ryan wouldn't say. What he would say was a name. Femi. It wasn't much but it was a start. For Zak Alquist to be involved in a murder and then murdered himself felt like far too much of a coincidence, whatever Bea might want Malton to believe.

If this Femi was involved in Carrie's death it wasn't too hard to imagine he'd had something to do with Zak's too.

Dean had done good. Malton was pleased how easily the boy seemed to pick up on what Malton was thinking and take the initiative. His suspicion that Zak's murder was only the tip of a much larger, murkier iceberg was looking more and more on the money. Hopefully Jordan Weekes would be able to bring this whole thing closer to a resolution and explain why drugs bearing his logo were found in Zak's flat.

The sooner he found Zak's killer the sooner he could pursue Bea's lead into James's murder.

Weekes's house was next to a park in Heaton Moor on a road of large, detached houses. Some retained their Victorian appearance but most had been renovated with white rendered additions, bonded driveways and – like Weekes's place – heavy security.

As a teenager Malton used to dream about the suburbs of South Manchester. Where the daily business of survival was replaced with what to him appeared to be a far easier way of living. Gently dilapidated houses, scruffy middle-class people whose clothes and cars had seen better days but who walked around like the world was theirs, always had been and always would be. A white world that made a mixed-race Malton wonder what his own white father had done to be excluded so completely from it.

'Thoughts?' Malton asked Dean. He saw that Dean had already been examining the entry system. Dean had about half a foot in height on Malton and had been peering over the gate.

'The dog looks like a Tosa,' said Dean.

One of the four banned breeds, Japanese Tosas were the dog of choice for criminals who wanted to flout both the law and their refined sense of violence. The dogs were bred for pit fighting and trained to attack in silence. Very pricey dogs. Jordan Weekes was doing OK for himself.

From the sound coming from the driveway Weekes had been neglecting his dog training.

'And the gate?'

'Easy enough, you want me to open it?'

Navigating security systems was just one of the many things Malton had taught Dean over the last year. Malton Security installed high-end systems and so Malton knew the schematics of every major security device on the market. From time to time Malton Security even employed a former military engineer when a client required an especially secure system. It meant that there was no security measure out there that Malton didn't know how to circumvent given enough time.

Sometimes there were fail-safes, other times it was a case of dismantling a system with great care – like defusing a bomb. Occasionally a heavy hammer would do the job.

'You do the gate; I'll get the dog,' said Malton.

Dean nodded, and standing on tiptoes, began fiddling with something on the other side of the gate.

Malton stood by the side of the gate that would open first. The growling got louder. A few times Dean flinched back. The Tosa was jumping up to try and bite him.

Malton slipped off the heavy, drill cotton chore shirt he was wearing over a fine, knitted, long-sleeve polo shirt. He took a couple of zip ties out of one pocket and stood ready, the chore shirt in one hand, the zip ties in the other.

Malton was no dog lover but he wasn't the sort of person who relished the idea of having to hurt an animal. In his experience if push came to shove he could get his jacket around a dog's head, disorientating it while he pinned the animal down and zip-tied its legs together. The dog wouldn't be best pleased, but it would be subdued without getting injured.

Hopefully Malton would be able to say the same.

Dean looked over. 'You ready?' he asked.

Malton planted his feet and got low, raising up his jacket like some kind of Mancunian matador.

He nodded to Dean who reached over the gate and pressed something that started the gate rolling back.

Malton heard the scrabble of paws on driveway as the Tosa scrambled from Dean's side of the gate to the other side where Malton was waiting. The growling fell silent. The dog was getting ready to attack.

As the gate opened he saw it. A tall, muscular dog with a short shiny coat. The genetic memory of the violence bred into it was impossible to miss. It stopped barking and took a step back waiting for the gap to be wide enough to make its move.

Malton fixed on its eyes through the gap. He felt himself squat lower, ready to power forward if necessary.

A split second later and the Tosa pounced.

Malton flung an elbow across his body, knocking the thickly muscled dog out of the air and back into the driveway. It was strong, maybe too strong to be wrapped up and hogtied.

As the dog scrambled to pounce once more Malton looked it in the eye and bellowed, 'DOWN.'

Malton saw Dean flinch at the sound of his voice. A deep, guttural command pitched at the animal subconscious.

The Tosa froze.

Malton took a step forward and drew up to his full height. He lowered his arms, unafraid.

'DOWN.'

The Tosa pawed the ground for a moment and then settled itself down on the driveway, looking up at Malton ready for its next command.

Dean was about to speak but Malton held up a hand. He wasn't finished. He walked up to the Tosa. Keeping his eyes on it the whole time. It was a magnificent dog. The result of generations of breeding and brutality had resulted in a creature with a superficial veneer of elegant respectability barely hiding a monstrous bone-deep savagery.

Malton couldn't help but feel he was looking into the eyes of a kindred spirit.

'STAY,' he commanded.

The Tosa did as it was ordered.

'You're on fucking camera,' called a voice from across the driveway.

A blonde woman with a lip-filler pout stood in the doorway holding a baseball bat.

'He's not here,' she said.

Malton could tell from the way she spoke that the baseball bat was no idle bluff.

'We're here to help Jordan,' said Malton, fixing the woman with the same calm deep stare that he had just used on the Tosa.

'I told you lot, I don't need the fucking police.'

Malton smiled. 'We're not the police.'

24

Between them Phil and Graham had taken next to no time to clear Kieran's Place of all the broken material. Whoever had smashed up the café hadn't been able to get into the kitchen and so once the debris had been cleared and the human shit scrubbed away, Lesha could get started on the day's business.

Phil helped her in the kitchen while a stream of workmen started arriving and under Graham's supervision a whole new café began to take shape before her eyes.

When Lesha had opened Kieran's Place four years ago she was alone. The furniture was begged or borrowed. The kitchen was the result of a funding application. Everything was scraped together with love and determination. And until this morning it had stayed that way.

But now Graham was here with his mates they seemed intent on not just replacing what had just been destroyed but remaking it entirely.

A couple of lads were installing built-in benches along the walls while someone else had turned up with a truck full of tables and chairs scrounged from an old pub.

Graham was helping to rebuild the counter, talking at length on the phone to a man about various measurements. Then another van full of fitters turned up and with Phil's help they carried out a glass food cabinet ready to be installed.

Kieran's Place had been ramshackle but it had been a testament to one mother's determination. In the past she'd resisted Graham's offers to reach out to his numerous contacts in the trades and upgrade the interior. For her the café as it was represented a defiant cry of grief.

Now thanks to Ani Delgado it was becoming an even louder cry. Not just of one woman but an entire community. Without even realising it Ani Delgado had given Lesha the chance to see just how much good she'd done these past four years.

The pace was frantic and the workmen had to work around the stream of regulars who still needed feeding but somehow the shock and fear of the morning had given way to a sense of proud defiance.

This was the Moss Side Lesha remembered.

Nearly two decades ago she had fled Ani Delgado's Moss Side with her son in a futile attempt to save him. But he'd been back on the bus and back into the Moss Side that had got him killed.

Now she realised that she was wrong to run. The only way to beat someone like Ani was to stand together and stand strong. Tell a better story. One of decency and hope.

A voice cut into her thoughts. 'You should tell them they're wasting their time.'

Lesha looked up and saw Ani standing in the middle of the debris. Her gut somersaulted over and she grabbed the food cabinet to steady herself.

Ani saw her reaction and smiled. She hated that he looked so handsome.

'You OK, mate?' said Graham, suddenly beside Ani. He was far bigger than Ani, and with the body of a man who built things for a living.

'He's just a well-wisher,' said Lesha unconvincingly.

'If you like,' said Ani with a smirk.

Graham didn't move. 'Sorry, mate, I didn't get your name,' he said coldly.

Ani darkened and in an instant both men knew what was happening. A few customers stood back. In the other corner the men building the benches carried on oblivious.

'You're Graham, aren't you?' said Ani. 'You know about your missus?'

'I know about you,' said Graham.

'Graham, don't,' said Lesha.

'Then you know what a fucking mistake you made hooking up with her,' said Ani.

He didn't get to say anything else because a giant, flabby arm had wrapped itself around his neck.

Phil, Lesha's most loyal regular, had grabbed Ani in a head-lock. Phil was at least a foot taller than Ani, his bald head not short of brushing on the ceiling.

'Phil, no!' screamed Lesha.

'Get away from her!' screamed Phil, his grip tightening.

Ani's face was pure shock. Part fear, part incredulity that this was happening to him. He flailed, his arms coming back and flapping uselessly against Phil's immense bulk.

'Phil, mate, put him down,' said Graham trying to keep the panic from his voice.

Lesha was out from behind the counter, a hand on Phil's shoulder. As calmly as she could she said, 'You have to put him down now, love. For me.'

But Phil didn't put Ani down. Instead he lifted him up. Ani's feet scraped the floor as Phil held him suspended in a choke-hold. Phlegm began to form on the edge of Ani's mouth. His eyes began to roll back.

Lesha looked up at Phil and somehow managed to keep her tone slow and even. 'I know you just want to help. But now you need to put him down. He wasn't doing anything. He's a friend. We're all friends here.'

Phil's face struggled to process this.

'He's a friend,' said Lesha firmly and all at once Phil let go.

Ani's body fell limply to the floor. Lesha was down beside him. This was bad. If Phil had killed Ani then he was a dead man. Wherever Ani's murderous twin Lani had ended up, as soon as he heard of his brother Ani's death he'd be back and Phil would die by inches.

As Lesha knelt over Ani for just a moment the smell of his skin took her right back to that summer when she'd been a too-easily impressed teenager and Ani had seen an easy mark.

Everyone in the café had stopped. They stood round watching, unsure what had just happened.

Lesha felt them watching her. Willing her to make things right. Now it was her who held Ani's life in her hands. All it would take to end it would be to do nothing.

That wasn't who Lesha was. But as she leaned in to clear Ani's airways his body suddenly spasmed.

Lesha jumped back as Ani sat up, groaned, turned and threw up on the café floor.

He looked up at the eyes watching him and scrambled to his feet, wiping his mouth with the back of his hand.

'You really are that fucking stupid,' gasped Ani, still struggling for breath.

Back upright Ani took in the scene and before Lesha could answer him, he spat on the floor at her feet, gave a defiant sneer and staggered out of the café, disappearing down the alleyways.

25

'You find my husband, you can slap him from me,' Lou Weekes told Malton, struggling to keep the squirming toddler on her lap from treating her like a climbing frame.

Lou looked every inch the drug dealer's long-suffering wife. Malton had seen her type before, ground down by life but still just about clinging on to some of the traces of the high-maintenance girl she'd once been. Now stuck at home with a kid and a husband who suddenly decided that now the cash was coming in maybe he had better places to be.

'Do you know where he might be?' asked Malton, looking around the front room of Jordan Weekes's Heaton Moor home.

The front room was huge. A pair of giant, L-shaped sofas in white crushed velvet bore all the stains of a house with young children. Large chrome and glass letters attached to the walls spelled out BLESSED, BE KIND and LOVE.

Piles of bright plastic toys were scattered across the grey carpet and one whole wall was dominated by a huge projector screen that rose out of a bespoke wooden unit. It was playing CBeebies with the sound off. The picture flickered in and out of focus as if the projector was broken. The small girl on Lou's lap wriggled and twisted, trying to get closer to the screen.

'He'll be out with his slapper,' spat Lou. 'First sign of trouble, he fucks off and leaves me and Daisy here like sitting ducks. I hope they fucking find him. See if she still wants him after they're done with him.'

'Who are "they"? Who's threatening you?' asked Malton.

Lou paused. It was obvious that as much as she wanted to vent about Jordan she was still rightly wary about the two strange men who'd turned up on her driveway.

'If you help me find Jordan I can protect you,' offered Malton.

Lou laughed. 'Can you fuck. What you going to do? Be here twenty-four-seven?'

'Yes,' said Malton and he reached into his chore shirt and handed Lou a card. She looked at it.

'Malton Security? That's you?'

'Yes. You help me and I'll have a man watching your house day and night. He can do it from inside or outside. He can be seen or be hidden. It's up to you. And I'll make sure your security is better than what you've currently got.'

'Took me about thirty seconds to bust open the gate,' said Dean with authority.

'That soft fucking dog,' muttered Lou. She looked from Malton to Dean, making up her mind. 'I don't know what that slag's name is. Only that I found all these photos on his phone. Silly bitch with her tits out and him promising her money. My fucking money. He's only doing it for the novelty.'

Malton inclined his head and let Lou continue.

'She's black isn't she? No offence.' Lou said this last part with the petty sneer of someone hoping very much to cause some offence.

The toddler nearly broke free. Malton nodded to Dean who stood up and held his arms out to Lou.

Lou eyed him suspiciously. 'Don't you fucking drop her,' she said, handing Daisy over. Dean took the little girl over to a pile of toys, sat her down on the carpet and began to talk animatedly with her.

Malton marvelled at how natural Dean was with the little girl. Just for a second Malton wondered if the unborn child Emily had sworn he would never see was a girl or a boy.

Snapping out of it, he turned back to Lou.

'Have you talked to the police?' asked Malton.

'Not fucking us. Nosey bitch next door gets spooked and gives them a call after catching someone trying to break in. Police said if Jordan did fancy being a grass then maybe they could help but otherwise fuck all. He told them to get to fuck. My Jordan's lots of things but he's not a grass. Whatever those pricks with their spray paint think.'

So the police hadn't made the connection from Jordan Weekes's drug business to Zak Alquist's murder yet.

'Did he ever mention someone called Zak Alquist?' Malton said, not skipping a beat.

Lou frowned. 'Who?'

Malton bought her confusion and moved on.

'Do you know how Jordan's drugs could have ended up at a crime scene?'

'Fucking obvious. Criminals do drugs.'

Lou shrugged impatiently but Malton held firm in his silence, allowing Lou to dwell on this until she tentatively added, 'What crime scene?'

'Zak Alquist was murdered. It's been on the news.'

'Told you I don't know who that is. I don't watch the fucking news. I've got a two-year-old.'

'Did Jordan ever sell to anyone from Moss Side?'

Lou took a beat, thinking hard before asking, 'Twenty-four-hour security?'

Malton nodded. 'For as long as it takes.'

She took a deep breath. 'You did not hear this from me, OK? Bad enough they *think* Jordan's a grass. He used to sell to this lot in Moss Side. Don't know their name. Something stupid and gangster rap. I only know that cos we were out once and this black kid came up and said hi to Jordan.'

'What did he look like?'

'Black,' said Lou unhelpfully.

Malton felt whatever lead Jordan Weekes could provide slipping away. Moss Side gangs getting supplied by white dealers higher up the chain wasn't unusual enough to point to anyone in particular.

'Did he have a name?'

Lou shrugged. 'Black name.'

In the corner, Dean was pulling faces for a delighted two-year-old and getting a better reaction than Malton was.

Beneath the glass and chrome BE KIND Lou Weekes sat silently scowling.

Malton didn't bother asking: *A black name like Femi?*

26

It wasn't a brick of cocaine but it was still drugs. A pebble-sized lump of cannabis bud that now sat on the table between Benton and her daughter Jenni.

Benton hadn't even been looking for it. It had fallen out of a pocket as she made a token effort to clear the mountain of laundry which, despite Benton being at work most of the day, Jenni had resolutely refused to help with.

She was stuffing random items into the machine when it had fallen out. It was a testament to how far behind on the laundry Benton was that she hadn't smelled it. Now the tiny lump sat on the kitchen table filling the whole room with its stale stench.

Despite being bone-tired and entirely focused on finding Femi Musa, Benton found herself forced to give 'the drugs talk'. Benton wasn't naive enough to imagine her teenage daughter wouldn't touch drugs; even so, after the day she'd had, this wasn't how she was planning to unwind.

'You know where that comes from?'

Jenni was silent. She was sulking.

'People get trafficked over here. They pay good money with the promise of a job. Then when they get here they get beaten, their passports taken and then they're locked in derelict buildings and forced to grow cannabis for criminal gangs.'

Jenni rolled her eyes. Benton could do without this.

Before leaving the office that night she'd learned that DCI Priestly had been round Jordan Weekes's house. It must have been the grenade logo that tipped him off. Apparently Priestly was too late. Weekes was in the wind and his wife refused to even let them in the door.

After what she'd seen at the Zak Alquist crime scene Benton felt like she was finally getting somewhere and now she had to give this talk to Jenni. Even if Simon had still been around it would be her playing the bad cop.

'They steal the electric to power the growing lamps and heaters. Sometimes that means cables that catch fire. And these farms, they're locked from the outside, so the workers don't escape. There was a fire at a place in Bolton last year. The fire brigade smash in the front door and this guy comes running out. He's screaming. He's on fire. His skin is dripping off him. Every step he takes he leaves a footprint, his own flesh sticking to the floor. Then he drops and dies. Right there in front of everyone. He was growing cannabis. Just like this.' Benton waved the bag at Jenni for emphasis.

'It's not mine,' said Jenni with a defiant smirk.

Benton thought about how much she missed her old beat dealing with violent gangland figures, pimps and drug dealers. It was much easier than this.

'I'm going to have to tell your dad,' she said.

Jenni shrugged. She knew just as well as Benton what a limp threat that was.

'That's all I've got,' said Benton defeated. 'You know what you did. I know what you did. That's it.'

'That's it?' Jenni sounded uncertain. Like this was a trap.

'That's it. I've got work to do. You have a room to go and sulk in. That's it.'

Half-heartedly Jenni flounced out of the room, swerved round several boxes and headed up the stairs, leaving Benton feeling a complete failure of a mother.

But she didn't have time to dwell on it. She'd already put the word out wherever she could, using all the connections she'd built up in Serious and Organised. The kind of connections that for all his degrees and promotions someone like Priestly would never make.

Benton wanted to speak to Jordan Weekes. Urgently.

She hoped when she did find him he might have some answers for the other thing that was playing on her mind. The thing she'd seen on the CSI footage of the murder scene just before Priestly had turned up and thrown her out of the evidence van.

Zak's murder scene was carnage. Blood everywhere. Exactly as you'd expect from a frenzied hammer attack.

But when the CSI had picked up that brick of cocaine there was blood underneath it. It had been placed there after Zak had been killed.

Just like someone had planted it.

27

Lesha watched Sergio and Raheem demolish their food and wished that she could be as happy and carefree as they so obviously were.

Graham was upstairs showering after working in the café all day. Lesha had the curtains closed. She knew someone would still be outside waiting. They were already there when they'd got back from the café, just like last night.

Once Ani was gone it had taken all afternoon for Lesha to calm Phil down. Gently reassuring him that he'd done the right thing.

Everyone was eager to forget what had happened and so that's just what they did. The work went on. The meals got served and before Lesha knew it, it was time to close up. It was as if it had never happened.

But it had.

It was only as the café emptied out and the pace slackened that Lesha had time to really digest what had changed.

Slapping Ani in the face in front of his friends put you on his shit list. Choking him out in public was a death sentence. Phil was a big guy but immensely vulnerable. She couldn't watch him twenty-four-seven; she was having enough of a time just keeping herself safe. Still, she couldn't just leave him and so Lesha had put in a call to his support worker and given an edited account of what had happened. She'd got promises that Phil would be watched more closely for the next few days. It wasn't much but it was the best she could do.

That left her free to go back to worrying about what Ani would do to her. There would be no more intimidation. No more threats. The boy outside watching the house was no longer a warning, he was there keeping tabs. Making sure Ani knew where Lesha was at all times. Giving him options for when he finally decided to make his move.

After what had happened at the café there would be no more long game. No more intimidation. Ani would strike. That much was certain now.

Graham came down glowing pinkly from his shower, filling the kitchen with the smell of soap. He was wearing an old T-shirt and tracksuit bottoms. He was smiling until he caught sight of Lesha.

He wrapped her up in his arms and held Lesha tight to him, letting her feel the warmth of his still-damp skin beneath his T-shirt. 'We got through today, didn't we?' he said nuzzling at her neck.

Lesha pulled away and spoke quickly: 'And tomorrow? And the next day? Ani Delgado is always the last man standing. I grew up with him. Him and his psychotic brother Lani, they outlived everyone. You know how? They killed them first.'

'They're bullies, that's all,' said Graham defiantly. 'I don't do bullies.'

The words were hardly out of his mouth when the brick came through the window, bringing a hail of broken glass with it before bouncing off the kitchen table and rolling across the floor.

Lesha and Graham were on the floor, instinct kicking in. Sergio and Raheem stood their ground, barking territorially.

The tiles felt cold and rough as Lesha pushed her face against them, terrified of what was coming next. She turned her head a little to where Graham had dived. He wasn't moving.

'Are you OK?' shouted Lesha.

Graham slowly lifted his head. 'Are you?'

Lesha flooded with relief. They were unharmed, but only for now.

Lying on the kitchen floor among the broken glass, Lesha knew beyond a shadow of a doubt that she would never be OK. Ani Delgado wouldn't stop now. He never did. Like a cat with a wounded bird, it was only ever a question of how long it would take for him to grow bored and end things.

It had been twenty years since she left him. Five years since he'd killed their son and hidden his body. But now Ani had finally decided her time was up.

28

Malton Security provided security for nearly sixty different venues in the city centre. Each one of those venues had at least one CCTV camera pointed at the street. Many of them had multiple cameras. All recording twenty-four hours a day and all of them backing up to servers at Malton Security HQ.

For the past few hours Dean had been pulling hundreds of hours of time-stamped footage off the cameras and assembling it into a coherent timeline.

Before they'd gone to Jordan Weekes's place it had felt like things were finally moving. Ryan Lewis had revealed Carrie's murder was a robbery gone wrong. Zak had been set up by Ryan at the behest of someone called 'Femi'. Although Ryan hadn't said it, Dean wondered if this Femi could be the third person in Bea's legal defence. Suddenly Bea's dry legal argument had a name. And then there was Lou Weekes telling Malton that Jordan was dealing to a Moss Side gang via a kid with, in her words, a 'black name'. It seemed like Femi was everywhere. Ironically that brought them no nearer to finding out who exactly he was and what his role was in all of this.

The grenade logo drugs found at the scene pointed to Jordan Weekes, and Izzy had confirmed it, but even Dean could see Izzy was lying about something. Either Weekes was involved somehow and had now been hung out to dry or he was an unfortunate random who someone thought fitted the bill to be the fall guy. Either way, until Weekes surfaced, they had hit a dead end. They needed something concrete to go on.

So when Malton had asked Dean 'what now?' Dean had blurted out his plan to compile the CCTV from every venue they worked within a mile radius of Zak's murder and scour the footage for anything that could confirm or refute the few facts they were working from.

It was a huge undertaking but Dean didn't mind. It felt like forward motion. What's more it meant he didn't have time to worry about losing Vikki to Goldsmiths in London.

She was making dinner in the kitchen while Dean sat on the sofa with his laptop on his knee and Fury lying prone beside him.

The comforting smells of hot fat, salt and paprika filled the house. Vikki was cooking chicken wings.

She came into the front room where Dean was working. She began clearing the table by the window and Dean watched her over his laptop. She was wearing unhemmed, wide-legged jeans and a baggy jumper.

'You ready to eat?' She smiled, putting a bottle of Pepsi Max on the table.

Dean nodded. She was pushing out the boat. Usually midweek they'd get an Uber Eats or he'd drive them up the road to the McDonald's drive-through. He wondered if this was her way of getting ready to tell him something difficult.

She peered over his shoulder at the laptop. Dean looked up proudly. 'See? I promised I'd stay safe. There's more than one way to do this job.'

Vikki made a noise that wasn't as impressed as Dean had hoped for and wandered off back into the kitchen.

Dean turned back to his laptop. It had taken a few hours of head-scratching but Dean had managed to line up the timelines of the footage taken on the night Zak Alquist was killed. With a few notable black spots Dean had created a web of surveillance that did a pretty good job of covering the area around Zak's flat and the immediate surroundings.

As his eyes shot over the footage he wondered what life would be like without Vikki in it. He'd go back to his mum's. He'd have to. Dean had moved out of the cramped flat he shared with his mum but he still made sure to come home every Sunday for lunch, bringing Vikki along with him. She and his mum instantly hit it off. Bonding over shared stories about Dean's domestic foibles.

As much as Dean loved living with his mum, returning alone would feel like a colossal failure.

Vikki began putting food on the table. The warm fat on the chicken wings glistened under the lights, and the smell of the spiced beans and rice made his attention wander. Dean was about to close the laptop when he saw something on screen that made him stop.

His eyes widened. He stopped the feed – the camera outside a sushi bar in Ancoats – and went back a few minutes, watching back now at double speed. Verifying what he thought he saw. His fingers hit the keys and it changed to a different feed – a sports bar on the edge of the ring road. Then another – an office space by the canal. Again he scrolled back and forward. Every clip bringing him closer and closer to Zak's flat. His excitement mounting as the time on the clips raced towards the time of Zak's death.

'What is it?' said Vikki, picking up on Dean's sudden laser focus.

Dean looked up with a huge smile on his face. He hit the space bar, freezing the image and pointed to the screen.

'A murderer.'

29

To call the terrace of 20 Stories restaurant spectacular would be something of an understatement. It was one of Manchester's most breath-taking bars. A two-storey-high space of glass and greenery provided the perfect location for a level of extravagance tailor-made to impress.

Watching Bea work the room, Malton imagined she could hold this event in a church hall in Moston and still be able to dazzle those in attendance with the sheer force of her personality. Bea's law firm was small but specialised in dealing with the kind of clients who treated having millions in the bank, blood on their hands and the constant threat of double-digit prison sentences as simply occupational risks of their chosen profession.

But tonight's gathering was a little different. Bea had made a name for herself dealing with the elite of Manchester's criminal community and now she had her sights set on a more respectable class of wrongdoer. A dozen or so of them were gathered in 20 Stories experiencing the full force of Bea's charm. Bea Wallace was reinventing herself. Just like the adopted city she called her home.

If anyone else had dangled the chance to find James's killer in front of him, Malton would have torn their arm off to find out all they knew. But that wouldn't work with Bea. She played the game just like Malton did. Out on her own, protected only by the cushion of competing interests surrounding her.

Malton's job to was to get answers by any means necessary. He'd built his career on never relenting. Once you hired Malton he'd turn the city upside down for you. There was no hiding place so remote or lie so convincing as to impede Malton in his search for answers. But the one mystery he'd never been able to solve was James's death. With the help of James's brother, heavyweight gangster Callum Hester, he'd pulled Liverpool and Manchester apart looking for answers. But when the smoke cleared all he was left with were questions and a gnawing grief that neither money, success, respect, nor fear could ever truly abate.

That was why when she sprang this meet-and-greet on him he'd held his tongue. Bea knew that by teasing Malton with a lead on James's killers she had his interest and she was going to see just how much that interest was worth.

Doing his best to contain mounting frustration Malton stood with his back to the bar and took it all in. The twenty or so guests invited by Bea were some of the most successful, wealthy people in Manchester. CEOs, commercial landlords and entrepreneurs. The latest generation of people to take up the mantle of making Manchester the greatest city in the world.

Looking out over the effortlessly elegant Italian suits and obviously expensive designer dresses on display, Malton wondered if any of these people had the first clue what really made Manchester tick. Every part of the city had its own criminal character. Malton knew them all. A lifetime of maintaining a strict neutrality combined with the unspoken knowledge of just what he'd done to survive as long as he had, meant that he could pass through worlds that most people would never imagine even existed.

But it was there, right beneath the surface. With its drugs and its cheap, undocumented labour and damp, crumbling HMOs. It was the rotten edifice on which their glittering, gilded Manchester rested.

Stood on the terrace of 20 Stories in his own very expensive, bespoke, cream linen suit and egg-shell blue Sunspel polo shirt, Malton felt utterly adrift.

This was Bea's world. The world of legitimate business. Of deals and contracts and laws. But when Bea's considerable powers ran out that was when it was Malton's time to shine. That was why he was there. Bea wanted to introduce him to her more respectable clients. Give them a small preview of the kind of services that thanks to Malton, she could now offer them.

Nate Alquist was just the start.

Malton distracted himself by going back over what he now knew about Zak's murder.

Zak Alquist had been playing at gangsters and, thanks to his dead girlfriend Carrie's brother, had met some very real ones. A boy called Femi and maybe others, according to what Dean had got out of Ryan. But Malton still had nothing to connect Zak to Jordan Weekes except for the cocaine in Zak's flat. Cocaine that Malton suspected had been placed with the same subtlety as the hammer attack that had killed Zak. Whoever had killed him wasn't used to covering their tracks. That said, they had enough money and drugs to go totally overboard trying.

From the man he'd left watching Weekes's place he'd already learned that the police had been round a few hours after him. He hoped he could keep one step ahead of them. GMP had millions of pounds, thousands of officers, the press and the public all behind them. But Malton had Manchester.

Weekes's wife said he was lying low with his mistress. So Malton had put the word out to all the clubs and venues he provided security for. As soon as Weekes surfaced he would know about it.

Whatever Weekes's involvement, it didn't answer his other question. What was Nate Alquist's angle in all this? First the meeting at his house and then the performance from Zak's living girlfriend Izzy whom Nate had sequestered away in a luxury hotel. His own son was dead but the first phone call he made wasn't to the police, it was to Bea Wallace. That told Malton that whatever Nate's game was the stakes were as high as they could possibly be. But was he playing alone or was someone forcing his hand?

Was that why Nate had asked for Malton to look into Zak's murder? A desperate cry for help? Something he couldn't go to the police with?

Malton's train of thought was derailed by the sight of Bea stalking across the room towards him.

'What are you doing lurking at the bar? The whole point of having you here is to show you off! Get you networking.'

Malton winced at the thought but kept quiet.

'Let me do some matchmaking,' said Bea looping her arm around Malton and leading him away from the bar. 'I'd like you to meet one of Nate's business partners. He's from Moss Side. Like you! He and Nate are working together on the new food hall in Moss Side.'

Malton was vaguely aware of the latest attempt to gentrify Moss Side. A food hall next to the Heineken Brewery. A market full of independent food stalls, bars and seating. Food halls had turned around Stockport and Stretford. Now Manchester Council were hoping to repeat the success with Moss Side. The Moss Side food hall had attracted generous interest-free council loans as well as several other incentives.

While Malton had read about it in passing he'd not bothered to look who was behind it. He was unsurprised to hear that Nate Alquist was involved.

Bea steered Malton between guests. As he passed among them he was aware of stolen glances, excited whispers. He felt like an exotic animal on display.

'I just know you two will have something in common,' said Bea as she expertly slipped into a small circle of people talking and sipping from their wine glasses.

Malton took a glance around the group and caught the eyes of a handsome, mixed-race man with a large, neat afro. Suddenly Malton's uneasy feeling solidified into a full-on red flag.

'Craig Malton,' said Bea, with a bright smile. 'Meet Ani Delgado.'

30

Malton felt relieved to be back at street level among the noise and the smell he recognised as Manchester. As much as the city changed it stayed exactly the same. Built on the same human frailties and virtues that made it the place it was.

His phone ringing in his pocket had interrupted Bea's meet-cute with Ani Delgado and now he was on his way to a city-centre bar with an urgency in his walk.

Ani Delgado was the last person he'd expected to meet at Bea's event. Malton knew all about Ani. They'd grown up together. Malton on the terraced side of Moss Side, Ani over in Rathbone Park Estate. Two kids with their own little kingdoms.

While Malton had left the city to make his way in Liverpool, met James, lost James and founded Malton Security, Ani had never moved from the same house in Moss Side. Involved in the Nineties gang violence, he'd survived into middle age thanks to a combination of ruthless self-interest, easy charm and his most valuable and dangerous asset: his twin brother Lani Delgado.

Ani and Lani had shared a womb but while Ani looked like any other mixed-race kid in Moss Side, Lani was white. Or at least white presenting. He still sounded and acted like a Delgado. But Lani could step outside of Moss Side and shake off the baggage that came with being mixed-race. At least until he opened his mouth.

As a 'white' kid on the Rathbone Park Estate, Lani radically overcompensated. While Ani was the brains, Lani was the ruthlessly uncompromising muscle.

The twins might have made it through Gunchester but they never left it. As far as Malton knew Ani was still calling the shots, with the latest incarnation of his gang going by the name the Chopboys. Ani was now removed enough from the streets to be a respected community leader, a public speaker and a mentor. But Malton knew for a fact he was the power behind the scenes.

As for Lani, he'd fallen foul of his brother's drive to publicly reinvent himself when he'd accidentally burned down the wrong house, killing a young mother and her baby. While officially Ani denied any knowledge of his brother's involvement, in private he had been forced to turn his back on Lani. The Manchester underworld tolerated many dark, terrible things but the murder of an innocent young mother and her child was not one of them.

Wherever Lani was, his brother Ani was at 20 Stories with Bea talking about the food hall he was building in Moss Side with Nate Alquist.

Malton wondered if Nate and Bea had any idea who they were getting into bed with, the three of them all working on the food hall project together. Or worse, if they even cared. Something about Bea waiting until her meet-and-greet to bring it up didn't quite sit right with Malton. Bea never did anything without a good reason. Whatever reason she had for bringing Malton and Ani together there was more going on than just canapés and small talk.

As he walked through the city centre Malton found himself wishing he was back parked up outside Emily's place in the hills. Watching from afar, touching from a distance. Removed so that he could never contaminate Emily with his world but close enough that should that world ever come calling he would be there to protect her.

But he was needed elsewhere. Ten minutes earlier, one of Malton's security guys had called with the information that Jordan Weekes had shown up drinking at a club called Bittersweet.

Bittersweet was a new addition to the Manchester bar scene. A bar done up like a tropical garden. A mixture of real and fake plants creating dozens of Instagrammable backdrops for patrons who would be so busy taking selfies that they'd barely notice the bar tab racking up as music rang out across the room.

A bouncer spotted Malton and walked over to him. Leaning in close he shouted to make himself heard.

'He's in the far booth. Made a scene, threatened a waiter. When we tried to talk to him he lashed out. I've got a couple of lads watching him. He's ranting. On something. Coke probably.'

Malton took all this in. 'Was he alone?' he shouted back.

The bouncer shook his head. 'Had a girl with him. She's in back. She seems really shaken by it all.'

Malton nodded. Thanks to the reach of Malton Security it was like having a thousand eyes on the ground. Better than any CCTV, Malton had decades of experience working for him. Every man was utterly loyal thanks to both the generous pay at Malton Security and the knowledge that their boss would never ask them to do anything that he wouldn't do himself.

Whatever discomfort he'd felt back at 20 Stories was long gone. This was his world and his word was law.

Malton walked through the elaborate garden décor of Bittersweet. It was a Tuesday night but there were still a handful of tables full up. A group of older women dressed for a rowdy night out who were seemingly not put off by whatever fuss Weekes had just caused. A young couple Malton guessed were on a first date sat watching awkwardly as the sparkler attached to the bottle of champagne they'd just ordered slowly burned down.

And there in the corner, watched by two monolithic slabs of muscle in Malton Security hi-vis armbands was Jordan Weekes. He wore jeans and a shirt unbuttoned to show a *Love Island*–ready body. Coke sweat poured off him. His skin greasy and slick under the lights. Dark patches soaking through his shirt. He was shouting at the two security men. His words lost under the echoing din of the music.

Malton stopped and took a second, his mind going over how he would handle the situation.

Just long enough for a figure to barge past him and walk up to Weekes.

Malton immediately recognised the purple anorak. DI Benton.

Malton had a very simple relationship with the police. He stayed as far away as possible. People came to Malton specifically to avoid the police and given some of Malton's more 'creative' investigation techniques he was happy for that to be the case. The one exception was Benton. Ever since she'd arrested him as a teenager he knew Benton was different. She understood how Manchester worked and like Malton she understood just how far you had to go to find out the truth. While each of them stayed firmly on their own side of the law, from time to time they'd meet in the middle.

Benton was flashing her ID and, as they were trained to do, the security men were stepping aside. Malton hung back and watched. He couldn't hear what was being said but it was clear whatever Benton was shouting in Weekes's ear was putting the fear of God into him.

Weekes rose to his feet and with Benton's hand on his shoulder moved to leave the club.

As they passed Malton, Benton caught sight of him and leaned in with a smile.

'We should talk,' she shouted in his ear.

Malton couldn't agree more as he watched Benton march Weekes out the club.

He approached the two men who'd been watching Weekes. He could see the look on their faces. The worry that they'd messed up.

Malton nipped it in the bud. He stuck his thumb up and shouted above the music. 'Good job. That's the training.'

A look of relief came over the men. The smaller of the two leaned in.

'The girl he was with is still in the back,' he shouted hopefully.

Malton gave a nod and the man led him through the club, past the bar and through the door that led behind the scenes to the guts of the operation.

The moment the door swung shut behind them the sound of music faded to a dull thud. Malton felt his hearing return as the shorter security guard opened the door to the staff office and stood aside for Malton.

He patted the man on the shoulder and turned to go into the office.

There sat waiting for him was Zak Alquist's girlfriend Izzy.

31

'Who would frame me for murder?' asked Jordan Weekes, his voice trembling.

'I was hoping you'd tell me,' said Benton. She leaned over from the driver's seat and opened the glovebox. An assortment of chocolate bars fell out. 'Help yourself,' she said.

Weekes grabbed a Mars bar and took a bite. He chewed it around his mouth for far too long before, with great effort, swallowing. He wasn't a handsome man but money had gone some way to making up for that. His teeth had been whitened, his skin tanned and toned. Benton recognised the neat, tattooed hairline of the clinic in town that made thousands of pounds charging bald men to permanently etch stubble over their shining domes. But there were still the signs of where Jordan Weekes started out. The smudgy Stockport County tattoo on his left breast, the battered, heavy hands of someone who's worked for a living.

Benton watched him eat. They were parked up in the shadow of Roach Court – a tower block just outside the city centre in Collyhurst. Sufficiently far from the tendrils of development, this part of the city was still home to enough areas of derelict buildings and empty waste ground to make Benton confident that she could question Weekes unseen.

She'd made it known she was looking for Weekes and after getting a call from one of the dozens of hospitality staff across the city centre she had got to know through policing the city for three decades, had rushed to Bittersweet hoping that no one had done anything as daft as calling the police.

The last person she expected to see there was Malton. She'd watched Malton go from a scrappy teenage thief to a mercurial, underworld fixer. Along the way she'd not been above offering the occasional titbit of information. For the right price. She would find out what he wanted with Weekes later but she knew that if Malton was involved then things had a habit of escalating. Time was running out.

Malton could wait. Right now she had the man whose drugs had turned up in both Femi Musa's bedroom and Zak Alquist's crime scene exactly where she wanted him – scared and alone in the passenger seat of her car.

Benton tried to focus. Ignoring the voice in her head whispering that maybe finding Femi Musa and solving Zak Alquist's murder were one and the same. That maybe this missing persons case might just be her ticket back into Serious and Organised.

'So you're telling me you didn't kill Zak Alquist?'

'Who?' said Jordan, his voice trembling.

Jordan Weekes looked genuinely terrified. Confused and scared. Benton's gut told her that the man sat next to her, tears running down his face, was no killer. But still, he *was* involved somehow. Whether he knew it or not.

'Where were you two nights ago?'

'Izzy, she were with me all night.' A look of relief came over Jordan. 'Ask Izzy.'

'Who's Izzy?' asked Benton.

Jordan looked shifty. 'My girlfriend.'

'I thought you were married?'

'I am,' said Jordan. 'But Izzy, she gets me. She were with me back at the club. Just ask her.'

Benton hid the annoyance she felt at missing that crucial detail. There was no chance that Malton hadn't picked Izzy up by now. If he couldn't get Weekes he'd make do with the girlfriend.

With all the talk on DLChat incorrectly fingering Weekes as a snitch there was every chance Malton was working for any number of aggrieved criminals keen to lay hands on Jordan Weekes. But Zak's murder raised the intriguing possibility that maybe Malton wasn't looking for a grass. Maybe he was looking for a killer.

'I didn't kill no one,' said Jordan more to himself than to Benton.

Outside the car Manchester was silent. A few lights on in Roach Court did nothing to alleviate the menacing darkness from the wasteland all around.

'Do you know Femi Musa?'

Jordan Weekes wiped his face with the back of his hand and crossed his arms. 'I'm not talking to you. I'm not a grass,' he said.

'That's not what I heard,' said Benton theatrically. If everyone else thought Weekes was talking to the police she may as well use it.

'I never said a fucking thing. I never,' shouted Weekes.

'That's a shame,' said Benton. 'Cos if you were an informant then maybe I could help you. As it is, I should probably just arrest you right now. Let Strangeways sort you out.'

For years now the ominous Victorian prison in the heart of the city centre had been rebranded HMP Manchester. Benton, like everyone else in the city, still called it its far more appropriate name – Strangeways.

'No, no, no, no. Don't do that. No,' said Weekes, backtracking.

'So maybe you do know who Femi Musa is?'

'They will fucking kill me if they know I told you about Femi.'

'Who?' said Benton, her interest piqued.

'Chopboys,' whispered Jordan. 'They used to buy off me. Femi, he was the guy they sent to do the deals. Nice lad. Shame he was wrapped up in it all to be honest..'

Benton felt her heart flutter with the feeling that made being a detective the best job in the world. That feeling when suddenly the jumble of facts begins to come into focus. The Chopboys. Two days earlier, at the scene of Tommy Fenwick's murder, Lesha Thompson had blamed them for Tommy's death. Femi's phone had been found in Tommy's flat. And now Jordan Weekes was fingering Femi as part of the Chop-boys gang. Jordan Weekes who sold drugs to the Chopboys via Femi. Drugs that Benton had found at both Femi's house and Zak's murder.

Femi's prayers for forgiveness were starting to make a lot more sense.

'Femi's missing,' said Benton and watched the colour drain from Weekes's face.

'You know anything about that?' she asked.

Weekes screwed up his face and looked like he was about to pass something solid. Finally he opened his eyes and let it all out.

'Last time I saw Femi was about a year ago, he turned up with this other lad. Right prick. Gobby little twat. You could tell he didn't have a fucking clue. Wanted to try the gear, like he were in fucking *Scarface*. I were going to tell Femi not to bring him round again.'

'But you didn't.'

'Next week that dickhead kid were on the news. He'd stabbed his girlfriend.'

'Zak Alquist?'

'Aye,' said Weekes. 'But I never knew it were him until I saw him on the telly. I got spooked and just stopped dealing with Femi and the Chopboys. No one gives a shit about black kids. Posh white kid though? That's a whole fucking lot of hassle I don't need.'

'And now Zak's dead.'

'Weren't you listening? I didn't want anything to do with it.'

'So how did one of your kilos end up in his flat?'

'Fuck alone knows,' said Weekes. The sugar hit was having its effect and he was starting to sober up. 'You going to arrest me?'

'Should I?' asked Benton.

Benton knew she didn't need to. The police had already connected his drugs to Zak's murder scene. DCI Priestly was on Weekes's trail. Even Priestly would find Weekes eventually. If that wasn't enough Weekes was on DLChat selling drugs.

Everyone on DLChat was going down. The evidence was right there on the computer screen. It was only a matter of time before GMP got round to Jordan Weekes and he'd be losing everything.

Jordan went quiet and grabbed a Twix out the glovebox.

'A couple of weeks ago I had a party. Me and Izzy. Couple of other girls. You know . . . girls.'

'So it was you, Izzy and some prostitutes. Was your wife there too?'

Weekes looked confused.

'Sorry,' said Benton. 'Carry on.'

'Anyway, we were all having a time. Having fun and that. Got a hotel room. You know how it is.'

Benton had no idea but she could imagine.

'I were pissed and showing off. Showed one of Izzy's mates what I had in my bag.'

'Which was?'

'Couple of kilos. I were giving it to a courier in the morning. Anyway, when we woke up her mate were gone and so were one of the kilos.'

Benton reeled. As a police officer the drug dealers she had most contact with were the ones who were bad at it. The ones who talked, the ones who posted on social media. The ones who got ripped off and pulled out guns on public streets. The ones who were too smart to get caught never showed up. But to hear Weekes casually mention losing something that had the cash value of a bar of gold was staggering.

'Did you not ask Izzy to find the girl?'

Jordan looked embarrassed.

'I didn't want her to feel bad about it. You know? I love that girl.'

This all felt like as much of a dead end as the roads around Roach Court. Jordan Weekes was clearly not a killer. And if he had been, given his competence as a dealer he'd have been found at the crime scene, waving a hammer about with his trousers round his ankles.

Whoever Izzy was, Benton would need to find her. Hear her side of the story. If Malton had her then maybe there was a deal to be done.

Ordinarily she enjoyed their back and forth. Malton giving her information that only he could provide and Benton giving Malton intel from over her side of the fence. But if Malton was straying into Benton's case then there was a real danger he'd be less of an asset and more of a liability. Benton felt a little frisson. She *was* getting somewhere after all.

'What's going to happen to me?' asked Weekes.

As soon as GMP got Weekes that would be one less lead she'd have at her disposal. The longer he was a free man the longer he was useful to her.

'Right now you're in a lot of trouble,' said Benton. 'Greater Manchester Police want you as a murder suspect. But more than that, did you see that man at the club? The short, built one.'

'The unit with a scar on his face?'

'Yes,' said Benton. 'That one. He is the most dangerous man you'll ever meet in your life. And for reasons I don't yet fully understand I think he wants a word with you.'

'I never did anything. I never!' wailed Weekes, sounding like a scolded child.

'That's why right now, I'm your only friend. I'm the only one who can protect you and the only one who'll believe you didn't have anything to do with Zak's murder. I'm investigating Femi Musa's disappearance. And until I find out what happened to him, I'm going to make sure you stay out of a prison cell and out of the clutches of that man with the scar.'

Jordan Weekes burst into tears.

'I'm sorry, I'm so fucking sorry,' he moaned.

'Just lie low, don't go home. Don't contact Izzy. Don't contact anyone. And whatever you do, don't leave Manchester.'

Benton sat back and watched him blubber. It reminded her of her ex-husband when she told him she wanted a divorce. Benton reached across into the glovebox and handed Weekes a packet of tissues. Weekes kept on weeping.

Benton wondered what she'd done in a past life to spend so much of this one taking care of pathetic men. She gave Weekes a reassuring pat on the back and slipped her card into his pocket.

But it would all be worth it if what Weekes said panned out and the Chopboys were in the picture. That was firmly back in Serious and Organised territory. What had started with Femi Musa had grown to something far bigger. While Weekes sobbed in the shadow of Roach Court, Benton couldn't help but smile. She was back in the game.

32

Dean turned over in bed and tried to ignore the argument he could hear going on in the street outside.

There was a street light directly outside the front of the house and it shone through the gaps in the curtains of the first-floor bedroom where he lay next to Vikki.

Beside him he could hear the gentle, distant murmur of her snoring, to which he'd grown comfortably accustomed. She woke early and went to bed late but when she was asleep next to nothing could wake her.

The light from the street lamp cast shadows across the ceiling as Dean strained to hear the words being shouted a few metres away outside.

A man's voice: '. . . going . . . bitch . . . be back . . .'

And a woman's equally fierce: '. . . pathetic . . . mistake . . . you?'

Their voices rang through the still night air. With no other background noises the sound bounced off the sleeping terraces and up into the night sky.

He wondered if Edith was listening. Writing it all down in her book.

Dean closed his eyes and tried to think about something else. About showing Malton the CCTV footage he'd discovered that evening. About how he still hadn't talked to Vikki about Goldsmiths. About what really happened to Carrie Lewis. So many different threads, all of them spiralling off into the unknown. It was too late and Dean was too tired. He had no answers, only the impossible carousel of his brain refusing to disengage.

Then he heard the punch.

The woman's voice again: '. . . bastard . . .'

Dean was out of bed and pulling on the tracksuit he wore round the house.

He was halfway downstairs when it occurred to him he was unarmed. Then he thought that was probably for the best. De-escalation. That was the key. That and protect the woman whose voice he could hear.

Pulling on his shoes, Dean opened the front door into the night.

He saw a man and woman standing in the road. She was dressed like all the girls from Number Twelve, balanced on platform heels and wearing a dress that barely covered her backside. He was in work trousers and a shirt that had been untucked. A Mercedes was parked outside Number Twelve, the lights on and the engine running. Dean guessed it was the man's car.

Dean didn't hesitate, walking across the pavement, through the spotlight of the street lamp and across the road towards where they were arguing. The man saw him first.

'Who the fuck are you?'

Dean ignored him and spoke to the woman. 'Are you OK?'

She smiled and Dean could see one side of her mouth starting to swell where the man hit her. 'Oh, he's fucked.' She turned back to the man shouting, 'You hear that? You know what he's going to do to you?'

Suddenly she had a phone in her hand and was dialling. The man went to grab it but Dean was there, his body between them.

The man staggered back momentarily.

'Out my fucking way,' he said. Since working for Malton Security Dean had been threatened enough times to hear the fear in the man's voice. He was already on his way out of the situation.

'You lay your hands on me? He will take you to pieces,' said the woman as her phone rang. Unlike the man there was no fear in her voice. Just glee.

137

Dean didn't know who she was calling but his gut told him that if whoever it was turned up this would escalate and quickly.

Dean turned to the man. 'GW4 7HG,' he said.

The man looked puzzled for a moment.

'That's your car. Or is it a company car? Or your wife's car? I don't know. I can find out. See that?'

He turned and pointed across the street, going from house to house.

'Camera doorbell, camera doorbell, camera doorbell.'

The man's brain scrambled to process what he was being told.

'They've all recorded you hitting her. Which is good. It means you got options.'

'Who the fuck are you?' repeated the man.

The woman was still waiting for her call to be answered, her eyes locked on the man.

'I'm with the neighbourhood watch,' said Dean truthfully. 'So do you want me to call the police? Or would you rather wait until whoever it is she's calling arrives?'

For the first time the man looked scared. Dean knew exactly what he was doing. When a person is arguing their brain is out of gear. They're driven by instinct. Rage and fear and aggression. When you make someone listen they suddenly have a chance to step back, evaluate the situation they've got themselves into. Just like the man was doing, stood in the middle of a street in Moss Side at gone one in the morning.

'There is a third option,' said Dean, watching the spark of hope ignite in the man's head.

'What?' he asked.

'You apologise to her. You pay her for whatever it was that went on this evening and you go home and never come back.'

The man hovered for a moment.

'Eight hundred pounds,' said the woman, lowering her phone and jumping into the conversation.

The man hesitated.

'It's up to you,' said Dean.

'Give me the bank details,' said the man, pulling out his phone.

Dean stood in the silence of the street and watched as the two parties back and forthed with their phones out until the woman's phone beeped and she smiled.

'And now you go home,' said Dean.

The man didn't wait to be asked twice. He stumbled into his Mercedes, pulled a nine-point turn in the narrow street and disappeared into the night.

As soon as he was gone the woman's demeanour changed. It was her turn to look scared.

'You don't tell anyone about this,' she half-commanded half-begged. Her mouth was starting to swell up badly.

'I just wanted to make sure you were OK,' said Dean.

The woman managed a pained smile at Dean. The kind you'd give to a clever child. 'Aren't you sweet,' she said, as she leaned in and gave him a peck on the cheek before turning and heading back into Number Twelve.

Dean stood for a moment, alone in the street.

When he turned to go back inside he saw Vikki's worried face watching him from the upstairs bedroom window.

33

The last time Malton saw Izzy she had looked scared for her life. Now, sat in the passenger seat of his Volvo estate, dressed in a white, sleeveless playsuit and strappy heels, she had the demeanour of a condemned woman.

Darkness had finally fallen over Manchester as he drove at a steady forty miles per hour, north out of the city towards a safe house on the edge of Bury. It was time to take control of events, starting with putting Izzy somewhere only he could get to her. Whether she was a witness or a pawn in a larger game, either way until Malton knew for sure what the truth really was he wanted to make sure that he and he alone had access to her.

It was too much of a coincidence for Nate Alquist and Ani Delgado to just so happen to have the same lawyer and be working on the same building project together. But now Ani was in the mix Malton felt strangely more at ease. Finally, a threat he knew how to deal with. Someone the police couldn't get anywhere near. He had an in. But where would it lead him?

The closed shutters of Cheetham Hill's textile district gave way to the scattered, suburban jumble of Crumpsall and beyond it the vast, green expanse of Heaton Park.

Malton drove in silence, ordering his thoughts. Working out what he needed to know from Izzy but also what he would have to tell Nate Alquist when it became clear she had absconded from the hotel.

They were heading down the edge of Heaton Park with the endless dark of the park on one side, houses on the other when Izzy finally spoke.

'I told him I couldn't come out tonight. He wouldn't take no for answer. He was going to come to the hotel.'

'Why would you give me Jordan Weekes's name, knowing full well that you were putting him in the frame for Zak's murder and then be out on the town with him the very next day?' asked Malton, his eyes going from the traffic lights to the scared young woman sat beside him.

'I felt sorry for him. I had to warn him.'

Malton thought back to Weekes in Bittersweet. Coked up and frantic like a cornered animal. He wouldn't be the first man with a wife and daughter at home and a girlfriend in the city but there was something about the idea of Weekes and Izzy as an item that just didn't add up.

'Sorry that he was being set up?' said Malton.

Izzy went silent.

'Because you know who really killed Zak don't you?'

Izzy turned to Malton. 'You have to take me back. Please,' she sounded desperate.

'I'm taking you somewhere safe,' said Malton as he slowed down to a halt at traffic lights.

'No,' said Izzy frantically. 'You don't understand. There is nowhere safe.'

'From who?' asked Malton.

Izzy's mouth moved but nothing came out.

The lights began to change and Malton started to move off.

It happened in a split second.

Izzy's hand was on the door handle and then the passenger door flew open as the car accelerated from the lights. Her seat belt was undone and before Malton could make a grab for her she was tumbling out of the car.

Malton slammed the brakes and in his rear-view mirror saw Izzy shedding her high-heeled sandals and fleeing barefoot into the dense blackness of Heaton Park.

Horns sounded behind him. With the passenger door still hanging open he hit the accelerator and without looking pulled his car across the opposite lane, heedless of oncoming traffic and headed after Izzy.

The Volvo smashed up over the kerb and Malton felt the tyres bite into the grass at the edge of the park.

His headlights carved a bright canyon through the gloom of the park and there at the very edge was Izzy, moving faster than Malton would have given her credit for.

Just as he put his foot down, the front of the car fell forwards and with a sickening crunch something smashed into the underside.

Malton didn't have time to worry about his undercarriage. Slamming on the brakes and leaving the keys in the ignition he bailed out of the car and tore into the park on foot.

By the time he'd run to the edge of light from the car's beams Izzy was long gone. Swallowed up by the endless dark.

34

'I want to live with Dad,' said Jenni over the breakfast table.

Benton was searching through boxes for the cereal bowls. Currently they were eating out of Tupperware. Without turning round she said, 'You think your dad is going to let you take drugs?'

She opened a box to find all her ex-husband's A-level Geography notes. Shutting the box, she struggled to lift it down, eventually dropping it to the floor where it gently split and a pile of papers started to slide out over the kitchen floor.

'At least he's there,' said Jenni.

Jenni was just like Benton in a lot of ways. She bristled against bullshit, said what she thought and didn't suffer fools. Unlike Benton she hadn't yet worked out that Simon, her ex, was an absolute waste of skin.

'Your dad doesn't have room,' said Benton.

'I stay the night there,' said Jenni.

'Yes, a night. In his bedsit. That I pay for. How would that work long term? Where would you do schoolwork? Get changed? Do anything?'

Jenni scowled and looked around all the boxes.

'No room here to do anything.'

Benton opened another box. It was full of tea towels.

'That's because your father is a hoarder and now I've got all his crap in boxes and I can't throw it away because he claims he's going to move into a bigger place although how that works, when he doesn't have any money or a job, fuck alone knows. Maybe when you move in with him you can ask him yourself.'

Benton hadn't meant to carry on talking as long as she had. Or to go from mild annoyance to full-on rant but she could see from Jenni's smug expression that she'd played right into her hands.

She was definitely Benton's daughter.

'So I can live with Dad?'

Benton sat down and poured herself a Tupperware container of cereal.

'Fuck it. Go live with him.'

Jenni smiled and got up from the table.

Maybe Benton should have gone after her. Maybe she shouldn't have lost her temper in the first place. Either way there was nothing she could do about it now. At least she was finally making progress on the case. Jordan Weekes had dealt with Femi and the Chopboys. He'd had some drugs stolen by a prostitute a couple of weeks ago and then his drugs show up, planted at Zak's murder. Could it be the same brick?

Femi was quickly moving from a missing boy to a killer on the run. But one thing still gave Benton hope. The cover-up. She could easily believe a kid caught up with the Chopboys would commit a murder. It was a stretch to imagine a murder quite as brutal as Zak's but still, it was possible.

But would that same kid go to such lengths to dress the crime scene to frame Jordan Weekes? That didn't sit right with Benton. And then there was the question of what Malton wanted with Weekes. Was he working the Alquist murder too? And if so, under whose orders?

She could hear Jenni angrily packing upstairs. As much as her daughter drove her crazy it still hurt to see her pulling away. Benton had done everything she could for Jenni, perhaps some time with her dad *would* do her good. Give her a chance to realise that Benton did more for her than Simon ever would.

Benton tried to put her chaotic family life out of her mind for a moment and focus on how to approach the one person she knew who could give her answers to the questions she had. The one person that might bring her closer to finding Femi.

The man behind the Chopboys.

35

Once upon a time when Malton needed to clear his head he'd visit a sauna, have sex with an anonymous man and head back out, his thoughts ringing with a newfound clarity.

Back then it seemed like the perfect solution. Malton had never felt like he belonged anywhere. He was tolerated or feared or indulged but never accepted. Growing up mixed-race with a dead black mother and an alcoholic white father he neither had a way into the black culture that surrounded him in Moss Side nor a warm welcome waiting for him in the white Irish of Moss Side who even back then were a dying breed.

Malton had hovered between worlds, wary of each and longing to belong to either. When he was still very young he realised that was an impossibility and he began to teach himself to survive as an army of one. He gathered all his softer emotions and packed them away deep inside his broad, light brown chest. Retreating from the expectation of anything as lofty as love he learned to read people, to pick them apart and anticipate them. He made sure that he would never need to rely on unexpected kindness or unforeseen charity. He taught himself to know how to intuit weakness. How to turn it to his advantage. Making sure he stayed one step ahead of the world at all times.

But once in a while that effort became overwhelming and he slipped. As a teenager he'd met a mixed-race girl just like him. Keisha. She had grown up his exact opposite. Able to insert herself anywhere. Make herself welcome with anyone. Yet he had learned that just like him she never lost the feeling of being on the outside. Both of them, in their own way, were mitigating the fear of being the only one and in doing so they found each other and fell in love.

Malton had walked out on her just after his sixteenth birthday. If Malton allowed himself to dwell on his mistakes he'd call this the biggest regret of his life. But regret was a luxury he didn't feel he'd earned.

It was then that he began visiting the saunas. Malton found himself attracted to men and women. Saunas provided the ideal way to scratch the one itch he couldn't reach. Brief physical intimacy and sexual release. Letting him keep a tight grip on his emotions.

When he met and fell in love with a man called James he thought that maybe he had a second chance at finally being happy. But by then he was so deep in the world of criminal violence that the dark currents swirling around him had engulfed James.

James had been kidnapped coming out of a pub late one night. Bundled into a van and whisked off into the night. While Malton frantically searched, James was slowly tortured to death over several days. By the time Malton found him what was left was barely recognisable.

James's death was the only crime he'd never got to the bottom of. Not for want of trying. Every day he thought about James. On good days he thought about his smile and his laugh. His Scouse sense of humour and how he looked at Malton with a pure love. On bad days he thought about what he looked like with all four limbs severed at the joint and neatly stacked up on a table beside where his body was found.

Twice Keisha had come back into his life and twice tried to win him back with a carnival of dark violence and seduction. But as much as Malton wanted to turn back time he couldn't let himself. Even when she revealed that when he walked out on her she had been carrying his son – Anthony. No sooner had he learned he had a son than she had told him how Anthony had arrived dead. A whole other life he would never know.

Since James and Keisha he had been alone. Sometimes alone with someone else – like Emily who was now carrying his child. A child who he had promised her he would never see, never expose to the danger of his world. Anthony's half-brother or sister.

Then there was Bea.

Compared to Keisha and James, Bea was just a stranger in the night. A warm body.

But if Bea really did have a lead on James's killer he couldn't wait any longer. He wouldn't wait for her to reward him with the information. He'd take matters into his own hands to find out what she knew.

But first he needed to clear his head. Malton didn't go to the saunas anymore. He had somewhere new to calibrate his thoughts.

A tiny stone in Southern Cemetery.

After Keisha told him about his son, Malton had done some detective work. Matching up the dates, he'd found Anthony's grave in Southern Cemetery. He was almost unsurprised when he discovered it had been dug up and the body taken. Keisha had been thorough in removing every trace of herself from his life.

But the stone was still there.

Anthony Malton 01.07.1992 – 01.07.1992

Malton looked out over the tiny headstones in the children's graveyard. His first thought was how they lay together. A kind of team, a family. Once again he felt desperately alone.

He reminded himself that was his strength. He was one man. The only way past him was through him. He had no one he cared for, no one who could be hurt to get to him. He couldn't be bought or threatened. He was untouchable.

Malton knelt down and laid the flowers he'd brought with him on Anthony's grave, next to the ones he laid there a few days earlier. Lately he'd found himself coming here more and more often.

As he did so, something caught his eye.

A card had blown across to the next grave and lodged itself in the dead flowers that covered it. But the card was much newer. It was small and plain, a picture of a teddy on the front.

Malton plucked the card from among the dead flowers and opened it up. Inside was a simple message.

TO ANTHONY. HAPPY BIRTHDAY. MUMMY XXX

Malton stood straight back up and spun around. He didn't quite know who he expected to see. Who he did see was someone he hadn't seen in nearly thirty years. A red-haired woman who he'd grown up with a lifetime ago in Moss Side.

36

'I never left. Why would I? This is my home,' Lesha said to the man sitting opposite her, as she picked up her mug of coffee.

Lesha hadn't spoken to Craig Malton in nearly thirty years. That didn't mean she hadn't heard about his reputation. When she was seeing Ani he had often talked about Craig. Joked about the rumours that he'd been sleeping with men over in Liverpool. Told her that he wasn't scared of Craig so many times that the message was absolutely clear – Ani was terrified of Craig.

After seeing him at Southern Cemetery a couple of days ago she'd held back unseen. Waiting until he'd left before she went to see what grave it was he was putting flowers on. Once she'd read the inscription on the stone she knew he'd be back sooner rather than later. And she'd be waiting for him.

'The worst part is they took the body.'

'I heard,' said Malton. In the thirty years since they last crossed paths he'd filled out. Been worn down by time. She wondered how she must look to him. Whether he even remembered her. They were sat in a café across from the cemetery. A glass-fronted place with tiled floors and insubstantial tables. A laminated A4 menu and a waitress who looked like she might be the daughter of the older man working behind the counter.

'That's what Ani does. He doesn't want money. He doesn't want territory. He's got Moss Side. He wants fear. He wants you to know he has power of life and death over you. Whenever he wants. But then you already know that don't you? You grew up with him. Same as me.'

Lesha watched whatever dark memories her words had dredged up flash across Malton's steely glare.

'But you aren't scared of him?' he said coldly.

'Me?' said Lesha. 'He killed my son and stole his body. What's left for him to do to me?'

She watched his face as she said this out loud. She'd seen the gravestone he was visiting and figured that if she could make a connection with him then maybe she could push further, ask about the rumours she'd heard about exactly what kind of business Craig Malton was now in.

'Do you have kids?'

Malton shook his head. Lesha felt a sting of cruelty in her words but she had no choice. 'When your child dies, it's like someone telling you the end of the film. You can keep watching, but everything . . . it doesn't matter anymore. You know how it all ends.'

Malton's jaw clenched.

'If someone choked Ani out in your café I can tell you exactly how it'll end,' said Malton.

Lesha looked down at her coffee. It was good and strong, a thick sludge at the bottom of the small cup, daring her to drain it.

'I heard you can help? People like me?'

Malton started to slowly shake his head.

Lesha jumped in, 'Please. Listen, I'm sorry. I saw you at the cemetery the other day and saw the grave. Your son? The dates, that was back when we were just kids. When you were going out with Keisha McColl, right?'

Malton was silent. Lesha felt him sucking the air out of the room with his wordless judgement.

She continued, 'I mean – you *know*. I know you know. When a child dies. It doesn't matter if he's seventeen years old or just a day. It changes everything. Makes just getting up in the morning a battle. And you can't tell anyone else. You can't put it into words. Sure, they know you're sad but it's not sadness is it? It's like everything stops making sense all at once. And so you have to relearn everything. Alongside the pain and grief.'

She looked into his eyes and saw that he understood every word she was saying.

'So what do you want me to do?' he finally said.

'I want you to tell Ani Delgado to let this one go.'

37

At breakfast Dean half hoped that Vikki would be angry with him. Last night when he had returned to bed freezing cold, still raging with the adrenaline of his encounter in the street she had said nothing. Just turned away from him and went back to sleep.

Dean had lain there listening as a second car pulled up outside. Whoever it was that the girl had called. As much as Dean wanted to see the man the girl was confident would teach her punter a lesson he'd never forget, he resisted the temptation and stayed in bed listening as a car engine cut off and a car door opened and slammed.

He had fallen asleep to the muffled sound of an argument coming from within the house across the road.

But as he drove Vikki to university she hadn't said a word about the night before. She had a fashion show coming up and spent the journey talking about the various internecine rivalries on her course. Dean loved to listen to her talk about fashion. While his idea of fashion extended little beyond ironing a crease in his trousers, hearing Vikki's passion flow out of her was incredibly seductive. He thought how much he'd miss her if she was down in London. They still hadn't discussed that application.

Malton wasn't at the office when he arrived. Dean's CCTV presentation would have to wait.

He passed the time in the canteen where the lads from the night shift were enjoying their free breakfast courtesy of Malton Security. Dean joined them, helping himself to a barm cake overflowing with sloppy fried eggs, crisp bacon and four sausages. It was more a case of keeping the sandwich together than actually consuming it. He listened as one of the night-shift team regaled the rest of the room with a story about how they'd caught someone putting a tracker on a promoter's car.

This was a relatively new tactic. While most club nights had gone cash-free there were a few notable hold-outs. This meant someone leaving a club at three in the morning was carrying maybe fifty thousand in cash. More at a weekend. It was such an obvious target that Malton Security walked promoters to their cars as a matter of routine.

Manchester's ever-resourceful criminal community had discovered that if you put a tracker on the car earlier in the night then you can tail the promoter home at your leisure and beat him up on his doorstep.

Having discovered someone attempting to do just that, the doorman had held the would-be thief until closing time at which point a couple of them had taken turns throwing the culprit down the club stairs before dragging them back to the top and doing the whole thing over again.

They'd left a semi-conscious thief at the bus stop outside Manchester Royal Infirmary with at least one broken leg and maybe worse.

The table ate the story up with even more gusto than that with which they consumed their free breakfast. Dean laughed along and wondered whether or not to tell Malton about this. While Malton was totally prepared to do whatever was necessary in his sideline serving the criminal underworld, he liked to maintain an absolutely clean slate with Malton Security. There was no point in having a dirty front business. Besides, Malton Security was more than a front. It had an impressive yearly turnover that Dean knew his boss was eager not to lose.

Finishing his breakfast, undecided whether to pass this information on, Dean went to wait for Malton in his office.

As he sat on the sofa looking at the map of Manchester that covered one wall of Malton's office, he considered the hundreds of pins that covered it. Each represented a job.

Dean's eyes lingered on Moss Side. The long rows of terraces. Princess Parkway. The site of Nate's new food hall. Moss Side sat surrounded on all sides by prime locations and yet there it remained, defiantly unchanged for all these years. What made Nate Alquist think it'd be any different with his food hall?

Suddenly Dean had a thought.

He fired up his laptop. Malton's lack of technology gave his office an almost nostalgic feel. As if it existed in another time. When the thought of solving all your problems with a few keystrokes made absolutely no sense at all.

Dean logged on to the property registry and picked a house at random. The nearest he could find to the site of Nate Alquist's food hall. Dean paid for the deeds and discovered that it had been bought by Nate's company a few months ago. He tried the house next to it. It hadn't been sold in nearly thirty years. It would either be home to an elderly resident or be derelict. He tried the next along. Another hit: Nate's company Upland Living had bought it only last week. Dean worked his way up and down the two nearest streets and found that over half the homes there had been bought by Nate Alquist in the past six months.

It suddenly made sense. If the food hall was built then all the surrounding land would suddenly shoot up in value. Nate was playing both sides. Getting money from the council to build the food hall and then benefiting personally from the uptick in property prices.

Dean wondered if there was anyone who might have discovered what Nate was doing and taken exception to an outsider gentrifying Moss Side? Murder felt a little much. Even for the Manchester property market. Still, he made a note to mention all this to Malton.

While he waited for Malton to arrive he managed to find some footage from last night of the doormen dragging a badly injured thief from the club, having tossed him down the stairs half a dozen times. He spotted that someone had already logged on to watch the footage. The IP address was the one he set up on Malton's phone. Letting his boss keep an eye on his security empire twenty-four-seven.

Malton had already seen it. That was the thing that never ceased to intrigue Dean about Malton. He knew what you knew even before you knew it. Dean went back over the footage from the night Zak was murdered.

Whatever Malton might know, he was pretty certain he didn't know this.

38

The silver Škoda Yeti on the driveway wasn't taxed or MOT'd. It was hardly a double-digit stretch but it was a foot in the door. Benton had done more with less.

She looked around the Rathbone Park Estate as she knocked. It had changed beyond all recognition. She remembered how it was when she was just starting out. More of a war zone than a housing estate. It *had* been war and it'd not been won by the gangs or by the police but by the people. The silent majority who just wanted to live in peace and bring their kids up in safety.

All around her now Benton saw that hard-won peace fraying at the edges. In food banks and damp temporary accommodation. In the casual slide into crime and the widening gap between the haves and the have-nots. The next few years would be busy ones for the GMP.

Ani Delgado opened the door wearing a dark suit and shirt with an open collar. Benton hadn't seen him up close for a good few years. His hair was neater and his face a little harder but he looked remarkably youthful for a man carrying as much on his conscience as he did. He was wearing a lot of aftershave, thick sandalwood tones. It smelled just as good as Ani looked.

'Yes?' he said, his face already clocking Benton as police.

'DI Benton,' said Benton breezily. 'I notice your car isn't taxed.'

'Not on the road, is it?' said Ani quick as a flash.

'That's true.'

Ani went to shut the door. Benton's foot in its size-seven rubber-soled boot was already there.

'Get the fuck out of my house,' said Ani, instantly slipping into a more familiar vernacular.

'I just wondered if I could ask you a couple of questions. As a community leader?'

Ani eyed her suspiciously. Benton knew she didn't have long. Behind him she could hear children's voices. His house was a three-bed but it was small. Dozens of coats hung in the hallway, a pile of shoes half blocked the corridor. An overwhelming sense of clutter.

'I'm looking for a boy who's gone missing. He's local and I know that the kids around here look up to you.'

From the intelligence Benton had seen, they did more than just look up to him. Ani was still very much involved. It was his good fortune that he'd never gone into dealing beyond selling on the street as a teenager. Untouched by the taint of the drugs world, Ani had been able to fly under the radar for decades while still keeping a firm grip on the Chopboys.

'What's his name?' asked Ani.

'Femi Musa,' said Benton, watching for Ani's reaction.

'Femi? Yeah I know Femi. Good kid. I did a talk at his school; he's a prefect. I'll put the word out yeah?'

Benton knew she shouldn't be surprised. Ani had spent the last decade rehabilitating his image. Positioning himself as a respected voice of the community. Anyone who knew better had the good sense to keep their mouth shut.

'If that's all? I got to go. My business partner's having a memorial for his son.'

'Oh?' said Benton.

'Poor kid was murdered. You lot should get on that.'

'What's his name?' said Benton, already guessing the answer.

'Zak,' said Ani. 'Zak Alquist.'

Benton tried not to show how pleased she was to have guessed correctly.

'OK, and make sure you get that car taxed yeah?' she said with a smile.

Ani frowned and shut the door.

Benton headed off to buy some flowers.

39

The house Malton had lent to Vikki Walker wasn't the only property he owned in Moss Side. Last night, after losing Izzy in Heaton Park, rather than go to Bea's flat or return to his house in Didsbury, which was still on the market – the price drop still not being enough to get potential buyers over the fact that it had been where two men had recently been beaten to death – he had gone home to the other house in Moss Side he owned.

Malton had millions in the bank but this house hadn't cost him a penny. This house had been left to him by his father.

It was on Stevens Street, one of the roads that spanned the entire length of Moss Side. It crossed the Princess Parkway boundary, connecting the two halves of Moss Side. The terraces on Stevens Street were deceptively large. Three big downstairs rooms as well as the kitchen and three large rooms upstairs.

Malton was living in Liverpool when he heard his father had died and left him his childhood home. He had done everything in his power to get away from that house and his father. He'd made a name for himself working doors in Manchester. He'd left the girl from Hulme he'd fallen in love with. He'd relocated to Liverpool and he'd met James.

Although he didn't realise it at the time Malton was running as fast as he could away from that house on Stevens Street and the memory of his father.

Rory Malton was a big man. Irish stock with a body built for the physically demanding work that a few generations earlier was all that the Irish in Manchester could get. Rory was the first generation to have the chance to better himself. To rise up on the sweat and blood and tears of the previous generations of Irish. The men who'd built Manchester.

But Rory drank. He pissed his parents' legacy up the wall. Lived in their house. Watched them both die young from the hard life they'd lived. He met a local girl and didn't listen when people said that she wasn't all there. He had a son and when it looked like becoming a father might be the making of Rory Malton, that local girl had taken a train up to Saddleworth Moor, walked out over the peat bogs and vanished.

They never found the body.

Rory and Craig were alone.

Upon returning to his childhood home after his father's death, Malton found it nearly unchanged. For all his faults Rory had kept his tyrannical obsession with order. His father never kept anything of sentimental or personal value. A couple of the upstairs rooms were completely empty. Only one bedroom had a bed, the bed where Rory's parents had slept. The bed where Malton was conceived.

Rory had slept on a camp bed in the middle room downstairs. His clothes hung up on a rail beside the bed. In the front room was a television and an easy chair where they'd found him after the neighbours complained about the smell.

The kitchen had an ancient gas cooker and dozens of tins of ravioli as well as Rory's final, untouched four-pack of Guinness.

Malton had taken an upstairs room. Cleaned it, carpeted it and put in new curtains as well as a bed and wardrobe. He also installed a floor-standing safe, clad to match the wardrobe.

Whenever he came to this house he came in the back via the high-walled alleyways. Snaking his way across from a few streets along. He could be seen from the upstairs back windows of the houses he passed but no one watching the house from the front would be aware anyone was coming or going.

Only Malton knew about this place. It was his little secret. Moss Side was lots of different things. It was a deprived suburb with a strong sense of its own identity. It was a spike in a graph of violent crime. It was home to famous poets, musicians, sportsmen and politicians. It was a twinkle in a developer's eye. It was Ani Delgado's personal fiefdom and it was the place where Malton felt most at home.

He belonged to Moss Side.

Malton had risen early. Dressed and let himself out the back, across several alleys to where he'd parked his car on the edge of Rusholme.

Driving to the office he did his best to shake off the past and focus on the urgent present.

If Ani Delgado was working with Nate Alquist, suddenly the puzzle of how Zak Alquist ended up in a flat, surrounded by drugs and money with his head beaten off, didn't seem anywhere near as complicated.

But Ani being in the picture wasn't enough to solve anything. It raised more questions than it answered. Was Zak involved with the Delgados? Was the Femi who Ryan Lewis told Dean about working with them? One of the Chopboys? Could Femi be Zak's killer? And what did Nate know about any of this? Had Nate bought Ani Delgado's public persona as a reformed gang member while at the same time, unbeknownst to him, his own son was dragged into the very gang his new business partner in the Moss Side food hall was still lording it over behind the scenes?

Nate had said Zak hadn't been quite as on the straight and narrow after the trial as he liked to make out. Was that him giving as much of an indication as he dared that he believed his partner in the food hall was behind the killing of his son? Had he reached out to Malton fearing confronting Ani head on through the police? Was Nate scared for his family? Or was he more worried about the damage to his business and his image as a respected businessman?

Then there was Lesha Thompson. If she'd been able to find him through Anthony's grave then anyone could. Malton resolved to stop visiting. It wasn't like Anthony's body was still there.

He hadn't told Lesha that. Hearing her talk about the heartache of not being able to bury her son had stirred something deep in Malton. He'd only found out about Anthony last year when Keisha, Anthony's mother, had told him the circumstances surrounding his birth and death. He thought about Anthony every day. Or rather he tried to imagine who he might have been, how being a father might have changed everything.

But it was too late. Malton had lived in the dark for too long. When his thoughts went to Emily and his unborn child all he could see were the shadows. The fear of something happening. The bloody vengeance he'd enact. Try as he might he simply couldn't imagine the good times. That bothered him.

He was still undecided if he was going to take Lesha up on her request for help. But running into her had let him know that despite getting involved with Nate, Ani Delgado was still very much how he was back when Malton knew him growing up.

Another son of Moss Side unable to shake off those terraces.

Malton crawled through the multiple lane complexity of the newly created traffic system that aimed to regulate the congestion coming into the city centre but in reality simply distributed that congestion over a far wider area. He passed the severe triangular building that would soon be home to some cutting-edge technology labs thanks to all the money that Manchester university's discovery of graphene had brought in, and he got onto the Mancunian Way.

Then there was Izzy. She was missing and scared for her life. That certainly fit with someone associated with Ani Delgado. From her rehearsed performance at the hotel it was clear someone was putting words in her mouth but from what she said last night in the car, it was certain she knew the identity of Zak's killer. Could that killer be Jordan Weekes? As hard as Malton found it to imagine her and Weekes together, if they were would she risk the combined wrath of Ani Delgado and Nate Alquist to protect him?

So much had happened in the past few hours that Malton hadn't even had time to process Bea's hint of a clue into James's killer.

Driving past the illuminated advertising hoardings that loomed over the Mancunian Way, he filed that away as one more plate to keep spinning. Right now he had more important things to do. As much as it pained him, he would have to go speak to Ani.

Ani was still in his childhood home in Moss Side. His nightmarish twin brother Lani had never settled anywhere, haunting the postcode like the malign ghost he was. A constant, unpredictable threat of Delgado violence keeping everyone in line. Where Lani was now was anyone's guess.

But that would have to wait. Nate was holding a memorial for his son around midday at the site of the food hall. Malton still didn't know all that much about Zak Alquist. Just what his father and the papers said. He hoped attending the memorial might give him a bit more of an idea of who exactly the boy had been. And if he got lucky maybe Ani Delgado would make an appearance.

Malton pulled into the Malton Security offices in Cheetham Hill. He saw that the van he'd lent Dean after he wrecked his last car was already there.

Nate would have to be told of Izzy's disappearance. Malton thought Bea could handle that. It would mean any questions Nate had about Malton's progress would have to go unanswered until Malton decided he was ready to answer them.

There was only one final loose end to chase. Benton.

Benton and Malton went all the way back to when he and his father lived together on Stevens Street. Back then she'd let him off whatever it was she caught him doing, knowing full well what he had waiting for him at home. She had recognised that Malton wasn't like the Delgados of this world. Malton lived among criminals, he thought like criminals, but Malton was something very different.

Still, if it came to it no amount of history would stand in the way of Malton doing the one thing he always did – finishing the job. That was the reputation he had. The thing that kept him bulletproof. If you hired him, he would finish what he started. No matter where it took him. No matter who it pissed off. That was how everyone in the underworld knew Malton never took sides. He operated above the fray.

Having parked up, the first thing Malton saw as he entered the office was Dean waiting for him, clutching his laptop.

The past year Dean had been invaluable. Malton was happy to admit that the world was changing at a pace he could barely keep up with. Not just technology, but the changing criminal mindset. Fists gave way to knives gave way to guns. A generation so scared of failure that they never start a fight that they don't intend to terminally end. A code of criminal silence gave way to online bragging, branded drugs and a reckless fatalism born of a quixotic desire to be seen, validated and celebrated for the kind of crimes that would put you away for life.

Dean kept Malton in the game. If he was in this early with his laptop that meant he had something to show him.

Ten minutes later, watching Dean play him the CCTV clip from the night Zak Alquist was beaten to death with a hammer, Malton couldn't be more impressed.

'There,' said Dean, pausing the footage. 'He's here, here and here.' Dean pressed a key and the screen flicked through several different CCTV feeds. All from Malton Security clients. Each time the same man appeared.

'There's no footage of him entering Zak's building but if you piece it together he approaches the flats, then leaves the flats, all within the timeline. We can see him walking into a blind spot,' said Dean, replaying a shot of the figure passing a CCTV camera and off the edge of the screen.

'But that blind spot is here.' Dean pressed another button and a Google Maps screen came up. He pointed a finger to the screen. To the outline of Zak's flats.

Malton sat back. It was impressive work.

But he wasn't thinking about who the unidentifiably blurry figure stalking towards Zak Alquist's apartment was. He was thinking about what wasn't there. For all Dean's work in establishing a visual timeline there was one glaring omission.

Dean had covered every inch of the approach to Zak's flat for the entire time of Zak's murder. But there was not a single frame of footage containing Izzy.

40

Dean guessed that Izzy wasn't more than twenty years old. That meant a lifetime on social media. While younger people had become more savvy to privacy settings it hadn't taken him long to cross-reference 'Moss Side' and 'Izzy' to find nearly decade-old posts uploaded by her parents.

A pre-teen Izzy playing in the street during a heatwave. Izzy at a family barbecue. Izzy in a school play.

Most importantly Izzy's first day of secondary school. A young Izzy stood in her brand-new school uniform, smiling for the camera in front of a house with a very visible door number.

A short drive around Moss Side and Dean had tracked the house down.

It was hard to know what Malton made of the CCTV. He'd watched it in silence before asking a few questions as to how he'd found it and pieced it together. After Dean had satisfied all his boss's questions Malton had abruptly changed tack.

He'd told Dean about the night before, Izzy fleeing into the night. Then Malton had asked Dean to track her down. Find the needle in a haystack. After what he thought was the break-through with CCTV, Dean had struggled to hide his disappointment at being given yet more hoops to jump through. But he learned long ago that Malton only ever asked him to achieve the impossible when he honestly believed Dean had a decent chance of pulling it off.

The idea of turning Malton down never even occurred to him and so he'd set about tracking down the young woman last seen running into the darkness of Heaton Park.

Now, stood outside the house where Izzy grew up, Dean tried to think of a decent story. He'd seen Malton lie countless times, never once giving any sign that he was being anything other than totally honest. But Dean couldn't lie. His face betrayed him. He instinctively started smirking and then the game was up.

The house was on the Rathbone Park side of Princess Parkway. As close to the main road as you could get. Over time the proximity to the outer edges of Chorlton had seen a few of the houses bought up and converted into handsome, multi-generational homes. Dean found Izzy's house unchanged from the photo of her first day at school. The front door was the same bright red, the planters still there, albeit now empty save for litter.

Dean decided that he'd just tell the truth. See how far it got him.

He knocked and took a step back, put on his game face and waited as the sound of someone undoing locks came from inside.

The door opened and Dean found himself staring at a face he recognised but took a split second to place.

It was the kid with the gun from the Moss Side Carnival.

41

Benton watched as the crowd of teenagers got ready to release helium balloons up into the air over Manchester. Hundreds of them. All with an image of Zak Alquist printed on the side.

She tried not to think about the farmer downwind who'd be finding a sheep choking on Zak Alquist's deflated face several days from now.

The memorial was taking place on the site of Nate Alquist's new food hall in Moss Side. It was no small affair either.

Nate Alquist had paid for a stage to be erected where there had been a brief set from a local singer who'd found fame singing on Manchester dance tracks in the Nineties. After an upbeat set of Mancunian anthems she ended on a pared-down, piano version of 'Atmosphere'.

Benton had hovered at the back and listened through several speeches about how much Zak would be missed. How he was one of a kind and lit up the room. A cheeky chap with an irrepressible sense of humour. An absolute legend who'd be partying up in heaven. A teenage girl had even got up and sung 'Hallelujah'.

All the boxes ticked.

No one had once mentioned Carrie Lewis. Looking around the crowd Benton saw a lot of sad faces. Almost all of them white. She saw DCI Priestly and another couple of liaison officers. A few councillors and a journalist. And there, stood beside Nate and his wife, was Ani Delgado looking appropriately sombre.

So far so expected. Benton wasn't sure what she was hoping to see but nothing so far had given her that fluttering feeling of things slowly beginning to make sense.

She stood back and looked round. The derelict houses that bordered the food hall and the first of the newly built flats that now lined Princess Parkway. The brewery towering over it all. Then she saw her. A middle-aged woman in a pastor's dog collar stood away to one side watching. No one paid her any attention. She seemed apart from what was going on but from the look on her face it was clear this was more to her than just someone else's tragedy. If Benton didn't know any better she'd say this woman looked disgusted.

Benton made a note to herself to find out exactly who she was and what she was doing there.

Nate Alquist was on the microphone. His wife stood silently beside him while her husband's voice cracked with emotion. Benton almost believed him. Nate talked about how Manchester was built on people like his son. People who seized life by the throat. The strivers and the doers. As Nate spoke Benton kept her eyes on his wife. Nate was on stage giving a performance. She had to stand beside him and control whatever thoughts were going through her head. All Benton needed was that one little tell. Something that would be enough to let her know that there *was* more going on than met the eye.

In her years of police work Benton had dealt with more bereaved parents than she cared to remember.

There was no standard way to handle the death of a child. The human brain isn't designed to cope with that tsunami of grief. Some people shut down. They removed themselves from the world. Others gave as many interviews as they could. Started foundations. Cried in public. They spent every last ounce of energy in a futile attempt to resurrect the ghost of their dead child through sheer force of repetition.

Then there were the ones who knew something more than they were letting on. Who were too helpful and then not helpful at all. Telling poorly thought out lies. Crying a little too easily. Clumsily inserting themselves into police investigations, confident that their status as a bereaved parent would protect them.

Until the truth inevitably came to the surface. They had been responsible for the deaths of their children. Benton never forgot those parents. But if Nate was one of those parents he was doing a damn good job of hiding it.

And there always close at hand was Ani Delgado. Stood behind Nate and his wife. Almost as if he was keeping an eye on Nate.

Benton waited until the time came to release the balloons before making her move.

As the sky filled with balloons and the site filled with people, their arms outstretched, filming it all on their phones, Benton saw Ani finally leave Nate's side and go over to talk to Priestly. From how Priestly nodded and smiled she guessed Ani was being his usual charming self.

She sensed her chance. Weaving through the crowd she made her way to the edge of the stage.

It was only a couple of feet high but Benton didn't try and climb it. Instead she stayed where she was, looking up at Nate Alquist. He looked smaller in the flesh. He was wearing a dark suit and white shirt, open at the collar. His trademark mop of hair had been elaborately styled to look like he'd just got out of bed. Benton noticed he was wearing leather trainers that looked like formal shoes but with thick, white soles.

'Mr Alquist, can I ask you a few questions about Femi Musa?' Benton shouted up.

Nate looked around for a moment before realising where the voice was coming from. He took a step back and looked down at Benton warily.

'Who?'

'Femi Musa, a young boy. Went missing a few days ago.'

An incredulous look came over Nate Alquist. A look that very quickly escalated into a sneer.

'This is my son's memorial. His killers are still out there and you're here asking me about some boy I've never met. Who are you?'

'DI Benton,' said Benton reaching into an anorak pocket only to discover that wasn't where she'd left her police ID. 'I think Femi Musa's disappearance might be linked to your son.'

'How? I've never heard of a Femi Musa. Neither had Zak.'

'That's funny,' said Benton. 'Because I found this on Femi's phone.' She held up a photo she'd taken of Femi's lock screen with her own phone.

Nate Alquist leapt down off the stage. The balloons were beginning to drift over towards the city centre.

The friendly, man-of-the-people Nate Alquist vanished in an instant. In his place was the Nate Alquist who had forged a multi-million-pound empire. The man who had graduated from a slumlord throwing tenants out on the street to the man berating councillors into submission as he slowly rebuilt Manchester in his image.

'You want to be very careful what you say to me,' he hissed, jabbing his finger at Benton.

'That advice goes both ways,' said a voice from over Benton's shoulder.

She turned to see Malton shouldering his way through the crowd. He put a firm hand on her shoulder and looked to Nate.

'Don't worry, I'll get rid of her,' he said before steering Benton round and guiding her back through the crowd.

As they walked away, leaving behind a visibly furious Nate Alquist, Benton turned to look at Malton.

'I'd like to see you try,' she said with a smile.

42

Graham had wanted Lesha to stay home for the day while he opened up Kieran's Place. But the thought of sitting in the house alone while other people ran the shop bearing her son's name was far worse than anything Ani Delgado could come up with.

Ani would never stop and neither would Lesha. His Moss Side wouldn't win. It couldn't.

Lesha's Moss Side was the parade at the carnival. It was the boxing gym that trained kids and produced champions. It was the Caribbean takeaways and the fabric shops and the memory of Maine Road. It was Alexandra Park and Moss Side Park and Platt Fields Park. It was residents greening alleyways and manning food banks. It was the sound of children in the primary schools, laughter and shouts echoing off terraces. It was thousands of people who had less of everything except pride in where they came from.

Up against that Ani didn't stand a chance. Besides she had Craig Malton on her side.

He hadn't agreed to her request to speak to Ani but he hadn't said no either. She didn't have to convince Craig about Ani. He knew. Craig was Moss Side born and bred. She hoped he was her Moss Side and not Ani's.

All day Lesha stood at the newly installed counter and served meals. Graham's lads were finishing off the café refurb. There were new seats and the front had been reconstructed with a freshly donated metal shutter. A local artist had already been in and offered to do a mural on it. Lesha had asked him to do a picture of Kieran.

When Phil had shown up that morning he acted as if the events of the other day hadn't even happened. Phil lived in the moment. He couldn't dwell on the past or worry about the future even if he wanted to. It was what made him so vulnerable but it was also what gave him an indefatigable sense of optimism. It was exactly what Lesha needed.

By the time she was closing up things almost felt normal.

Wiping down the kitchen and listening to the radio, Lesha's arms bulged with the effort. Her breath grew short as she scrubbed and scrubbed, as if hoping that all the fear and worry would disappear along with the grease and dirt.

She was backing out the door with the bin liners when she stopped dead. There above the roofs of the houses she could see the sun hanging in a cloudless sky. Like a child's drawing, bright yellow against the blue. She felt its warmth on her bare arms. On Kieran.

She opened the bin and hauled the rubbish in.

As she pulled down her brand-new shutter and closed up for the day she felt a pride swelling in her chest.

The right Moss Side had won.

43

'Who's Femi?' asked Malton.

He and Benton were sitting outside the Abbey Taphouse. Having led her away from the site of the food hall, they'd made small talk while strolling up through Moss Side and into the Science Park that marked the end of Moss Side and the beginning of the universities.

While the park was made up of anonymous, light industrial buildings housing laboratories and in one case a small hospital where members of the public were paid handsomely to serve as guinea pigs for new medicines, there remained a single reminder that at one time it had been just like the rest of Moss Side – dense terraced streets.

Nearly seventy years ago a local boxer by the name of Len Johnson had been told the Taphouse didn't serve blacks and instead of knowing his place had rallied a couple of hundred locals, black and white, and along with the Mayor of Manchester's backing overturned the pub's colour ban.

Malton still remembered first hearing about Len Johnson as a teenager. Learning that just like Malton Johnson was mixed-race. It was the first time he got the idea that maybe there was more to where he was from than people like Ani Delgado. A whole hidden history of Manchester that wasn't taught in school. A black history.

Len Johnson showed Malton that there was more than one Manchester. Sitting on top was the Manchester that everyone knew about. Mills and the Hacienda and the football. But then beneath that lay a dozen different Manchesters all at odds with each other. It was from these competing subcultures that he had created his own vision of his home city.

'Who do *you* think Femi is?' said Benton, answering Malton's question with one of her own.

Malton knew Benton well enough to understand how this worked. They both had their own worlds. Benton, the world of law enforcement. Malton, the world of law breaking. Each could go places and do things the other couldn't. Usually this sort of conversation was mutually beneficial to all parties. But ever since he bumped into Benton at Bittersweet and she'd whisked Jordan Weekes out from under his nose he'd known that this moment was coming.

Malton took the bait. 'I think Jordan Weekes was selling drugs to the Chopboys and Femi Musa was the point man.'

'Point *kid* – he was only sixteen.'

'Was?'

'He's missing. Last few days.'

Malton had almost expected this. Femi's name had kept coming up and yet Femi himself was nowhere to be seen. It was a setback but if Femi was missing then it weighed heavily in favour of Femi's involvement being key to the whole jumbled mess.

'So why the interest in Nate Alquist?' asked Malton.

'I could ask you the same,' said Benton.

They sat in silent impasse. Each one trying to work out just what the other knew and what they hoped to get out of this conversation.

Benton finished her packet of crisps and began to fold the wrapper into a tight, greasy knot.

'OK, let's stop fucking around. I can guess that you've been hired by Nate Alquist to look into Zak's murder. I can also guess from you turning up to grab Jordan Weekes that you've seen the murder scene. Seen Weekes's drugs. And we both know you're not stupid so I'm guessing, like me, you didn't buy Weekes as a killer, which means you're missing a suspect. Which means Femi.'

She paused and Malton felt her watching him for a response. He gave a little smile but held back from letting her know how on the money her guess was.

Benton pulled out her phone. Malton looked at the second-hand photo of Zak and the boy he assumed must be Femi. 'So if you do fancy Femi for Zak's murder and you do want to know more, then it's your turn.'

Malton ran over everything he had learned in his head, trying to locate the least valuable thing he could throw to Benton. While he knew Benton liked to work her own case, she was still GMP.

'The girl who was with Weekes last night, Izzy. She's scared,' said Malton.

There was no way for Benton to easily connect Izzy to Zak. Least of all because according to Dean's CCTV montage Izzy was nowhere near Zak's flat on the night of his murder.

'Scared of what?' said Benton.

Malton shrugged. 'Chopboys? Femi Musa?'

'Ani Delgado?' Benton let the name hang. Malton felt her watching him for a tell. All he gave her was a shrug.

'Don't know. She was about to tell me who killed Zak but then instead jumped out a moving car,' he said.

'You let her escape? You're slipping. All that soft living up in the tower block with Bea Wallace,' she teased him.

Malton hadn't kept his relationship with Bea a secret. While Malton's job required a low profile, Bea was the exact opposite. She made it her business to be the smiling, blonde face of her law practice.

'You know they're using you, Craig. Right? Putting a shine on a botched job.'

Malton didn't like hearing his deepest suspicions out loud.

'With your ex Keisha, at least you knew what she wanted. To bump you off in the worst way possible.'

This was true. A year ago, she'd nearly succeeded too. As of now she had vanished off the face of the earth. After the last time they met Malton wondered if she was gone for good this time. The card at the cemetery suggested otherwise.

Benton continued, 'Bea? She's a sly little bitch. All blonde hair and a giggly Geordie accent. Wouldn't surprise me if she's in on this too. Protecting Nate, her client.'

Again Malton did his best not to let Benton see how accurately she was mining his fears.

'But me? What you see is what you get,' she said, wiping her greasy hands on her trousers. 'So let me tell you what I think happened. Femi and Zak were mates and buying drugs for the Chopboys. Zak fancied playing at dealers and Femi was glad to have a rich kid along for the ride. But things go south and Carrie gets killed and the Chopboys drop him like a bad habit.'

Malton kept quiet and listened. He knew if Benton was outlining all this for his benefit that what she was keeping back must be even more revelatory.

Benton continued, 'Somehow thanks to your missus Bea Wallace, Zak gets off a murder charge, at which point his old friend Femi comes calling. Zak Alquist has maybe had a change of heart about the whole drug dealing thing and next thing he knows he's getting a visit from someone with a hammer. Case closed.'

Benton held his eye. 'But I don't think Femi killed him. So now it's your turn.'

Malton thought through what he knew. Benton had already thrown Ani Delgado into the mix.

'You wondering whether to mention the fact that Nate Alquist and Ani Delgado are working together?' said Benton.

Now Malton was surprised. Benton was further along than he thought. The nagging worry he'd had ever since Bea introduced him to Ani the other night resurfaced in his mind. What if the Chopboys had killed Zak, and Ani Delgado was the one who suggested Nate get Malton involved? What if Ani Delgado saw his stake in the food hall at risk from his gang connections and thought he had more chance of controlling the narrative with Malton looking into it than the police? What if Nate Alquist wasn't the one playing games? What if he was the one getting played?

Benton saw Femi as a boy sucked into the middle of something beyond his control. Malton saw him as just another of Ani Delgado's disposable foot soldiers.

Things were about to get complicated in a way that he couldn't afford to drag Benton into.

Malton rested his hands on the table, the fingers interlaced into a giant club.

'I've always respected you,' he said. 'But you know what I do. You know that if I've been asked to find Zak Alquist's killer before the police that means I'll do whatever it takes.' He fixed Benton with a cold stare.

Malton knew this day was coming. For all their history they were still on opposite sides of the law.

'And you know I'll do whatever it takes to bring Femi home alive,' said Benton, unmoved by Malton's gentle display of intimidation.

Malton said nothing.

One thing was certain – one of them would find Femi Musa first. As a lost boy or as a killer.

44

In Dean's experience when people opened a door and found Malton stood waiting for them, they knew that they were in trouble. Malton was an expert at allaying those fears, subverting expectations and winning trust. But that first impression was always there, lingering with menace at the back of their mind.

When people first saw Dean they generally wanted to try and help him. He had the air of someone who had got lost, wandered in where they weren't meant to be and now needed gently guiding back onto the straight and narrow.

In the heat of the carnival and surrounded by people, the man who he now knew to be called Taymon had had no choice but to defend his bruised ego with aggression. But when he'd answered the door and Dean had quickly explained why he was there, it was obvious that Dean was absolutely no threat.

In fact, when Dean had told him just enough about Nate Alquist and the meeting with Izzy at the Paramore hotel, Taymon had realised Dean was on his side. He'd invited him in and made him a coffee. Dean half wished Malton could have seen him.

'When did you last see your sister?' asked Dean. He was sitting on a leather chair while Taymon sat opposite on a matching sofa. Both were covered in heavy, clear plastic covers, which amplified every little move into a cacophony of angry squeaks.

'Couple of weeks ago? She doesn't live here,' said Taymon. 'She's got a flat in town.'

'What does she do for money?' asked Dean as politely as he could.

'This and that,' said Taymon, looking guilty.

'Average flat in town is nearly a couple of grand a month. Does this and that pay that well?' asked Dean sounding a little more forceful.

Taymon looked away. 'I know what she looks like. I know what that means. Ever since she was little she had men round her. At first she hated it but eventually she gave in. Learned to play them. On her terms.'

Dean looked round the room. A lot of colourful art. Laminate floors, blinds over the windows. He wondered just what 'on her terms' meant and just how much of what Izzy did to make rent on a city-centre flat really was 'on her terms' and not on the terms of someone like Jordan Weekes or Nate Alquist.

'You said you saw her at that hotel?'

'Paramore. But she isn't there anymore. She ran off.'

'Ran off?' said Taymon, shifting anxiously in his seat, the plastic sofa cover giving a nervous whinny.

'I think she might be in trouble,' said Dean. 'I'm trying to help her.'

'You?' said Taymon. 'Why?'

As briefly and discreetly as he could Dean explained what he did for Malton and how they'd been hired to look into Zak's murder.

'I told her they'd kill him,' said Taymon angrily. 'I told her that. She thought she could save him.'

'So she *was* in a relationship with Zak?' Dean couldn't hide his surprise. At best he had imagined Izzy as some kind of hanger-on, exploiting a rich kid eager to live the lifestyle. He'd never pictured her risking her own safety for Zak.

Taymon laughed almost theatrically. Rocking back on the sofa, causing it to squeak along with him.

He regained his composure and said, 'No. They made her. They wanted a way to make sure his dad did what he was told.'

'Who's they?'

For the first time since Dean had sat down, Taymon was silent.

'You're not from round here, are you?' he said after a moment, leaning forward.

'I live up on Morton Road,' said Dean confidently. The seat cover beneath him squeaked in agreement.

Taymon shook his head. 'That don't mean anything. I mean you're not from here. You didn't grow up here. You don't know here. You think you do. You don't know shit. How it really works.'

'At the carnival, you had a gun. Those lads you were casing. Is that who you're talking about?'

Taymon smiled. 'I should thank you, you know? You saved my life, back there. That's not me. I'm not running about making trouble. Nah. Yeah, I know them, but I'm not like them. Izzy wasn't like them. Not 'til they got into her. What was I thinking? One guy against all of them? Should have just shot myself. Been quicker yeah?'

'Did those guys get your sister to go out with Zak?'

'The thing you got to understand. Gangs and that. It's not like *The Godfather* or nothing. Gang's just a bunch of guys. They got a name but that's not them. That's a name. I know their real names. Ali and Romeo and Mike and Mitchell and Carl. And I went to school with all of them. I know their mums. We play football and that. We did. But then they decided they wanted more. They wanted money. Wanted people to look up to them. Be scared of them.'

'So who made your sister go out with Zak Alquist?' Dean sensed Taymon losing focus.

Taymon took a breath. 'I'm only telling you this cos you stopped me doing something wild. Cos I owe you. Not cos I'm a grass.'

Dean nodded. He understood just how important that distinction was.

'When those boys get told to pick up my sis and tell her she's going to go out with this little dickhead Zak Alquist, only one man telling them to do that. The man they all wanna be some day.'

Dean realised how still he was sitting. The seat cover beneath didn't make a sound.

'You tell anyone this, I'm dead. Yeah? Man who pulls the strings. Man who ruined my sister? Ani Delgado.'

45

St Barnabas was still a working church. The pews were lined with hymn books. A modern PA sat nestled at the front of the church and all the appropriate health and safety signage indicated a place of worship that was still very much in use.

'The council had promised us that land,' said the pastor sat at the back of the empty church. She was around Benton's age, that same careworn look of someone who rarely got a chance to sit down and catch their breath. She wore a black shirt and dog collar underneath a tatty fleece top.

'It was going to be an outdoor worship area and sports facility. Basketball courts, a five-a-side pitch. Community resources.'

This was news to Benton. It was hard enough to keep up with the currents of Manchester's criminal underworld, never mind the backstabbing world of Manchester property development.

She'd left Malton feeling like she'd given more than she got. Malton was after Femi and that made her worried. If anyone could find a missing boy in the torrents of the Manchester underworld it was Malton. That wasn't what worried her. If Ani Delgado and Nate Alquist were business partners just how much of what Malton found out for Nate was being fed back to Ani? If Nate thought Ani could help him build a food hall might he think Ani could help him find his son's killers? In his rush to find out who killed Zak could Nate Alquist actually be setting up the murder of Femi Musa?

While she was still in Moss Side, Benton had decided to follow up on a hunch. The pastor she'd seen at the memorial.

Something about the way she watched the memorial. Seeing through Nate Alquist's pomp. She had the look of someone who'd seen too much to be bullshitted, bullied or bought.

'Then one day I get a visit from the council. Some junior clerk telling me that the permission had been withdrawn. Withdrawn!'

The pastor's voice rose with outrage and echoed off the high ceiling.

'We'd already been fundraising for two years!' She pointed to a board at the front of the church where someone had painted a vertical line to indicate current funds. It stood at fourteen thousand pounds.

There were a handful of churches within walking distance of the food hall site. Benton had gone to two others before she found the woman she was looking for. Angrily hoovering her empty church.

'So what changed?' asked Benton.

The pastor's fire dimmed a little. She turned to Benton. She looked tired. 'Sorry, tell me again, why are you here?'

Benton smiled apologetically. 'When I said I was asking about Zak Alquist's murder, well, that was a lie. Truth is I saw you at the memorial for Zak Alquist. You didn't seem to be getting into the spirit of it. I wondered why.'

'Don't get me wrong, I feel nothing but heartache for a murdered child. A father losing a son. But seeing the carnival that Nate Alquist made of it. Everyone there ready to jump in their car and drive back to wherever it is they came from. Somewhere rich and white where they think they can walk into Moss Side with money and have everything their own way.'

The pastor sighed. 'This has been going on for so long. With the land. Seeing Nate Alquist use the death of his son as some kind of victory parade. It felt . . . wrong.'

Benton nodded along. 'A victory parade?'

The pastor looked sad. 'We were dealing with a man from the council. A man in planning. After they withdrew permission I wanted to know why he didn't tell me to my face.

I thought he was a coward. I went to the town hall myself. In person. To demand answers. I found him in his office. Cowering.'

'What did he say?'

The pastor let out a sigh. 'Someone had broken all the fingers on his left hand. He didn't need to say anything.'

Breaking fingers didn't sound like Nate Alquist's style. It sounded a lot more like his business partner – Ani Delgado.

Before Benton could say anything further the pastor stood up and crossed her arms. She was suddenly stern. 'Nate Alquist isn't from Moss Side. He has no idea who he's getting into business with. Or what the price will be. Evil men do not understand justice, but those who seek the Lord understand it completely.'

'Amen,' said Benton and meant it.

The pastor headed off down the middle of the church and disappeared into the vestry, leaving Benton alone.

It would seem Nate Alquist had made a deal with the devil and now, whether he liked it or not, Malton was dancing to Ani Delgado's tune.

With nothing better to do, Benton bowed her head and said a little prayer for the continued good health of Femi Musa.

46

'Chop, chop, stab. That means you got to get at least two chops with the machete.' Ani Delgado mimed a chopping motion with his right arm. 'Arms, legs, head, face, don't matter. You bring that blade down hard. Chop. Chop.'

He paused for effect. Every single one of the two hundred teenagers sat watching in the school hall were silent. Hanging on his every word.

'Then you got to stab. And remember, you're not killing no one. You kill a man you're going away. Don't matter who you are. So where do you stab? Favourite place? Right here.' Ani grabbed his crotch and rode the wave of sickened groans coming from his audience.

'Chop. Chop. Stab. You're in the gang.'

★★★

Malton was waiting for Ani outside the school gates. It was a quiet street; large, detached houses with small driveways and mature trees breaking through the wide pavement.

The memorial had wound down and Ani was nowhere to be seen by the time Malton had returned to the crowd after leaving Benton back at the pub. But Ani was easy enough to track down. In his new role as self-appointed community leader he was working the ex-gang member angle for all it was worth. Giving talks to schools all over Manchester. Today he was at a school in Sale where despite the million-pound houses and leafy, suburban respectability they felt hearing from the man who had survived the Chopboys would be a helpful lesson for their pupils.

Ani had killed at least three people that Malton knew about and there were rumours of a dozen more. He'd armed kids to settle debts; he'd tortured rivals and threatened hundreds of people. Just one man, Ani was like a criminal black hole, dragging everything around him into the void.

But that wasn't the Ani Delgado who'd come out to Davyhulme Grammar to give his talk about gangs. That Ani was repentant, a victim, a cautionary tale with just enough of a hint of danger to make the message palatable.

Walking out the school gates, Ani caught sight of Malton and waved.

'Craig!' he shouted, a huge smile breaking across his face as if greeting an old friend.

That was the other thing about Ani Delgado. He was a cruel, ruthless bastard but he was also impossibly charming.

Ani crossed the road, his arms open. Malton resisted the invitation to hug but Ani didn't seem to mind.

'I keep missing you! First the other night, then I saw you at the memorial. Bad business. Seems like things never change. Still, great to see you, bro.'

'I'm not your bro,' said Malton before he could stop himself. Something about Ani got under his skin. The way he coerced the world into playing along with his fantasy of a redeemed criminal.

Ani didn't drop a beat. 'You missed a great talk in there. Important stuff. All the naughty shit we used to get up to. Making sure the next generation don't fuck up like we did!' He laughed.

Ani wasn't going to give up a thing. Malton would have to make the first move.

'Nate Alquist asked me to look into who killed his son.'

It was mid-afternoon and the road outside the school was deserted. Just two boys from Moss Side shooting the breeze.

'Terrible what happened. And anything I can do to help, you just ask. My name carries a lot of weight in places the police can't go. Anything you need?'

'What are you doing in business with Nate?'

Ani lit up.

'Fucking exciting times, Craig! We're building a food hall in Moss Side.'

Malton noted the use of 'we'.

'Gonna be just what the place needs. You got all the new flats and stuff. New faces. Moss Side's changing. So I said to Nate, what's in for us? People like you and me? People who make Moss Side? You know you can't just come in here and start throwing your weight around. It don't work like that does it?' Ani laughed as if he expected Malton to be in on the joke.

'How does it work?'

'Partnership. Nate saw me, saw someone who's respected in the community. Someone they look up to. He saw someone who could help him realise his vision.'

'What is that vision?'

'A new Moss Side. Money. People. Growth. We're going to build a food hall but it's not going to be the usual artisanal bollocks. I'm getting the community involved. The guys who do the barbecues, the mums who make the patties. I'm going to make sure when you eat in Moss Side food hall, you're eating proper Moss Side. Local food. Local jobs.'

Malton had to remind himself who Ani Delgado was. A gangster and a killer. Right now he was doing a brilliant impression of a visionary entrepreneur. Malton could feel Ani's sales pitch getting under his skin.

'Sounds exciting,' said Malton noncommittally.

'It fucking is, Craig. It really fucking is. Time I did something right for once.'

'What's in it for you?'

Ani gestured to an imaginary audience. 'Fucking Craig Malton. He knows the questions to ask. He's the man! It's money, isn't it. These days I don't just do the speaking. I'm in property. Like Nate. That's why the food hall's fifty-fifty. Me and Nate. We're a team.'

Malton didn't bother to hide his surprise. He figured some kind of shakedown but this felt like Ani Delgado had walked in and taken over.

Ani sensed Malton's reaction. 'I know! Scally like me getting into something like this.'

'And if anyone gives Nate any bother?'

Ani frowned. 'Moss Side's changed. It's not like that.'

'And the Delgado name doesn't hurt?'

'That's bang out of order, Craig. That was years ago. Whatever my brother Lani did or didn't do, that's not me.'

Malton remembered Lani all too well. Growing up a white-presenting mixed-race kid in a black community, Lani always had to be tougher and meaner and give less fucks than the black kids around him. Mean enough to burn a house down around a mother and child.

Ani spread his arms. 'I'm an open book. Ask Nate. Ask your missus. If there's anything I can do to help you get to the bottom of what happened with Zak, just ask.'

'Am I asking you or am I asking the Chopboys?' said Malton.

Ani frowned. Finally his good humour left him. But only briefly before a more clipped, severe Ani regained control.

'You always did think you could get away with it, didn't you, Craig? You want to be careful who you piss off. It's not like it was. Kids running about with guns and knives. This is big-boy stuff now. You go and play Miss Fucking Marple and let me help Nate move on. Focus on doing some good. OK?'

Ani turned to go to his car. Malton reached out, wrapped a giant hand around Ani's arm. Compared to Malton Ani was slight but he shook off Malton's grip and turned on him fearlessly.

'You want to start something?'

'One more thing,' said Malton. He wasn't going to bring this up but Ani had pissed him off and so now he wanted to return the favour. 'Lesha Thompson.'

Ani turned and spat on the ground, inches from Malton's feet.

'That's what I thought,' said Malton. 'I'm asking you nicely. Let it go. If what you say is true, you're a changed man. About to become a very rich man. You don't need to risk all that over a stupid beef. Her son's dead. Let sleeping dogs lie.'

'I'm not risking a fucking thing,' said Ani with a sneer.

He didn't wait for a reply. He barged past Malton, got in his car and drove away.

Malton watched him go. Now everyone involved had given their own version of events. Nate, Bea, Izzy and finally Ani. It was time to find out which version was the truth.

47

Graham had insisted on meeting Lesha to walk her home. He said he'd come to inspect the work on the café but Lesha knew that was just him sparing her pride.

He'd been off on another job and was still dressed in overalls, covered in paint and plaster dust with heavy, steel-toe-capped boots poking out the bottom. He wore a T-shirt under his overalls, his arms bare in the late afternoon sun. His arms were a mess of random tattoos. Symbols, words and pictures.

Lesha had never imagined getting tattoos until Kieran died. She never would again. Two was enough to keep her son with her.

As they walked through Alexandra Park Lesha felt Ani Delgado's grip begin to relax. When she had first met him all those years ago, they had barely been together a couple of months before Lesha discovered she was pregnant.

Maybe Ani still had feelings for her after all those years. Maybe the sight of her and Kieran living a happy life without him felt like a slap in the face. Lesha didn't know why Ani suddenly came back into her life and took her son away from her. But he had and once again Ani Delgado had thrown her life off course.

She was determined he would not do it a third time. Seeing the café come back together and hearing from all the customers worried about her after the brick through her window the other night, Lesha had begun to feel like maybe Ani Delgado wasn't as all powerful as he'd like to think.

Graham had stood by her from the start and now they walked hand in hand out of the park and towards the house.

'I told you,' he said proudly, 'you stand up to bullies.'

The board was still over the front window of the house, the memory of their smashed window still raw. Graham had hoped to get it replaced today but someone had let him down at the last minute. He promised Lesha it'd be done by tomorrow.

As they crossed the road Lesha could swear she saw curtains twitching. She couldn't blame them. They couldn't have missed the commotion last night. The breaking glass and Sergio and Raheem barking long into the night. It had taken a couple of hours to settle them down. Eventually Lesha had kicked Graham out of bed and he'd slept on the sofa while Sergio and Raheem slept with her.

She was so caught up in thinking about what to tell the neighbours that she had her key out before she noticed that the door was already open.

Lesha didn't even know why but the first words out of her mouth were: 'Sergio! Raheem!'

She was home and her dogs weren't in the corridor barking with excitement. Somehow deep down she already knew what she'd find.

A flat, sick feeling begin to churn in her throat. That dull white noise began to expand in her brain as she left Graham behind and rushed into the house.

First the kitchen then the living room and the back room. They were empty. Just as she'd left them. Untouched.

Back in the hallway, Graham opening his mouth. Saying something she couldn't hear. Only the blood pumping in her ears and the dull thud of her feet on the stairs as she raced upstairs and into her bedroom where she knew they'd be.

And they were. In the bed where just the night before they'd slept, their soft, warm bodies pressed up against her own. All three of them looking out for one another.

The bed was a sickly, moist red. Cold, wet blood covering the white sheets and matted into the white fur of Sergio and Raheem.

Lesha's hand was at her mouth too late, she turned and threw up on the carpet, emptying her body before she turned back to what was left of Sergio and Raheem and let out a bottomless howl.

48

The music was too loud for Dean to think about Izzy or her brother Taymon. About Ani Delgado or Zak Alquist or any of it.

On the dance floor at the White Hotel all he could do was dance alongside Vikki and a couple of hundred other clubbers who had braved their way into the scruffy guts of Cheetham Hill to find themselves in one of Manchester's most out-of-the-way venues.

Once upon a time the White Hotel was an MOT garage. Now it was a dance floor, art space and bar. A place to hear music that you couldn't get anywhere else. Esoteric dance music, innovatively fucked-up bands and art pieces that would get you thrown out of any respectable gallery.

Vikki had dragged him down to listen to a band he'd never heard of and Dean had willingly come. Not just to escape the muddle of new facts echoing round his head but to enjoy every minute he could with Vikki.

Since she closed her laptop a couple of days ago there had been no mention of London or Goldsmiths. Dean was almost letting himself believe it was just a passing fancy that he'd let himself blow out of all proportion.

But deep down he knew why he'd not simply come straight out and asked her. As soon as he asked the question he'd get the answer and if the answer was that she was leaving him to go to London it would break his heart.

Onstage a man and a woman were surrounded by boxes covered in knobs. Not anything Dean could readily identify as an instrument. They hunched over these boxes, turning dials and nodding along as the music soared and fell, washing the concrete dance floor with grinding beats.

He hadn't told her that he'd met the guy from the carnival with the gun. That while they weren't exactly friends there was now no bad blood between him and Taymon. And he wasn't going to tell her that he was about to get mixed up with someone far more dangerous than a protective brother with a handgun.

Dean had heard Ani's name in passing a few times over the last year while working for Malton. Nothing he heard gave him any enthusiasm about the prospect of having to get involved with him in person.

So he kept on dancing. Shaking his gangly frame to the music and looking like one of those inflatable figures you'd find on the forecourt of a car showroom.

Vikki looked gorgeous. Her body half swamped, half revealed in the sleeveless, black maxi-dress she wore. Dean had come in jeans and a T-shirt. Opting to look as incognito as possible rather than risk trying to blend in.

The music crescendoed and Vikki flung her arms around him and before he could respond she was kissing him. She was nearly as tall as he was and her lips held him as their two sweaty bodies moved together, drowned in sound.

Then suddenly they broke apart and Vikki was leading him by the hand. Past the carnage of the unisex toilets and into the bar. Almost dragging him, her face set forward, pulling Dean through the tightly packed throng.

Dean felt the cooler air of the bar and then they were outside with the smokers and the reluctant dancers.

Something had changed. The joyous energy of just a few moments ago had vanished. Instead as they stood shivering a little in the cool night air, Vikki could hardly meet his eye.

When she did her face was solemn.

'I can't put it off any more,' she said. 'There's something I've got to tell you.'

49

Benton had been so absorbed in the day's revelations that she was halfway through shouting upstairs to ask Jenni what she wanted for tea before she remembered that her daughter had upped and gone to live with her ex-husband in his flat on the edge of Levenshulme.

The house she was renting while they finalised the divorce was as near to their old house in Chorlton as she could afford. That meant it was all the way out in Stretford. Within spitting distance of Stretford Mall, which was improbably becoming the focus of an overly optimistic attempt to brand Stretford as the new up-and-coming area for young hipsters.

The fact that Benton lived there gave the lie to that one.

It was as impersonal as all rental properties. White walls, no pictures or photographs. Solid carpets and laminate and the cheapest appliances money can buy. It didn't help that every surface was still covered in cardboard boxes.

Padding into the kitchen, Benton felt guilty savouring the stillness of a silent house. As much as she missed Jenni, right now her daughter was hard work. Having tried everything else she hoped that some time apart might be just what both of them needed. She hung up her anorak, opened the freezer, took out a ready meal for one and stuck it in the oven.

Benton took a chair in the kitchen and sat watching the oven heat up her food.

She knew so much, so why did it feel like she was missing something? Femi and Zak. Nate and Ani. Two bodies, Zak's and Tommy Fenwick's, both murdered with hammers and both connected to Femi. One through the drugs left at the scene of Zak's murder, one through Femi's phone left at Tommy's flat.

Then it hit her. The thing she'd never once questioned. Femi and Zak. It was one thing for a rich kid to play at being a drug dealer. But how on earth would he end up meeting someone like Femi in the first place? They didn't share schools, post-codes, social groups. So what was the connection?

Benton had a thought. She jumped up and reached into the pocket of her anorak, pulling out the stack of IDs she'd found in Femi's bedroom.

Glad she'd conveniently 'forgotten' to log them into evidence, she cleared a space on the kitchen table, pulled off the thick elastic band and set the cards down on the table.

There at the top was Tommy Fenwick.

Benton started going down the pile. There was a mixture of driving licences, college and work IDs and even a membership card for the Portico Library. All with photographs of their owners.

Tommy Fenwick. James Nolan. Sally Farrow.

Some faces ravaged and in decline. Some fresh and filled with optimism. All of them somehow in Femi's orbit.

Elliot Moor, Mitchell Carson, Alfie Hackett.

And then there it was. Near the bottom of the stack. A student ID.

Ryan Lewis. Brother to Carrie Lewis. Zak Alquist's dead girlfriend.

Benton had seen Ryan from all the coverage of Zak's trial a few months ago. Facial tattoos and saggy grey skin. But that wasn't the Ryan on the ID. This Ryan had a healthy, pink complexion. He was smiling. Frozen at a time when he had no idea what was coming for him.

That was what put Femi and Zak together. It was Ryan Lewis.

She thought back to the trial. To the shock at Bea's defence team producing the evidence of a third person present. There had been speculation it was Ryan who was present. But Benton couldn't think why, if that was the case, Zak would risk prison just to protect him. Far more likely Zak Alquist wouldn't want to identify a gang member he'd just seen murder his girlfriend.

It made less sense for him to then become best mates with Femi. After Carrie's death surely Zak would want nothing to do with the drugs scene that got her killed? But there he was on Femi's phone.

And what about Femi's dropped phone? If Femi was this ruthless killer, moving unseen through Manchester would he really leave his phone at Tommy's murder scene? Had he been disturbed?

For a moment hope swelled in Benton's chest. If someone took Femi from Tommy's flat could they be Tommy's killer? And maybe Zak's too? Even Carrie's? Was Femi just unlucky enough to have been present at three separate murders?

Then it hit her. Even if that was true and Femi wasn't just an innocent bystander it meant he was probably dead. There was only one person who would have the motive and the means to be cleaning house like that. Ani Delgado as he reinvented himself as Nate Alquist's partner in the food hall.

Benton looked at all the faces on the IDs spread across the table. Femi's client list for shifting drugs. Each one a tragedy. Someone sucked into the orbit of the Chopboys and Ani Delgado. The lucky ones would be forever scarred, the unlucky ones dead. On paper she was looking for Femi Musa. In her heart she knew she was looking for a body that would take her straight to Ani Delgado.

She realised she still didn't know anything.

The oven timer beeped. Her tea was ready.

Benton ate alone, Ryan Lewis's ID propped up on the table watching her as she did.

50

Emily was laughing so hard she had to put her hand over her mouth. Her whole face creased with joy. Malton felt like he could almost hear her.

But he couldn't. He was sat in the darkness on the other side of the field beside Emily's cottage. He was watching her through binoculars. All he could hear was the complete stillness of the countryside.

The sounds of Uppermill in the valley below didn't travel this far up. In the past hour a single car had gone past. They wouldn't have even seen Malton, parked up in the lay-by, until they were on him and by then they would already be on their way. Nothing but another car in the night.

Emily was standing up, her body straining to balance the weight of her pregnant belly. Mayer was on his feet too, crossing the kitchen to help her. He was laughing. Happy in the warm glow of their little cottage.

Malton wasn't under an illusion that Ani Delgado would take notice of his warning to leave Lesha Thompson alone. Ani Delgado would do whatever Ani Delgado wanted to do. He felt sorry for Lesha. When she approached him in the cemetery he knew she'd try and win his sympathy. Bring up her dead son and try and link it back to Anthony. It was a clever move in that it had worked despite Malton seeing it coming.

You couldn't be hard with a family. If there were people depending on you then you couldn't walk through life utterly unconcerned. That was a problem. Malton liked to move forward. You didn't have to watch your back if you were constantly on the move. It was only when you settled and got soft that suddenly things became complicated.

Things getting complicated had killed James. It had lost him Emily. It was stopping him going back into the city to confront Bea.

Malton felt himself losing focus. He put down the binoculars and rubbed his eyes. He was tired but he didn't feel he deserved sleep.

Instead he closed his eyes and went through his plan one more time. It was a trap for whoever it was that was lying to him about Zak's murder. He'd thought it through clearly, made sure that everything was clean and neat and simple. There was no ambiguity and no way out. Once the trap was set there would be no going back.

He felt himself slipping under and jolted awake. He looked up; the lights were off in the cottage. They'd gone to bed.

Malton turned on the car engine and kept the lights off until he had rounded the corner, out of view of the cottage before he stuck them on full beam and drove back into the city ready to confront whoever was behind Zak's murder.

51

The light went green and the heavy metal gate that covered the stairs leading down to the basement opened. A deep silence came up from below, the thick walls smothering the sound of the busy city-centre street that Lesha had just left behind. She looked up at the multiple cameras filming her every move and slipped through the gate, hearing it click shut behind her.

Craig Malton had let her down. Sergio and Raheem were dead. Graham wasn't listening when she told him how pointless it would be to get the police involved.

This wasn't a police matter. Not anymore. Now it was just her and Ani.

Lesha walked down a marble staircase and through a second heavy gate. She found herself in an airless lobby with a desk along one side. Across from the desk, through an open door she saw the safe room. Rows and rows of security deposit boxes. It went back at least thirty feet; a vast subterranean space where anyone who wanted to pay the monthly fees could store whatever they wished, safe in the knowledge that it was protected by steel and stone and CCTV.

She handed her membership card to the man on the desk. This was only the second time she'd come here. The first was to make her deposit five years ago. This had been the best place she could think of for what she needed to store. Something she hoped she'd never ever be back for but which she couldn't risk anyone else ever knowing was in her possession.

Having verified her membership, the security guard led her into the secure room and indicated to a small booth where she would be free to examine the contents of her box in privacy.

Turning to a wall of safety deposit boxes, the guard inserted his master key and looked to Lesha. Lesha inserted her own key and they both turned at the same time. Like a miniature safe, the door swung open to reveal a bright red, metal storage box within.

Lesha nodded to the guard who left the secure room and returned to the desk. Finally alone, Lesha slid out the red box. Feeling the weight, she knew at once it was still there.

She lugged the box to the private booth, shut the door behind her and opened it.

It was five years ago when Lesha had found drugs on Kieran and learned he was dealing for the Chopboys. She gave him an ultimatum. Leave the gang or she'd call the police on him. Kieran had called her bluff leaving her no choice but to call the police and have him arrested. She knew the police wouldn't charge a kid his age with the amount of drugs she found but she hoped the experience would be a wake-up call for her son.

She never got to find out if it worked. Kieran was shot dead on his way back from the station. His body scooped up and spirited away.

In the months that followed as Lesha tried to scrape her world back together she'd finally got round to clearing out Kieran's room. He'd grown up in that room. From a little boy with his collection of cars and tractors to a giggly pre-teen who loved nothing more than days out with his mum. Lesha had wrapped her son in as much love as she had in her body. It wasn't enough.

She took down the posters of United players. She boxed up his PlayStation and games for the charity shop. The smell of his freshly laundered clothes was nearly unbearable but she persevered, filling a bin liner with them to be donated.

There at the back of the drawer she found it. The final proof of what Kieran had died for. A handgun he had been given by the Chopboys to hide. That was how it worked. Let the younger kids take the risk of holding firearms while the older members kept their hands clean. A small, cold lump of metal that had cost her son his life and wiped out the last seventeen years of hers.

Lesha could barely stand to look at it. But she knew she must. One day the Chopboys would be back for that gun. She couldn't bear the thought of it being used to kill another child.

After a sleepless night with it under her pillow she'd left the next day to a place in town where for a fee she could keep it under lock and key.

Lesha sat in the small booth just off the strong room. She closed the door behind her. She could hear the slow whine of the air conditioning pumping fresh air from street level down into this silent, sealed basement.

She opened the red metal box and there was the gun. Just as she had left it five years ago.

She picked it up and felt nothing but the purest, burning rage.

52

'We've found Izzy,' said Malton solemnly.

'About time. First Bea tells me you pick her up in a club and then lose her, then nothing.' Nate seemed about to continue his rant but then stopped and took a breath. He looked past Malton and Dean, through the glass walls of his extension and out towards an unseen point in the garden.

Dean couldn't help but notice Nate wasn't his usual easy-going self. It looked like he hadn't been sleeping.

The giant glass box that grew out of the back of Nate's Victorian mansion and served as his office was strewn with paperwork and takeaways. It looked like Nate had been living there. A couple of pillows and a blanket on a nearby sofa confirmed the impression.

'Bea said you were the best. So what have you actually found out?' said Nate, the edge behind his friendly tone now barely disguised. 'Bad enough that idiot Priestly calling every day to tell me just how little progress the police have made. At least I'm not paying him five grand per diem,' said Nate looking straight at Malton.

Just as Dean would expect, Malton remained unmoved by Nate's outburst.

On the way over Malton had explained the plan to Dean. The trap they were going to lay. Dean had to admit it was clever. If it worked then they'd have Zak Alquist's killer and not only that, they'd have unravelled why he wound up dead.

Nate's impatience would be a key part of the plan.

It was all a welcome distraction from thinking about Vikki and the bombshell she had delivered at the club last night. It was only a year-long fashion course in London but as far as Dean was concerned it was as good as the end of their relationship. They'd gone back to the house in Moss Side together but had gone to bed in silence. Each of them retreating to their own side of the bed.

Malton clasped his hands together. 'We are looking for a man called Jordan Weekes.'

'You think that's news to me?' said Nate, his voice finally raising in anger. 'Bea gave me a transcript of everything Izzy said in your meeting. The meeting I set up. I got you that name. Me. And now it seems like I'm doing all the work and paying you for the privilege.'

'If you're not happy with the job we're doing, I'm sure DCI Priestly will find your son's killer. Eventually,' said Malton calmly.

Dean said nothing. He just watched as Malton slowly drew Nate in.

'What Bea won't have told you is that we spoke to Izzy again. Just me and her,' said Malton.

Dean saw the look of confusion on Nate's face. 'What did she say?' snapped Nate urgently.

Malton leaned forward and did his best impression of apologetic.

'That's just the thing. She's scared. She won't tell us of what, but she's not talking.'

'Let me speak to her,' said Nate. 'She knows me. She knows she can trust me. I mean, what was she even doing outside Paramore?'

'We found her in a club with Weekes.' Malton let that hang for a moment, gauging Nate's reaction. 'We're going to keep her safe,' he continued. 'And as soon as she talks we'll let you know.'

'Where is she?' Nate demanded.

Malton's face rearranged itself into something approaching regret. 'She asked not to see you. My personal opinion? I think she feels guilty about what happened to Zak.'

Nate took a moment, doing his best to walk back from the edge of the full-blown tantrum Malton had led him towards. 'I just want to know she's safe is all,' he said with a strained sincerity.

'Trust me. She's at a safe location. Bea knows all about it.'

Nate took a beat. His eyes never left Malton's face. Dean held his breath as he watched Malton's trap close around Nate without him ever once suspecting it.

'As long as Bea thinks it's secure?' said Nate warily.

'I run every detail past Bea,' said Malton.

Dean breathed out, making a conscious effort not to smile at the balletic display of manipulation he'd just witnessed.

There was only one thing that could go wrong – if Malton had made a miscalculation and Bea Wallace wasn't lying through her teeth.

53

Bea's hands and mouth were covered in sticky, sweet sauce as she devoured the takeaway container full of wings. She'd tied her blonde hair back and wrapped a plastic apron around her work clothes before going to town on the wings.

'Despite your vanishing act I had quite a bit of interest after last night,' she said to Malton. 'In fact seeing you rush off like that ended up being quite good PR.'

Malton sat across from her in the kitchen of her apartment. Watching her eat, having declined any himself. He wasn't hungry. The plan was in motion. First Nate and now Bea.

Bea finished the wing she was on and tossed it onto a small pile of greasy bones before beginning to lick her fingers.

Realising Malton was watching she made a joke of sucking each finger seductively as she talked.

'Obviously I couldn't tell them what you were doing but I did tell them you were on twenty-four-seven. Like the other night when you didn't come home,' said Bea leaving a pause long enough to leave Malton in no doubt it was his turn to fill the silence.

'I was busy,' said Malton. He'd been at Bea's for nearly an hour now and she hadn't got anywhere near asking him the one thing he was here to tell her – the location of the safe house where he was keeping Izzy. Or more accurately the location of the house where he wanted Nate Alquist to think he was keeping Izzy.

'I'm thrilled you dropped by and the wings were great, but as much as I'd love to fuck, I've got a lot on.'

Malton wondered if he'd made a miscalculation. Maybe Bea really wasn't in on this. Maybe she was simply Nate's lawyer and that was it.

Watching Bea clean her lips with a wet wipe, suddenly all thoughts of Nate Alquist and Ani Delgado vanished from his head. He thought about how Bea's hair smelled. How her soft, naked body felt warm and vulnerable snuggled against his own hard, battered frame. The sound of her laughter and the fact that she seemed utterly unfazed by any part of the hell that Malton dragged around with him.

If Bea wasn't in on this and Izzy was in the wind, it would mean going back to square one. But that wasn't a huge stretch. Dean had found Izzy's brother in Moss Side. They could start with him. Lean on him. Buy him off. There were a million different subtle and not so subtle ways to erode a person's loyalty. Everyone, in Malton's experience, had a breaking point.

But more than that it would mean he could still have Bea. He didn't quite trust her and that was what made him want her. It was like she knew that more than love or stability what Malton needed was the challenge. To lock horns with someone who wasn't scared of what he was. Someone who wouldn't be dragged under like Emily or James.

Bea scooped the bones back into the takeaway box and dumped them along with the wet wipes in her desk bin before heaving out the bin liner, tying it tightly and offering it to Malton.

'Can't have the place smelling of fried chicken, can I?' She laughed.

Malton took the bag off her, even managing as close to a laugh as he could remember. Their fingers touched and she smiled up at him.

'I haven't forgotten about the witness statement. James? How about this evening? I'll be sure to "accidentally" leave it on my desk and you can "just so happen" to catch sight of it. All nice and legal.'

She let out an infectious Geordie giggle.

Bea was already head down, back at her work as Malton turned and headed to go. Perhaps there *was* room for just a little softness in his life.

He was at the door when she called back to him, 'Oh, I nearly forgot. You any closer to finding that girl Izzy?'

Somewhere deep inside Malton an impossibly small flame trembled, dimmed, and went out.

54

Ani Delgado's website described him as one of Manchester's most celebrated motivational speakers. It had photographs of him shaking hands with local celebrities and politicians. Stood in front of groups of beaming kids and poised, mid-speech.

Ani Delgado used to be a hardened criminal but now he had seen the light and wanted to use his experience to help others.

You could book him to talk in schools or youth groups. But he could also give talks to companies and business conferences. Applying the lessons he learned from being involved in street-dealing to the world of legitimate business.

He had it both ways. The glory of his crimes and the praise due to the repentant criminal.

Lesha watched as Ani left his house wearing a suit and tie, got into his silver Škoda Yeti and drove off towards town. He had an appointment. Lesha knew this because she was the one who'd booked him. A last-minute fill-in at a team-building away day.

Ani Delgado had already been paid the five-hundred-pound appearance fee and was off to inspire some sales reps. Or at least that's what he thought he was doing. As long as he was out of the house for the next thirty minutes or so that was all Lesha cared about.

She'd arrived early enough to watch Ani's partner pile six kids into her car and head off on the school run, leaving only Ani inside. Then ten minutes later Ani too had appeared at the door.

Lesha waited another few minutes until she was confident he wasn't coming back and then, having made sure the gun was safely tucked away in an inside pocket, she got out of the car and without breaking stride, walked round the back of Ani's house and let herself in to the garden.

55

Moss Side's streets had been drawn at right angles to each other. Long rows of terraces, back to back with yards and then cobbled alleyways between those yards. The alleyways had been partially gated before the council ran out of money meaning that unless you had a key at a certain point you would find yourself stuck facing a twelve-foot, metal alley gate and a dead end.

Stevens Street and Dover Street were two of the longest roads in Moss Side, each lined with larger, three-bedroom terraces and both backing onto each other with an alleyway in between. Every six houses there was a break in the terrace and an alley leading towards the main alley that ran between the two streets.

Dean set off up Stevens Street making sure, as discreetly as he could, that at every break in the terrace the men who he had positioned were ready and waiting. He was gratified to spot only one of the Malton Security men, his bulk sticking out from behind a communal bin down one of the alleys.

At the top of Stevens Street he turned right and then proceeded down Dover Street in the opposite direction, again making sure that at every alleyway there was someone waiting.

Happy that the entire block was manned Dean walked back up Stevens Street and ducked into the cul-de-sac on the other side of the road opposite the house that sat slap bang in the middle of Stevens Street. The house whose address Malton had made sure to leak to Bea in the hope that she would in turn leak it to Nate Alquist.

Who Nate Alquist chose to leak it to was the whole point of the operation. Thirty Malton Security men covered every inch of the block ready to spring the trap that had been set around the house on Stevens Street. Anyone could get in but once the house was breached no one was getting out.

The men had been briefed to expect trouble. Malton hadn't told them to come armed but from the tone of his briefing he left it in no doubt that if anyone did come armed, he wasn't going to stop them.

Stevens Street was a terrace of twenty houses. A large area but small enough for the men to feel confident that whatever was coming their way, they could deal with it.

The final part of the trap was Malton himself, sat waiting in the house where, as far as Bea and hopefully Nate Alquist knew, Zak's girlfriend Izzy was being kept safe.

When whoever it was that she was being kept safe from turned up, it was Malton they would meet.

If Malton failed to subdue them then the net of bodies Dean had marshalled around the house was there as plan B.

From what they'd discovered, Femi Musa was the prime suspect in at least three murders. Dean knew Malton didn't like to deal in speculation but from the manpower on the ground it was clear that Malton was expecting more than just a sixteen-year-old kid to show up.

Dean shuddered to think who would be able to overpower Malton. He knew full well why so many of the guys were in fact armed with clubs and brass knuckles. If they had to go into action they knew they were going up against someone who had taken out Malton. And Dean had never seen anyone take out Malton.

Dean thought about how Malton had described Zak's injuries and shivered.

He checked his watch. It was still early. Moss Side was quiet. The traffic down on Princess Parkway was just about audible as was the occasional blaring exhaust of a driver hammering through the narrow streets well over the twenty-mile-per-hour speed limit.

Dean took a long breath and tried to stop his heart beating quite so fast. He felt guilty. Vikki was right. This job would get him killed eventually. But it wasn't that simple. He loved this job. A terrible thought hit him – did he love it more than Vikki? And if he did what did that say about their future together?

From his vantage point Dean was pleased that the men were doing a good job of staying out of sight. Whoever showed up they were ready for them.

With time to kill, Dean turned on his walkie-talkie and made sure everyone was in position.

56

Stalking through Sunshine Plants and Flowers garden centre Benton felt a twinge of guilt about the state of the garden in her old house. Long hours, a teenage daughter and a useless husband meant that by the time they had sold the house it was little more than a large patch of chest-height weeds.

When they'd first moved in the garden was the whole point. They were young people turning their backs on the thrills of the city to embrace a suburban mortgage. All because Benton was pregnant with Jenni. The little girl who had run around that garden singing, dug in the mud, planted sunflowers and danced through the sprinkler.

It was only as Jenni got older that things began to fall apart. Benton realising that whatever the dream she and Simon had had when they bought that house it was no longer one they shared. Jenni became a teenager, they drifted apart and the garden became a mess of weeds.

With a failed marriage and a daughter who didn't want to know, Benton had thrown herself into her job heart and soul.

Maybe that was why every time she'd been slapped down by GMP she hadn't walked away. As much as it stung getting reprimanded by the job she loved, it would hurt even more to leave it completely. So Benton had gone back to uniform after a trumped-up discipline charge. She'd done a year in traffic rather than end up on the desk-job-to-early-retirement pipeline. And when they'd recently moved her from Serious and Organised to the general pool she'd said nothing.

But now she was on the brink of something huge. Corrupt land deals, cover-ups and at least three murders, all seemingly connected.

She saw Ryan Lewis at the far side of the outside area moving pot plants. Then she saw the other kid.

Even before he drew his gun he stood out a mile. The only customer under fifty in Sunshine Plants and Flowers. He was all in black, hood up and walking with purpose towards an oblivious Ryan Lewis.

Benton was already moving.

'Hey!' Her shout got both Ryan Lewis and the kid's attention.

First Ryan saw her but then he turned and saw the kid in black pulling a handgun and quickening his pace.

Ryan froze to the spot, ready to die.

Benton had other ideas. Mid-run she grabbed the nearest thing to hand: a potted hebe, and without breaking stride, she hurled it as hard as she could at the kid's head.

As the hebe connected and knocked him sprawling, his gun went off, the bullets all landing well wide of Ryan Lewis.

BANG. BANG. BANG.

As the kid hit the ground, his gun flew from his hand and slid under a table of lavenders.

Benton started towards him.

'Police! Stay down!'

The kid did the exact opposite. He took one look at Benton, his eyes peeking out from the ski mask he wore under his hood, got to his feet and started to run.

'You OK?' Benton shouted at Ryan, who nodded dumbly. That was good enough. She spun round and tore after the gunman.

Past the horrified customers and upturned displays she followed in his wake through the inside area of the garden centre.

By the time she broke out the entrance she could see the kid at the far end of the car park, jumping onto a trailbike and racing away.

Exhausted, Benton bent double, heaving in air. As the adrenaline of the chase wore off a terrible thought occurred to her. She'd run out of time.

57

Dean was getting bored of waiting. They'd all been in position now for a couple of hours. The morning lull was giving way to the lunchtime traffic. Feeling the need to be in motion, he'd checked in once more with Malton before heading off to do another circuit.

He walked along Dover Street, the road that ran parallel to the back of Stevens Street where Malton was waiting. He looked carefully at each house. He couldn't put his finger on it but it felt like he was missing something.

A collection of family homes and rental properties. Some tatty, some well cared for. Long gone were the days when a skinny, white man walking in Moss Side aroused suspicion, but even so Dean was careful to keep moving. To not make eye contact when he spotted one of the Malton Security guys waiting.

Reaching the end of Dover Street, he turned into the alley-way that ran between it and Stevens Street.

Something was wrong. A pair of legs lay sticking out from behind the communal bin.

Dean rushed over, already on his walkie-talkie. It was Djama, the young lad who'd saved his bacon at the carnival after-party. He lay very still across the cobbles among the rubbish and the grime. Blood was pouring from his head.

Dean knelt beside him and felt for his pulse. It was there. He was alive.

'Femi's here!' hissed Dean into the walkie-talkie. 'Give me a report.'

One by one the men reported back in the order they'd practised earlier that morning. Starting with the bottom of Stevens Street before working around in a circuit first up Stevens Street and then down Dover Street.

Dean felt his heart race as one by one each reported back negative. They'd not seen anyone.

Dean looked down at Djama then looked up, whipping his head around.

He stood and ran from the alleyway back onto the street. Nothing.

He ran out onto Stevens Street. It was deserted.

Dean could hear his breathing, heavy and frantic. He looked down the face of the terraces. There in the middle was the house where Malton was waiting. But for what?

Suddenly something struck him. His eye was drawn to the roofline. A continuous line of tiles and topping stones broken only by a clutter of aerials and satellite dishes.

Dean turned and ran back to where Djama lay. He still hadn't moved. Dean stepped over his body, round the bin and tried the back gate of the end house.

It swung open. The lock was hanging off.

Dean ran into the backyard where he saw the kitchen door had been kicked off its hinges.

Rushing across the yard, he jumped over a broken child's bicycle, through the kitchen and into the back room where he saw an elderly woman, an oxygen mask over her face, a look of terror in her eyes.

Dean didn't have time for the wave of empathy that flooded over him.

'Where is he?'

All the old woman could do was raise one shaky arm and point.

Up.

58

Dean's voice came frantic and urgent over Malton's walkie-talkie.

None of the monitors Malton had set up in the middle room of the house where his father had once lived showed any sign of life.

'Hold. Everyone hold,' said Malton calmly into his walkie-talkie before turning it off completely. If someone was coming he wanted to be ready for them. Not distracted by panicked chatter.

The house was empty once more. As silent as it had been since the day Rory Malton passed on.

With the monitors still showing nothing, Malton rose from his seat and grabbed the polished steel hatchet that he had laid on the table beside the monitors. He walked out into the hallway. There was no one behind the glass of the front door. No one looking the other way past the back room and into the kitchen. No sign of life in the yard. The gate sturdy and sealed.

Malton closed his eyes and listened. He heard something.

It was faint. A muffled, dull sound. But it was coming from inside the house.

With his grip firmly on the hatchet Malton began to pad upstairs. Just as he had done as a kid when late at night he needed the bathroom and didn't dare disturb his sleeping father.

His footsteps as light as a child he heard the noise louder now. Smothered by brick and plaster, it was getting closer.

He looked up. It was coming from above him.

Malton was on the landing when the noise stopped. He stood dead still, his eyes held on the small hatch on the landing leading to the roof cavity.

He'd not been up there in years. The hatchway was tiny, built in an age when men the size of Malton were a distant dream.

Malton retreated slowly into the back bedroom, and hidden behind the open door, he watched as the hatch lifted up and disappeared into the darkness of the attic.

A second later he saw Lani Delgado awkwardly slip through the open hole and land on the carpet outside the master bedroom.

59

Dean was halfway up Stevens Street when Malton came crashing through the front door of the decoy safe house and landed heavily on the tiled path.

As he scrambled to his feet, hatchet still in hand, a second man appeared in the doorway. He was white and shorter than Malton but wide with it. His hair was shaved close at the sides and long on top. Blood was streaming down one side of his head and when he turned to clock Dean, Dean saw that he was missing his front teeth.

He wore a football shirt covered in blood and in one hand held a bloody claw hammer.

Dean had stood up to men twice the size and even stared down the barrel of a gun. But there was something about the way this man looked at him that turned his stomach to wet concrete.

'He's done the gas!' cried Malton to Dean before turning back to face the toothless man.

The man raised his hammer and hurled it straight at Malton. Malton raised a forearm and took the full force of the blow. Without waiting to see the damage, the man in the bloody football shirt vaulted onto the path of the next-door terrace, ran out the front gate and off down Stevens Street.

Malton clutched his arm and cried, 'Get on the walkie-talkie. Evacuate the street. The fucking lunatic's ripped the gas main open.'

Dean had never seen Malton like this before. Beaten, bloody and talking as if he were scared.

Without a moment's hesitation Dean was on the radio.

'Stevens Street side, break cover, knock on doors. Evacuate the street. Dover side, same, break cover, knock on doors. Get everyone out. NOW!'

Dean rushed to Malton's side. His boss was in a bad way. He'd taken a hell of a beating.

'You take that side,' said Malton, pointing towards Princess Parkway with his good arm.

Dean did as he was told. Soon he was joined by a couple of other Malton Security guys. He grabbed the nearest one.

'The end terrace, it's an old woman on an oxygen canister. She can barely move. You're going to have to carry her out.'

The hulking Malton employee nodded and rushed off. It was then that Dean remembered – Djama was still lying unconscious in the alley.

Looking up Stevens Street he saw Malton and the others emptying the terraces at a pace. Thousands of hours working doors had given them the ability to give clear, concise orders and expect them to be followed.

He raced into the alley. Djama's feet were still poking out from behind the bin.

Dean rushed to where he lay, bent down and hooked his arms under Djama. He was a dead weight but Dean had no choice. He took a deep breath, bent his knees and began to haul Djama out of the alleyway. One cobble at a time.

60

With Ani Delgado's background, a tip-off about a handgun would be enough to provoke an armed police response. And once they found the gun then Ani would have more pressing things to worry about than Lesha.

The idea pleased her. This gun was the dreadful legacy of Kieran's murder. A constant rebuke to Lesha and anyone else who believed in some kind of justice and order. In Ani's world it would be used to exact violent gangland justice. Lesha would show him that she was better than that. That justice and order still existed, even for Ani Delgado.

He had killed Tommy, he had trashed her shop and he had murdered her beloved dogs. That couldn't go unanswered.

Stood alone in the garden, Lesha froze for a moment. Her eyes travelled up to the back bedroom window. Ani's old room. It was where over two decades ago he had seduced her. If it could be called seduction. Back then everyone knew Ani. To be singled out for his attention was irresistible.

In those days his mother was still alive, his twin Lani living in the bedroom across the landing. Two brothers raised to believe that the rules didn't apply to them. Whatever they wanted they should take. Whoever stood in their way they should crush.

It was Ani's mother who had told Lesha she wasn't to see her son again. She'd given her a couple of hundred pounds to get lost and told her to get an abortion. Lesha had given her the money back.

The garden was cluttered with plastic furniture, broken children's toys and a trampoline stacked on its side against the fence. If only she hadn't gone to check on Tommy. Or it hadn't been the anniversary of Kieran's death. Or Ani hadn't given her that sneering look. Anything to have not marched into that garden and struck Ani across the face. A single gesture that had already cost the lives of her beloved dogs and put everything she'd built since Kieran's murder at risk.

Lesha focused. Ani could be back at any moment. She didn't have the luxury of time. A large wooden summer house dominated the back of the garden. It had a small porch and a window behind which a large piece of cardboard blocked any view inside.

That would be where Lesha would hide the weapon.

She was unsurprised to find the door unlocked. The Delgado house used to always be unlocked. It was the family's way of showing the world they feared no one. While Ani and Lani made enemies all over Manchester no one would have the guts to walk into their estate, much less into their house. Moss Side was their kingdom. Their reputation, the fortress that kept it inviolate.

Lesha stepped inside and found an immaculate recreation of a pub. Not any pub either, the kind of pub that died out in Moss Side over twenty years ago. Solid, carved wood. Stained glass and thick, smoke-saturated carpet. Beer towels and optics, a dartboard and even an old vending machine screwed up on the wall. It looked like Ani had been collecting from pubs as one by one they had closed. Creating a small time capsule here in his summer house.

There was a reason why Ani had never graduated up the criminal hierarchy. He loved Moss Side. His Moss Side. He could no more leave than he could flap his arms and fly. It wasn't in him.

Lesha was searching the bar for somewhere to hide the gun when she heard the phone go off. A soft buzzing was coming from the nook of seating on one side of the shed. She paused. She'd already been here too long. It was only a matter of time before someone came back.

Between her fear and her curiosity, curiosity won out. Pocketing the gun she went towards the sound. She stood for a moment in silence listening. Trying to pinpoint where she could hear it coming from. The noise stopped.

Lesha started pulling off seat cushions, hoping that she had correctly identified where the sound had come from.

There it was. Under a cushion, a cheap, disposable mobile phone. Vibrating against the wooden seat.

Lesha picked it up. There was a message.

From 'L'. It said: FUCKED.

As she was about to try and open the phone to find the contact 'L', the roar of a giant explosion rang out over Moss Side.

61

Nate Alquist pouted like a sultry rock diva. His long Ventile raincoat billowed out dramatically in the wind. Behind him the Manchester horizon was his backdrop.

He was doing a photo shoot for a colour supplement profile. The location – his brand-new block of student accommodation dubbed The Tyre Factory. Yet another Upland Living development. Sat on the edge of the city it loomed over the Mancunian Way, looking out over Hulme and Moss Side. A development in progress, there was currently little to it save the concrete floor and the lift shaft running up the middle of the building. Temporary guard rails lined the edge, and beyond was a lethal drop from the thirtieth storey down to street level. The whole thing was exposed to the elements, unguarded beneath the City-Blue Manchester sky. Malton shivered as the wind whipped around him. Howling as it raced in and out of the skeletal, concrete structure.

As Malton stood by the builders' lift watching, Nate didn't look like a man who'd just lost his son.

Bea had given Malton the address of the photo shoot. He was tired of running around trying to figure out the things he wasn't being told. Less than an hour ago an explosion had not just wiped out his childhood home but levelled half a street in Moss Side. Stevens Street and Dover Street had both been evacuated and there was already talk that the entire row of terraces might have to come down.

The explosion hadn't just ripped a hole in Moss Side, it confirmed all his worst fears about the Alquist job. He was being played. Now the only question left was by whom and to what end.

Nate caught sight of Malton and signalled to the photographer to wind it up.

'What is this about?' Nate called out to Malton as he strode towards him, pulling his raincoat around him against the cold.

Malton kept quiet. Let Nate come to him.

Beneath his heavy cotton jacket Malton could feel the bruises blossoming across his arms from where he'd deflected a hammer thrown with malicious intent by Lani Delgado. The sharp cold of being this high up and without shelter shook off any lingering stupor from his fight.

Lani had dropped down the hatch with his back to Malton. Even from behind Malton instantly recognised the taut, dense frame of Lani Delgado. He knew the moment he saw Lani that he would have to strike first. Take Lani out before Lani returned the favour.

When Malton had first tackled him he hadn't known Lani was carrying a hammer. He soon found out.

As the two of them sprawled onto the floor of the front bedroom, his father's room, Lani had twisted round and brought the hammer down on Malton's ribs. Years of violent muscle memory and weight training meant that a blow that would have broken a regular man's ribs merely hurt so much Malton wanted to throw up and pass out.

He'd done neither. He got to his feet and drew the polished steel hatchet he carried with him everywhere. The axe he'd brought to a hammer fight. An evil joy came over Lani Delgado as they squared off. By the time it was over Malton was covered in bruises and had a couple of broken fingers, which he hadn't yet had time to strap up. He did his best to ignore the sharp pain that shot up his arm every time he tried to move them.

For his trouble Lani Delgado had lost an ear. But he'd got away.

Nate reached Malton. He was about to speak when Malton said, 'Someone just blew up my father's house in Moss Side.'

Nate did a very good job of feigning surprise.

'We heard something up here. I didn't realise it was so close. Why would someone blow up your father's house?'

'To kill Izzy.'

'Izzy was at your father's house?' said Nate, a note of genuine anxiety creeping into his voice.

Behind Nate the photographer was taking advantage of the view to shoot some panoramic shots of the city.

'She's fine,' said Malton.

Nathan faked a smile. 'Thank God. I need to talk to her.'

'She's fine because she was never there. I don't know where she is.'

Nate paused and for a moment he eyed Malton, trying to figure out just what was happening.

The photographer was coming over. Malton caught her eye and held open the cage that contained the builders' lift.

'Can I . . .' started the photographer but Malton cut her off.

'Mr Alquist will follow you down,' he said brusquely.

The photographer looked to Nate who quickly waved her into the lift.

He and Malton stood side by side watching as the cage slowly descended. The photographer slowly receding away until it was just the two of them. Alone, thirty storeys up.

'What do you mean you don't know where she is?' said Nate, retreating into a well-worn tone of impatience.

Despite himself, Malton was impressed. Now he and Nate were alone there was nothing he couldn't do to Nate if he wanted. Rather than give in to the fear, Nate was making a stand. Showing he wouldn't be intimidated.

Malton looked away and brushed past Nate as if avoiding the question.

Sensing weakness Nate followed.

'I asked you a question.'

Malton stopped just before the temporary barriers, where Nate had been standing for his photo. He had a clear view of the thirty-storey drop.

He turned to Nate.

'I told Bea that I had Izzy there. Bea told you. And then a man called Lani Delgado shows up, tries to kill me with a claw hammer and when it looks like I've got the upper hand he tears out the gas pipes, blowing up the house and taking half the street with it.' Malton paused, seeing how this information was sinking in. 'Do you know who Lani Delgado's brother is?'

Malton saw Nate's eyes look past him towards the concrete edge. His courage deserted him.

'I can explain everything,' he said.

62

Benton enjoyed the look on Priestly's face as she ran through all that she'd discovered in her search for Femi Musa.

Jordan Weekes and the connection between him and the Chopboys. Ryan Lewis and how the death of Tommy Fenwick was connected to Carrie Lewis's murder and the killing of Zak Alquist.

Priestly had gone especially pale when Benton began explaining just what she'd learned about Nate Alquist and his connection to Ani Delgado. That the council had been terrorised into greenlighting Nate's food hall development.

After half an hour of debriefing she was coming to the end.

'This is pure speculation but I'd say someone is tidying up loose ends. Zak Alquist, Femi Musa and now someone's just tried to kill Ryan Lewis. All connected to Carrie Lewis's murder.'

'You don't think Zak Alquist did it?' asked Priestly.

'I think whoever did kill Carrie set off a chain of events that is rapidly getting out of control. Whether or not Nate Alquist knows it, he's hitched his wagon to a ruthless criminal who'll stop at nothing to be the last man standing when the smoke clears.'

Priestly was silent for a few moments.

Ryan Lewis was already being guarded in a police station out towards Oldham. Officers had been sent to Nate Alquist's home as well as the homes of Ryan Lewis's parents and of Femi's mother. Before Benton even began she had given Priestly a list of names of potential targets.

To his credit Priestly hadn't asked questions, he'd simply made sure units were heading out to throw a wall of steel around anyone else who could find themselves in the crossfire.

What Benton hadn't mentioned was Malton. Not that she would ever talk about him to the police. But more than that. Now Femi Musa was a prime suspect in a murder she was no longer working his case as a missing person. It would be folded into Priestly's investigation. The last chance she had to find Femi Musa and bring him home to his mother would be Malton.

'One thing I don't get,' started Priestly.

'Which bit?' asked Benton.

'Why is a detective as good as you not a DCI by now. Or higher?'

Benton smiled. 'You just answered your own question,' she said.

As she walked out the office she could see Priestly's team already scrambling to process all this new information.

For a moment her thoughts strayed from all the violence and intrigue all the way back home. Jenni was still with her dad. Benton had spent so long trying to find someone else's child that she'd barely noticed when she'd lost her own.

Maybe this was for the best? A chance to slow down and work out what post-divorce life looked like. Not just for her but for Jenni and Simon too.

Benton didn't envy Priestly's job now. Back when she thought that maybe she could bring in Femi there was no pressure. No one watching her try to land the big white whale. With Nate's connections that went all the way to the top of the council and on to Westminster, Priestly had potentially the most sensitive murder inquiry in GMP's history on his hands.

Strolling out of the station, Benton was thinking about ringing Jenni to see what takeaway she fancied for tea when her phone rang and she was dragged right back into the fray.

63

Thirty storeys below, the noise of the city was barely audible. It was drowned out by the wind blowing through the empty concrete shell of The Tyre Factory.

As Nate talked, Malton had slowly moved so that Nate's back was to the temporary barriers – the only thing between them and the drop to street level.

Nate was too busy spilling his guts to even notice.

'I think their plan was just to take Zak's money. He was only a boy. You know what kids are like these days?'

Malton had an inkling but he let Nate carry on.

'It's my fault. It's the job. It's like an addiction. Doing the deals, setting things up. When someone tells me I can't do something, I've got to prove them wrong.'

So far so much PR, thought Malton but nodded along doing his best not to wince as every little movement sent new shooting pains through his body. In his pocket his broken fingers felt like they were on fire, his bruised forearm was already swollen and hard. He wanted nothing more than to lie down and sleep for a week but he was getting close now.

'I wasn't around for Zak. It was hard, growing up with me for a dad. I think he wanted to show me he could do something for himself. That's what he was doing with the drugs and the gang stuff. That wasn't the real Zak.'

'How did you find out what he was up to?' asked Malton reserving judgement on who exactly the 'real Zak' was.

'It's funny really,' said Nate about to slip into raconteur mode before seeing Malton's face and deciding against it. 'It was Ani Delgado tipped me off.'

Malton shifted a little too quickly and the broken fingers in his pocket screamed out. He sucked in air through his nose and clamped his mouth tight shut to not cry out.

'You knew Ani?' was all he said.

'I'd bumped into him before. At council things. Whenever they needed community voices it seemed he'd turn up. No one really said what he did or who he was. He played the part.'

Malton could well believe it. Ani Delgado had survived for this long living in Moss Side, up to his neck in violence. He was hiding in plain sight.

'He comes up to me at this fundraiser, really charismatic guy. Tells me that he wanted to give me a heads-up, that Zak was getting involved with some heavy people in Moss Side.'

'And you believed him?'

Nate sighed. 'I guess I knew something was up. I'd found . . . things at the house. Drugs. But that's just teenagers right? But then there was Ryan Lewis. I always hoped Carrie would just be a phase you know? Schoolboy crush. Get it out of his system.'

Malton imagined throwing Nate Alquist over the guard rail. The thought was enough to distract him from his injuries.

'If he hadn't got involved with her then he'd never have got into the gang stuff. It was all her brother. He's a drug addict. Did you know that?'

'Did Ani offer to help?'

Nate shook his head. 'I didn't want him to. I was grateful for the heads-up but to be honest – Ani, he's not the kind of person I deal with. I'm more about following the money. Big fish.'

Malton thought about how pleased with himself Ani had been at Bea's event the other night. He wondered how he'd feel hearing his business partner Nate talk about him like this.

'So you can imagine the fucking chaos when he turns up on my doorstep with Zak and tells me that Carrie's dead.'

'Did he say who killed her?'

Nate hung his head. Very slowly he said, 'It was Zak. He admitted it to me.'

'So you called the police?'

Nate looked straight at Malton. He steeled himself and said, 'My son had just told me he stabbed someone. I was panicking. So when Ani told me he could deal with it . . . what would you have done? With your son?'

Malton felt utterly unqualified to answer that so kept quiet.

'I know it was stupid. But he was my boy.' Nate looked like he was trying hard not to cry.

'But then Zak told the police that he'd killed Carrie. Ani went nuts. Talking about how he'd put himself on the line for Zak and now he was going to get in trouble himself. If Bea hadn't got involved I don't know what would have happened.'

Justice, thought Malton but said nothing. If a man like Nate Alquist could do something like this for his son, Malton didn't want to find out what lengths he'd go to, to protect his offspring. In a few weeks' time a child would be born with his blood. The only way he had to never be put in a situation like Nate's was to never ever know that child.

Malton's phone beeped. A message from Benton. It could wait.

'What did Ani want in return?'

Nate sighed. 'Ani Delgado is like a vampire; once you've invited him in he's never leaving. Before the trial he found out about the food hall, insisted I cut him in. Made it clear if I didn't then not only would Zak go to prison but he'd also make sure that once he was there he wouldn't last a week. By then I knew exactly who Ani Delgado was.'

That was how Ani lasted as long as he did. He never threatened. He never fought. He had Lani for that. Ani just charmed. He was your mate. He helped you out. He went above and beyond. Until the day he turned around and asked for something in return.

Over Nate's shoulder Manchester looked vast. Yet it only took a single man like Ani Delgado to poison an entire post-code.

'Zak tried to move on. He met Izzy. I thought at least she might take his mind off it all. But Ani was getting too much. He was always calling. Always badgering me about the food hall or some other half-baked scheme of his. I told him I wanted him out.'

'How did he take that?' said Malton already knowing the answer.

'He told me that there was no "out". I got mad. I threatened him.' Nate looked down. 'It was the most stupid thing I've ever done in my life.'

Malton thought for a moment. Trying to square everything in his head. Carrie's murder giving Ani Delgado a window into Nate's world. Nate letting him in and then realising too late there was no turning back.

'Do you think Zak really killed Carrie?' asked Malton.

Nate looked up, suddenly fierce. 'Not Zak. I know that much. He felt so guilty for her death he confessed to it but Bea showed me all the evidence. He couldn't have done it.'

'The third person?'

'One of Ani's goons probably,' said Nate angrily.

Malton had his own suspicion of exactly who that goon might be. Not Femi Musa as he'd previously thought. The same goon who'd just blown up his father's house. Ani's favourite attack dog. His brother Lani.

Soon enough Ani would get wind of the trap Lani walked into. The trap Malton had set for Nate. After all this, Nate would have to go to ground. Radio silence. Then it wouldn't be long before Ani put the pieces together and did the one thing he did best. The thing that had kept him out of prison all this time – he would set Lani loose on anyone who could possibly link any of it back to him. Scorch the earth and move on. Very bad things were about to happen.

Nate took a step backwards and feeling the barrier against him, spun round, seemingly surprised to find himself so close to the edge. He turned back to Malton, both hands firmly gripping the barrier behind him.

'When I hired you I knew that Ani Delgado had my son killed. And I knew that they'd make me cover it up for the police. Bea said you were the best. That you would find the truth.'

Right from the start something had been off about Nate. The sort of people who called Malton always had something to hide. That was why they called him. The satisfaction at his hunch finally paying off was nearly enough to make Malton forget his injuries. But there was still one more suspicion he needed clearing up.

'Bea knows all this?' asked Malton.

Nate nodded. 'It was her idea. She said if you found out about Ani we could use that against him and if you got sucked into the cover-up then it would convince Ani that me and him were good. She said it gave us options.'

Malton felt that same glimmer of sadness that he'd had when Bea had asked him where he was keeping Izzy. She had done what she always did – whatever she needed to do to come out on top. That included using Malton. He silently raged, but not at Bea, at himself for falling for it.

All he could do now was try and bring this to an end.

Nate interrupted Malton's internal recriminations. His grief was suddenly gone. He was back to the ruthless man who'd made a fortune building Manchester in his image.

'I've done some bad things but nothing that deserved losing my son like that. I've dedicated my life to this city. I'm not going to stop now. Bea didn't want to make the call and I was too scared to do the right thing. I don't want options anymore. I know what I want. Bea told me that you can do anything. For a price.'

Nate looked over Malton's shoulder and out across the exposed concrete plateau that formed the top floor of the building. Confirming they were alone.

'I want you to kill the Delgados.'

Before Malton could reply his phone beeped again. He got it out ready to call Benton back and check she was OK.

It wasn't Benton. It was an unknown number. A single photograph taken from some distance away through the window of a cottage.

A photo of Emily.

64

'I didn't tell them shit,' said Taymon.

He was sat on the floor, leaning against the fireplace, his legs splayed out on the carpet, his face an unrecognisable mess of blood and bruises. The violence still fresh in the air.

'Fucking Chopboy pussies.' He spat a thick gob of blood and mucus onto the grate.

As soon as Dean had got the call from Malton, he'd rushed round to warn Taymon. He was too late.

The front room was trashed. The heavy plastic covers on the sofa and chair were both liberally splashed with blood. Pictures had been ripped off the wall and the front room window had been broken but still hung in there, a jagged crack across the pane.

'What did they want?' asked Dean, handing Taymon a tea towel he'd grabbed from the kitchen.

Taymon wiped his bloody face and inhaled, sucking snot and blood down his throat and clearing his sinuses.

He smiled.

'They wanted Izzy. And I gave them fuck all.'

Dean couldn't believe it. It looked like at least six or seven men had given Taymon the kind of kicking that most people don't get back up from. But from what Malton said he might just have got lucky.

Lani Delgado, the man Dean had seen fighting Malton, was out there cleaning house. Dean had no doubt if it had been Lani who'd come calling he wouldn't be having this conversation with Taymon right now. He'd be dead and wherever Izzy was, so would she.

'There's a man coming for you,' said Dean.

'Lani?' said Taymon. 'Fuck Lani.'

As much as Dean admired the sentiment he knew going up against Lani was suicide.

'I can help you,' said Dean.

Taymon started laughing before the pain of doing so brought him coughing and wheezing to a halt.

'What the fuck can you do?'

'I can make sure you and Izzy are somewhere safe. My boss can talk to Ani Delgado, make a deal to get them off your back.'

Taymon was shaking his head.

'Whoever your boss is there's no way he's talking to the Delgados. They'll kill him. Like they kill anyone who gets in their way. Me and Izzy are going to take our chances.'

'My boss is Craig Malton,' said Dean. He didn't often drop Malton's name. People either knew him or they didn't. Besides, he wanted to do things his own way. If the only trick he had was to wave Malton's reputation around then pretty soon someone would call his bluff and it would all be over. But time was against him and he knew that if Taymon wasn't scared of Lani Delgado there was no way he'd look to someone like Dean for help.

Taymon went quiet. His eyes narrowed and he looked at Dean, trying to figure him out.

'The guy who crippled Leon Walker?'

Of all the pins in the map on the wall of Malton's office, it was his fight in a multi-storey car park with Vikki's father several years ago that had reached Taymon's notice.

Dean nodded.

With great difficulty Taymon hauled himself to his feet. He winced in pain with every step.

He looked Dean square in the eye for one last, lingering examination.

Then he hobbled over to the sofa and without taking his eyes off Dean he grabbed the heavy plastic cover and hauled it off. Beneath the plastic the white leather was as immaculate as the day it was bought.

'Come out,' he said loudly.

For a beat, nothing, then very slowly, before Dean's eyes, the sofa began to unfold. It was a sofa bed. The mechanism slid up and out and as it did so, from underneath it all, stepped Izzy.

65

'I remember Kieran,' said Benton. 'Back when he was with the Chopboys. You could tell his heart wasn't in it.'

Lesha had arranged to meet Benton outside Kieran's Place. The café had been closed all day. Yesterday after gently collecting what was left of Sergio and Raheem, she and Graham had buried the dogs in the garden. Lesha had planted a small lavender bush to mark their final resting place. Something lasting and beautiful that might just make the heartache she felt at losing her two boys that little bit more bearable.

After going through all that she couldn't bring herself to see anyone.

A pile of food donations sat rotting on the pavement. Someone had daubed CHOPBOYS on the new shutters.

'What more was I meant to do?' asked Lesha sadly.

'Don't blame yourself. GMP's got a three quarters of a billion pounds a year and nearly ten thousand bobbies and Ani Delgado's still walking about.'

'Four days ago I accused Ani of killing Tommy. Since then he's smashed my windows, wrecked my café, and murdered my dogs.'

Benton puffed out her cheeks. 'He's a prick like that.'

Lesha and Benton were alone outside Kieran's Place. It gave Lesha plenty of time to look this woman up and down and wonder if she had made the right decision calling her. Something about the way she'd carried herself made Lesha feel there was something different about Benton compared to the other coppers she'd dealt with.

'I don't know much more about Tommy's case, I'm afraid. But the detective working on it is good. She'll get to the bottom of it,' said Benton.

'Will she?'

Benton grimaced diplomatically and leaned in.

'Between you and me, yes. Obviously. But officially?' She shrugged.

'Officially nothing gets done?'

'We've been in special measures for over three years now. Believe me, if he'd got murdered back then I wouldn't even be having this conversation. You could forget about it. I guess what I'm saying is there's a lot of good people working on it but I've learned through bitter experience, there's no open goal that GMP can't sky the ball over and then pass the buck.'

Lesha had been here before. When the idea that the police existed to keep you safe from the bad guys had met the hard reality of Greater Manchester Police. But something about Benton made her push on.

'You still looking for Femi?' she asked.

Benton shook her head. 'Afraid not. Another one that got away. He's a suspect in multiple murders. Your Tommy's included.'

'You think he did it?' asked Lesha.

Benton was silent for a moment. She seemed to be wrestling with something. Finally she spoke. 'I know that I don't want him to have done it. And I know that every murderer has a mum and a family. Every killer was a kid once. But something about Femi. What I've learned. I just don't think he's a killer. If thirty years on the force counts for anything that's my gut. He's involved, but I don't think it's him doing it.'

Lesha breathed a sigh of relief. Whatever Benton would have said she had made up her mind before she'd even called the number on the card. But hearing her say she didn't think Femi was Tommy's killer made what came next much easier.

'So you're off his case?' she asked.

Benton smiled. 'Well, I am and I'm not. I'm not officially looking. But obviously, if something comes along, I'm going to follow it up. At least until I can decide if it's something I should pass over.'

Lesha felt the fingers in her pocket wrap around the phone from Ani Delgado's shed.

'Some coppers they're all about the glory. Serious and Organised? That's the department if you want to make your name. That's just below murder that is. Big drug busts. Angry-looking mug shots. Police confiscation. The sort of stuff that makes the police look good. Whereas missing persons? A black kid from Moss Side? Missing? You're getting fuck all if that gets solved.'

Lesha must have been frowning because Benton quickly hurried up to her point.

'Thing is, I don't give a shit about glory. I give a shit about people like Ani Delgado walking around thinking they can fuck up people's lives and never have to answer for it. Fuck glory, I want justice.'

Lesha remembered what the papers had said about Kieran when he was killed. It still made her mad even now.

Lesha looked Benton up and down once more and made her decision.

'They killed Kieran because I spoke to the police. Ani wanted me to know there was nowhere I could go. No one who could protect me. He put his pride over his own son's life. To let the world know just how far he'd go. Then he took the body. That was just to hurt me. Just to show me how cruel he could be.'

'I'm sorry,' said Benton, the indignation going out of her for a moment.

'But he's wrong. He couldn't kill Kieran. Not as long as I'm here.' She pulled up her sleeve and showed her tattoo. 'He's here now. I'm his resting place. And this . . .' she motioned to the shop '. . . this is so the world can remember Kieran Thompson as something other than what they said in the papers. Not a gang member. Not a drug dealer. Not a black kid from Moss Side. My son. Who loved people and football and films and his mates and who could have done anything.' She looked up at the café front with tears in her eyes before turning back to face Benton. 'Are you a mother?'

Benton nodded.

'I carried Kieran for nine months inside me. I can carry him for much longer than that. Whatever Femi did, I know he's got a mother out there. I know how she feels.'

Lesha reached in her pocket and took out the phone she'd found in Ani's shed.

'I got into this whole mess cos Ani Delgado's gang of parasites killed someone I cared about,' she said. 'I don't know if seeing Tommy there, like that, reminded me of Kieran or if I just couldn't stand to let it slide. I never liked bullies.'

'I'm sorry about Tommy. Hopefully they might get some answers.'

'It's not enough though, is it? Answers. I know who killed Kieran. You think that makes it better?'

'I'm not going to help you do anything illegal,' said Benton quickly.

Lesha laughed. 'Calm down. I don't want your help. I want to help you.'

She turned the phone on.

'You said you were looking for Femi?'

Lesha held the phone up for Benton.

There on the screen was a shot of Femi Musa holding up a Man City match-day programme from the previous weekend. He looked thin and scared but most definitely alive.

'It's Femi, isn't it?' said Lesha.

Benton took the phone off her and peered at the image. It was taken in the back room of a terrace. Bare boards. Several different layers of wallpapers on the walls. Her face lit up.

'That's Moss Side,' said Benton confidently. 'Of course it is. The Delgados never leave Moss Side. They can't. This is their kingdom. This is where they do what they want.'

Benton pinched the image to enlarge it with her fingers. She squinted at the screen and seemed to be thinking.

Lesha took the phone off her and moved the image closer.

'See that?' she said pointing to the window in the background. There was sky and then to one side the backs of terraces.

Benton's face lit up as she realised what Lesha was getting at. 'It's not back to back; it's a junction.'

Lesha had recognised it straight away. In Moss Side there were terraced streets that met at right angles where some houses backed onto not the back of other houses but an alleyway running between the backs of two further sets of terraces. Forming a kind of T-junction in the alleyway. And out of the back windows of those houses you could see sky.

'And there . . .' said Lesha pointing. There in the alleyway someone had fly-tipped a child's trampoline. The top of the frame and mesh netting visible over the top of the yard wall.

Benton took the phone off her, clearly animated with excitement.

'There's about a dozen streets like that in Moss Side but I bet there's only one with a trampoline dumped there.'

'And you don't want anything in return?' said Benton.

'No. I do. I want you to bring him back to his mum. Alive.'

66

The road suddenly dipped and Malton felt his car leave the tarmac as he neared eighty miles an hour on a straight of country lane. For a split second the Volvo was airborne, the countryside rushing by on either side before it crashed back down onto the road, the solid suspension crunching rigidly with the impact.

He'd left Nate Alquist with instructions to get home, lock his doors and sit tight. It was sloppy but he had something far more important to worry about.

Somehow Ani knew about Emily. He'd sent him the photo. He was there. Outside. Now.

Malton was right; Ani was clearing house and Emily had been sucked into the chaos.

He tore round a blind corner and had to pull out into the opposite lane to avoid ramming into the back of a slow-moving car. Jinking back into his lane just in the nick to avoid a head-on collision with a tractor, Malton put his foot down, willing a few more miles per hour out of his car.

He was high up on the edge of the Peak District. Closing in on Uppermill and Emily. As he started to descend into the valley he tried to focus.

Now he knew exactly what Nate Alquist was feeling when he'd asked him to kill the Delgados. The only difference – Malton would gladly kill whoever it was that was threatening Emily. Back before she fell pregnant he knew that Emily would always be in danger of finding herself enveloped by the darkness he carried with him. But it had been a theoretical danger. Like every other obstacle he'd faced in his life, Malton was sure he could overcome it.

After the loss of James, he had developed a total disregard for his own safety and a complete lack of sentiment for every aspect of his life. Malton stayed alive for as long as he had by not caring about dying. Enshrouded in the protective cloak of his own private death wish. But now with Emily and their unborn child things were different. There was something new. Fear.

He slammed the brakes, ground down into third and hauled the car round ninety degrees, accelerating off up a narrow road that would take him past Dobcross and on to Uppermill from where he could climb up the valley to Emily's cottage.

His mind felt refreshingly blank. The mystery of the past few days was all but solved. Ani Delgado had wormed his way into the lives of Nate Alquist and his son Zak. There were details left to resolve but now that Ani was in the picture the whole bloody mess was ripped wide open for all to see.

Malton nearly lost the road again as he flung his car around a hairpin bend and tore upwards in second gear. The road began to climb away from Uppermill and slowly the stone terraces thinned out into farmland. He was so nearly there he could feel his heart tight with anticipation. Visions of dark violence and terrible loss hovering just beyond his horizon.

The car screamed to a halt outside the cottage. Malton was already out and rushing to the front door.

He could barely feel his injuries. The fear and adrenaline working better than any painkiller.

Without breaking stride he threw a size-ten double-soled Tricker's boot with all his weight behind it and the door smashed inwards, Malton following close behind.

The cottage was empty.

He pulled out his hatchet and paused a moment, listening for any sound.

From the bedroom he heard the deep, resonant snap of a shotgun being closed.

'This is your only chance to come out,' he said slowly. 'If you don't take this chance you will have weeks and weeks to regret it before I finally let you die.'

He heard his own voice issuing bloody threats like some kind of unhinged gangster. The very men he strove so hard to not become.

The bedroom door opened and the long barrel of a shotgun emerged. From behind it stood Mayer Haim. Emily's father.

'Get out,' Mayer said, his voice deep and uncompromising.

'Where's Emily?' barked Malton, confusion beginning to flood in.

'At the hospital. She went into labour. I came back for her stuff. How did you find us?'

'You're in danger,' said Malton.

'I know,' said Mayer, not lowering the shotgun.

Malton's phone began to ring in his pocket.

'Get out of my house,' said Mayer.

***

It took until the outskirts of Manchester for the numbness to lift and for Malton to remember to check his phone.

He had a missed call from Lou Weekes.

67

With every red light Dean's paranoia grew. Malton hadn't answered any of his calls and so he'd had to make a decision. He'd ordered Taymon and Izzy to pack a bag each and be ready to leave in the next five minutes.

With Taymon lying in the back, still badly wounded from his beating, and with Izzy sat up front, Dean had driven south, through Whalley Range and Chorlton, specifically to avoid crossing back through Moss Side.

He told himself this was the call Malton would have made. Every moment they spent back in Moss Side was more chance for the Delgados to come back and finish the job. Malton Security taught their doormen a simple acronym: ACE. Anticipate. Control. Escape.

In a dangerous situation they were to anticipate the threat. Read the body language. Assess the situation. See the danger coming before it got there. Moss Side was Ani's home turf. The Chopboys already knew where Taymon was and it was clear they were looking for Izzy. There was every chance they'd be back and this time they'd make sure they got answers.

Then you contain the situation. Remove a violent punter. Steer them to the exit if possible. Signal to colleagues to subtly put themselves between a potential flare point and any vulnerable punters. If need be, use force. Use it first and use it hard.

Dean didn't have that option. He wasn't arrogant enough to imagine he'd have a chance against one Chopboy, much less a gang. No one could win at those odds. Well maybe one man but right now he wasn't picking up his phone.

So Dean contained the situation by removing Izzy and Taymon to his van and heading for the hills.

That was the third part – Escape. You can't confront violence without risking getting hurt or even killed. If the odds are overwhelming then you need to get out of that situation. That was when doormen were trained to call the police. But Malton never called the police. He made it clear to Dean on his very first day that calling the police wasn't just not an option, it was an active failure.

Right now Dean was escaping as fast as he could safely drive.

With every mile they drove from Moss Side it was as if the spell of the Delgados grew weaker. It was impossible to imagine the Delgados in Urmston or Trafford or Stockport or anywhere that wasn't the small pond they'd been churning up their entire lives.

As he waited for the hundredth red light to change Dean heard a noise coming from the back of the van. It took him a moment to realise what it was. Taymon was laughing.

'Take it easy,' said Dean.

'Nah, it's funny though right?' said Taymon.

Dean failed to see what could possibly be funny about getting beaten half to death in your own home.

'You saved my life twice in a week. Like you're my guardian angel.'

Dean almost chuckled. It was kind of funny.

'We're not clear yet,' he said. 'I'm taking you to a safe house out in Stockport.'

'If they come again, I'm ready for them,' said Taymon, his voice suddenly serious.

To Dean's horror Taymon's arm leaned over from the back of the van. He was holding the same gun Dean had seen back at the carnival.

'Put that away!' Izzy chided her brother.

Taymon sucked his teeth and pulled his arm and the gun back.

'And stay down. You're badly hurt,' she said.

'I'm fine.'

'Stay down,' commanded Izzy again and Taymon went quiet. 'Can I put the radio on?' she asked Dean.

Grateful for the distraction, Dean nodded and Izzy put on some music.

As he drove out of town towards the safe house, Dean wondered what his next move was. More than that he wondered why on earth Malton wasn't answering his phone.

68

Benton peered through the alley gates that barred the way between two gable-end terraces. She moved from side to side trying to see past the end of the yard walls and round the corner into the alleyway that ran along the back of the terraces. It was impossible.

She pulled out her phone and checked Google Maps again. This was the fourth T-junction alleyway configuration in Moss Side. The first two hadn't been gated. At the third she'd found the alley gate hanging open with no one around. She was beginning to run out of options.

But this alley gate was shut up tight, a twelve-foot-high steel grille barring entry. The alley itself was obviously cared for. Planters had been placed along the sides of the houses and blossomed with colourful flowers and even a small tree. At the bottom someone had put a bench up against the back wall that faced down the alley Benton couldn't quite see. They'd also put up trellises. Vines crawled up and down the brick walls.

It looked idyllic but Benton was none the wiser as to whether or not there was a trampoline dumped there. The trampoline in the photo of Femi from the phone Lesha Thompson claimed she'd found in Ani Delgado's back garden.

She walked back into the street and stood in the road looking at the terraces trying to work out which one might be hiding Femi Musa. Some houses had been better tended than others but one stood out like a smashed thumb. The front door was covered in a metal shutter, as were the downstairs windows. The upstairs windows were rotten, wooden sash windows, and a bush in the small front garden had grown high enough to nearly cover the lower part of the house. If you were looking for somewhere low-key to hide someone it definitely looked the part.

When Lesha showed her the photo she'd felt the rush of excitement. The chase was back on. She could postpone real life for something far simpler. Right now bringing Femi Musa home alive seemed far more possible than healing the rift between her and Jenni.

'Are you here about the noise?' called a voice from across the road.

Benton wheeled round to see a smart, elderly lady clutching a notebook.

'I call the council every day, report everything,' she said sternly.

Benton had already pulled out her ID and was walking over. 'DI Benton, yes. We got all your reports . . . ?' Benton held, waiting for a name.

'Edith, Edith Morrisson.'

'Yes of course,' mugged Benton. 'Mrs Morrisson. So, you've been writing it down?' She pointed to the notebook the woman was holding up.

The old woman smiled.

'Everything.'

69

It had been twenty minutes since Lou Weekes had called Malton. As he leapt from the car, Malton could hear fighting coming from behind the heavy gate that covered Jordan Weekes's driveway.

At one end of the driveway the gate had been hauled open a few feet, brute strength going against the gears and brakes in the opening mechanism. The kind of strength that Malton's battered body remembered only too well from his last encounter with Lani Delgado.

He had left one of his best men watching the Weekes house for the past few days. A kick-boxer called Illian. Illian was a taciturn, six-foot unit who all the other bouncers hated being paired with. He almost never spoke, didn't drink or take breaks and spent all his free time training at his local gym in Ashton. Usually Malton valued someone who could talk his way out of a situation. He knew all too well that there was always a bigger guy. Or in the case of working doors, there was always a carful of guys. Often carrying weapons. It didn't matter how tough you were. The best way to walk away from a fight was not to have the fight in the first place.

Then he'd seen Illian demolish an entire rugby team single-handed. While the other two men on duty had barricaded themselves in the venue, Illian had gone out the back way and stood between the door and eight burly, drunk rugby players, all of them nursing bruised egos.

By the time Illian had finished with them it wasn't just their egos that were bruised.

So Malton had kept him on. One of a handful of men he had whom he trusted to be able to deal with whatever level of violence Manchester could throw at them.

Squeezing through the gap in the gate he wondered just how long Illian could hold up against Lani Delgado.

The bonded driveway was covered in blood.

Illian staggered in a kick-boxing stance. His head was pouring blood. He had to reach up to wipe it from his eyes. From the way he dragged his left leg it was clear that he could barely stand. But he wasn't backing down.

Across the driveway from him Lani Delgado swaggered. The heavy crowbar he carried in his hand had a bloody clump of hair stuck to one end. He was dressed in jeans and a clean football shirt. His right ear was missing, courtesy of Malton's hatchet. A rancid dressing, brown and damp with blood had been wrapped around his head, his hair plastered down across his face with perspiration.

Malton's head felt clear. The pain from his injuries receded. Nate and Bea's double cross, Ani's bluff, Zak's murder; they all became distant side issues. The Delgados had threatened Emily. Now he was going to end them. This was a simple question of violence.

Lani sensed Malton's presence just a second too late as Malton swung a tight punch at the back of his head. With not enough time to fully dodge the blow, Lani twisted his body, bringing the crowbar towards Malton in a sweeping arc, the gap-toothed hook of the weapon making a path straight for Malton's head.

Malton was forced to pull his punch in order to get under the crowbar. What was intended as a knockout blow to the back of Lani's head became instead a hit to the kidney.

Malton knew from experience that a blow to the kidney could end any fight. The electric shock of pain that spreads out from a solid blow to the kidney is like nothing else. Your entire body goes into violent, immediate shock. It's enough to bring trained heavyweights to their knees.

Lani Delgado stumbled a few steps back but kept his feet and turned to face Malton with a look that muddled extreme pain and intense delight.

Malton had lost his biggest advantage – surprise. Now he would have to once again pit himself against a man whose violence surprised even Malton. Lani Delgado didn't fight like a big man. He fought like a man who wanted to bite your face off just for fun.

'What are you doing?' screamed Lou Weekes from behind an upstairs window.

Malton glanced up to see her clutching her infant, her face a mixture of fear and indignation.

'It's over, Lani. I know about Nate,' said Malton, ignoring the distraction.

Lani shrugged and lunged for Malton with the crowbar. Malton stepped back and then back again as Lani dived towards him, the solid metal bar cleaving the air.

Ordinarily Malton could read a man's body. See what attack he was planning and respond in kind. But Lani was in a frenzy, each attack a maddening continuation of the last.

Lani was shorter than Malton, less muscle, but he seemed to possess a limitless strength. His face was screwed tight with a lifetime of baked-in hatred for the world. Lani could easily pass as white. Only the slight curl to his hair and a fullness to his complexion gave any idea of his true origins.

Malton almost felt sorry for him. Growing up mixed-race in Moss Side Malton knew what it was like to be on constant notice from the black community while still getting to enjoy all the negativity from the white world that came from looking like he did. Trapped between two sides.

Malton had left Moss Side when he was a teenager for all manner of reasons but chief among them was the desire to find somewhere he belonged. Lani Delgado would never leave Moss Side. He couldn't. The Delgados were every bit as much a part of Moss Side as the terraces and the carnival and the Rathbone

Park Estate. And so Lani Delgado found himself an outcast. An unwanted afterthought.

Lani Delgado's world turned its back on him. Just like Malton's. While Malton left to find a new home Lani had turned all his hatred back on the place that rejected him.

Illian was slowly flanking Lani. Malton saw how the kickboxer staggered. He had lost enough blood that it was taking its toll even on a man like Illian.

'Whose idea was it to go after Emily? Ani? Nate? Bea?'

Malton was playing for time and he knew it. Lani would never talk. Men like him would rather die than submit. But Malton could see the damage Lani had done to Illian. He started to feel his own wounds once more, still fresh and raw from the last time he and Lani met earlier that day. For the first time in Malton's life a thought passed through his head – *I might lose this fight*.

Then he remembered the photo of Emily. The brazen threat to the one thing in his life that made his calloused heart beat a little faster. Losing this fight wasn't an option.

'Half-caste cunt,' spat Lani, literally. Without thinking, Malton put up an arm to block the phlegm heading his way. Quick as a flash Lani swung the rounded butt of the crowbar into Malton's gut, knocking the wind out of him.

Malton sank to his knees but before Lani could land another blow Illian launched a flying knee towards Lani's head.

Lani brought up an elbow and with a hideous crunch, bone met bone as he batted Illian out of the air.

The momentum of the attack staggered Lani and he took a few steps back. But still, he was on his feet. Illian and Malton were on the ground.

Malton felt the surface of the driveway through his rough fingertips. Grasping for a sensory anchor to cling on to consciousness, he savoured the blood in his mouth.

Looking up he saw Lani steadying himself, his eyes malicious pinpricks. His breath hissed hot and bloody from the gap in his mouth where his front teeth once were. The hate that consumed Lani Delgado's life was in the driving seat. Whatever was left of Lani was simply floating helpless, trapped in an engine of pure violence.

Then beyond Lani he saw something even worse. Jordan Weekes's Tosa.

The dog was pacing behind a gate that separated the driveway from a path leading to the back garden. Malton saw the look in its eyes. It was a coiled spring of muscle and teeth. A triumph of centuries of breeding – a silent, brutal weapon made flesh.

Someone just needed to pull the trigger.

Illian tried to get up but finally his legs gave way and he thudded back on the driveway. Lani turned to Malton.

His mouth was moving but his brain was swimming in a sea of adrenaline and endorphins. All that came out through his smirking lips was: 'Fuckin' . . . fuckin' . . . fuckin' . . .'

Malton only had seconds left. He looked past Lani and locked eyes with the Tosa.

'GO!' he screamed, pulling air deep from his diaphragm to make a noise that could pall the devil himself.

Even Lani paused for a moment. Long enough for the Tosa to take a step back and launch itself over the gate and straight for Lani.

In the time it took Lani to turn around the Tosa was on him. It bit a chunk out of the arm he raised up to defend himself. Lani dropped the crowbar in shock, the metal clattering on the driveway.

But Lani didn't back down. Ready now, he turned to face the dog. Two purebred killers staring each other down.

'You know you can't win,' shouted Malton.

Lani didn't budge. The idea of backing down had long since disappeared from Lani Delgado's thinking.

'Fuckin' . . .'

The Tosa jumped straight for Lani's face. Lani grabbed it out of mid-air and the two bodies went to the ground. Lani's hands wrapped around the Tosa's front legs as its snarling mouth tried to take a bite out of him.

Malton was on his feet now. He came towards Lani, kicking the crowbar away as he got nearer.

He could see the look of primal fury on the Tosa's face. And looking straight back up at it that same look on the face of Lani Delgado.

This would only end with one of them dead.

'STOP!' shouted Malton and it was like a switch went off in the Tosa's head. It shook itself free and backed off from Lani.

'Fuckin' . . .' muttered Lani, turning to look back in time to see Malton kick him as hard as he could in the head. And then a second time to make sure he wasn't getting back up.

70

The old woman wasn't lying when she said she'd written down everything. Benton watched as she turned the pages of the little red notebook to reveal neat columns of dates, times and incidents. Late-night parties. Sunday morning construction work, domestic arguments. Fly-tipping, double parking, graffiti and all the other needless annoyances that plagued Moss Side.

'Yes,' she said, smiling at the acknowledgement. 'The house opposite. Number Twelve. I think it's a brothel.'

'Oh,' said Benton, looking at the house the woman was pointing to; the one next door to the derelict wreck.

'And what about the house next to it?' said Benton, directing her attention back to the dilapidated one. The old woman's face pursed with distaste.

'Disgusting. It's an absolute disgrace. It shouldn't be allowed. I've tried to find out who owns it. No one knows. I'm amazed we don't get rats.'

'Anyone coming or going?' asked Benton.

The woman shook her head. 'It's sealed at the front and back. But that's not what I called about. It's Number Twelve. There are girls in that house. A people carrier comes twice a day. Taking them out, bringing them back.'

Benton reached over and took the book off the woman and idly flicked through it looking for something that could help. Loud music. Men arriving late at night. Noisy car exhausts. Then a thought hit her.

Next to several entries she saw the name 'Dean'. 'Dean called.' 'Dean had a word.' 'Dean talking to council.' For a moment Benton wondered.

She flicked back to just over a week ago. The day Femi went missing. Nothing.

But then the next couple of days there were several entries marked 'Building work Number Twelve.' The house Edith said was a brothel. Next to the derelict house.

'I don't suppose you remember what this is?' asked Benton, pointing to the entry.

The woman shook her head with displeasure. 'Oh yes I do. Earlier this week. Two days it went on. All hours of the day and night. It sounded like they were knocking out bricks. Disgraceful it was.'

Benton looked back at the two houses. There was no way in or out of the derelict house. Unless you made a way.

She handed the book back to the woman.

'So what are you going to do?' asked Edith. 'Write to the council? Open a file?'

Benton shook her head with a smile. 'I could do that but why bother when I can just take a look myself?'

With that she walked across the road and knocked on the door of the alleged brothel. While she waited for an answer she waved Edith back into her house. Edith took a few steps back towards her front door but stayed firmly on the street watching the show.

The door opened a crack and before anyone even appeared Benton's hand was round the door, pushing it wider and stepping past a young woman and into the house.

'What is this?' she said, in an accent Benton recognised as somewhere Eastern European.

She shouted, 'Police,' over her shoulder and carried on walking down the hallway. Despite it being daytime the lights were all on and curtains drawn creating a sickly, mid-afternoon gloom.

In the front room the word 'police' was having the desired effect. A couple of women in jeans and cardigans were tidying something away. Benton didn't have time to investigate.

She kept on going through to the back room. These terraces were small. Just two-up two-down.

She walked into the back and immediately saw what she was hoping to find. There was dust and debris everywhere. In the wall shared with the derelict house someone had freshly smashed out a rough doorway in the alcove to the side of the chimney breast, joining the two properties. Acro props had been used to hold up the now unsupported wall.

Without pausing Benton ducked through the hole. She thought to herself how if she was in America this would be the point she'd take out her police weapon. But this was Moss Side and right now she wasn't acting as a police officer never mind one with a gun.

Behind her she could hear people fleeing as she stood up in the back room of the derelict house.

The carpet was faded green and the room smelled of damp. Something growing in the backyard completely covered the back windows and the room was dark.

Benton checked the kitchen was empty and made her way into the hallway.

There were crates of bottled water stacked up against the front door.

Benton stopped for a moment and looked up the stairs. If someone was up there who wanted to do her harm she was alone and unarmed. No one except Edith even knew she was there. She most definitely didn't have any legitimate reason to be there.

But she had a reason that overrode all of that. Tejumola Musa and the promise she'd made to Lesha Thompson.

Benton sprinted up the stairs, her thick, rubber-soled boots thudding on threadbare carpet, sending plumes of dust up into the still, dead air.

Her shoulder made short work of the flimsy padlock on the door to the back bedroom and she crashed into the room, squinting in the bright light.

There was a mattress and bucket on the bare floor and cowering in one corner of the room – Femi Musa.

71

'I swear I didn't know they'd kill him.'

Dean was making his way through the outskirts of Stockport. In the back of the van Taymon had gone quiet. Dean hoped he was just sleeping. For the past twenty minutes he and Izzy had been driving, listening to the music in silence.

They were pulling into the driveway of the safe house when she'd finally spoken.

'Ani has girls. Lots of them. They work for him. He's got places in Moss Side. Houses where they live.'

She looked at Dean, willing him to fill in the blanks.

Dean suddenly thought back to the house across the road from him and Vikki and understood everything.

'Is one Twelve Morton Road?' he asked.

'Yeah,' said Izzy, sounding surprised.

'And you worked there?'

Izzy shook her head. 'No, that's the foreign girls. His brother Lani, he deals with that side. Ani had a couple of girls from Moss Side. He keeps us for special jobs.'

Izzy's voice was trembling but she continued.

'That's what Zak was. A special job. Ani had some business with his dad; he wanted leverage. That was me.'

Izzy looked down into her lap.

'I didn't think they'd kill him.' She looked to Dean, her eyes damp and pleading.

'It's not your fault,' said Dean half-heartedly. He wondered if he should reach out and comfort her and decided against it. Taymon was still silent in the back.

'Ever since I was little, I knew what I looked like. When I was nine I started getting attention. Suddenly the world stopped being about being me; it became about being something for other people. For men.'

Dean felt relieved he'd decided against giving her a hug.

'And what about Weekes?'

Izzy scowled. 'I thought it was just stealing. Ani wanted me to get close to him. Find out when he had drugs on him and take them off him.'

'You were just meant to steal from Weekes?'

'That's what I thought. That's what he told us to do. A kilo. God knows what for. Ani doesn't sell drugs. He says that sort of thing gets you killed.'

Dean nodded. That made sense. The Delgado twins had survived more than one drug war. They'd learned their lessons and moved with the times. That's what the food hall was. Simply the latest evolution in their money-making machine.

'Then Ani calls me and says Zak's dead. I never saw his body. I just did what I was told.'

'Which was?' asked Dean softly.

'Call up Nate. Tell him Zak was dead, that I'd found him. Mention the drugs and the money. Say it was a gang thing.'

'Was it?'

Izzy shook her head. 'Zak was just a kid. Most of the time all we did was talk.'

'About what?' said Dean.

Izzy shrugged. 'His girlfriend Carrie. The one who got killed. Next thing I know Zak's been murdered and Ani tells me I've got to tell his dad that Jordan Weekes did it. He texted me the whole story. Made me learn it by heart. Told me to delete it. I didn't.'

She pulled out her phone and handed it to Dean. There was a long WhatsApp message of bullet points. Izzy's story about how Zak died and who killed him, the story he and Malton had heard her give at the Paramore hotel.

Dean couldn't believe it. It was as good as a confession. It was evidence. He swallowed and tried to hide his excitement.

'I'm going to need this phone.'

Izzy shrugged. 'It doesn't matter now does it? He's going to kill me.'

'No!' said Dean. 'No. You're safe here. Malton will sort this out. He always does.'

Izzy laughed. 'You can't sort Ani. He thinks you're up to something, he'll send in his boys.'

The images of CB tattooed on Ryan Lewis's face suddenly came to Dean's mind. CB. Chopboys. Ani had branded Ryan's face. Ani Delgado was a bully who surrounded himself with weak people who'd do anything he asked. Even sell out their flesh and blood.

'Is that what he did with Zak? Send someone round? You ever heard of Femi Musa?'

Izzy frowned. 'Femi? Femi was helping Zak. Before Femi came along all Zak had was guilt about what happened to Carrie. Femi was the one who convinced him to do something about it.'

'Femi didn't kill Zak?' said Dean, unable to hide his astonishment.

Izzy let out a little laugh before catching herself and falling silent.

'No. Femi wouldn't hurt anyone.'

Dean had no idea what was coming next.

'Femi was there when Carrie was killed. It had been his idea to set Zak up. He met Zak through Carrie's brother Ryan. Femi and his Chopboy mates were cuckooing Ryan. Staying at his place, taking his money. Ryan put them on to Zak. Zak liked hanging around with them. They treated him like a big deal and he got to play at being a gangster. Then Ani found out and he made sure they dragged Zak in as deep as you can get. Zak had no idea it was Ani behind everything.'

Izzy began to well up.

'Why?' asked Dean, already knowing the answer.

'His dad. Ani wanted something he could use against Nate. That's what he does – he sucks you in and then once he's got you, that's it. He never lets go.'

Izzy looked away, lost in her own regrets.

'So how did Carrie end up dead?' asked Dean. He felt bad pushing Izzy but he knew he had to ask. More than once he'd seen Malton keep the pressure up long after someone had broken. Squeezing every last piece of information out of them. This was when the truth always came out in the most painful way possible.

'Zak was going to buy drugs off the Chopboys,' said Izzy. 'Ani told Femi to sell him a whole kilo. Can you imagine? But when Zak came to the meet, Carrie was there. It all went wrong.'

'And Zak killed Carrie?' said Dean, still focused on the one thing Izzy seemed to be skirting around.

Izzy shook her head. 'No. I think he really loved her.'

'But he confessed.'

Izzy laughed. 'That was Ani's idea. He was waiting to hear Zak had bought the brick so when he hears Carrie's dead he suddenly shows up. Takes over and tells Zak that unless he took the rap then his whole family was in danger. Zak was so cut up about Carrie that he just went along with it. Poor kid.'

'How do you know all this?' asked Dean, eager to verify her story.

'Femi told Zak everything a couple of months ago. The plan to set him up. Femi begged for his forgiveness. Femi was trying to convince Zak to talk to the police. Said he'd go with him. Tell them what really happened with Carrie.'

'And Zak told you?'

Izzy hung her head and looked away.

'How did Ani find out Femi and Zak were going to go to the police?' asked Dean.

Izzy gasped quietly to herself. She was trying not to cry.

'You've got to understand. Ani's in here,' said Izzy tapping the side of her head. 'He makes me do things that make me feel sick with myself. But I still do them. Every time. I don't know if I'm scared or deep down I want him to like me or what, but whatever he said I did. So when he asked me about Zak I told him everything. What he and Femi were planning.'

Izzy burst into tears. Dean wished he could tell her it wasn't her fault. In a way it wasn't. She was put in an impossible situation. What little choice she had was hemmed in by violent coercion and a will ground down by years of abuse. But at the end of the day it *was* her telling Ani Delgado that Zak was planning to go to the police with the truth about Carrie's murder that got him killed.

Dean felt sick. Now everything made sense. Femi wasn't in hiding as a killer; he had been disappeared by the Delgados after betraying them.

'I didn't want to tell your boss who killed Zak because if I did it would mean I'd have to tell him why they killed Zak and then you'd know it was my fault.' Izzy began to cry.

Dean resisted putting an arm around her. He still had one last question.

'So who killed Zak?'

Izzy looked surprised. 'You haven't worked it out? It was the same person who killed Carrie.'

72

While Manchester rises into the sky in steel and glass and money, beneath the pavements the rotting remains of what it once was lie untouched, a buried secret. Clues to the real nature of the city that lurk sleeping beneath the fever dream above.

Basements, passageways, rivers, railways, even entire buildings. A city beneath the city. Wrapped in thick darkness, air heavy with mould and poisonous gases. A ready tomb for the unwary.

Perfect for what Malton had in mind.

He'd taken an unconscious Lani Delgado from Jordan Weekes's bloody driveway and dragged him to the basement of a block of flats just off Canal Street. A block he owned.

There in the far corner of the basement was a heavily locked door.

Behind that door lay a labyrinth of corridors and yet more sealed doors, each leading to yet more darkness. Damp and neglect made sure that every surface was wet and crumbled to the touch. Torch beams showed entire universes of particles swirling in the uninvited light. Paint, dust, asbestos, mould and skin. The old city waiting to invade the lungs of interlopers.

Dragging Lani Delgado over discarded shop fittings, broken glass and pigeon carcasses, Malton finally came to a second locked door.

Behind it lay the abandoned nightclub where Malton brought Lani's unconscious body.

Nearly twenty years ago the street-level entrance had been filled in with concrete and new buildings erected on top. Now it belonged to Malton.

The nightclub was low-ceilinged with a raised DJ booth at one end of the long room and a bar to one side. Old flyers littered the floor. Faded posters offering drinks at prices that could only have come from decades earlier.

In the middle of the dance floor was Malton's only addition to the room – a high-backed, metal chair had been riveted down into the concrete floor.

Lani Delgado sat on this chair, each hand cuffed to a chair leg with rigid, police-issue handcuffs. His legs had been fastened to the chair legs with multiple zip ties, holding him firm. Finally a thick, leather belt had been wrapped around his neck, securing him to the back of the chair and limiting any movement to a bare shuffle.

Malton sat on his own chair a few feet away, watching as Lani slowly came to. Malton wore a mask over the lower part of his face, twin air filters on each side of a moulded rubber housing, protecting his battered lungs from the decay in the air. His eyes hung in his face like dying stars, filled with the promise of unlimited explosive energy.

He'd brought an electric lantern down with him, which he plugged into a small battery pack in one corner with a long flex and placed down on the floor between them. The lantern threw out a large, yellow circle of light, beyond which the recesses of the derelict club faded back into the subterranean night. The beam uplit Malton and Lani's faces, giving both of them an appropriately macabre cast.

This was a netherworld where terrible men could do terrible things unseen by prying eyes. This was Malton's Manchester.

A loud, hissing sound came from Lani as he sucked air in through his teeth. Then a spluttering as he began to choke on his own spit before with great effort he spat onto the floor between them.

The wet dollop of bodily fluid sent dust spiralling up into the lantern's light as it hit the long-disused dance floor.

Malton watched as Lani slowly realised his predicament. First his arms, then his legs and finally his neck. In a few short seconds Lani learned that there was nowhere to go. Nothing to do. This was where it ended.

'Fuckin' . . . fuckin' . . . fuckin' Malton.'

Malton didn't react.

Lani tried to look around but with his neck held firm he could barely move. Instead his eyes shot from side to side like a trapped animal.

Malton reached up and pulled the mask off his face. With one giant hand he wiped the perspiration from round his mouth and nose. He clenched his jaw and pictured himself swallowing his rage about Emily. For now at least. It was time to get some answers.

'You never did leave Moss Side, did you?' said Malton.

Lani smiled. 'That bitch shouldn't have been there. Baby shouldn't have been there. Fuck off.'

Occasionally amidst the constant news flow of suffering and misery a story stands out that shocks a desensitised population back to some kind of shared sense of moral decency. The murder of a mother and child by Lani Delgado was one such story. The community had decided that it was Lani who shouldn't have been there, indeed shouldn't be showing his face anywhere in Manchester much less Moss Side.

'Did Ani decide that you didn't quite fit the Delgado brand he was building for himself? Local boy made good doesn't work if his brother's out burning women and kids to death?'

'Fuckin' Ani.'

It looked like Lani was trying to shake his head but unable to move he just shuddered on the spot.

Malton continued, 'I told Bea Wallace a lie about where the girl would be. She told that lie to Nate Alquist. Who told it to Ani. Who told it to you.'

'Sorry about your old man's house,' Lani said with a laugh. 'All those happy memories.'

Malton knew well enough that Lani's upbringing was no more stable or loving than his and so let that comment go.

'You and your brother are extorting Nate Alquist, right? You even killed his son to send a message.'

Lani was laughing again, a wet rasping sound. His tongue shot out between his missing front teeth and licked his lips.

'If you want,' he said.

'I don't need you to talk,' said Malton. 'I can leave you here. No one will come looking.'

A look of thwarted rage came over Lani. He began to bellow. Not words, just fury made into guttural noise. His eyes bulged and despite being securely restrained the threat of his physical presence filled the empty nightclub.

Malton watched him slowly peter out.

'No one can hear, can they?' said Lani with a defeated grin.

Malton shook his head.

He hadn't decided exactly what he was going to do with Lani yet but it didn't hurt to lead with the line that he was about to leave Lani down here to starve to death alone in the dark.

Lani licked his gums and said nothing.

'You know Nate Alquist has asked me to kill you and your brother?' said Malton.

Lani growled a little but kept his mouth shut.

Malton carried on, 'How'd you two even get involved with a man like Nate? When your boy Femi killed Carrie?'

Malton hoped Lani would take the bait.

Ever since he saw Lani dropping down from the attic of his father's old house Malton had radically revised his theory as to Femi's involvement. Nate Alquist had fingered the Delgados for Zak's murder. Given the brutality of the scene, that had to mean Lani Delgado. All that was left to clear up was who was responsible for Carrie's. Malton had heard Nate's side of the story, now he wanted the real version.

Lani started to laugh. Then wheeze, then choke.

'Femi Musa? You clueless cunt.'

Lani paused and then with every sinew of his body he pulled against his bonds. With his eyes locked on Malton, his arms bent back as he tugged on the solid metal cuffs. His thighs swelled with blood as his legs fought the zip ties. Even his neck bulged with primal fury as the leather belt held.

Until it didn't. The cuffs and the zip ties stayed firm but the leather of the belt tore open, flopping uselessly over Lani's chest. He flexed his neck and spat once more, this time directly at Malton. He missed by inches.

Malton was impressed. Having fought Lani twice he knew he was a tough son of a bitch but this was going some. As tough as he was he'd just taken the bait and was halfway towards confirming what Malton already suspected.

Malton feigned surprise. 'So if not Femi? You?'

Lani looked proud.

'Fuck it. Fuck it. Nate's kid wanted to be a dealer. Ani found out he was hanging out with Femi and so Ani's got to be clever. Fucking Ani. Gets Femi to sell the kid a kilo. A fucking kilo? Get him on the hook. Roll him up to his dad.'

'So what went wrong?'

Lani shook his now-free head.

'Ani asked me to go along, make sure Femi didn't fuck it up. Useless prick. Then Zak's fucking girlfriend turns up and starts making a fucking scene.'

Malton gently leaned away from the light, lest Lani Delgado see a glimmer of satisfaction on his face. He'd been wrong about Femi before, but now he had his confirmation of who the real killer was.

Malton played dumb. 'And so what did you do?'

Lani grinned with silent malice. 'I made sure she stopped making a fucking scene.'

Finally he was starting to see the bigger picture. Zak wasn't Carrie's killer. It was Lani Delgado.

'But something went wrong? Did Femi grow a conscience? Was Zak going to change his story? Ani gets scared? Asks you to make it go away? So you kill Zak? Kill Femi. Ani gets the added bonus of showing Nate what happens if he steps out of line?'

273

A low, rasping growl welled up in Lani Delgado's chest and oozed out of the gap in his teeth, filling the empty nightclub with a deathly white noise. It put Malton in mind of an animal getting ready to pounce. Lani's eyes were wide open, peering across the illuminated gloom straight into Malton's soul. Thin trickles of blood ran down the side of his neck from where his ear used to be.

He looked like the devil himself.

'You stupid bastard,' said Lani, growling out his words. 'Nate Alquist? He knew. He made a choice.'

'It's never a choice though is it?' said Malton. 'Not with your brother.'

'You think Nate's the victim? Shows what you know. Fucking Moss Side half-caste cunt. Out playing in the city. Thinking they all look up to you. They're laughing at you. People like us? They know what we are. They won't ever let us fucking forget. So me? I don't ever let them forget it either. They can build this city into whatever they want. I'll burn it down it over them every fucking time.'

As he processed Lani's words Malton felt the solid, Manchester earth beneath his feet. All at once he realised he was still operating from a second-hand version of the truth. They were all telling their own version of events. Bea, Nate, even Izzy. The only one who knew for sure was sat right in front of him, seething in the dark.

'Nate Alquist knew you were going to kill his son?' The words sounded insane. Malton knew Nate was holding something back, but this?

'Ani's just like you. Thinks everyone looks at him and sees someone. They don't. They see another black kid from Moss Side. Fucking idiot. He thought he could strong-arm Alquist. After the trial, turns out Nate had recorded everything. Had him on the hook. Made my idiot brother an offer. Like a fucking fool he lapped it right up.'

'What did Nate offer him?'

'Thing Ani's always wanted. Moss Side. Nate buys up the houses. Him and Ani do the food hall together. Ani finally gets to be the king of the castle with the bank balance to match.'

Lani was breathing heavily. Rage and adrenaline were keeping him upright and talking. It felt to Malton like a confessional. A lifetime of pent-up rage at being the 'other' brother. The violent one. The 'white' one. The one who wasn't Ani.

'And what did Nate want in return?'

'Council had given the food hall site to some church. Years back. When no one wanted anything to do with Moss Side. All Ani had to do was convince the council to change their mind.'

'And he convinced them?'

Lani smiled. 'I convinced them.'

Malton shook his head. It was too incredible. His mind raced over everything he knew. Probing for a weakness in what Lani was telling him. This couldn't all have been a setup from the start. A man wouldn't possibly allow his own son to be killed. And for what?

'No,' Malton started. 'Even if all that's true . . . why would he agree to you killing his son? He didn't have a choice. How could he say no to you?'

'That little shit Femi got into Zak. Got him feeling guilty. Got him ready to talk to the police. When Nate found out, he knew how that would go. If people knew the truth about Carrie Lewis that's one thing. But to know that he made a deal with her killers? How's that going to look? Your problem is you think cos he's rich and white he's the good guy. They taught you to hate yourself so much that you can't see what's right in front of you.'

The worst part was Lani was right. Malton had seen Nate as the victim. He'd been blinded by his money and his success and standing. By his whiteness. The ultimate social status craved by a mixed-race kid who no one wanted.

Then he saw Lani Delgado and realised just how foolish he'd been.

Right in front of Malton was everything he feared about himself. The violence, the self-loathing, the poisoned knowledge of the eternal outsider. But he refused to let himself feel anything for Lani Delgado. Lani was a cold-blooded killer. He thought of Emily in hospital. By now he could be a father. Instead of being at her bedside with a fresh new life, he was down in the dark and the filth with a monster.

'Now he thinks he can get you to kill us both. Cover it all up. So go on, you cunt. Be a good little boy. Do what he fucking says.'

Lani thrust his head forward, daring Malton to move on him.

Malton felt himself standing up. He imagined how good it would feel to wring Lani's neck there and then. Watch the cockiness drain out of him. Hear him beg.

'You shouldn't have threatened Emily,' he said and walked towards Lani.

'Who the fuck's Emily?' said Lani.

Malton stopped. There are dozens of ways to tell someone's lying. They over-elaborate; they tell you details they don't need to. They qualify and hedge. They can't look you in the eye; they fidget and shake. Lying well is an art form that very few possess.

Lani Delgado barely had enough emotional intelligence to qualify as human. He held the world around him in violent contempt. It wouldn't occur to him to lie. Why would he need to?

'You dumb?' said Lani. 'Emily? Don't know an Emily, mate. That your missus? Your bit on the side? Bea know about that?' he said with a leering grin.

A terrible thought hit Malton. Could it be Bea threatening Emily? Or at least making it look like someone else was? Keeping him off balance so he wouldn't see through her? He shuddered, less at the possibility and more at how far down this rabbit hole of paranoia he'd gone.

Suddenly Lani's words came back to him. *They taught you to hate yourself so much you can't see what's right in front of you.*

He felt an icy calm come over him. For the first time he felt his eyes adjusting to the gloom. He saw the dried blood and phlegm on Lani's face. The swollen spot on his temple where Malton had kicked him unconscious. The rotten teeth either side of the gap in his mouth. The dead eyes.

Malton took a step back and sat down again. Emily was safe, for now. It was time to finish up with Lani.

'Where do you fit in with the food hall then? Ani wants to be the local hero. Nate wants to be the man who rebuilt Moss Side. Where does his murderous brother fit in to that?'

Lani's eyes softened just a fraction before he caught himself and sucked that tiny shred of humanity back down into the pit he called a soul.

'I don't want to run a fucking market full of wankers. Fuck that. Ani's started believing his own shit. Reformed gang member. Fucking mentor. He wouldn't last a fucking hour without me.'

'What say I leave you down here and we test that out?' said Malton calmly. Now he saw it all. Everything finally made sense. He only had one thing left to clear up. 'Why do *you* think Nate hired me?'

Lani shook his head.

'That's your fucking missus that is. Stupid bitch. Nate came to her when he found out his son was about to spill his guts. Nate told her about how he'd played Ani at his own game. Turned a girl's murder into profit. She told him that she could help make it all go away. Just like she did the last time. Only this time there's got to be a price. His fucking son. He sold out his own fucking kid.'

Malton felt the last piece of the blood-soaked puzzle slot into place. The picture he saw horrified him. Nate Alquist was made to choose between his empire and his son. He'd chosen bricks and mortar over flesh and blood.

'And that's where you came in?' he said, feeling his revulsion for Lani Delgado coming roaring back.

Lani shook his head. 'Problem with Ani, he's like you. Likes to think he's clever. So him and Bea and Nate cook up a story.

Set up that sorry cunt Weekes. Give me a hammer, some coke and some cash and tell me to make it look like a drug deal gone wrong. And to make sure they sell it? They bring you in. I'm bored now. Fucking get it over with.'

Malton was silent for several seconds. With everything now clear in his head everything was immediately much simpler. He was back in charge. It was up to him now how this whole thing ended.

'I have a deal for you.'

'Fuck your deal,' said Lani.

'Well I'm going to tell you anyway because if you don't want it, I'm leaving you here to starve to death.'

Lani held his tongue.

'Nate Alquist wants me to kill you.'

'Pussy can't do it himself, can he?'

'He was happy to kill his own son to protect his business.'

'Happy for me to kill his own son,' said Lani. 'Keep his fucking hands clean. Just like Ani. Same as it always was. I can't show my face in Moss Side, but soon as Ani got a problem he's on the phone to me. I solve problems.' Lani laughed at his own joke.

A thought suddenly came to Malton.

'Did you kill Kieran Thompson?' he asked.

'Cleaning up Ani's fucking mess. Again,' grumbled Lani as if murdering his teenaged nephew was just another bit of housekeeping.

Malton had what he needed. Now everything made sense. It was his turn to decide what to do with the information.

'What do you think he and Ani will do once the food hall is up and running? You think they'd risk having you in the background? The famous baby killer?' said Malton.

Lani's face clenched tightly and for the first time he looked away. Malton recognised the tell. A man barely in control of his emotions, desperately trying to marshal the storm within. He knew for a man like Lani that was an impossibility. He knew because it was exactly the same for him.

'So here's the deal. I give you Nate Alquist.'

Lani turned back to face Malton, his eyes lit up. He shook his head and laughed. 'What?'

Malton continued. 'I give you Nate Alquist. Let the two of you sort it out between yourselves.'

'I'll fucking kill him.'

'Maybe.' Malton shrugged. 'But it's between you and Nate. No one else. And after that, however you and Ani want to settle things, well, that's between brothers, isn't it?'

'You know if you let me go I'm going to rip Nate Alquist to pieces and then I'm going after my brother.'

'I don't care,' said Malton. 'But only them. No one else gets hurt. They do, you'll find yourself back down here. Only difference, I'll have brought my power tools with me.'

Lani shook his head. 'You can take the boy out of Moss Side.' He was suddenly serious. 'Deal. So what do you want in return?'

73

'He turned up at the café in bits. Said there were some lads outside his flat threatening him. I didn't know where else to take him, so I brought him back to ours.'

Graham motioned to the kitchen table where a thoroughly shaken-looking Phil was devouring a packet of biscuits.

Lesha put all thoughts of the photo of Femi and the gun in her pocket out of her mind and sat down next to Phil, placing a hand on his immense arm.

Phil turned to her, his face red and swollen.

'Are they going to kill me?' he asked, wide-eyed with fear.

Lesha looked at Phil and calmly said, 'They're going to have to get through me first.'

'This can't go on,' said Graham over her shoulder, his fists bunched up with silent anger.

'I didn't mean to hurt that man,' said Phil.

'It's not your fault,' said Lesha. 'You were protecting me. You did the right thing.'

Phil smiled weakly and stuffed another biscuit into his mouth.

'They can't get away with this,' said Graham. 'Terrorising Phil here? He didn't know what he was doing.'

'I was protecting Lesha!' repeated Phil with stubborn pride.

This was exactly what Ani Delgado did. He strung out the pain. For him it was the agony of the wait before the killing blow that fed him. But Lesha refused to live in fear.

'We've got to go to the police. I'll talk to them myself,' offered Graham.

Lesha shook her head. 'It doesn't matter. The police need people to help them. People are scared.'

'You're not scared,' said Graham. 'You told me how it used to be round here. How people stood up. Stood together. Why can't that happen again?'

It was a good question and one that Lesha had been avoiding for the past few days. Kieran's Place was her stand to show the world that the darkness wouldn't win. Not only had it been trashed, but someone had also broken into her home and slaughtered her dogs. Going after Phil was just the latest nasty reminder that it would never end until someone stood up and refused to let it continue.

It only took one person.

Lesha stood up.

'I need to go for a walk.'

'I'll come with you,' said Graham too quickly.

Lesha shook her head. 'No. I need you to take Phil back to his flat. Make sure he's settled.'

'What if they come back?' said Phil urgently.

'I promise you,' said Lesha. 'I'm going to make sure they don't. Do you trust me?'

Phil sniffed loudly and for the first time since he'd arrived in Lesha's kitchen he smiled.

'I trust you,' he said.

She looked to Graham and could tell he was aching to say something but that he knew her too well so all he said was: 'You know what you're doing.'

Feeling Graham watching her from the kitchen window as she headed off towards the Rathbone Park Estate, Lesha felt the weight of the handgun still in her pocket and wondered if he was right.

74

Dean watched Taymon breathing for several minutes until he was satisfied that he was indeed just sleeping and not slowly dying from some unseen internal wound courtesy of his beating.

He had called Malton several times. Each time his phone going straight to voicemail. It had long since gone dark outside.

He wondered what Vikki was doing right now. He'd barely seen her this last week. Chasing Zak Alquist's killer had been wrapping him up and robbing him of the time to process what she'd told him back at the White Hotel. She was leaving to go to London for the year.

Maybe it was for the best. Look at Malton. Whatever relationship he had with Bea Wallace was hardly healthy. Then there was Emily, who'd fled pregnant with Malton's child. And of course Keisha. The childhood sweetheart of Malton who had shot Dean point-blank in the face. This line of work didn't seem great for stable, sane relationships.

Perhaps he did have to choose between Vikki and the job. The thought made him sad. He worried he'd make the wrong choice.

He left Taymon sleeping and went to check on Izzy in the front bedroom of the safe house. She'd told him that it was Lani Delgado who'd killed both Carrie and Zak. Dean had seen Lani fight Malton to a standstill. Zak and Carrie never stood a chance. Would Malton?

He stopped outside Izzy's door. The light was on. He knocked gently.

'Hello?'

Nothing. Dean wondered if he should knock again. But what if something was wrong?

'I'm coming in,' said Dean, knocking again and gently easing the door open.

The box room was empty. The small single bed was still made, Izzy's bag resting on top of it. Unopened.

Dean shot out the room and back into Taymon's. He was still sleeping. No Izzy.

'Izzy!' he called out, checking first the bathroom and then the toilet.

Both were empty. Like he knew they would be. She'd gone.

Before he could think what to do a terrible thought hit him.

He raced back into the room where Taymon lay, dead to the world.

He dived into Taymon's open holdall, pulling out clothes, a phone charger and some toiletries.

But no gun.

75

Tejumola's front room was immaculate. Despite the parade of police who had been in and out in the past day, everything remained in its place. Ornaments on ledges, doilies arranged on tables, photographs neatly framed on the walls.

The only thing that had changed was Tejumola. She couldn't stop smiling. Femi had been found alive and nothing else mattered.

Tejumola sat opposite Benton. She was still neatly dressed as if to defy the police who had come to visit her with their questions about Femi. A show of elegance and pride against the dirty world that had reached up and swallowed the happy little boy in the photographs that looked down on her.

Right now Femi was being held in a secure location by the police but it would only be a matter of time before he was back home.

Through the lace curtains Benton could just about make out the armed guard stood outside the house in the darkness beneath the street light.

Whether or not Femi talked made no difference to the people who he could incriminate. The killer of Tommy Fenwick and Zak Alquist wouldn't be taking any chances and so neither would Benton.

To his credit Priestly had quickly agreed to the armed guard. She had called him the moment she had Femi away in her car. Driving round South Manchester, keeping moving, watching for anyone following. She didn't have a destination in mind, just as long as she could keep Femi near her and away from the Chopboys until GMP arrived.

She was passing Southern Cemetery when she realised there was a police roadblock up ahead. Police vans, cars, the whole works. Priestly wasn't messing about. He was going to make sure Femi passed from Benton into police custody in one piece. In the seat beside her Femi had recoiled in fear at the show of strength while Benton did her best to reassure him.

The same reassurance she was now trying to give to Tejumola.

'They told me it was you who found him?' asked Tejumola warily.

'Yes.'

'How?'

The question put Benton on the spot. As much as she trusted Tejumola she couldn't risk compromising Priestly's investigation or betraying Lesha's confidence. Benton settled for: 'I never gave up looking.'

Tejumola gave Benton an understanding nod. Benton took it as a cue to start on the plate of biscuits that had been set out for her.

'The guns and the police?' said Tejumola, her real question too scary to contemplate saying out loud.

'Some of the people Femi was involved with are known gang members. Some of them are suspected of crimes of serious violence.'

Benton saw Tejumola's smile dim just for a moment.

'But,' cut in Benton quickly, 'Femi is somewhere very safe. And as soon as we're done questioning him he's coming right back here. To you.'

Right now the police were going through the phone that Lesha Thompson had given to Benton. The phone with the photo that had helped her track down Femi. Armed with the texts on that phone and Femi's testimony it would only be a matter of time before Ani Delgado got a knock on the door.

Tejumola examined Benton, looking her up and down. Benton knew exactly what she was doing. Trying to decide if she could trust this woman with the safety of her boy.

Benton leaned in closer. 'I can't say for definite, but from what I've gathered, I think Femi got caught up in something bad and was trying to make things right. I think he was trying to help.'

Tejumola grabbed on to this slim twig of hope with both hands.

'He wanted to pray with me. For forgiveness. I should have done more to bring him back to Jesus,' said Tejumola.

Benton immediately thought about Jenni. She'd not spoken to her daughter in nearly two days since she left for her dad's. Partly the case, partly a desire to let her ex see how intensive it was raising a kid on your own and partly out of a hope that Jenni too would appreciate what life without her mum looked like.

But it was more than that. Like Tejumola she saw her little girl growing up into an adult over whom she had next to no control. Just as the world reared its ugly head she was meant to accept that she could no longer keep it at bay. The drugs she'd found on Jenni could be nothing or they could be the tip of the iceberg. Like Tejumola she was simply overwhelmed.

'You did the only thing you can do. The only thing *we* can. Surround them with love and let them know that whatever happens we'll always be there.'

No sooner had Tejumola raised a hand to her face and dabbed away a tear than in the near distance gunfire erupted.

76

Being the mother to a murdered son was a club no one wanted to join. Its members regarded each other with a mixture of compassion and horror. Seeing a mirror of their own trauma looking back at them. Scrutinising each other for the tell that might somehow give them an unwanted insight into their own suffering.

Lesha had been to the groups. Heard the talks, even given them herself. Kieran's Place had been born out of the strength and solidarity those women had given her. But it had also been born out of a desire to move beyond that. To no longer be defined by Kieran's death. She wanted to live in the future. Making Moss Side somewhere that couldn't possibly let it happen again.

She realised now that, no matter what she built, it wasn't enough. Not as long as Ani Delgado was there in the background, corroding the foundations of hope and decency. Parading his bogus redemption for praise from people who had the privilege of living somewhere like Didsbury or Chorlton or Cheadle or anywhere that would never live in fear of a man like Ani.

She'd been standing across the road from Ani's house for long enough to see the sun set over the estate and the street lights begin to come on. She'd seen cars returning from jobs and school runs. Families going back into their homes. Safe for the night.

That morning she'd hoped that planting the gun would be enough but she saw now that was just wishful thinking.

Ani's road was a cul-de-sac of semi-detached houses. The saplings planted when the Rathbone Estate was built were now large, mature trees that covered the road in shade. A verdant contrast to the red-brick canyons of Moss Side's terraces.

She felt an impossible guilt for what she was about to do. The stain she was about to impose upon their worlds. But she knew that, like a surgeon, if you wanted to cut out a cancer then there would be blood.

What happened next was an afterthought she had yet to get around to. The news that Ani had the Chopboys stalking Phil was enough to let her know that there was no more time. All those years ago she'd made the mistake of thinking someone else would fix things for her. She'd gone to the police and it had got Kieran killed. She still hadn't learned. She'd approached Malton expecting that maybe his reputation was enough to keep Ani at bay. He too had failed her.

She had to do this herself.

In her pocket was the gun Kieran took in for the Chopboys. It was time for it to come home. It and the three bullets in the magazine. Back to where they belonged.

She hoped that Benton had managed to find the boy. Femi. Whatever he'd done she couldn't bear to think of yet another mother joining that wretched club. She wondered if Tommy Fenwick had a mother somewhere mourning his death. She imagined that, after years of watching her son fall so far, the news of his death might come as some kind of relief. The cruellest kind of closure.

It would all end tonight.

The sound of a car pushed Lesha back into the shadows. Ani's silver Škoda Yeti came round the corner. He was at the wheel. He was alone. Lights were on in Ani's house. It would have to be done on the driveway. When it was just him and her. The father who killed his own son and the mother who would finally make him pay.

Ani pulled up into his driveway. Lesha was already moving, out from the darkness and into the street lights. Her arm hung loosely at her side, the gun in her hand.

Ani killed the engine.

She was across the road and at the kerbside. A few metres between her and the driver's side of the car.

Ani hadn't seen her as he opened the car door to get out.

But he hadn't seen the other woman either. Nor had Lesha.

The first Lesha knew of her was when she walked up to Ani Delgado and before he could even turn to face her, fired eight bullets into him, killing him instantly.

77

'Where are we going? What's the threat?' Nate Alquist's voice rang out.

Malton kept one hand on Nate as he led him through his house, past his wife and past the three Malton Security men he'd had stationed and towards the back garden. With a police car parked out front of the house he'd need to go the long way round.

The multiple fireplaces scattered throughout the house lent the air a heavy, warm grip. The smell of firewood soaked into everything with its reassuring solidity. This wasn't a home where bad things happened.

Nate's wife Amelia ran after them into the large hallway with its parquet flooring and yet another fireplace.

'Where are you taking him now?' she demanded frantically.

Malton turned, his hand still on Nate's shoulder and said, 'I know who killed your son. And I know why. Now, I need your husband to sort it all out, once and for all.'

'Sort what out?' She turned to Nate. 'This has gone too far. You need to go to the police, tell them everything.'

'No,' said Nate too quickly.

'This is nearly over,' said Malton and then turned to Nate. 'We need to go. Now.'

Nate shot Amelia one of his billion-pound-property-magnate smiles. A smile to let the world know that everything was under control. Whatever happened Nate Alquist was coming out on top and it'd be better for everyone if you just made peace with it now.

'This is what I'm paying for,' said Nate reassuringly to his wife. 'This is what Bea does – she handles this sort of thing. After last time, you think we can trust the police?'

He looked to Malton. 'Let's go,' he said. A command not a request.

When Malton had first seen Nate's house he'd been over-awed. The mountaintop of nice, white wealth that he'd been clawing his way towards his entire life suddenly receded away. Without ever letting the words coalesce into a belief, Malton had always told himself that there was a sum of money, a size of house, a way of living that would eventually silence the doubts of a little boy whose mother preferred losing herself on the moors to raising her son and whose father reminded him daily of that fact. Seeing Nate's house he realised there would never be enough wealth to put clear water between him and his demons.

He'd envied Nate. But then Lani Delgado had told Malton the true price of that house. Nate had sacrificed his own son. Malton's mind went to Anthony's empty grave in Southern Cemetery. The child being born at this very moment in a private hospital somewhere in Greater Manchester. Far from Malton and all his damage.

Focusing now on the task at hand, Malton led Nate out into the back garden, through a gate that led to the golf course behind the house and into Malton's waiting Volvo. He made sure the doors were locked before he turned on the ignition and started driving back into town to where, unbeknownst to Nate, in a long-abandoned nightclub, hidden beneath the city, Lani Delgado was waiting for them.

78

'If you hadn't shot him I was going to,' said Lesha as she put her kettle on.

The woman who'd given her name as Izzy sat in silence at the kitchen table. Between the two women sat Izzy's now-empty handgun. A murder weapon.

'He made me a killer,' said Izzy flatly.

'You don't have to explain anything,' said Lesha.

Izzy looked up and shook her head. 'No, you don't understand. There was a boy and he made me go with him. Watch him. And when that boy grew a conscience about what Ani had done I went back to Ani and told him everything. And now that boy's dead. I killed him.'

'What was the boy's name?'

'Zak,' said Izzy and finally burst into tears.

Lesha's brain scrambled to piece together what she was being told. Tommy's death and Ani's vendetta had been so all consuming that the outside world had barely registered. But it had been impossible to miss the murder of Zak Alquist. It was front-page news.

'Ani Delgado killed Zak Alquist?' she asked.

'His brother did,' wept Izzy. 'And all because of me.'

Lesha hadn't seen Lani for years, not since he'd gone into exile for his sins.

After watching Izzy gun down Ani, Lesha had gone into pure survival mode. She'd thrown an arm around the girl and without giving her time to object had guided her at speed out of the estate. Before doors started opening and police started arriving.

That was half an hour ago. Now they were both back in Lesha's kitchen. She set a cup of tea on the table in front of Izzy and sat down herself, still unsure exactly what her plan should be.

'You need to call the police,' said Izzy sadly.

'Maybe,' said Lesha.

For the first time something like comprehension came into Izzy's eyes. She looked at Lesha anew.

'What do you mean you were going to do it?' she asked.

Lesha pulled out her own gun and put it on the table. Izzy looked from Lesha to the gun and back to Lesha, her eyes wide and fearful.

'He killed my son,' said Lesha.

'He was going to kill my brother. Kill me too,' said Izzy.

Lesha was glad she'd come home to find that Graham was still out settling Phil in his flat. But he'd be back soon. Lesha needed a plan.

'I can't go back,' said Izzy.

Lesha knew she couldn't stay here either. There was no way that she hadn't been seen. And even if she hadn't been, there was too much to tie Lesha to Ani. A dead son and five years of waiting on a grudge. The police would be here soon enough asking questions that Lesha couldn't answer.

'It's all going to be OK,' said Lesha.

Before Izzy could ask how she could possibly know that, the doorbell rang.

Out of the kitchen window Lesha saw DI Benton waiting at the front door.

79

When Bea Wallace was trying to impress someone she would either choose her best RP or her broadest Geordie, depending on just who she needed to impress. Whether she was going to be the implacable lawyer laying out her case to an Etonian KC or a giggly blonde promising the world to a violent criminal.

Right now Bea was swearing more than Dean had ever heard her swear.

'I put a fucking tracker on his fucking phone. I tell Craig to keep Nate safe. And now he's gone. Fucking gone!'

When Dean had been unable to get hold of Malton there was only one other person he could think of who might know his whereabouts.

Bea spun round the laptop on her desk to show Dean an open app that displayed a map of Nate Alquist's last location.

'There! There should be a fucking dot. A fucking dot that tells me exactly where Nate Alquist is at all times. Can you see a fucking dot?'

Dean could not.

'You have any idea how much fucking money he's worth?'

'Maybe he turned the tracker off?'

'Listen to you. What a clever fucking lad. You can't turn it off. Even if the phone's off, this tracker's on the fucking battery. It's proper Mossad shit. Part of my extravagantly large bill. None of which matters if he's fucking disappeared off the face of the fucking earth. And where the fuck is Craig? I put him on this job for this exact reason.'

Dean wished he knew. He had hoped Bea might be able to tell him that. Unwilling to leave Taymon alone, he'd packed him, half-asleep, into the van and driven back into town. As he drove it occurred to him he had no plan as to how he would track down Izzy. Izzy who had escaped the safe house with a gun.

'Ani Delgado's dead. Did you know that?' Bea snapped at him.

Dean didn't.

'Shot on his fucking driveway. Twenty million. That's what that food hall's costing. Ten per cent of that is legal fees. That's me. Now Nate's gone and Ani's dead. Fucking two million quid down the shitter. What are you even still doing here and who the fuck is that bleeding in my waiting room?' She gestured towards an unconscious Taymon.

Dean had never seen Bea like this before. She was rattled.

He tried to imagine what Malton would do in this situation. How he'd take control and calm things down. He thought how Malton always moved that touch slower. Let the world readjust to his speed. Never rushed. Never panicked. It was a great trick. If you could pull it off.

Dean thought of his plan as he said it. 'I'm going to find Malton. Wherever he is, he'll know where Nate is. Nate's the property developer. Ani's a gangster. Nate doesn't need him.'

Bea was about to argue the toss but Dean was on a roll.

'Think about it,' said Dean. 'You have Ani why? Protection? From who? Ani. Now he's dead. Nate's clean. Next time he needs help he can call the police like any normal businessman.'

'That would be totally true if only for one thing. Ani's psychotic brother Lani. Who, when he's not trafficking whores, enjoys nothing more than beating people to death.'

'You've met Lani?' said Dean, genuinely shocked.

Bea shuddered. 'Just the once. I was meant to be meeting Ani to discuss this house in Fallowfield he wants to do up and rent out. He's paying my rate to ask advice about being an amateur landlord? Fucking hell, I swear you drag these dipshits to water but they're still fucking idiots. But I need him for the food hall so I turn up. But it's not just him, it's this white guy, missing all his teeth, wearing a football shirt with a haircut like an internet Nazi. Ani tells me it's his fucking brother Lani.'

Bea looked out the window, as if the memory was something she couldn't quite bring herself to face.

'I've met murderers; I've met men who kill people for less than a grand. Guys who've casually given the word and had entire families tortured. For stupid, petty shit. Men soaked in violence. Broken little boys who grew up to be the worst people in the world.'

She turned back to Dean and managed to flash a dazzling, white grin through her lipstick-red lips.

'You've seen my wall of fame out there,' she said, pointing to the waiting room. 'But something about Lani Delgado. The way he just stood and watched as me and his brother talked about this chicken-shit rental. I've had men's eyes on me since I was young. I know what they want. It's always the same thing. Not this sick fuck. I swear, the way he was looking at me, it was less like he wanted to fuck me, more like he wanted to break me into pieces and eat me.'

She grimaced and swallowed down the image like so many sundered limbs.

'So yeah, I met Lani. And if you're asking would I fancy him for killing his brother? Fucking yes I would. And if he did kill Ani, that means he's not following the party line anymore. Which means Nate's fucked and, to be honest, I'm not even sure Craig stands much of a chance.'

Dean had been in the police interview room when spree killer and father to his girlfriend Leon Walker had tried to murder Bea. Leon Walker was a six-foot-six giant. A one-man gang. Yet he'd never once heard Bea talk about him in those terms.

Dean looked again at the map. There was nothing on the screen. No dot. No Nate. Either the phone had been destroyed or wherever it was the signal was being blocked.

His mind went back to the map on the wall of Malton's office. All of Manchester. All those pins. A history of violence. Malton must be out there somewhere.

Suddenly Dean had a crazy idea.

80

'Someone just shot Ani Delgado dead outside his home,' said Benton, watching the two women for a reaction.

The young woman, barely more than a girl, sat at Lesha Thompson's kitchen table looked like she'd been crying but said nothing. Lesha simply stared back at Benton.

'Did you find Femi?' she asked.

'I found him,' said Benton. 'He was being held hostage in a derelict house next to what looked to be a brothel.'

At the mention of the brothel, the younger woman looked away guiltily.

'I don't know if any of those women hung around for the police,' said Benton. 'My bet is they'd been told who to call and they're so deep into it all they didn't recognise a chance to escape. Right now they're being distributed back out all over Manchester.'

'Where is he now?' asked Lesha.

'Somewhere very safe. Which considering what just happened to poor old Ani, is probably for the best I reckon.'

Benton could swear she smelt cordite. The peppery smell of a recently discharged gun.

'Ani kills Kieran. And Tommy. And now he's dead. You know how that looks right?' said Benton.

Benton knew exactly what was going on here. One or both of these women had shot Ani Delgado. Right now she was trying to figure out what exactly she was going to do about it.

The younger woman opened her mouth to speak but a look from Lesha shut her down.

It had been a short walk here from the Musa household. Benton could hear the sirens heading to the Rathbone Park

297

Estate. The din of multiple units responding to a shooting. By the time she was nearly at Lesha's place the helicopter was up and hovering over Princess Parkway.

In all her time at Serious and Organised this is what Benton fought to avoid. The cascade of violence that always threatened to erupt somewhere in the city. Too many guns and gangs and drugs and money and feuds. Like rats in a barrel. The trick was to find the right moment to reach in and pull out the right rat to calm things down. The problem was one rat looked pretty much like the next and every time you put your hand in that barrel every single fucking rat tried to bite it off.

'Why are you here?' asked Lesha.

Lesha's tattoos stared back at Benton. Kieran's face. IF LOVE COULD HAVE SAVED YOU, THEN YOU WOULD HAVE LIVED FOREVER.

It was hard to find anyone in Moss Side with love for Ani Delgado. Benton had been in the police long enough to know that the system was irretrievably broken. For every victory there were a hundred losses. Every crime that secured a conviction stood in front of tens of thousands that the police didn't even know about. To pretend that the system worked was insanity. Benton had kept her head as long as she had by making sure that when and where the opportunity arose she put her thumb on the scales just a little. Made sure that there was one less glaring injustice in the world.

Did it make a difference to the vast ocean of criminality in which she swam? Of course not. Did it help Benton sleep easier at night? A little.

'I'm here to take the gun that shot Ani Delgado. I don't want to know which one of you did it. I don't want you to even tell me that it was the gun. I just want you to give it to me and I will make it disappear.'

The room fell silent. Benton had made her offer. Taken the risk. Every time she set aside the rules that the police insisted she follow and chose her own brand of justice she was taking that risk. For the last twenty-odd years the angels had been shining on her. But that didn't mean that the next time she rolled those dice, it wouldn't finally throw up snake eyes.

Her search for Femi had left her in no doubt that something violent and rotten was coming to a head in Moss Side. The last of the old poison bubbling up to the surface. While Serious and Organised were busy combing the phones of every drugs gang in the city, a whole new gang war was threatening to break out.

Nate Alquist and his food hall had stirred old ghosts. The rats in the barrel were getting restless and it felt like Benton was the only person who saw it.

Not quite the only person. Someone had beaten her to it. Reached into the barrel, braved the rabid teeth and frantic claws and removed the most dangerous rat of all – Ani Delgado.

On paper it was murder. In practice it had probably prevented a dozen more murders.

Which was why when it came on her radio that Ani Delgado had been shot dead her first thought was Lesha. The mother whose grief for her son was still so raw.

Lesha had helped her rescue Femi. Now it was Benton's turn to repay the favour. Whoever the young woman in the kitchen was she didn't want to know. There wasn't any more time.

Benton looked between the two women, gauging their reaction. 'Or do I call the police?' she said.

The younger woman looked down at the table but Lesha held Benton's gaze. Both women full well knowing the truth, both of them feeling out whether or not they dared speak it out loud.

It was Lesha who looked away first. She knelt down, opened a cupboard by her knees and brought out two handguns, which she set on the table.

'Touch them,' Lesha said to the young woman. The young woman looked confused until Lesha grabbed her hands and laid them on the guns, all the while keeping her eyes on Benton.

'You saw her touch them,' said Lesha. 'And me too,' as she handled the guns herself. 'Our prints will be all over them.'

'Mine too,' said Benton, reaching over and taking both guns. She put them in a pocket in her anorak as if it were the most normal thing in the world.

'If I were you two,' said Benton, 'I'd maybe think about treating yourself to a few days away.'

81

'Where are we going?' asked Nate, as he stumbled down the unlit passageway, his footfall illuminated by the beam of Malton's torch behind him.

The questions had started almost as soon as they were in the car. Nate throwing his weight around, demanding to know if this was about his request to kill the Delgados.

Malton had kept silent, driving at a steady speed towards the city centre. In time Nate read the situation and had grown quiet.

It was dark by the time Malton's car began to slip between the skyscrapers and viaducts. The lights of Mayfield Depot greeted them as they came off the Mancunian Way and dog-legged back into the city past homeward-bound commuters.

Nate passed the time on his phone. Shooting glances into the front of the car where Malton sat alone driving. Malton was pulling into a private parking spot behind the main drag of the Gay Village when Nate spoke, glancing up from his phone screen.

'Someone shot Ani Delgado.' His voice was a queasy blend of surprise and exhilaration. He was so carried away in the news that he didn't notice the brief moment of surprise from Malton.

Malton might have had all the pieces but it was clear he didn't know all the players. With unknown fires still to fight, the best he could do was to extinguish the ones he knew about. One blaze at a time.

Whoever had shot Ani, his death made what Malton had planned for Nate and Lani much neater.

'Was this your doing?' said Nate. He sounded like a giddy schoolboy. Malton's silence was all the confirmation he needed. Nate sat back in his seat in a daze.

'You asked me to do a job,' said Malton, letting Nate's imagination tell the story for him.

Nate shook his head in disbelief. 'You know, I remember my first million. I'd just sold these flats in Levenshulme. Used to be a community centre. Been derelict forever. I got it cheap, knocked it down, built a block of flats, sold them all before I'd even finished building them. I wasn't even thinking, I just had a cheque to pay in and I noticed my account. The seven-figure balance. The money for the flats had cleared. I was a millionaire. That's how this feels right now. Wow. Bea was right; you are the man to go to.'

Malton let Nate enjoy his fantasy. Like father like son. Something about having money and power was never enough for some people. They craved a taste of something darker. Their natural risk taking leading them to stay at the table playing long after they should have cashed out.

Malton remembered his own first million. He'd been given it in a carrier bag by Callum Hester, the older brother of his dead lover James. Callum had handed it over in the knowledge that Malton would never stop looking for James's killers. He'd called it paying in advance. Malton hadn't wanted the money, but he knew better than to offend a man like Callum. Despite their shared grief over James, Callum still commanded dozens of men all over Merseyside who would happily kill men, women and children on his command.

'Is that what we're here to do? Finish the job?' asked Nate. He sounded exhilarated.

A nod and slight smile from Malton was more than enough encouragement to get Nate out of the car and following him into a nearby block of flats behind the Gay Village. They were some of a handful of flats that had existed in the city centre prior to the IRA blowing it up in the Nineties. Malton had once lived there and when he'd come into money he had bought the entire building. Now it was worth millions but he'd never sell it. Not as long as he needed access to the underbelly of the city.

Malton and Nate walked down into the silence of the basement. It occupied the entire footprint of the building. But with no natural light it had been relegated to being home to washing machines, drying rooms and bicycle racks.

They crossed the floor to the far corner of the room where Malton unlocked the door that would take them deep underneath the city.

Ten minutes later, whatever enthusiasm there had been had long since vanished into the dead, particle-filled air. Nate stumbled through the soupy blackness into the guts of the city.

The two men moved wordlessly forward. Occasionally Malton's torch would turn for a moment through an open doorway. A brief snapshot of a whole new subterranean world leading off into dark forever. Then before fear even had a chance to spark, the torch beam would be back onto the passageway and they would continue, Nate silently glad not to be going into whatever unlit bowels they had just glimpsed.

Occasional groans from pipes echoed out of the darkness. The unmistakable scrabble of vermin somewhere in the walls. Once in a while everything shook as they passed beneath tram tracks on the street above.

They'd been going for nearly quarter of an hour by the time they reached the second locked door. Nate got there first. With nowhere left to go he turned to face Malton, holding a hand up to his eyes against the torch beam.

Malton could see he was scared. His earlier excitement long since extinguished by the underground trek.

'You shouldn't have brought me down here. The whole point of getting you to do this is that I'm not involved.'

'You're involved,' said Malton and brushed past him to unlock the door.

From beyond the open door came a howl.

Nate stumbled backwards, nearly bumping into Malton.

'What is that?'

'The man who killed your son,' said Malton and headed through the door, taking the torch with him.

'Wait!' called Nate, hurrying after him. 'Lani's in there? What are you doing bringing me down here?'

Malton had his final confirmation. He'd never given Nate Lani's name.

He turned and reached into his jacket. He pulled out a gun. A small-calibre Glock 43. The weapon looked dull under the torch beam.

'You asked me to kill the Delgados. I'm not a murderer. But that doesn't mean I can't make murder happen.'

'I'm not going to shoot him,' said Nate.

'Right now, we don't exist. There are no phones, no outside. No light, no eyes. Nothing. Just us in the dark. And what happens in the dark will stay in the dark.'

Malton swung his torch around and for the first time Nate saw the nightclub. The chipped paint and the busted dance floor. Piles of discarded flyers and abandoned catering equipment.

'This is Babylon City. Isn't it?'

Malton smiled. It was.

'I used to come here. It closed decades ago. What's it still doing here?'

'The future is always built on the past. Doesn't mean the past isn't there if you go deep enough.'

'Fucking come on!' bellowed Lani's voice from somewhere in the darkness.

Nate suddenly looked unsure. 'He's back there waiting?'

'Waiting for you,' said Malton. Still holding the gun he headed off into the ruins of the nightclub.

82

'When it was just Malton not answering his phone, I thought maybe he had it turned off.'

'He never has it turned off,' said Benton as she followed behind Dean.

'No. I know. But then when Bea showed me the tracker she put on Nate's phone, it just wasn't there.'

Dean wouldn't have described Benton as Malton's friend but in the time he'd been working for Malton she was the closest to it he'd seen. Malton and Benton had, if not an affection for each other, a comfortable acknowledgement that they might be the only two people in the whole city who saw what was really going on. And as such, from time to time, they would reach across the divide and offer assistance.

Dean pushed open the door to the basement level of the flats. With Malton missing in action and Bea losing her mind there was only one other person he could think to call.

Benton stopped at the bottom of the stairs and shook her head. 'So obviously they must be underground?'

Dean saw Benton looking around the basement, taking in the washing machines and bicycles. She saw a clean, well-lit space, conspicuously absent of Malton or Nate Alquist.

'Not just underground,' he said, crossing the basement. 'There's a place. Malton showed me once. A club he used to work for. Abandoned under the city.'

When he'd called Benton, he'd been cagey with the details. Malton was in trouble. Nate Alquist's life was in danger. There was no one else to turn to. He kept things deliberately short.

Now, as he explained his theory to Benton, he was glad he had. Saying it out loud sounded insane.

'Thing with Craig,' said Benton, trotting along behind Dean, 'He likes everyone to think he's this invincible, unfeeling, unmoving brick shithouse. And that suits. He's a man who's made his career out of taking money from one set of criminals to stitch up another. A job like that you can't show weakness. Ever. It's why I'm amazed you're still around.'

'I'm not weak,' said Dean, turning to face her.

'Course not, love, but you're also not the product of a violent, loveless home who came of age slap-bang in the middle of an unprecedented epidemic of gang violence.'

Dean thought back to everything Vikki had said. It all boiled down to the exact same thing. He was too nice for this sort of work.

'See this,' said Dean, pointing to his face. 'Keisha shot me. I lost six teeth. Broke my jaw. Never went to hospital. Never spoke to the police.'

'I know but . . .'

'And when Leon Walker tried to murder Bea in a police interview room? I fought him off!'

'As I remember it,' said Benton, smiling, 'it was Bea who stabbed him in the neck with one of those ridiculous heels she's so fond of.'

'The point is, whatever you think I am, I can do this. I've lived in Manchester my whole life. I know this city inside out. I know why someone from Droylsden thinks someone from Audenshaw is posh and why someone from Didsbury thinks someone from Audenshaw is scum and why everyone thinks everyone from Chorlton is a bearded, vegan wanker. I can tell you the names of every major criminal family in the city. I can tell you every fatal shooting for the last three decades. Who's inside for life and who's still out and living on the profits in Hale. I didn't grow up surrounded by criminals, but I grew up in a city shaped by them. I had my eyes open.'

Benton puffed out her cheeks. 'Quite a speech.'

'I mean it,' said Dean.

'Quite a speech to be wasting time on if you really do think Malton and Nate are doing God knows what in a disused club under the city,' said Benton with an infuriating grin.

He'd won her back. 'Follow me!' he said and headed for the far corner of the basement.

'There's a locked door that takes us to . . .' He stopped dead. The locked door wasn't locked anymore. It hung open in the corner of the basement.

Dean rushed over and hauled it fully open. The long, dark corridor stared back at them. The stink of stale, dead air began to creep out of the darkness and into the basement, fouling the smell of fresh laundry.

'Did you bring a torch?' asked Benton.

Dean silently cursed.

'I've got my phone torch,' he said, getting out his phone.

'Brilliant, so you're just as well prepared as I am to go wading into this obvious suicide mission,' she said peering into the darkness.

Dean hovered for a moment. She was right. He knew from the only time he'd been down here with Malton it was a long walk along a litter-strewn corridor. There were plenty of dead-ends and wrong turns. Without a light it was complete darkness. You only had to walk a few metres from the basement of the flats to lose all light completely.

Then before he could think of a compelling reason why they should risk plunging into the belly of the city with nothing more than a couple of phones and his hunch, the argument was made for him.

The clear sound of a gun being fired came from far away in the darkness. Muffled and faint but definitely gunfire.

Benton was already barging past him, her phone in one hand and to Dean's shock, a gun in the other.

'Come on then,' she said and took off into the dark.

Dean took a last look at the strip-lit certainty of the basement before following, close on Benton's heels.

83

'You pull the trigger and that's it,' said Malton, the gun still smoking in his hand.

He'd pocketed his torch and the lamp that sat in the middle of the floor shone upwards, giving the derelict club a suitably gothic cast. Paint flaking off faded purple walls, posters for long-forgotten club nights and the dust dancing in the beams as if in terrible mockery of the disco ball that hung long dead from the ceiling. To complete the horror of it all, on the other side of the dance floor, still strapped to a chair, was Lani Delgado, his face a mask of blood and sweat.

'Fuckin' kill you,' he huffed into the still air, his eyes frigid pinpricks locked on Nate Alquist.

As Malton handed the gun to Nate a smile broke across Lani's face. He began to laugh. He'd only been down in the derelict club a few hours but already the noxious air was in his lungs and his laughter lurched between barking wet grunts and tight, hacking coughs.

'I can't kill him,' said Nate.

Malton had been waiting for this.

In all his time working for Manchester's criminal firmament Malton prided himself on one thing above all others. He'd never once killed someone. Had he broken limbs? Of course. Had he threatened people's families? If it needed to be done. And had he delivered countless people into the hands of his criminal employers in full knowledge that the best they could hope for was a swift death? That was the job.

But Malton himself had never once directly taken a life. He knew what a fine distinction it was, but it was a distinction that mattered to him. Malton did what he did by staying apart from the violence. He could partake but he could never become it. He'd seen what happened when the violence got in your soul. How it corrupted you completely, dragged you down. There was already more than enough churning away in his head. He couldn't risk letting the violence in.

As much as something inside him demanded to tear Nate Alquist to bloody pieces for his part in the death of his own son, Malton resisted his darker urges. He fell back on that fine distinction that had kept him alive until now.

Nate held the gun out to Malton. 'You do it. I'm paying you.'

Malton shook his head. 'I don't kill people. That's not what I do.'

'What about Ani?' said Nate.

'Ani's dead?' barked Lani. 'Ani's dead?' A sudden shock seized his body and he went back to wildly bucking against his restraints. Bolted to the floor the chair held firm but it didn't stop Lani thrashing like an animal in a trap. 'My fuckin' brother! You killed my brother!'

Malton shook his head. 'No. Not me.'

'You said . . .' started Nate, looking confused.

'I didn't say anything. I don't know who killed Ani. But it wasn't me. I told you already. I don't kill people.'

'What's happening here?' uttered Nate, suddenly painfully aware of his predicament.

'You wanted me to kill the Delgados; that's what I'm doing. That gun is untraceable. Down here no one can see or hear us. Lani Delgado is tied to a chair a few metres away. The rest is up to you.'

Malton saw it dawning on Nate what was happening. The smallest of smiles spread over his face.

'You're a clever fucker, aren't you? Like you've transferred your conscience to some offshore tax haven. Plausible deniability.'

'No,' said Malton coldly. 'I'm not a killer.'

'You won't shoot me,' barked Lani. 'You're a pussy, just like your son.'

Nate stiffened. He raised the gun and pointed it at Lani. Lani leered back at him.

Both men were so locked into their standoff that neither of them noticed Malton step back from the light and begin to slowly cross the room to where Lani was tied up.

'You killed my son,' said Nate. For the first time since he'd met Nate, Malton detected a faint tremor in his voice. A flicker of genuine grief.

'Your choice,' Lani spat back.

'What choice did I have? You tried to set me up. Your fucking brother. Imagining he was some kind of big-shot businessman. In his fucking council house in Moss Side. I'm going to build that food hall, then I'm going to knock down as much of that fucking place as I can. Rebuild the lot. Fill it with people who've never heard of Ani Delgado or his sick fuck brother.'

'You also hired me to find the man who killed your son,' said Malton from the darkness encircling the dance floor.

Nate peered beyond the light looking puzzled.

'What? Yeah, he's here. Lani.'

'I never told you that,' said Malton. He was behind Lani now, a Stanley knife in his hand.

'You did, you said it was Ani's goons,' said Nate, a note of panic in his voice.

'I never mentioned Lani. You mentioned Lani. Back there, I told you I had the man who killed your son. You immediately knew who that was. Because you knew all along.'

Nate raised the gun in front of him.

'Where are you? What are you doing?' he shouted, trying to see into the dark.

Malton had quietly unlocked the cuffs holding Lani's arms to the chair. Lani had the good sense to keep his arms behind his back while Malton started to cut the zip ties holding his legs.

'You could have gone to the police. You could have told them about the Delgados. But it was too late by then. You'd decided to work with killers. And, when your son finally grew a conscience, you set those killers on him.'

'That's bullshit. Did he tell you that?' said Nate, waving his gun at Lani. 'You believe him? Fuck that. I'm paying you. Where are you? Stop fucking around and do your job.'

'I've done my job,' said Malton from the darkness. Lani's legs were almost free; only a handful of ties still bound him to the chair. Lani sat perfectly still. He knew what was coming next. Malton could feel his body tense and ready to go. 'I found your son's killer. And I've given you the chance to kill him.'

'You think I won't?' said Nate, stiffening.

Malton had cut all but one of the zip ties holding Lani. He rested the blade of the Stanley knife on the final tie and felt it go tense against the knife's edge. With his other hand he reached down to the cable that ran from the lamp in the middle of the floor to the battery in the corner of the room. He felt for the connection between the lamp's plug and the extension cable from the battery pack. His fingers wrapped around the plug while his thumb held the socket firm.

'Then do it,' said Malton as he cut the final zip tie and at the same time, in one swift movement, pulled out the plug.

The light went out.

Lani Delgado surged forward with a roar and Nate Alquist opened fire.

84

Benton was running full pelt, both hands out in front of her. In one she held her phone with its torch beam cutting through the dark; in the other, one of the two guns she took from Lesha Thompson.

Her boots tripped over rubble and debris. A couple of times she nearly fell face first into the mess of broken bricks, wires and litter that covered the floor of the corridor. But her momentum kept her upright and moving forward towards where several more gunshots had just erupted.

Behind her she could hear Dean keeping pace, his phone torch shining past her, casting her shadow in her own torch beam.

If it had been anyone but Dean she wouldn't be here. But she'd seen how the boy had a sixth sense for being in the right place at the right time. Trouble stuck to him like gum on the bottom of a shoe, so when he said he thought Malton had taken Nate Alquist beneath the city she was at least prepared to entertain him.

Now as she slammed through the open door at the end of the corridor she was glad she had.

She nearly fell over as her feet hit bare concrete floor. Her torch beam spread out into a much larger room. Turning it from left to right she realised she was in some kind of night-club, long since abandoned to decay.

Dean was beside her.

'This is the place,' he said, out of breath.

Without time for caution they ventured further into the club. It was all small spaces, all on different levels and connected by one or two steps. A warren of places for clubbers to dance and drink and get up to whatever they wanted unseen.

Benton recognised it at once. It was Babylon City. A stalwart of Nineties Manchester that like almost every other club from that time had succumbed to changing tastes and the rapacious desires of men like Nate Alquist.

There on the wall a poster boasted '50p Drinks Night'. Benton suddenly felt very old.

'Fuck,' Dean's voice echoed in the dark.

Benton followed the sound. Beneath her feet the concrete had changed to sprung floorboards. A dance floor. And there to one side of it was a metal chair, riveted to the floor.

Dozens of bloody zip ties were scattered around the chair along with two sets of police handcuffs and a leather belt that had been torn in half.

The club was empty.

Benton took a breath and almost immediately started to cough. The air was foul. She raised a hand to her face, attempting to wipe it from her nose and lips.

Before she could think what to do next a scream followed by another gunshot came from close by.

Benton was already moving, her phone up, her gun out. Dean hot on her heels.

'They're down here,' she said, her eyes fixed forward. Her shadow was back taking point, bouncing and staggering in the torch beam. 'Where does this head to?'

'I can't remember,' said Dean. 'But it's all connected. You could get lost down here.'

Benton had been trying not to think that thought. As she hurtled through a door in the club she found herself in yet another service corridor, this time with a lower ceiling and bare brick walls that dripped with damp.

You definitely could get lost down here. And when your phone battery ran out, you'd be lost in the dark. It made her grateful for the distraction of the pursuit.

'Can you hear something?' shouted Dean.

She could. Previously the only sounds had been pipes expanding and contracting. Water flowing through them and the occasional grumble of traffic. But now there was another sound. A continuous low roar.

The air was changing too; the stale dustiness was replaced with the cold, damp taste of rot. Benton noticed that they were running through more and more puddles.

Another scream from up ahead. Lower this time and a gun-shot.

'Whoever's shooting, hopefully they're running out of bullets,' Benton called back. She only had the three that had been in one of the two guns. The other was empty. She imagined all those bullets were now in Ani Delgado.

Suddenly her phone torch beam dimmed and was competing with the weak glow of natural light.

'It's the river,' shouted Dean. 'That noise, we're near the river.'

Nate Alquist wasn't the first person to leave his mark on Manchester. What were once villages, became the city, became the slums. What were once rivers and bridges became giant culverts and cathedral-like archways, guiding water deep underground as the city grew above it.

Each successive generation of building simply grew on top of the last. There was no order or planning, just stone that gave way to brick that gave way to concrete. A warren of waterways taming nature down dark, biddable tunnels.

As they got closer it was clear the light was coming from an opening up ahead in the corridor wall. Benton reached it first. It was a doorway leading down into a new tunnel. A fast-flowing river thundered through it, the sound of the water echoing off the brick roof. At some point the tunnel had been improved with concrete and now a narrow walkway ran along-side the water.

Looking down into the tunnel, Benton saw the thin daylight of early morning, a tiny glimpse of the sky at the end. She considered the drop down. Metal footholds had been cemented into the wall leading to the narrow concrete ledge. The ledge looked dangerously slick with water.

Halfway up the tunnel she saw two figures. As the furthest figure neared the light she saw the unmistakable choppy haircut of Nate Alquist. The figure following it was limping and as Benton's eyes adjusted she saw a messy trail of blood smearing the concrete behind it.

Benton was already scrambling down into this new tunnel, feeling her rubber soles slide on the wet steel footholds. With one hand she held her phone and gun while with the other she clung on to the freezing cold metal of the handholds.

She descended as fast as she could. At the bottom her patience deserted her and she jumped down feet-first onto the concrete ledge beside the river. Almost immediately her feet went out from under her.

Her phone flew out of her hand, skidded across the ledge and into the river. She barely held on to the gun as she spread herself wide and low and just about held herself still.

Dean was down beside her now, an arm steadying her.

She shook him off.

'There's no time!' she shouted and, as fast as she dared, she raced down the narrow ledge towards the light, Dean following close behind.

In the distance the tiny figures of Nate Alquist and his pursuer were still just about visible, framed against the light.

The air was clear now. Cold and wet. Water dripped down from the arched, brick ceiling of the tunnel and occasionally Benton had to dodge old tyres or bags of rubble that had somehow been discarded this far underground. It didn't matter where you went in Manchester, Benton reflected, someone was always going to have got there before you and fly-tipped something.

The sound of water was getting even louder as they neared the end of the tunnel. First Nate vanished from sight and then his pursuer.

'It's Lani Delgado!' shouted Dean from behind Benton.

Benton knew the officer who had been first on the scene at the house Lani had burned down. He'd ended up taking early retirement. Unable to unhear the sound of a mother and her baby screaming for their lives, trapped in a fire he couldn't get through to save her.

Everyone knew Ani Delgado was lying when he said he had no idea where his brother had fled to. His public denouncements rang particularly hollow for everyone involved in the case and its tragic aftermath.

She also knew Lani Delgado's reputation. It made her glad to have the gun.

The mouth of the tunnel expanded outwards as Benton finally reached the end and had to stop herself. There was a sharp drop nearly ten metres down to where the river joined yet more water in a canyon.

Walls that started first as rock then stone, then brick, then concrete and steel rose up either side of the river, wet with moisture and covered in plant life and mosses. From street level it was at least twenty metres down and impossible to access.

Looking up, Benton could make out the edge of Victoria Train Station. They'd come out on the River Irk to the east of the city centre. She turned back to the river. It was flowing at speed, hemmed in by the steep walls before heading down manmade rapids, which dropped a couple of metres and disappeared into black vaults beneath the station.

She could see that Nate Alquist had somehow climbed down and was wading along the very edge of the riverbed. The water up to his waist.

A few metres behind followed Lani Delgado.

Whatever Nate was planning he was about to run out of river. Up ahead were the rapids. The water hit a row of concrete stanchions, breaking up into a roaring, white foam before racing down underneath the city.

'Stop! Police!' screamed Benton, her voice bouncing off the walls either side of the river.

Nate looked up briefly and caught her eye. She saw he was carrying a gun. Lani Delgado kept moving.

'STOP!' she screamed again, as loud as she could.

Lani Delgado didn't hesitate. Nate was a few feet from the edge now and Lani was still coming. He broke his gaze away from Benton and turned back to Lani.

'We've got to do something,' Dean called out to her.

No sooner had he spoken than Lani charged Nate. Nate fired his gun at point-blank range into Lani's face. Lani wrapped his arms around Nate, taking both of them forward and down the manmade rapids.

For a moment both bodies vanished, lost in the white foam. Then just briefly they rose, still locked together, now moving at speed with the current.

Nate Alquist looked up. Benton saw a look of utter terror in his face, before he and Lani fell beneath the water and disappeared into the darkness beneath the city.

85

Bea watched bemused as, still caked in the filth of the tunnels beneath the city, Malton pulled another drawer from the filing cabinet. He swept her desk clear, scattering papers all over the office floor, before dumping the contents of the new drawer out onto the desk.

'You could just tell me what you're looking for?' said Bea, her voice soft and playful.

Malton looked up from the mess of papers. Rationally he knew he was looking for a needle in a haystack. A few lines in a deposition that referenced James. But he couldn't bring himself to ask for anything from Bea. Not after what she'd done.

He dived back into the papers, pulling them out at random, eyes running down lines and lines of dry legal text.

'You after the deposition that mentioned James?' said Bea conversationally.

Leaving Nate Alquist and Lani Delgado to sort things out between themselves, Malton had headed back to Bea's office, half-hoping she wouldn't be there so early in the morning. Out of everything that had happened in the past few hours what stuck with him most was knowing that Bea was in on all of it. Lani had made it clear that ever since Carrie's murder over a year ago, Nate had been involved with the Delgados.

The wounds from not one but two brutal encounters with Lani were finally catching up with him, he'd yet to sleep, Ani Delgado had been shot dead and the last time he saw Dean the boy was going to warn Izzy's brother that his life was in danger. But all he could think about was Bea's betrayal.

If Bea had lied to him about Nate Alquist, could she be lying about the lead in James's murder?

He'd found the door to her office locked and before he knew what he was doing, he was smashing through it with the hatchet he always had concealed in his jacket pocket.

He'd got through the door to find Bea stood in the middle of her waiting room pointing a taser straight at him. Behind her a battered-looking young lad was sprawled across the chairs in the waiting room sleeping. Apparently unmoved by the sound of Malton breaking down the door.

Malton went straight past Bea and into her office. It had taken every last reserve of self-control not to take the hatchet straight to her. She had used James against him. He hadn't told her more than the bare facts of James's murder but she'd sniffed out his weakness. The instincts that made her such a great lawyer had been turned on Malton and she'd found the one thing that would leave him incurious to the truth. The possibility of finding James's killer had stopped him looking deeper into Nate Alquist's lies. It had taken Lani Delgado to · finally rub the truth in his face.

Finally the head of steam that had brought him here was dying down and clarity was descending. He looked up from the desk to Bea. He noticed she was still holding the taser.

'You set me up,' he said, doing his best to make it sound like fact and not an accusation.

'How? You mean I got you a job with Nate Alquist?'

'You knew that Nate Alquist was blackmailing Ani Delgado.'

'I knew that when Nate Alquist found out Ani Delgado was trying to use his son against him that Nate did what any father would do, he looked out for his son.'

'By covering up Carrie Lewis's murder?'

'What choice did he have? Zak had already confessed; if it wasn't for me he could well be in prison. If someone did that to your flesh and blood would you just stand by and do nothing?'

Malton was stunned. He'd expected contrition and explanation, instead Bea stood her ground doing what she was paid to do – arguing Nate's case.

'I wouldn't trade my son for my business,' said Malton.

Bea was silent for a moment, debating something to herself.

'I had my suspicions that Nate knew about Zak's death,' said Bea. 'But that's where you came in. To find out the truth.'

'You used me to work out your next move?' said Malton, his voice breaking with exhaustion and pain.

Bea gave him a look. He'd seen it before. It was the look she had whenever she had to face down a client on the verge of tearing her apart. The kind of look you give a rabid dog that you know you can't fight and you can't outrun.

'You think what you do is sort things out behind the scenes. That's not what you do,' said Bea, her Geordie accent in full effect. 'Me? I sort things out behind the scenes. You? You're petrol on a fire. You're a provocation. You go into a situation and you have this terrible habit of escalating everything to a point of no return. Don't get me wrong, that is a skill.'

Malton was lost. Whatever Bea's end game was he could no longer see it. He was bone-tired, his injuries screamed for attention and worst of all he no longer cared.

He turned back to the papers on the desk. With his one good hand he tore through legal documents, his eyes darting across lines of text, hungrily seeking out anything that could lead him to the clue Bea had dangled in front of him.

The words began to blur, his fingers moving faster than his eyes, his frustration and rage overwhelming him. A lifetime worth of fury was getting ready to erupt when Bea said, 'It's a good thing. Trust me.'

Malton looked up, his face lit with menace. He was done with this bullshit. He knew instantly she could see the change. She stood her ground. Her face hardened.

I was sharing a cell with this bloke, I think his name was Gaz, maybe Chris. Actually I'm not sure what he was called. He was a Scouser. Said he was a hitman. Claimed he'd bumped off Callum

Hester's brother,' parroted Bea, the words obviously learned by heart.

She reached past Malton and with unnerving precision picked a single sheet of paper from the mess on her desk and handed it to Malton. He looked down the page and saw the words Bea had just recited.

His heart stopped for a moment as he read the line one more time. Callum Hester's brother. James.

'What is the name of the man he shared a cell with?'

Bea shrugged. 'I don't know. That was the only part in hundreds of pages. It wasn't relevant to my client's case so I didn't pursue it. Of course at the time I had no idea that Callum Hester's brother was James. Or that he was your ex. But when I did find out it seemed worth setting aside. For a rainy day.'

'How long have you known?' demanded Malton.

'Before we ever got together,' said Bea. 'It was only when you mentioned James's surname that I remembered I'd heard that name before. Took me a while to find it again but I did.'

'And you didn't tell me?' Malton's head felt like it was about to crack open and everything he'd been holding inside all this time would spill out all over the floor of Bea's office.

'I was right not to tell you. Look at you. If I told you what would you have done? Fallen to pieces. That wouldn't help anyone. I needed you to somehow get Nate away from the Delgados. And if you started to get cold feet then I had a little titbit to keep you keen.'

Bea was smiling. She couldn't help it. It was obviously how in love she was with her own cleverness.

Malton gripped the desk to stop himself tearing Bea in two. 'What's the client's name?'

'I can't tell you that – it's privileged.'

Malton moved out from behind the desk and advanced on Bea, who picked up a folder sat atop a pile of papers and held it out for him.

'But for you I'll make an exception,' she said handing him the file.

Malton took it but didn't back away.

'Ani's dead,' said Bea.

'I know,' said Malton, not wanting to give Bea the satisfaction of yet again being one step ahead of him.

'I'm sure you've got an alibi,' said Bea flippantly. 'Gunning someone down in their driveway isn't quite your style. Dare I ask about Nate?'

'He's dead,' said Malton definitively.

Bea couldn't hide her disappointment. 'And Lani?' she said the hope in her voice giving her away.

Malton shrugged. It wouldn't hurt for Bea to be looking over her shoulder from here on in.

'How do you fancy some close security work?' she joked.

'We're done,' said Malton, refusing to take her bait.

Bea shrugged. 'Worth a try, pet.'

Malton didn't move.

'I thought we were done,' she said, her voice slipping just a little into stern RP.

'You sent me a photograph of Emily,' said Malton. His voice resonant like tectonic plates. A white-hot rage bleeding any cadence from his words.

This time Bea appeared to be surprised. She shook her head. 'Don't know what you're talking about.'

'You said yourself, you wanted to keep me under control. You thought threatening my unborn child was the way to do it?'

Bea gave a little shrug. Her face an unreadable grin. Her hand held the taser a little tighter.

'No I didn't. And I wouldn't. I know you. I know what buttons to press to make you go and what buttons to press to melt you down. Besides, even I've got standards. What makes you think it wasn't Ani?'

'Ani Delgado spent his whole life telling the world he was a reformed character. He started to believe it himself. When I met him the other night at your meet-and-greet, he was different. Nervous, out of his element. He wanted to be the man he told everyone he was so much he started to believe it himself. Sure he'd slip back into his old ways but I don't buy Ani threatening women and children. Not after what his brother did.'

'So it was Lani,' said Bea.

'You met Lani. You think oblique threats are his style?'

Bea let out a little laugh and stopped herself. 'Have you ever thought that maybe you're spoiled for choice when it comes to people with a grudge against you? Thinking off the top of my head, I'd say I fancy your deranged ex who's tried to kill you at least twice.'

Keisha. Malton had done such a good job of closing that chapter of his life that it had never even occurred to him. He had taken her at her word that she was gone from his life forever. Even the card he'd found on Anthony's grave hadn't quite shaken his belief that he would never see Keisha again.

But if she knew about Emily? If she was watching?

'You've got your file. Now get the fuck out of my office and take that derelict Dean dumped in my waiting room with you,' said Bea. Her fear had been fleeting. She was back now. The fearsome, five-foot-four blonde in stiletto heels. 'Before I call the police.'

86

Dean watched Benton's backside move from side to side above him as she climbed the metal footholds upwards towards the light.

He was exhausted. It had been nearly two hours since they saw Nate Alquist and Lani Delgado carried away beneath the city. Since then they had returned to the underground warren beneath Manchester and begun to try to retrace their tracks.

They'd spent their time slowly moving through trial and error across the city centre, all the while underground. They'd passed through the abandoned underground line linking Piccadilly Station to Victoria before finding a door that took them into the remnants of what looked like public baths. By now the sound of trains passing nearby had become unmissable. Reasoning that they must either be at Piccadilly or Oxford Road Stations, they'd pushed on along a modern drainage tunnel until the sound of trains had died down.

Finally, Benton seemed satisfied that wherever they were it was worth the risk to break cover and so they'd located a ladder up to the surface.

Dean emerged by the side of a canal, surrounded by fields.

Looking round he realised they'd got as far out as Pomona Island, the unadopted waste ground just beyond Deansgate. Waterways and scrubland had become home to hundreds of different species of wildlife. Thriving, indifferent to the vast, bloated city less than a mile away.

But even now the city was coming. Looking round, Dean saw the hoardings promising more of the same. More flats, more luxury living. Pomona Island wasn't long for this world.

He found Benton a little way away, doing her best to wipe herself down with a packet of tissues. She offered one to Dean.

For the first time he saw how filthy he was. Down in the darkness it was impossible to gauge but up in the unforgiving sunshine of Pomona he saw his suit was ruined. The trousers soggy and torn, his jacket smeared with mud and old flaking paint and mould and every other damp stain he'd brushed up against down beneath the city.

He made do with wiping his face down.

'You can't report this,' said Dean, trying to sound stern.

Benton turned to him and burst out laughing. First a chuckle then an outright cackle. She didn't stop. The laughter barrelled out of her and every time it looked like she might have recovered she looked at Dean in his soiled suit and creased up all over again.

'Oh, God, I'm sorry. It's nerves. It's not you. It's nerves.'

Dean found himself laughing along. He wasn't sure what he was laughing at, but it felt better to be laughing with someone than being laughed at.

Benton sat down on the grass and composed herself. Dean sat next to her. They were facing back towards Manchester. The phalanx of new buildings obscured all trace of the old city.

'Sorry,' said Benton. 'Yeah, I'm not going to report to my boss that I was chasing a property billionaire and a murderer through underground tunnels, both of us armed, and then I watched them get carried away to their deaths. As shit as GMP is at follow-up? I think they might follow up that one.'

Dean realised she was right.

'And what about the gun?' he asked.

'What gun?' said Benton, holding up her empty hands dramatically.

'Where did you ditch it?'

Benton shrugged. 'If you ever find out be sure to let me know.'

Dean was on the verge of enjoying the closure of it all when he remembered his boss.

'What about Malton?' he said.

Benton turned to him, a look of pity on her face.

'He's a big boy,' said Benton. She didn't quite sound like she believed it.

Dean's hunch had paid off. Malton had been down there. He'd used the entrance in the basement of the flats he owned. But whatever happened down there he was long gone by the time they arrived on the scene.

'But he was down there. With them both.'

'And you saw what happened. Tell me that wasn't his plan all along? Thing with that one, just as it looks like it's all gone to shit suddenly you realise he's been playing both sides the whole time. He's always one step ahead.'

This time Dean wasn't so sure. He hadn't spoken to Malton since Lani Delgado blew up the house on Stevens Street. He'd never seen Malton like that before. On the verge of being physically bested by another man. It had shocked him.

Since then, Malton had been out of contact, which was completely unlike him. Dean gazed out over Manchester and hoped Benton was right. That somewhere out there Malton was sitting back pleased at how things had gone exactly as he'd planned.

'You know you're too nice to be doing this?' said Benton, her eyes fixed on the city.

'I've been told that,' said Dean.

'By your girlfriend?'

Dean felt himself blushing a little. 'She's not going to be my girlfriend for much longer.'

He had managed to avoid thinking about Vikki when they were chasing down Nate Alquist. But on the long, dark trudge through subterranean tunnels all the way out to Pomona Dean'd had plenty of time to glumly ruminate on Vikki's plans to move to London.

'Planning on dumping her?' asked Benton.

'No! She's going to London. Doing a fashion degree.'

'Not London?! That place on the other side of the world! With trains three times an hour from Manchester Picca-dilly? Not that London?' said Benton with mock outrage. 'Yes, London is a toilet. Yes, everyone who lives in that toilet is a terrible human being, but no, it's not the edge of the world. It just feels like it.'

Dean could sense the goodwill beneath Benton's teasing. He appreciated the effort.

She lowered her voice and looked him in the eyes. 'But it doesn't matter how easy it is to get to London if you're lying dead somewhere. Which is what tends to happen to people who spend enough time around Craig.'

'You're doing OK,' said Dean.

Benton turned to him, a look of incredulity on her face. Before he could say another thing, she burst out laughing again.

As the sound of it carried over Pomona, Dean couldn't help but join in. The pair of them sat at the final untouched edge of the city, laughing together as the Manchester sun slowly baked the filth of the undercity into their clothes.

87

Graham had got into fights for Lesha. He'd rebuilt her café and he'd cleaned up the remains of her slaughtered dogs. He'd never once stopped to ask questions. He saw what she needed and because he loved her he was there to help.

But even he was struggling with this.

'Where are we going?' he asked as Lesha stuffed clothes into the suitcase lying open on their bed.

'I don't know yet,' said Lesha honestly. Ever since Benton had left, taking the two guns with her, Lesha had been in motion.

'And who is the girl?'

Izzy was in the bathroom showering. She was coming with them. From what little she'd told Lesha it was clear she was as much one of Ani's victims as Kieran. Another associate, brought close, used up and discarded. The only difference, Izzy got the chance that Kieran never did. She'd seen through Ani and hit back.

'She needs my help,' was all Lesha had to say on the matter.

'No,' said Graham.

His tone made Lesha stop her packing.

'You can't do this. I don't know what you think there is left to tell me? What do you think I'll do? Do you think I'll be scared off? People have been killed. Raheem and Sergio . . .' His voice trailed off and for the first time since she'd known him the faintest trace of a tear appeared in his eye.

'You just have to trust me,' said Lesha.

'Then you have to trust me,' said Graham. 'And that means you tell me everything. Absolutely everything.'

There was no time for this. At any moment the police could be there. Or the Chopboys or someone else. There was no time to think this through. By the time she had sorted things out in her head it could well be too late.

Lesha took a deep breath and took the biggest risk of her life.

'When Kieran died I found a gun in his bedroom. I've been keeping it in a safety deposit box in town. After what happened to Raheem and Sergio I was planning on planting it on Ani, but then when he threatened Phil I realised that wasn't enough.'

Graham kept quiet but behind his eyes Lesha could see his mind struggle to process what she was telling him.

'So I took the gun and went to shoot Ani outside his house. But Izzy beat me to it. She shot him down like the animal he was and I brought her back here. Then a Greater Manchester detective took my gun and Izzy's gun and told us to leave town for a few days while she covered it all up and that's why you need to pack a bag and we need to go. Now.'

Graham didn't say a word. He turned to the wardrobe, pulled out a rucksack and began stuffing it with clean clothes. Lesha couldn't have loved him any more if she tried.

Izzy appeared in the doorway, wrapped in a towel.

'I've set you out some clothes in the spare room,' said Lesha kindly. She was at least a couple of sizes bigger than Izzy, if not more, but she hoped that the sportswear she'd picked out would do for now. They'd stop at a supermarket somewhere along the way, buy her a cheap new wardrobe. It didn't matter. Moving was the only thing that mattered now.

Get out before things caught up with her.

Lesha closed her suitcase and hauled it off the bed, the weight catching her by surprise as it landed on the bedroom floor.

She looked up at Graham.

'I know how mad all this is,' she said.

'Ani got what he deserved,' said Graham the anger in his voice tempered by a grim satisfaction. He softened. 'I love you and this will all work out.'

For a moment Lesha believed him. Then the doorbell rang.

Lesha froze. Inside she could feel everything falling down. She had so nearly outrun it all.

Graham was looking out the bedroom window.

'It's some bloke, doesn't look like police.'

Fear flashed inside Lesha as she rushed to the window.

There stood on the doorstep was Malton.

★★★

'Lani Delgado confessed to killing my son and you let him go?' roared Lesha, unable to keep the anger from her voice.

'Maybe Nate Alquist killed him, maybe he killed Nate Alquist. Maybe one or both of them got back out. Maybe neither. Not my concern.'

Lesha was livid. The Craig Malton she'd let in to her kitchen was a very different man to the one she'd met in Southern Cemetery. Previously his still, brown eyes spoke of a deep, churning process. A mind that was absorbing everything and evaluating every word and action. This wasn't that Craig Malton.

He seemed leaden. Slow but with no purpose. The mercurial air of brutal intelligence was gone. The man who lumbered into the kitchen and sat himself down unbidden was all physical menace. Whatever spark of animation long extinguished.

He was filthy. His chore shirt smeared with mud, the top underneath saturated with tiny specks of filth. From the trail he left on the kitchen floor it looked like he'd been wading through the sewers.

But Malton was oblivious to it all. He barely looked at Graham or Izzy. Just Lesha as he said his piece.

'You came here to tell me that?' said Lesha.

Malton shook his head. 'No,' he said, leaving an agonising pause before continuing, 'When I let Lani go I gave him two conditions. One, he was to never contact you ever again. Not him, not anyone else. You and the Delgados are done.'

Lesha laughed. 'You think it's that easy? I know Ani's dead. That doesn't change anything. He killed my boy; you wouldn't understand.'

For just a moment a dull glow of something terrible flared in Malton's eyes. He sniffed heavily, looked away for just a moment and when he looked back the dead, blank expression was back.

He fixed Lesha with those empty eyes. She felt the terrible pull of the abyss that lay behind them.

Finally, he spoke.

'Two. He had to tell me where they buried Kieran.'

88

Ani Delgado was dead. Femi Musa was in protective custody. Lani Delgado and Nate Alquist were both missing and Benton had just realised that she didn't have anything in for tea.

She called to the front room where Jenni sat watching TV.

'Chinese or Indian?'

'Chinese,' came the reply.

Jenni hadn't even properly unpacked at her dad's flat. Benton only had to fill ten minutes of awkward conversation at the door with Simon while Jenni hurriedly gathered her things.

Benton and Dean had ridden the tram back into town, smelling so bad that even the junkies who jumped the Metrolink to beg in the city centre had given them a wide berth. Then they had gone their separate ways. After showering and bagging up her filthy clothes, Benton had headed straight over to Simon's place to see her daughter. She wasn't sure if Jenni would come home, but after the last few hours Benton just needed to see her.

Jenni hadn't apologised or explained away the drugs or thanked her mum for coming to pick her up. Jenni had headed out to the car in silence, put the radio on during the drive home and let herself back in the house with her key.

Benton couldn't be more pleased to have her home.

As she rifled through boxes upon boxes of Simon's belongings looking for plates she suddenly had a brilliantly awful idea.

Twenty minutes later she and Jenni were stood in the back garden watching a boxful of back issues of *Cycling Monthly* gently burning.

'We should get marshmallows,' said Jenni mischievously.

The night nipped around them but the heat from the fire was more than enough to keep them warm. It lit up the garden, casting their faces in a soft, comforting glow. Benton stole glances across at her daughter, marvelling that someone like her could create such a beautiful human being.

'Don't tell your dad we did this, OK?' said Benton, adding a delicious layer of conspiracy to the already bad behaviour.

She was sick of the boxes and half-suspected that two days with Simon's untidiness was enough to risk suggesting they burn some of his stuff to Jenni. Her face had lit up at the suggestion.

The two of them huddled together in the dark watching the flames.

'I've got a box of A-level Geography notes or a box of instruction manuals for what looks like a board game about orcs playing rugby,' said Benton, pointing to the pile of boxes they'd both dragged into the garden.

'Why not both?' said Jenni.

Benton knew there'd be hell to pay but she was too busy letting the feeling of closeness with her daughter fill her up. With everything finally squared away, her brain lingered on the human tragedy of the past few days. Parents would be burying children.

While Jenni was alive and above ground Benton resolved she should be spending every minute she could with her daughter.

The phone call she'd received from DCI Priestly shortly after returning home, only convinced her of her decision. Jordan Weekes had turned up dead. Shot, gangland style and stuffed into the boot of a stolen car. Tortured into the bargain. Weekes had been a lot of things – a drug dealer, a cheat, a husband and a father. But he hadn't been a grass. In amongst everything that had happened these past few days something about Jordan Weekes's death struck a chord with Benton. The unfairness of it all.

While Jenni was inside making a pot of tea, Benton discreetly stuffed the bag of her soiled clothes between Simon's burning possessions. By the time Jenni came back out it was all just flames.

Benton had laughed off Dean's worries but now she found her thoughts turning to Malton. She knew what he'd made himself into, but she also knew what he was back at the start. A scared little boy living in a house with a broken-hearted alcoholic. A house that was now nothing but rubble.

As they both stood watching Simon's possessions burn, Benton racked her brains for the right thing to say to tell her daughter how much she loved her, how much she hoped for her and how she would do her best to protect her from all the darkness that there was in the world. When she couldn't find the words, she settled for squeezing Jenni's hand tight in her own and saying nothing at all.

89

Malton saw his mother sometimes. In his dreams. He'd seen the handful of photos that his father had kept. But those photos had been destroyed in the explosion. Now all he had was his memories. Memories he wasn't even sure were his to remember.

In his dreams she was always dressed the same. A fashionable white PVC raincoat that reached just above her knee. A patterned dress that stopped considerably further up and shiny, black shoes with a block heel and a buckle. Her skin was a fabulous shade of dark brown. Much darker than Malton's own skin. Her hair combed out into a neat afro, she looked out at Malton. She was smiling, a brilliant white smile that threatened to break into a laugh. Eyes that told him he was in on the joke. He was in on everything. Here was where he belonged. She was who he belonged to. She was here to make everything make sense.

He knew that he couldn't possibly have seen her like that. He knew that it was a photo of her and not a memory. But even so when he closed his eyes he saw her as clear as day. Not faded or static but moving, living flesh. There against the terraces of Moss Side she was waiting for him.

Then he opened his eyes and she was gone again. Out there somewhere on a lonely moor.

The tiny baby looking up at him had his mother's eyes. He felt them staring up at him and suddenly there were tears in his eyes.

'This is once and once only,' said Emily.

Malton pulled himself together. But before he could stop himself he was reaching out a hand to the tiny baby Emily held in her arms. His battered, scarred skin looked obscene against the fresh new-born. But it was the same colour. That same light brown.

Malton had a daughter. She would grow up to have her grandmother's eyes and smile. He might never see her again but finally he wouldn't be alone.

'My dad doesn't know I called you,' said Emily.

Malton turned away from his daughter and tried to find words.

He'd been back in his old house in Didsbury when Emily had reached out. All traces of the events in the club beneath the city had been disposed of. Dean had left him half a dozen messages. He'd listened to them all one by one before leaving a message for Dean telling him to be in work the next day. He had just realised he'd not eaten in the past twenty-four hours when the phone lit up.

Stood in the maternity wing of Manchester Royal Infirmary everything he feared about becoming a father hit him at once. This tiny, delicate person was the only thing that mattered now. He would do absolutely anything to protect her.

He knew what that meant. To keep his daughter safe he could never see her again.

Emily continued, 'He said you broke into the cottage.'

Malton sighed. 'I thought you were in danger,' he said.

'Were we?'

Malton wished he could lie. But in the face of new-born innocence he found himself incapable.

'Someone knew you were there.'

'Who?'

'I don't know,' said Malton honestly. 'But I'll find out.' He had a very good idea who that person might be but said no more.

Emily had started to cry. 'I knew I shouldn't have called you. I don't know what's worse. Knowing or not knowing. Either way, this is what happens. This is who you are.'

336

It was true. When he stood alone in the face of the criminal conspiracies of Manchester's underworld Malton was invincible. He couldn't be bought, bribed or beaten. But now it was like all his vulnerability had been poured out of his body into one tiny, perfect child.

He couldn't continue what he did and be a father. He had to choose. Deep down he knew the choice would be made for him.

'I know how much it means to you. To see someone who looks like you. Like your mother.'

The tiny baby's mouth opened and her little lips suckled the air.

'That's why I wanted you to see her. For the first and last time.'

Malton saw a flash of his mother in her white mac. She was walking out along an endless moor and he knew she wouldn't ever turn back. Not even once to wave goodbye.

He looked down at his newborn daughter and it took every last ounce of strength he had in his body not to cry out.

90

He's buried in Hollinshead Hall.

The early autumn sun snuck through the trees, painting the green forest floor with its generous warmth.

The only sounds in the entire world were the gentle murmurs of nature and Lesha's footsteps as she made her way towards the hall.

Kieran was buried in Hollinshead Hall. That was what Malton had told her. That was what, he claimed, Lani Delgado had told him in exchange for his freedom.

Lani Delgado the child murderer. His word was all she had to go on.

Lesha, Izzy and Graham had spent nearly a fortnight at an Airbnb in Wales. Every day they'd walked on the beach, read by an open fire or just lay in bed trying to process what they'd been through.

Every day Lesha expected the knock to come. A police car, custody, questions. It never did. After the first week Graham went back to Manchester to properly close up the café and make sure things were taken care of.

Izzy and Lesha spent their time alone talking about the one thing they had in common – Ani Delgado.

Izzy had asked about Kieran. That was all Lesha needed. She painted the picture of the headstrong child, raised out in Whalley Range away from the baleful influence of his absent father in Moss Side. She talked about the dawning reality of seeing her child sucked into a world of gangs and criminality. How unjust it was that by accident of birth a young boy was forced to make the kind of choices that would leave most adults wanting. There was no right way to navigate what Kieran went through. All Lesha could do was let her unconditional love be the north star that would eventually bring him home.

But Kieran never came home.

As great as Wales had been, with Ani dead and their secret safe with Benton there was nothing keeping them there. Back in Manchester Izzy returned to live with her brother and Lesha came home to find everything just as she left it. Not quite everything. Graham had a surprise waiting for her. The surprise leapt on her as soon as she was in the door. An Akita puppy. A tiny, white ball of fluff, looking for all the world like a child's toy. It ran towards her, pressing between her legs and racing around her excitedly.

As everything settled back down to as normal as things would ever be again, Lesha knew there was only one thing left to do.

That morning Lesha arranged to collect Tommy Fenwick's unclaimed ashes and headed off alone to finally be reunited with her son.

She had looked up Hollinshead Hall. Spent hours staring at it on her phone. A ruined country house just outside Tockholes. Hidden in woodland. Just about accessible by car but remote enough to bury a dead body away from prying eyes.

Her directions had led her down increasingly narrow country roads. Slowly but surely the trees got closer and closer until their numbers swelled enough to allow their branches to cover the road. The waning September sunshine dipped briefly and in the half-light Lesha felt like she was heading to meet Kieran halfway between the world of the living and wherever it was he now found himself.

The road ended in a small car park. Lesha's was the only car there. She'd never been afraid of being alone. She'd never really been afraid. As she hauled on the rucksack holding the sturdy plastic urn containing Tommy's ashes she wondered if perhaps that was what had caused all of this. Maybe a little fear would have made everything different.

But that wasn't who Lesha was. If you were scared then you were powerless and Lesha refused to live her life like that.

The path through the trees was well trodden but deserted. The soft, deadening silence of the British countryside filled her up. It made her senses sharp and her head clear.

As the trees began to give way she glimpsed Hollinshead Hall. Or rather what was left of it. In a clearing the size of a football pitch, the ruins of the house walls and outbuildings rose up out of the grass. As if the earth was slowly expelling it. Pushing it into the air for all to see.

As she broke cover of the trees she felt the sun wrap itself around her and she staggered to a stop.

She would never find Kieran. There was too much ground. Too many places to look. If he was even here.

She turned and glanced at the tattoo on her arm. Kieran smiled back at her and she felt tears pricking her eyes.

'Morning!' a voice from behind her caused her to spin round, wiping her eyes dry as she did so.

An older woman with a dog emerged from the trees. Her hair was white and she wore hiking shorts and boots, her fleece top open over a faded shirt. Her dog was a scrappy-looking mongrel who was already racing around the ruins, unable to contain its excitement.

'It's amazing, isn't it?' said the older woman as she drew level.

Lesha nodded silently. She wasn't in the mood for small talk but the woman didn't seem to notice.

'I used to come here with my husband. Liked to imagine it was our little spot. But we were happy to share!' She laughed and Lesha couldn't help give a little smile. Wherever this woman was from, her voice had the bouncing optimism of a private education and family wealth.

She finally looked at Lesha and her smile quickly turned into something more thoughtful.

'I like your tattoo. Is that your son?'

Lesha found herself nodding along, unsure whether to tell this stranger to mind her own business or tell her every last detail about Kieran's life.

Before she made up her mind the woman was reaching into her pocket. She pulled out a tatty wallet and extracted a photo. She held it up for Lesha to examine. It was a smiling, older man. Grey hair, shorts, walking boots and fleece. Just like the woman. He was stood in front of Hollinshead Hall. It looked no different in the photo to how it did on that morning.

'My husband,' she said. 'Always take him with me. Maybe I should get myself a tattoo like yours. In case I lose my wallet!'

'My son was murdered,' said Lesha, out loud before she could stop herself.

Finally, the woman went quiet. She stood watching her dog run around the ruins until eventually she said, 'I know how sad I was when Charles died. He died an old man, in his bed, me beside him. I can't imagine how strong you must be to lose a child like that and even get up in the morning. Last thing you need is me prattling on. I'm sorry'

She gave a smile that hovered between reassurance and pity and started off towards her dog.

Lesha watched her pick her way between the ruined walls of Hollinshead Hall.

She found herself calling after the woman, 'I get up every morning because Kieran can't.'

The older woman stopped and turned back. She said nothing; she just listened.

'And I know too many people who should still be here,' Lesha continued. This had been inside her all this time but it was here with a stranger at the place where Kieran's body was buried that it finally came to the surface. 'And maybe love couldn't have saved him, but it's all I've got.'

'That's all any of us have got in the end,' said the woman. Her dog ran over to her and started pacing at her feet, its tail wagging. 'And dogs.'

Lesha let out a laugh.

'Take care,' called the woman and with that she turned and headed off into the woods leaving Lesha alone again.

To her surprise she found herself smiling.

Lesha reached into her backpack and brought out Tommy's ashes.

She looked out over Hollinshead Hall. Somewhere nearby was Kieran. He'd found his way home. And now he and Tommy would never be alone again.

91

The concourse at Manchester Piccadilly teemed with life. Beneath the arrivals and departures board hundreds of passengers and their families darted in and out of the shops, queued at the ticket machines and rushed back and forth through the gates to the platforms beyond.

The sound of dozens of conversations mixed with the foggy blare of the PA, a constant hum of noise instantly recognisable in any British railway station.

Dean could see the trains lined up waiting to depart. There on platform five was the train that would take Vikki to London and away from him.

He stood with her two suitcases, watching the clock tick down until her departure time. Everything Vikki owned in the world was squeezed into those two suitcases. Ready to go and make a new life in London.

Ever since he and Benton had emerged into the Pomona sunlight and she'd told him what he already knew about the inevitable conclusion of working for Malton, he'd been struggling to make his decision. Vikki or the job.

Malton had returned to work a changed man. He seemed distant and cold. He disappeared for days on end, delegating a lot of the day-to-day operation to Dean. Suddenly overwhelmed with work, any thoughts of quitting seemed impossible.

Thanks to Femi Musa, GMP now knew the full extent of Nate Alquist and the Delgados' roles in the deaths of Zak and Carrie along with several other deaths. It was still an ongoing investigation. One that Bea Wallace seemed to revel in, plunging into the thick of the mess and putting herself forward as the saviour of the Moss Side Food Hall. A project she was now touting as a tribute to Zak Alquist.

Days became weeks became months and before Dean knew it, it was time for Vikki to be heading off.

Even as the day approached, still he hadn't made his mind up. The guilt he felt at abandoning Malton somehow outweighed the agony he felt at watching Vikki slip away. Either way, by not making his decision he postponed having to face up to the most difficult choice of his life.

The time leading up to now had somehow been the happiest time of all. With the immediate future mapped out Vikki had embraced the present. She and Dean ate out, went clubbing, went to gigs and museums and art happenings. Dean thought his trip beneath Manchester had been eye-opening but Vikki showed him a whole new Manchester again. Not the dead, buried Manchester of the past but the vibrant, modern Manchester of the future. Where youth and love and possibilities meant far more than stale nostalgia.

With his responsibilities at work came a pay rise. Suddenly there was a brand-new car parked outside the house in Moss Side. He'd taken them to every fancy place in the city he could think of. While Vikki knew where the cool people went, Dean at least knew where the rich people hung out.

Between them they'd turned Manchester into their own private playground.

The booming voice of the PA told Dean that all that was now over. Vikki's train was boarding.

He turned and saw her rushing out of WHSmith clutching a handful of magazines for the train journey.

It was now or never. Time to choose.

'I don't think they'll let you through the gate,' said Vikki, pointing over to where a small crowd had started to filter their way through onto the platform.

'You got everything?' asked Dean pointlessly.

'I bet they've got a few shops in London,' said Vikki with a smile. 'I'll be good.'

She put her arms around Dean.

'London's not so far,' she said.

'I'm going to leave my job,' said Dean all at once.

Vikki's face fell for a moment. Then she shook her head. 'Why? You're great at it and from what you said, Malton's gone AWOL, so you're basically running things.'

It was true. Dean hadn't seen Malton in at least a week.

'But then I can come to London. With you. You said your-self, it's going to get me killed.'

Vikki suddenly looked very serious. 'Life will get you killed,' she said. 'Don't you dare quit. I love you and I know you love me and I know you love your job. And as much as it terrifies me knowing what you do, if you leave the job you love for me that means eventually you'll realise the huge mistake you made and blame me for it. I'm not having that.'

'I won't,' said Dean half-heartedly.

Vikki's eyes darted up to the clock. Fast but not so fast that Dean didn't notice.

'Dean,' she said. 'I love you and I'm coming back. Maybe not straight away, but I'm coming back. These past few months?'

'It's been amazing,' said Dean, finishing her sentiment.

'Yeah.' She smiled. 'And now we get to do that all over again. In London.'

'It won't be the same,' said Dean.

'No. It'll be different. And that'll be good. Because that's what I love about you, about this city and the people who live here. It's about not doing the same things over and over. It's about taking risks and making a world you want to live in. You can take the girl out of Salford but I'm fucked if I'm going to end up in London for the rest of my life.'

Dean couldn't help himself; he leaned in and kissed Vikki there under the announcement board for as long as it took for the PA to remind travellers that the 13.10 to London Euston would be departing in five minutes' time.

He watched Vikki hurry through the gates, give one final wave and then haul her suitcases up onto the train after her.

A few moments later the train doors closed, a man on the platform waved a flag and the train pulled away.

Dean walked out of Piccadilly Station, past the staggering statues of squaddies blinded by gas and on down towards Piccadilly Gardens where he spent half an hour trying to feel sorry for himself.

Finding himself surrounded by the mercurial, filthy, brilliant, obstinate, optimistic people of Manchester he found it all but impossible.

Epilogue

Malton ran a hand over his head. He hadn't shaved it in a few days. Long enough to feel the beginnings of hair. When he was fourteen Malton had stolen some clippers from a shop in town. He'd taken them home and shaved off his curly hair. He'd never had hair since.

The haircut could wait. He was so close he could feel it.

He sat in the corner of the pub in Speke, his back to the wall, an untouched pint on the table in front of him. The air was thick with cigarette smoke. Apparently no one had told the landlord that smoking inside had been illegal for nearly two decades.

From what Malton had learned it wasn't the only illegal thing that went on in this pub.

It was a plain-looking detached pub. Built to ape the larger, Victorian pubs in Liverpool's city centre, it stood on the edge of an estate where its attempt at grandeur was made all the more obvious by the uniformity of the houses surrounding it.

Malton had stepped around half a dozen bicycles on his way inside. Their riders clustered about a pool table, shouting and laughing. Confident that no one would be touching their bikes.

The folder he'd got from Bea had contained the testimony and a name. A name was all he needed. It was the name of the man who'd got a visit in the middle of the night, waking up to find Malton holding a hatchet to his neck.

He'd been very helpful and given Malton more names. He hadn't known the exact name of the man who had told him

347

he'd killed James but he knew where he was from. Who he might know. Just enough for Malton to get to work.

But Liverpool wasn't Manchester. It had been over a decade since Malton worked in Liverpool and although to his relief it hadn't embraced change at quite the pace of Manchester, nevertheless he was on foreign soil. He had no reputation, no contacts, no Malton Security. He'd left Dean back in Manchester running the company. Finding James's killer now consumed his every waking moment.

He'd chosen not to wonder if his new daughter was safe. He'd decided to ignore the tracker he'd found on the underside of his car or his suspicions that it was Keisha who'd sent him the photo of Emily. All he worried about was pulling the thread that he hoped would lead, eventually, to James's killer.

That thread had brought him here.

The lads at the pool table kept looking over. It was clear he'd been noticed. His investigation told him that someone in this pub had managed to go the last decade openly challenging Callum Hester and yet was still alive to tell the tale. The kind of man who'd think nothing of killing the brother of a man like Callum Hester. Or robbing him. Or doing any number of things that any right-thinking criminal would know equated to a death sentence.

That meant the man who drank in this pub had power.

Malton thought through all the Manchester criminals he'd faced. Psychopaths like Danny Mitchum. Violent narcissists like Ani Delgado. Unbound monsters like Leon Walker and Lani Delgado. He'd seen them all off. But that was back in Manchester. In Liverpool they did things very differently.

The smell of cannabis joined the cigarette smoke. A joint was being passed round the pool table where the lads had stopped playing pool altogether and were now looking across at Malton.

Malton slid a hand into his inside pocket and wrapped his fingers around his hatchet. He'd sharpened it just that morning, running a whetstone over the blade until it was sharp enough to slice paper at the mere touch. With all the weight that Malton could put behind it he'd be able to take apart every single person in the pub.

One of the boys left the pool table and made his way to the middle of the pub. He was grinning, glancing back to his mates.

Malton instantly knew he had a gun. The boy was barely sixteen, hardly ten stone. The confidence he displayed approaching Malton could only mean one thing. He was armed.

Malton wondered how he could close the distance. Currently the lad was at least ten foot away. Easily enough to get a shot off. Malton would need to be nearer if he was to close down the advantage of the firearm.

Without hesitation Malton got up and started to the bar. He kept the boy in his peripheral vision. He could hear high-pitched laughter coming from the pool table.

The boy started walking towards Malton. As he passed the mirror behind the bar Malton could see his arms were by his sides, the gun still hidden.

'Who the fuck are yous?' said the boy, now only five foot away by Malton's estimation.

Malton discreetly slipped the hatchet out of his pocket, careful to keep it hidden beneath his coat.

'I said,' started the boy. In the mirror behind the bar Malton saw his hand going into his trousers for a weapon. 'Who the fuck . . .'

'ARMED POLICE. EVERYONE DOWN!'

The boy spun round, his hand out from his trousers and holding a handgun, to see four Firearms Officers in full-body armour pointing MP5s straight at him.

Before he could say a word they opened fire.

Malton hit the deck as bullets pumped into the boy. The close range and the professionalism of the men firing meant every bullet hit its mark. The gun flew from the boy's hand and he fell to the ground torn to pieces.

But the armed police weren't through. They kept moving across the pub floor. Towards Malton.

He looked up to see an officer pointing the gun down at him.

'WHERE'S THE BLADE?' he screamed at Malton.

Malton's eyes went to his pocket.

'HANDS BEHIND YOUR BACK! NOW!'

Malton did as he was told. A second officer appeared beside Malton, clamping handcuffs onto his wrists. Yet another officer was in his pocket.

'Shit!' the officer shouted, pulling his hands back, blood dripping from his fingers, the hatchet in his hand.

'It's sharp,' said Malton blankly.

Malton was hauled to his feet and hurried out the pub past the remaining armed officers who were already beginning to realise the full extent of the fuck-up that had just taken place.

There was a police van waiting outside the pub. Its back doors were already open, revealing the reinforced holding cage in the back.

Malton was tossed in and the cage closed.

A young man appeared from round the side of the van. He was in a suit and tie. Malton thought he couldn't look more like police if he was in full dress uniform.

'Craig Malton,' he said. 'My name is DCI Priestly, and I'm arresting you on suspicion of murder.'

Acknowledgements

I would like to thank Dr Hughes for all her insight and input. My literary agent Gordon Wise for getting all this off the ground in the first place. My TV agent Michael McCoy whose enthusiasm encouraged me to turn a script into a novel into a series of books. Beth Wickington my editor for all her notes, thoughts and help. Helena Newton for her air-tight copy editing. Elliot Sweeney for taking the time to read a rough and ready version and give some great pointers for making it slightly less rough and ready. Rob Parker for running Crime Central in Manchester. Heather Burnside for the reassurance and advice. Fenchurch for the jokes. I'd also like to thank my family and parents for their continued support.

Finally I'd like to thank everyone who's sat down to read or listen to a Manchester Underworld book. I love Manchester and love getting to write about every part of it. None of that would happen without readers.

Read on for a sneak peek of the fourth book in Sam Tobin's gritty Manchester Underworld series.

Out April 2024.

Prologue

Jake lay back on the bed and enjoyed the smell of freshly laundered sheets. His clothes were still scattered all over the floor of the bedroom. The darkly stained jeans and filthy anorak. Trainers held together with duct tape. They lay in jarring contrast to the pristine, white of the hotel room carpet.

The older man had insisted Jake shower first. Jake didn't object; it had been nearly two weeks since he'd showered at his former sheltered accommodation. He'd had to sneak back in after being banned for stealing from the other residents.

Jake let his battered body sink into the soft mattress as he looked up at the ceiling. The sex had been gentler than he was used to. But then this would usually happen in a back alley or, if he was lucky, the backseat of a car, parked on some deserted North Manchester industrial estate. To be taken to an expensive hotel, paid three times his rate and then get to do it on a king-sized bed was a rare luxury.

The older man's aftershave was imprinted on the pillows. A dark, floral bouquet that spoke of wealth and respectability. His clothes were folded neatly over a nearby chair, beside the large suitcase he'd brought up to the room.

From his luggage Jake assumed the man must be visiting Manchester for business. Maybe he had a wife and family and was taking advantage of being away to spend time with someone like Jake. Whatever his story he'd hardly said two words to Jake. And when he did speak it was in barely audible mumbles. But Jake recognised guilt when he saw it. As if to confirm Jake's intuition the entire time they'd been together the man had been furiously puffing away on a stylish, chrome vape pen.

Shrouding the both of them in a sickly sweet, white smoke which smelled familiar in a way Jake couldn't quite place.

The older man had been in the bathroom for nearly ten minutes now. If he hadn't have taken his wallet in with him Jake would already be gone. But he could wait.

He looked round the room. There was a football theme. On the wall a framed Manchester City shirt bore Yaya Touré's name and what looked like his signature.

He rose off the bed to take a closer look at the shirt. It was the 2013 season. Back then Jake had been only eight years old. He lived and breathed football. His parents had got him the home and away kits just so he had a spare kit to wear while the other one was in the wash. Jake was always out in the street kicking a ball. The Etihad was only down the road. As a boy, it had seemed inevitable that one day he'd be playing there himself.

That was before the drugs.

Jake heard the toilet flushing and he hurried back to lay on the bed, doing his best to make his battle-scarred, nineteen-year-old body look as inviting as possible.

It was time.

He draped one arm over the side of the bed, ready to reach into his bag for his knife.

He'd let the man come back onto the bed, naked and vulnerable, ready for round two. Then before he knew what was happening, Jake would have the blade at his throat. By the time Jake was done the man would be heading back to wherever he came from, desperately inventing a story as to how he lost his wallet and phone and money. A story he could tell his wife and kids.

The bathroom door opened and despite the best efforts of the extractor fan a cloud of sweet-smelling vapour wafted into the room. There in the middle of it the older man stood for a moment looking at Jake. He was good-looking man in a way, but then there was something about his face, a haunted quality that lent him a darker air. He'd never once smiled since he'd picked Jake up by the canal side a few hours ago.

Jake guessed he must be in his fifties, but he looked younger. Where Jake's body was rail thin and riddled with scabs and tattoos the other man's body was toned and lightly tanned. When they'd had sex, Jake almost enjoyed it. Almost.

The older man started to approach, his bare feet padding across the thick pile of the carpet. The deep smell of his aftershave mingled with the clouds of white smoke. A decadent, heady aroma.

Jake reminded himself what he was here for. Unseen, his hand slid down the side of the bed, into his bag, searching for his knife. He kept eye contact with the older man, smiling seductively as his fingers rooted through the detritus of his bag. The half-drunk bottle of vodka, the shoplifted make-up palettes and phone cases. Where was that knife?

The older man was kneeling over Jake now. He stroked Jake's sunken chest with one hand and smiled for the first time.

The man's teeth were brown and rotten.

'Looking for this?'

There was a flash of silver in the corner of his eye, and before Jake could comprehend how his knife had ended up in the other man's hand, he felt the blade slide deep into his side.

Jake thought how strange it was that he hardly felt any pain. He tried to look up into the face of his murderer but all he saw was a smothering darkness as the light in the room slowly dimmed to nothing.

1

'No offence son, but you seem like you're out of your fucking depth here. You understand what I'm saying Dean?'

Dean did his best to nod politely as Janet Farr came to the end of yet another long, rambling monologue. Janet was pure south Manchester. Every other word out of her mouth was 'fuck' and she always made sure to end her sentences with a question to confirm the listener was following her free-form train of thought.

The Farrs lived in a house in Bredbury, just outside of Stockport. At one time the building must have been some kind of farmhouse, out in the open country with only a collection of strange, half-built outbuildings for company. Over time it had been added to, with a large, ground floor extension, and more recently a conservatory, with the yellow expanding foam still visible around the joins.

But just as the house had grown, so too had Stockport. Now their land was overlooked by a tower block to its rear while across the road a newly built estate of over fifty homes stood in sharp contrast to the Farrs' ramshackle collection of buildings.

The extension had been built to accommodate a western saloon-themed pub. Swing doors led from the front of the house into a room covered in wood panelling with various Confederate flags, guitars and posters hanging up on every available surface. Behind the bar there was a tap serving Budweiser and a shelf with nothing but Jack Daniels. Dean sat across from Janet Farr at a pub table beneath the centre piece of the entire room: a giant mural of a cowboy wrestling a steer to the ground.

The Farrs were thieves, opportunists and for the past two years drug dealers and this was what they spent their ill-gotten gains on.

'See, when we came to you we thought we were getting the other bloke. The black one,' said Janet, leaning back into the built-in seating that ran along the walls of the 'bar'. She was thin, almost boyish, but Dean knew she was far stronger than she looked. A lifetime of corralling her family along with the augmentation of Botox and fillers had turned Janet Farr's face into a permanent scowl.

Dean had never seen her in any colour other than black. She was currently in head-to-toe black Balenciaga. It matched her mood.

The man she was talking about was Dean's boss, Craig Malton. For the last three months Malton had been locked up in Strangeways prison on remand for murder. Malton had ignored Dean's multiple requests for a visiting order or phone call and so, without any further instructions, Dean had done his best to carry on business as usual.

Day to day that meant managing Malton Security, a firm that employed nearly sixty people and ran doors for half the nightclubs, restaurants and bars in the city. On top of that Malton Security guarded high-worth individuals' homes, provided close protection and any other service you could imagine that lay in the grey area between lawful vigilance and semi-legal violence.

But what Malton was really known for was what Dean was currently engaged in. It was why Janet Farr had reached out in the first place. The security work was the official business but what Malton really did was far darker.

Malton solved crimes for criminals. People who for whatever reason didn't want to get the police involved. Kidnapped drug dealers, unsolved gangland killings, missing product. Whatever the issue, the Manchester underworld knew that if you had the connections and you had the cash there was nothing Malton wouldn't do, nowhere he couldn't go, no one who he wouldn't lean on, just so long as it produced results.

Malton had lived in Manchester his entire life. From a scrappy kid in Moss Side through to the power behind a multi-million-pound security firm. In that time he'd forged connections with the people who made Manchester work. The gangsters, the dealers, the slumlords, the corrupt politicians and the crime families who were the real power behind the city.

But Dean wasn't Malton. Malton was a middle-aged, eighteen-stone, mixed-race wrecking ball of a man whose reputation alone got people talking without saying a word or lifting a fist. Dean was a nineteen-year-old, six foot bean pole with good manners and a face that made people want to mother him.

On the other side of the room the tinny sound of a karaoke track started up. Words appeared on the large TV hanging on one wall and Janet Farr's daughter Marie got ready to sing.

Janet turned and cheered at the sound.

'Go on Marie!' she cheered, clapping in support. Janet's face shone with delight through her perma-glare.

Despite how much trouble they were giving him, Dean found it very hard to dislike the Farrs.

Marie was in her twenties, built like her mother, slight but with a natural fighter's posture. Always on the front foot. Fearless. Like her mother her face was plumped up with fillers but unlike Janet, Marie had led a life of having her every whim indulged by her mum. When Marie smiled it didn't look like a prelude to violence.

Behind the bar the sound of Marie about to break into song caused Janet's son Carl to briefly look up from his mobile. His eyes blank and uninterested. The most striking thing about Carl was his head, a giant, shaved boulder plastered with a permanent look of unreadable passivity. Carl was huge; fat but clearly terrifyingly strong with it. His hands were like paving slabs, stubby fingers fumbling at his phone's touchscreen.

As Marie started to sing Carl went back to listlessly staring down at the glowing screen and Janet turned back to Dean. Her face stopped smiling.

'Over three months now since we got robbed. And what the fuck have you got to show for it?'

Dean wracked his brains. What did he have to show for it? The Farrs sat slap-bang in the middle of the pecking order of Manchester's drug economy. They were far below the rarefied air at the top where a handful of gangs and individuals with a global reach negotiated with South American cartels and European crime gangs to bring millions of pounds of uncut drugs into the country. But they were also several rungs above the hand-to-mouth street dealers who would be found in every part of the city, their pockets stuffed with tiny wraps and filthy cash.

The Farrs had a tyre garage which was the perfect cover for bringing drugs into the country, stuffed into the rims of performance tyres. From what Janet had told Dean, the Farrs bought cocaine wholesale from a UK-based importer who put the product in the tyres while they were still overseas. Once the tyres were through customs the Farrs paid a courier to remove the drugs. The chain of custody broken sufficiently to insulate the Farrs, the drugs were then delivered to them at a later date once the coast was clear.

The tyre garage gave the Farrs a plausible explanation as to why they were involved in bringing things into the country but the courier meant they could stay one step removed from the illegality of the process. Should the drugs be found before the tyres had passed through customs, they could plead ignorance. Should the courier be caught with the drugs once in the UK there was nothing to tie him to the Farrs.

That was the plan and it had worked for nearly two years, but three months ago someone had robbed the courier bringing the drugs from the latest tyre shipment. The Farrs had hired Malton to find those drugs. A week later Malton had been arrested and sent to Strangeways.

'As I've said, it would really help if you could give me the name of the man you buy from?' said Dean as politely as possible. This had become something of a sticking point.

'And I fucking told you, I'm not a grass.'

Dean appreciated the Farrs' respect for the basic tenets of criminality but it didn't make his job any easier. Malton never let something like that get in his way. He thrived on the unknown. He told Dean that he'd rather people didn't give him the information. People lied, people omitted, people had their own agenda. When Craig Malton got information out of someone, he knew that information was true.

Dean wished he could say the same. Where Malton relied on reputation and menace, Dean relied on curiosity and smarts. But try as he might he kept hitting brick walls with the Farrs' stolen shipment of cocaine. Nearly two hundred grand's worth.

The drugs hadn't appeared anywhere obvious. He'd kept an eye on everyone associated with the Farrs to see if they changed their behaviour. Usually, the kind of criminals who ripped off other criminals lacked the basic impulse control not to immediately spend their sudden windfall. But the missing drugs had yet to make their presence felt in the underworld economy. And so Dean was left with nothing.

Malton had taken a chance on Dean, given him a job, and trained him up as his second in command. In the time he'd been working for Malton, he'd been shot in the face, nearly beaten to death and he'd saved Malton's life more than once. Malton had seen past Dean's age and innocent looks and recognised someone just as adept as he was at navigating the dangerous currents of the Manchester's criminal networks.

However much he wanted to walk away from the Farrs and their missing drugs, Dean knew he couldn't let Malton down.

'Mate, I've told them to move on. It happens,' came a voice from behind Dean. He turned to see Janet's son-in-law Martin awkwardly negotiating the saloon doors that led into the room.

Marie was halfway through a Shania Twain number and turned, flirtatiously directing her singing towards Martin.

'Fuck off Martin,' said Janet. 'I tell you what, if my Mickey were here now he'd fucking slap you for that.'

Keeping a safe distance from his mother-in-law, Martin sat down across from Dean, sharing a look of exasperation. From the three months Dean had been dealing with the Farrs, Martin had struck him as the reasonable one. Ever since the patriarch Mickey Farr had got locked up for punching out a female police officer at a derby match, it had been Martin running the show. The Farrs sold to a string of gangs who in turn supplied the street level dealers. They were close to the violent, free for all of the lower levels but with just enough of a buffer to not get involved.

'This investigation is costing us money. For what?' said Martin.

Martin obviously used steroids; his arms bulged out of his t-shirt, swarming with tattoos. His hairline was in retreat to the back of his head but he still had a youthful optimism about him which showed in how he dressed – tight jeans and fashionable knitwear under a padded gilet.

Despite all his toned muscle, Dean was sure that the chubby, untoned arms of Carl Farr could snap Martin like a twig.

Dean hadn't even brought up just how much the Farrs now owed. Without results he felt guilty even mentioning it. One more thing that Malton would have easily taken in his stride.

'I want my fucking drugs, Martin. You understand?' said Janet, turning on her son-in-law. 'I paid for Craig Malton and I get this fucking kid?' She turned back to Dean. 'No offence son,' she said.

Dean nodded and kept quiet.

'Thing is, I think you're not even fucking trying. So I've had to take matters into my own hands. Sorry love.'

For a moment Dean felt a flood of relief. Right now he was single-handedly running Malton Security and this side of the business was too much to be doing on top of all of that. If Janet Farr could help this along then he wasn't too proud to accept assistance.

'I had a word with my Mickey,' said Janet with smile.

On the other side of the bar, Marie missed the high note by miles.

'See, he's banged up with your boss,' Janet carried on. 'No point giving you a kicking, need you to get the fucking job done.' She smiled. 'But your boss, sat on his arse in Strangeways? I reckon he could stand to have a little reminder of who it is he's fucking about with. Give you a bit of an incentive to pull your finger out and find my fucking drugs.'

Marie finished her song with a flourish. Janet turned and applauded wildly. Carl kept on looking at his phone. Martin looked away, doing a bad job of hiding his annoyance. Dean said nothing. If what she was telling him was true then things were about to get messy.

He almost felt sorry for Mickey Farr.

Go back to where it all started with
book one in the series!
There's only room for one boss in this city…

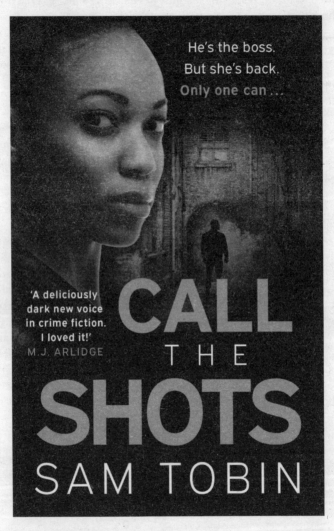

He's the boss.
But she's back.
Only one can…

'A deliciously
dark new voice
in crime fiction.
I loved it!'
M.J. ARLIDGE

CALL
THE
SHOTS
SAM TOBIN

Meet Craig Malton and Keisha Bistacchi in the first book
in Sam Tobin's Manchester Underworld series.
Available now.